ISSUE 15, EARLY SUMMER 2020

CONTENTS

Page 6: **Editorial**

Page 10: **Graham Masterton interview and analysis of *Mirror* by Marc Damian Lawler**

Page 31: **World exclusive extract from Graham Masterton's *The House of a Hundred Whispers***

Page 36: **Aidan Chambers interview and review of *Dead Trouble & Other Ghost Stories* featuring exclusive illustrations by Randy Broecker**

Page 49: **Lynn Lowry interview**

Page 61: **The Many Faces of Frankenstein… and His Creations**: feature by John Gilbert

Page 70: **Stephen Jones' *The Best of Best New Horror: Volume One***: review/feature by Trevor Kennedy

Page 74: **John Stewart: A Forgotten Artist of Fantasy and Supernatural Horror**: feature by James Doig

Page 88: **Lynda E. Rucker interview**

Page 97: **Simon Fisher-Becker interview**

Page 106: **The Many Wars of the Worlds**: feature by Raven Dane

Page 112: ***Planet of the Apes* (1968)**: feature by Dave Jeffery

Page 122: ***Phantasmagoria* Fans' Euphoria**

Page 126: ***Phantasmagoria* Fiction**:

Page 127: **The Fragile Mask On His Face** by David A. Riley
Page 145: **Fair Dues** by Mike Chinn
Page 151: **The Amazing Xandra Lee vs Ned Swann** by Adrian Baldwin
Page 160: **Prey** by Joe X. Young
Page 163: **A Place For Junkmen** by Connor Leggat
Page 180: **Greasehead** by Conor Reid
Page 183: **My Pillow is a Ship** by Marc Damian Lawler
Page 185: **I Should Not Be** by Richard Bell
Page 187: **As Silver Dusk Suffuses Red** by David A. Riley
Page 188: **Byron's Burning Bones** by Emerson Firebird

Page 190: **Batman Triumphant**: feature by Nathan Waring

Page 201: ***Aliens vs Predator – Requiem***: feature by Owen Quinn

Page 208: ***Twin Peaks: Fire Walk With Me* (1992)**: feature by Michael Campbell

Page 215: ***Twin Peaks: Fire Walk With Me*-inspired artwork** by Franki Beddows

Page 217: **Byddi Lee interview**

Page 224: **Casey Biggs interview**

Page 230: **1960s Horror films**: feature by David Brilliance

Page 236: **Reading R. Chetwynd-Hayes** with Marc Damian Lawler

Page 247: ***Phantasmagoria* Reviews**

Page 298: **Acknowledgements**

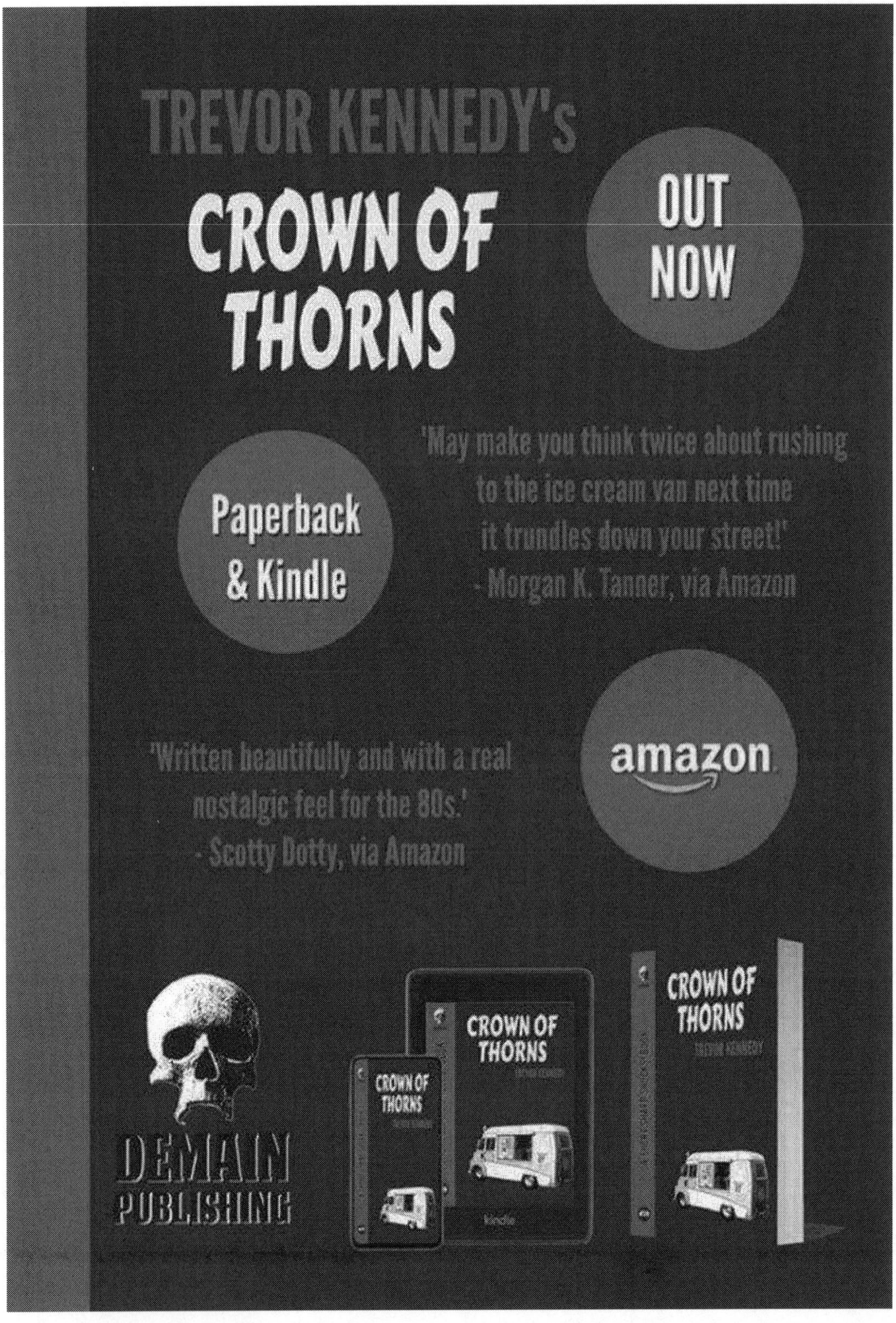

TREVOR KENNEDY's
CROWN OF THORNS
OUT NOW
Paperback & Kindle
'May make you think twice about rushing to the ice cream van next time it trundles down your street!'
- Morgan K. Tanner, via Amazon
amazon
'Written beautifully and with a real nostalgic feel for the 80s.'
- Scotty Dotty, via Amazon
DEMAIN PUBLISHING
CROWN OF THORNS
TREVOR KENNEDY
kindle

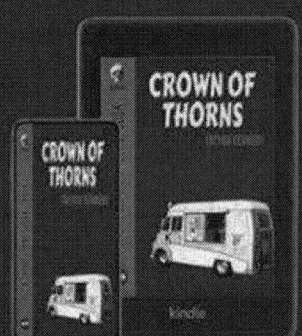

PHANTASMAGORIA MAGAZINE

Editor: Trevor Kennedy

Co-Editor: Allison Weir

Editorial Team: John Gilbert (Consultant Editor), Adrian Baldwin, Helen Scott

Cover and logo design: Adrian Baldwin, www.adrianbaldwin.info

Front cover artwork: Jim Pitts
based on the David A. Riley story "The Fragile Mask on His Face"

Interior artwork: Franki Beddows, Randy Broecker, Dave Carson, Mike Chinn, Stephen Clarke, Peter Coleborn, Allen Koszowski, Jim Pitts, David A. Riley and John Stewart

Contributors: Abdul-Qaadir Taariq Bakari-Muhammad, Richard Bell, David Brilliance, Michael Campbell, Mike Chinn, Con Connolly, Raven Dane, James Doig, Emerson Firebird, Ethan Horner, Dave Jeffery, Carl R. Jennings, James Keen, Doreen Kennedy (administration), Marc Damian Lawler, Connor Leggat, Graham Masterton, Barnaby Page, Owen Quinn, Conor Reid, GCH Reilly, David A. Riley, Michael Stephenson, Sarah Stephenson, David L. Tamarin, Nathan Waring and Joe X. Young

With thanks to Stephen Jones, PS Publishing and The Alchemy Press

COPYRIGHT NOTICE:
I (Trevor Kennedy) have endeavoured to source the copyright details of all pictures and artwork we use within *Phantasmagoria Magazine* but would be glad to appropriately right any omissions in the next issue.
Please contact: tkboss@hotmail.com

COPYRIGHT INFORMATION:
Entire contents are copyright 2020 Phantasmagoria Publishing/TK Pulp (Trevor Kennedy) and the individual contributors. No portion of *Phantasmagoria Magazine* may be reproduced in any form without express permission from the authors. All rights reserved.

Published by Phantasmagoria Publishing/TK Pulp though KDP

EDITORIAL

THE CASE FOR CATHARSIS

WE ARE LIVING in very strange times. At time of writing and publishing, much of the world is still in lockdown due to the coronavirus pandemic, the death toll tragically and dramatically rising on a daily basis, although, I hope, the peak is now truly behind us, with a working vaccine well on the way. Every one of us has been affected by the situation in some shape or form, our once bustling city centres turned into ghost towns, the pubs, restaurants, cinemas, theatres, sporting arenas etc all closed. Same thing for businesses, with many people working from home where viable and only essential workers still out there on the front line, such as our amazing health workers, supermarket employees, postal staff and others, and we salute (and applaud) every single one of them and wish those suffering from COVID-19 a very speedy recovery. Our thoughts are with the families and friends of those who have been taken by this virus, many of whom having contributed to our genre in various ways.

It really is like something from an apocalyptic horror film, and that is not in any way me making light or trivialising what some of us are going through – I personally know people who have been infected and have lost family members to it and it is truly awful. What I do find fascinating, though, is how some people – myself included – often turn to (sometimes very bleak) fictional horror during dark times as a form of escapism and cathartic release from the very real-life horrors of the world. There has been serious scientific research done on this topic and it is always profoundly intriguing to me from a psychological point of view about how the human psyche works, especially in times of crisis.

Generally speaking, most of us love a good thrill and scare from a safe place. That's why roller-coasters were invented, after all. And it can be very good for our mental health and well being as well, purging our inner fears and demons through make-believe situations on the page or screen. They educate us and fuel our imaginations greatly too, so surely this can only be a good thing?

Of course, horror (and sci-fi and fantasy) isn't for everyone and that's perfectly fine too – each to their own. I have, however, heard serious claims that certain films (and by extension, books) of a more heavier nature have caused people to become clinically depressed. If that is indeed the case then it goes without saying that it is best to stay clear of those types of films and perhaps the holding up of the mirror to real societal issues is too uncomfortable for some, but in my opinion, it is imperative that these things *are* dealt with in some manner, whether this be through fiction or other means. On a personal level, fiction – books, films and especially my own writing and publishing ventures – has been the most important factor in my recovery from addiction-related troubles, after many years of attempting other means unsuccessfully. I cannot stress this enough. It has been my saviour, my returning fully to who I was before all my problems began in my youth. To those of you who have supported me on this journey, I cannot thank you enough!

During the current lockdown, I have been even more so indulging myself in books, films and television series of a strange variety, including *A Field in England* (I can't believe this modern folk horror classic slipped under my radar until now!), and revisiting classics such as John Carpenter's *The Thing*, Robert Egger's *The Witch*, Clive Barker's *Hellraiser* and *Nightbreed*, *District 9*, some of David Lynch's back catalogue and Romero's original *...of the Dead* trilogy, along with a large selection of books, which really have helped to get me through the long days and nights. Heck, I even watched that superbly deranged *Tiger King* documentary series from Netflix.

I suppose we all have our own specific ways of dealing with life's trials and tribulations when they come along, but never underestimate the power of a good book or film to take us away, albeit temporarily, to fantasy lands and situations where we can lose ourselves for some hours. They help us understand the world and who we are a little bit more, collectively and on our own, while at the same time greatly entertaining and inspiring us too, making life much more exciting, thought-provoking and worthwhile. And you'll not get any better value than that, my friends!

Welcome to *Phantasmagoria* issue 15! Last time we spoke I reported that

Stokercon 2020 and the Great Yarmouth Sci-Fi Weekender had been very understandably postponed due to the pandemic outbreak. Stokercon has now been rescheduled for Thursday 6th August 2020 to Sunday 9th August (situation permitting), whilst the Great Yarmouth Sci-Fi Weekender will be held in March 2021. *Phantasmagoria* plans to have a strong presence at both of these so we hope to see as many of you there as possible.

In other news, we should be stocked in the shops again soon too, namely Forbidden Planet Megastore London, Forbidden Planet Belfast and Coffee & Heroes (Belfast) as soon as they re-open. In the meantime, all of our back issues are still available to purchase throughout the world from Amazon, including the two Specials so far, based around *The Lovecraft Squad* and R. Chetwynd-Hayes. Two more Specials are currently in the works and will be centred on a couple of literary legends, namely M. R. James and Karl Edward Wagner.

For this issue, we have another fine selection of material from our talented team for your consideration. There's interviews with a couple of British horror author greats – Graham Masterton and Aidan Chambers – horror/cult film acting legend Lynn Lowry, *Doctor Who* and *Harry Potter* star Simon Fisher-Becker, along with authors Lynda E. Rucker and Byddi Lee, and *Star Trek* actor Casey Biggs. On top of this, we've been given the honour of something of a world exclusive in the form of an extract from Graham Masterton's brand new novel – *The House of a Hundred Whispers* – due for release in October. Randy Broecker exclusively provides us with some of his sublime illustrations from Aidan Chambers' new book – *Dead Trouble & Other Ghost Stories* – as well.

Also included are features on Frankenstein, Stephen Jones' *The Best of Best New Horror: Volume One*, the artist John Stewart, *The War of the Worlds*, *Planet of the Apes* (1968), *Batman Begins* from 2005, *Aliens vs Predator – Requiem* (2007) and David Lynch's *Twin Peaks: Fire Walk With Me* (1992), whilst David Brilliance gives us his thoughts on the horror films of the 1960s and Marc Damian Lawler checks out another classic R. Chetwynd-Hayes story. As always, there is a large variety of high quality fiction, artwork (on top of the wonderful original cover painting by Jim Pitts based on David A. Riley's story "The Fragile Mask on His Face", which also appears!) and reviews on display from the regular team too.

Phantasmagoria will return later in the summer with issue 16 and one of those aforementioned Specials, so until then, please take care and stay safe and well.

Trevor Kennedy,
Belfast, Northern Ireland
June, 2020

PHANTASMAGORIA SPECIAL EDITION SERIES

ISSUE #2: THE LOVECRAFT SQUAD

RETAILING FROM AMAZON, FORBIDDEN PLANET MEGASTORE LONDON, FORBIDDEN PLANET BELFAST AND COFFEE & HEROES (BELFAST)

(Cover artwork by Douglas Klauba.
Cover and logo design by Adrian Baldwin, www.adrianbaldwin.info)

LOOKING INTO
GRAHAM MASTERTON'S ЯOЯЯIM

A brand new interview with the author by Marc Damian Lawler

*Marc Damian Lawler chats in-depth to legendary horror (and other genres) author **Graham Masterton** about his novel **Mirror** and more, in an interview that also features extracts from the classic work, which Marc takes a detailed look at, whilst a certain ghost even gatecrashes the interview at one point too.*

When I look into Graham Masterton's *Mirror*, I see back to when I looked into the mirror on the cover of the first paperback edition (Sphere, 1988) and marked the words written in red on the silvery surface:

**ON THE
OTHER SIDE
OF THE
MIRROR
LIES A
NIGHTMARE**

...and indeed there was: rushing towards me on the inside cover, blazed Satan in the fiery form of a bad ass dragon; its shiny black claws dangerously close to my fingertips.

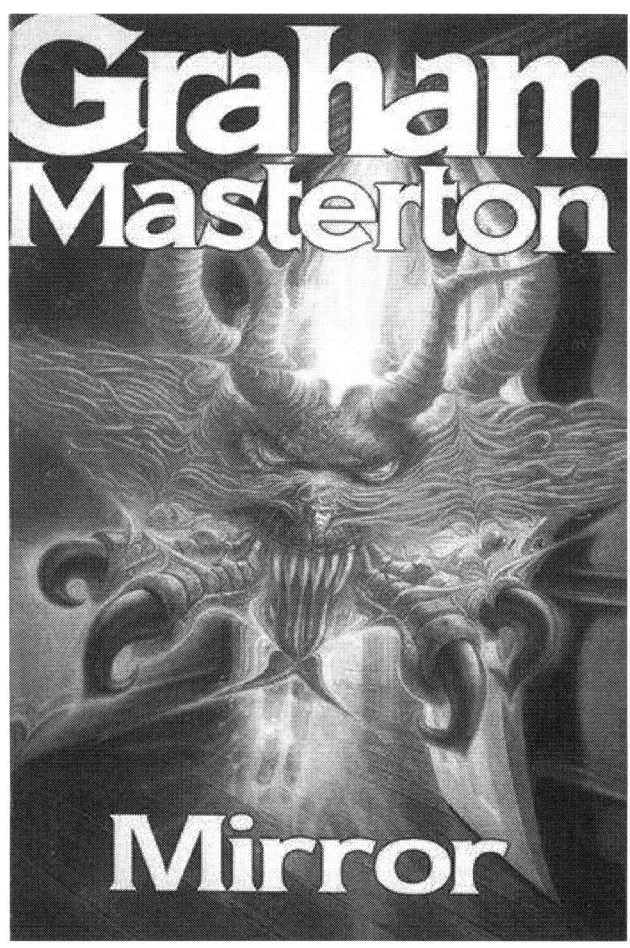

The blurb:

Screenwriter Martin Williams is a man possessed. His obsession – 'Boofuls', the darling boy-angel of 30s Hollywood, whose horrific death was more spectacular than anything Hollywood ever dreamed up...
   Now fifty years later all Martin wants is to make the movie that will bring Boofuls back to life. He can't believe his luck when he manages to buy a mirror from his idol's house. But that mirror was there when Boofuls died, and it has seen many things, more than the human eye can imagine...
   Strange things happen in the mirror. Stranger things happen to people who try to probe its secrets. And Martin is about to enter the gateway through which all hell will break loose...

Marc Damian Lawler: Where were you when Boofuls flickered to life on the silver screen of your mind?

Graham Masterton: Boofuls appeared in my mind during one of our many stays in Hollywood. I was negotiating the contract for *The Manitou* movie and apart from that my publishers Pinnacle had moved out to Los Angeles. It was while I was sitting by the pool at the Sunset Marquis reading about the child movie stars of the 1930s and 40s. I was interested in particular in the tragic story of Scotty Beckett, who appeared in *Our Gang* and several notable movies with major stars before his career collapsed and he ended up drunk and on drugs and involved in petty crime. Scotty had first been noticed as young as three years old, because of his singing voice.

'Metro held a 'Name the Child Star' contest in the newspapers, and the short list of names was sent to Louis B Mayer. Mr. Mayer read them, hated them all, and scribbled in the margin, B. Awful'. This half-illegible comment was taken by a wholly illiterate secretary to be Mayer's own suggestion for little Walter's new name, and she typed it and sent it to the publicity office. At least, that was the way Mr. Mayer told the story, and Boofuls himself never contradicted him.' (p. 27)

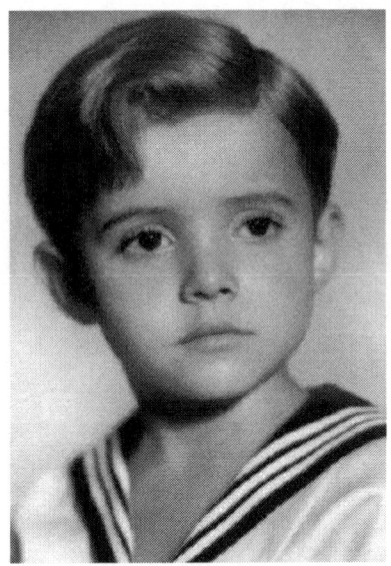

(Tragic child star Scotty Beckett)

MDL: How did the name 'Boofuls' come to you? Is it a play on the word, 'beautiful' – or is it named after a Jelly Baby? Apparently, the green ones are called 'Boofuls'.

GM: As you suggest, 'Boofuls' is just a childish way of saying 'Beautiful'. I also liked the way it suggested 'boo!' which is used to scare children.

MDL: Was *Mirror* written during one of your stays at Rancho Santa Fe in San Diego?

GM: I didn't write when we were staying in Rancho Santa Fe, because they really were restorative vacations and there was plenty to occupy my time apart from writing; like swimming and sunbathing and taking our sons to San Diego Zoo. We went to Rancho Santa Fe so often that we made good friends there including Neil Reagan, Ronald Reagan's older brother, who gave me one of those 'Reagan Country' election posters. My son still has it framed on his living-room wall. We were also invited to judge the Rancho Santa Fe flower show.

MDL: That was where thirty-nine members of the UFO doomsday cult, Heaven's Gate (inc. their leader, Marshall Applewhite), based in San Diego, checked out of planet Earth in the belief their souls would be picked up by an extraterrestrial spacecraft tailing comet Hale-Bopp and transported to another "level of existence above human". Did you read about their dotty delusion and consider it as a possible inspiration for a San Diego-set sci-fi / horror novel?

GM: I read about this cult, although it didn't inspire me to write a novel about it. I prefer characters who are evil rather than deluded.

MDL: *Mirror* reads like it was penned by an Angeleno. You must have taken special care to achieve an authentic narrative voice to match the setting.

GM: We visited LA so often that it wasn't difficult to pick up the expressions and the intonations. I was trained as a newspaper reporter so I was always careful to listen to the way that different people expressed themselves and the words they used to emphasise what they were saying. Apart from that, I have always been interested in local dialects and slang. I have written many novels featuring American characters, from Harry Erskine, the fake fortune-teller in *The Manitou* to Jim Rook, the remedial English teacher who has the ability to see demons and ghosts from every kind of ethnic mythology. When my late wife Wiescka and I went to live in Cork, in southern Ireland, I was immediately fascinated by the accent and the slang, which led me to create Detective Superintendent Katie Maguire... whose adventures now span 11 novels. In Cork, shopping is 'the messages', a haircut is a 'bazzer' and to give somebody 'down the banks' is to give them a good telling-off. A Cork accent is very different from other Irish accents and I spent a long time trying to copy it. The only problem with immersing yourself so much in the language and the thinking of another country is that it takes a long while to get over it. I still say 'thanks a million' and 'that's grand altogether', after nearly a decade. Wiescka used to complain that I talked like an Angeleno after I had finished *Mirror* and like a Corkonian after the first Katie Maguire novel *White Bones*.

GM: *'I have to be frightened by what I'm doing. There has to be at least one moment – hopefully it's underlying through the whole experience – when there is a true feeling of fear in me.'*

MDL: Can you remember what that moment was when you were writing *Mirror*?

GM: I was in the Plaza hotel in New York. I could see a reflection of myself crossing the foyer, and close behind me was a small boy wearing a gray sweater and short pants. When I reached the desk, I turned around and there was no sign of him. It was only later that I was able to see that there was another mirror which gave a double image, rather like a hall of mirrors in a funfair. I have always thought, too, that the visual effect you sometimes experience in hotel bathrooms where you see yourself reflected about a hundred times over is quite spooky. What if that 'you' in one of those myriad reflections is the real you, and you yourself are just one of those images.

"'I was like the guy who buys Playboy *and tells himself he's buying it for the articles.'"* (p. 2)

MDL: Part of your job as the deputy editor of *Mayfair* magazine, and the executive editor of the UK edition of *Penthouse*, was to commission the articles between the photo spreads – referred to as the 'excuse material'. Do you have a funny anecdote that you can share with us about it?

GM: When *Penthouse* was starting up in the US in 1969, I started to visit New York regularly. I soon got to know American publishers, such as Howard Kaminsky of NAL, who encouraged me to write my first sex how-to book *How a Woman Longs to be Loved*. (Howard Kaminsky, apropos of nothing at all, was the cousin of Mel Brooks, whose real name is Mel Kaminsky). That first sex book was published under the name of 'Angel Smith', and there was a picture of Angel on the jacket in a wet T-shirt. The book sold a huge amount of copies (remember that these were the days when about the only non-medical sex book was *The Joy of Sex*) and Angel received heaps of fan mail, including proposals of marriage. One morning she received a padded postal package and when I opened it I found a letter inside that read 'Dear Angel, I adore you... I would do anything to meet you and show you how much I have learned from your wonderful book. I have included a gift just for you.' Inside the package was a condom, and the letter went on to say, 'I have rolled this on myself and rolled it off again. I hope you appreciate it.' If there is a world record for how far and how fast a condom can be flung across a room, I hold that record!

After that, I insisted on writing sex books under my own name, such as *How to Drive Your Man Wild In Bed*, which sold half a million copies in six months, and enabled me to give up working for *Penthouse* and make a good living as an author. (Again, apropos of nothing at all, *How to Drive Your Man Wild In Bed* is one of only 26 books still banned in the Irish Republic, but is still a massive seller today in Poland under the title *Magia Seksu*.) It wasn't too long, though, before the market for sex books was flooded, and my publishers said they didn't want any more. I pointed out that they were already contracted to publish my next book, *How To Turn Yourself On*, but if they didn't want that, I could send them a horror novel that I had written for my own amusement in between sex books. That was *The Manitou*. The publishers liked it, apart from the ending, in which Misquamacus the vengeful medicine man was killed off by Vietnam Rose, the venereal disease which Karen Tandy's boyfriend had given her after serving in Saigon. That was a deliberate echo of the H. G. Wells novel *The War of the Worlds* in which the Martians succumbed to the common cold, and also to the reality of the thousands of Native Americans who died from the smallpox that the settlers brought with them (and it has chilling echoes, too, of today's pandemic!). I wrote a new ending in which Misquamacus was zapped by computers, and that's the version that was filmed, with Susan Strasberg's nightgown conveniently dropping down to her waist.

MDL: *Mirror* is a fantastic evocation of the time period it was written in; especially when it comes to mentioning the big TV shows and monster film hits of the 80s:

"'Touch this desk and you die, suckah!'" (p.5)

*"'It beats me, you know, how **Rambo** can gross seventy-five million dollars, with all its shooting and killing and phoney philosophy… and here, here"* – *slapping his screenplay in the palm of his hand* – *"is the most entertaining and enchanting musical ever made, and everyone sniffs at me as if I've trodden in something.'"* (p.34)

'He wondered mischievously if Kit the talking car could turn out to be gay: if he could come out of the garage, so to speak.' (p. 56)

*'It may not be foolproof, but could you use a rope when you go into the mirror, just like in **Poltergeist**…'* (p. 317)

Am I right in thinking that the year the story takes place in is 1985? Martin says he has some work to do on a **Knight Rider** teleplay, and the last episode of that show was filmed at the beginning of '86. It also ties in with the release of **Rambo** (May '85) and the start of the fourth season of **The A-Team** (Sept. '85), when the show was still at the height of its popularity and working on it would have been considered (perhaps not financially, because Martin has only $578 in his savings account) a big deal for a screenwriter.

GM: Yes, I think 1985 is a pretty good guess. Our three sons were all addicts of those TV shows and the **Rambo** movies in those days so I got to see them whether I liked it or not. In fact they still quote **Rambo** today, especially when one of them tells a bad joke and they post the clip of Sylvester Stallone falling into the tree and saying 'Jeeeezzuss!'

MDL: I love the lyrics to / info. about Boofuls' songs; especially

'Heartstrings':

> *You play such sweet music*
> *How can I resist*
> *Every song from your heartstrings*
> *Makes me feel I've just been kissed*

'Whistlin' Dixie, *of course, became one of the most successful musicals of all time. Boofuls' show-stopping song 'Heartstrings' sold more copies than 'All My Eggs in One Basket'; and when he accepted his Oscar in 1937 for* **The Story of Louis Pasteur**, *Paul Muni joked that he had only beaten Boofuls for the award 'because they thought it was too heavy for him, and he might drop it.'* (p. 27)

GM: Those songs were all written by me. I am always writing songs in my head. It's actually quite a nuisance. I tried to purge myself of the habit by writing a humorous novel called *If Pigs Could Sing* about two country boys who become famous rock singers and make so much money that they can afford to pay a special guy to pick the pineapple off their pizzas.

> *The girl I love is a goddess on earth*
> *But one day she fell out of a blimp*
> *She hit a haystack at 54 ½ miles an hour*
> *And she now has a left-footed limp*

MDL: Was this extract your inspiration for the transformation of Ramone's cat?

'How would you like to live in Looking-Glass House, Kitty? I wonder if they'd give you milk in there? Perhaps looking-glass milk isn't good to drink.' — Lewis Carroll, *Alice Through the Looking-Glass*

GM: Yes, a lot of the logic and the atmosphere of *Mirror* comes from *Alice*.

"Here, Lugosi!" called Wanda. "Here, pussy-pussy!"
  It was then that Martin heard the faint thump-thump-thump of a furry tail on the floor, and the low death-rattle sound of a cat purring.
  "Sounds like he's under the desk someplace," he told Wanda, and hunkered down to take a look.
  Thump, thump, thump. Prrrrrr-prrrrrr-prrrrrr.
  "Lugosi?" he asked, and his voice was clogged with phlegm. Two eyes opened in the darkness. Two eyes that burned incandescent blue, like the flames of welding torches.

"Lugosi?" asked Martin, although this time it was scarcely a question at all.

Something hard and vicious came flying out from under the desk and landed directly in his face, knocking him backwards onto the floor. He was so surprised that he didn't even shout out, but Wanda did – a startled wail, and then a piercing scream.

He felt claws tearing at his neck; claws tearing at his cheeks. His mouth was gagged with soft, fetid fur.

Panicking, he seized the cat's body in both hands and tried to drag it away from his face, but its claws were hooked into his ears and his scalp, and he couldn't get it free.

"Aaahh!" he heard himself shouting. "Wanda, help me! Wanda!"
Wanda came blustering into the room and slapped at the cat, but didn't know what else to do. Martin rolled over and over on the floor, tipping over his chair with his pedalling legs, colliding against his desk; but the cat clung viciously to his head, lacerating his face with claws that felt like whips made out of razor wire.

My eyes! thought Martin in terror. It's trying to claw out my eyes!' (p. 86)

MDL: I don't know what effect milk has on cats in Hollywood the Other Way Around, but that certainly wasn't Lugosi that slinked back out of the mirror.

'... he thought he heard a child's voice, close to his ear, whisper, 'Pickle-nearest-the-wind'.

He sat up... The drapes stirred a little as if a child was hiding behind them, but Martin realized it was only the morning breeze.

Pickle-nearest-the-wind. What the hell did that mean?' (p.69)

Apart from it being quirky and mysterious and, of course, referring to Boofuls' cat, is there a deeper, hidden meaning to 'Pickle-nearest-the-wind' that the reader isn't privy to?

GM: I seem to remember that it's a paraphrase of a metaphor in a foreign language, but for the life of me I can't remember what it was or what it meant. I thought it might be Polish (my late wife Wiescka being Polish) and I have asked several of my Polish friends but so far no luck! If I ever recall what it was I'll come back to you!

MDL: Apart from Boofuls, my favourite character is Homer Theobald.

"'I'm not a medium or a spiritualist or a psychic. I'm a sensitive. That means my mind is sensitive. What you have in this apartment is a raging beast, my *friend. It's already tried to claw you to pieces, but only your face. If I go in there, it's going to claw my mind to pieces. I'm sorry, I understand your problem, but I don't wish to spend the rest of my life with the IQ of a head of broccoli.'"* (p. 133-4)

You describe him as looking like Uncle Fester, but on the audiobook he sounds more **Breakfast at Tiffany's** than **Addams Family**. Is Truman Capote a comparison too far, or is the narrator, Robert Slade, on the right vocal track?

GM: Homer Theobald is a complete invention, so he can sound like anybody you like!

MDL: Which one of Boofuls' mirror murders was your favourite to write?
My favourite to read is Dr. Rice's:

"'Tell-tale-tit, your tongue shall be split, and every cat and dog in town shall have a little bit!"
Dr. Rice cut into his own tongue with the hairdressing scissors. There was a terrible crunch of flesh that he could feel down to the roots of his tongue, right down to the pit of his stomach. His throat muscles contracted in an attempt to scream, but the grip on his neck remained, and there was nothing he could do but choke and struggle.' (p. 163)

GM: To be honest with you, *Mirror* was written a long time ago on a planet far, far away, and I have written about 75 more novels since then, so it is hard to remember every scene. For me, though, the key moment will always be when the ball comes bouncing into the room in the mirror... but not in the real room.

'... he saw a child's blue and white ball come bouncing through the open door behind him, and then roll to a stop in the middle of the varnished wood floor.
He stared at it in shock, with that same shrinking-scalp sensation that he had felt this afternoon when he had seen Mrs Harper floating in midair. "Emilio?" he called. "Is that you?"
There was no reply. Martin turned around and called, "Emilio?" again.
He got up out of his chair, intending to pick the ball up, but he was only halfway standing when he realized that it wasn't there anymore.
He frowned, and walked across to the door, and opened it wider. The passageway was empty; the front door was locked. "Emilio, what the hell are you playing at?"
He looked in the bedroom. Nobody. He even opened up the closet doors.

Just dirty shirts and shorts, waiting to be washed, and a squash racket that needed restringing. He checked the bathroom, then the kitchen. Apart from himself, the apartment was deserted.

"Hallucination," he told himself. "Maybe I'm falling apart." He returned to the sitting room and picked up his glass of wine. He froze with the glass almost touching his lips. In the mirror, the blue and white ball was still there, lying on the floor where it had first bounced.

Martin stared at it and then quickly looked back into the real sitting room. No ball. Yet there it was in the mirror, perfectly clear, as plain as milk.

Martin walked carefully across the room. Watching himself in the mirror, he reached down and tried to pick the ball up, but in the real room there was nothing there, and in the mirror room his hand appeared simply to pass right through the ball, as if it had no substance at all.

He scooped at it two or three times and waved his hand from side to side exactly where the ball should have been. Still nothing. But the really odd part about it was that as he watched his hand intently, it seemed as if it were not the ball that was insubstantial, but his own fingers – as if the ball were real and that reflection of himself in the mirror were a ghost.

He went right up close to the mirror and touched its surface. There was nothing unusual about it. It was simply cold glass. But the ball remained there, whether it was a hallucination or a trick of the light, or whatever. He sat in his chair and watched it and it refused to disappear.

After half an hour, he got up and went to the bathroom to shower. The ball was still there when he returned. He finished the wine, watching it all the time. He was going to have a hangover in the morning, but right now he didn't much care.

"What the hell are you?" he asked the ball.

He pressed his cheek against the left side of the mirror and tried to peer into his own reflected hallway, to see if it was somehow different. *Looking-Glass House*, he thought to himself, and all those unsettling childhood feelings came back to him. If you could walk through the door in the mirror, would the hallway be the same? Was there another different world in there, not just back to front but disturbingly different?

In his bookshelf, he had a dog-eared copy of *Alice Through the Looking-Glass* which Jane had bought him when they were first dating. He took it out and opened it up and quickly located the half-remembered words.

Alice was looking into the mirror over her sitting room fireplace, wondering about the room she could see on the other side of the glass.

'It's just the same as our drawing-room, only the things go the other way. I can see all of it when I get upon a chair – all but the bit just behind the fire-place. Oh! I do so wish I could see that bit! I want so much to know whether they've a fire in the winter: you never can tell, you know, unless our fire smokes, and then smoke comes up in that room, too – but that may only be pretence, just to make it look as if they had a fire. Well then, the books are something like our books, only the words go the wrong way: I know that, because I've held up one of our books to the glass, and then they hold one up in the other room. But now we come to the passage. You can see just a little peep of the passage in Looking-Glass House, if you leave the door of our drawing-room wide open: and it's very like our passage as far as you can see, only you know it may be quite different on beyond.'

Martin closed the book. The ball was still there. He stood looking at it for a long time, not moving. Then he went across to his desk and switched off the light, so that the sitting room was completely dark. He paused, and then he switched it back on again. The ball in the mirror hadn't moved.

"Shit," he said; and for the very first time in his life he felt that something was happening to him which he couldn't control.

He could have gotten Jane back if he had really wanted to – at least, he believed that he could. He could have been wealthier if he had written all the dumb teleplays that Morris had wanted him to write. But he had been able to make his own decisions about things like that. This ball was something else altogether. A ball that existed only as a reflection in a mirror, and not in reality?

"Shit," he repeated, and switched off the light again and shuffled off to the bedroom. He dropped his red flannel bathrobe and climbed naked onto his futon. He was about to switch off his bedside light when a thought occurred to him. He padded back to the sitting room and closed the door. If there was anything funny about that mirror, he didn't want it coming out and jumping on him in the middle of the night.

Irrational, yes, but he was tired and a little drunk and it was well past midnight.

He dragged the covers well up to his neck, even though he was too hot, and closed his eyes, and tried to sleep.

He was awakened by what sounded like a child laughing. He lifted his head from the pillow and thought, Goddamned Emilio, why do kids always have to wake up at the crack of dawn? But then he heard the laughter again, and it didn't sound as if it were coming from downstairs at all. It sounded as if it were coming from his own sitting room.

He sat up straight, holding his breath, listening. There it was again. A small boy, laughing out loud; but with a curious echo to his voice, as if he were laughing in a large empty room. Martin checked his clock radio. It wasn't the crack of dawn at all: it was only 3:17 in the morning.

He switched on his light, wincing at the brightness of it. He found his bathrobe and tugged it on, inside out, so that he had to hold it together *instead of tying it. Then he went to the sitting room door and listened.*

He listened for almost a minute. Then he asked himself: "What are you afraid of, wimp? It's your own apartment, your own sitting room, and all you can hear is a child."

He licked his lips, and then he opened the sitting room door. Immediately, he reached out for the light switch and turned on the main light. Immediately, he looked toward the mirror.

There was nobody there, no boy laughing. Only himself, frowzy and pale, in his inside-out bathrobe. Only the desk and the typewriter and the bookshelf and the pictures of Boofuls.

He approached the mirror slowly. One thing was different. One thing that he could never prove was different, not even to himself. The blue and white ball had gone.

He looked toward the reflected door, half open, and the peep of the passageway outside. It's very like our own passage as far as you can see, only you know it may be quite different on beyond.

How different? thought Martin with a dry mouth. How different? Because if a ball had come bouncing into the reflected room, there must have been somebody there to throw it; and if it had disappeared, then somebody must have walked into that reflected room when he was asleep and picked it up.

"Oh God." He swallowed. "Oh, God, don't let it be Boofuls."' (p. 21-24)

(RORRIM S'NATAS, the French edition of *Mirror* from 2003)

'Martin opened his eyes wide and stared. The shock of waking up and finding that Boofuls was actually holding his hand was so violent and numbing that he couldn't do anything at all, he couldn't move, couldn't speak.

"Did I frighten you?" asked Boofuls. His voice was clear and reedy, with the precise enunciation of prewar years. "I didn't mean to frighten you. You knew I was coming, didn't you? You did know?"' (p. 174)

MDL: The emotional experience at the heart of the story is Martin Williams' journey from Boofuls' number one fan to his number one enemy.

The phrase, 'You should never meet your heroes', could have been especially written for Martin Williams. (For me, it's Anna Maxwell Martin – a bloody good actress, but an absolute cow to meet; and Donovan – who almost single-handedly destroyed my hope that the hippie dream had been real.) Is there someone famous that you held in high regard, but changed your mind after you met them?

GM: I don't like to speak ill of anybody. We all have our foibles, but sometimes fame does make some people foibler than others, to coin a word. I was a big fan of Allen Ginsberg's poetry when I was about 15. Poems like *Howl* showed me that you could write without fear about anything you wanted, and in the most straightforward language. Years later when William Burroughs moved to live in London, he and I became friends, and I regularly used to drop in to his apartment in Duke Street. Several well-known Beats used to show up, including Alex Trocchi and Brion Gysin, and one evening Allen Ginsberg appeared. To say that he was up his own rear end would be an understatement. Nobody else could get a word in edgewise. Then he declared that he was jet-lagged and lay on the living-room floor to have a rest, draping his greasy black curls all over one of my brand-new pale suede Italian shoes, which left a stain I could never get rid of. I also spent an afternoon round at Christopher Lee's apartment in Hollywood, discussing a movie project with my agent. Let's just say that in real life I didn't find him very different than his character in **The Wicker Man** – or **Dracula**, for that matter. One horror movie actor I really adored was Ingrid Pitt, who had actually appeared in **The Wicker Man**, too, and **Countess Dracula**. She lived in London and we talked about doing a movie together (the details of which are a long and unbelievable story in themselves). Ingrid was Polish, like Wiescka, and the two of them got on really well. Sadly Ingrid has gone too.

MDL: Do you have a favourite line or passage in the book? Two of my favourites are:

'The mirror remembers Boofuls being killed.' (p. 140)

GM: I like that line too.

'They took hold of the mirror. Mr Capelli chanted, "One-a, two-a, three-a –"

Without a word, both Martin and Ramone released their grip, and stood up, and stepped away. They looked into each other's eyes; and each of them knew that the other had shared his experience.

'When they had tried to lift the mirror, a strong dark wave had gone through each of their minds, black and inhuman but undeniably alive – like centipede legs rippling, or the cilia of some soulless sea creature, cold, pressurized, an intelligence without emotion and without remorse and with no interest in anything at all but its own supremacy and its own survival.' (p. 116)

GM: I rarely have favourite lines or passages in books. I have favourite books, of which *Mirror* is one because I was entranced by *Alice Through The Looking Glass* when I was young, and also because it reminds me of good times in Hollywood, where I still have friends in the movie business. You mentioned that Donovan disillusioned you about hippiedom, but his rendition of *The Walrus and the Carpenter* from *Alice* on his album *HMS Donovan* is really worth a listen.

MDL: I love it when you offer us a fictionalised glimpse into Lewis Carroll's mirror:

"'I believe I came as close to death as a man may go and yet return to the real world. I saw darkness; and I saw unimaginable beings; human beings with heads as huge as carnival masks; creatures with hunchbacks; dogs that spoke. It seems to me now like a dream, or rather a nightmare, but I was convinced that I saw Purgatory, the realm in which each man takes on his true form. In the land beyond the looking-glass, in the world of reflections, is the life after death, and the life before death. I understand now the closeness of Christianity, which teaches each man that he will have his reward or his punishment in the world beyond, and the Hindu religion, which teaches that a man will be reincarnated according to the life he has led.'" (p. 233)

GM: It was Alice that started my fascination with mirrors; particularly Carroll's notion that if you could somehow see beyond the reflection –

through the door and along the corridor – you would find yourself in a world where the normal rules of existence were back-to-front... I used to press my cheek against my grandparents' mirror as close as I could, trying in vain to see through their drawing-room windows, and into the gardens beyond, where I was sure that I would see different people walking about, and different weather. But all I ever managed to do was to leave a hot cheek-shaped oval on the glass.

There are myths and superstitions about mirrors in almost every culture. In the Jewish religion, it is important to cover all mirrors in a house where someone has died while the family is sitting Shivah (the seven-day mourning period). It is said that if the mirrors aren't covered, the spirit of the deceased may become trapped in one and not be able to move on to the afterlife. Some cultures took this further, insisting that mirrors should be covered at night and when people in the house are sleeping, to make sure that a dreamer's wandering soul doesn't get trapped in one. In Serbo-Croatian culture, a mirror was sometimes buried with the dead, both to prevent the spirit from wandering and to keep evil men from rising. Then, of course, there's the superstition about holding a candle up to a mirror and saying 'Bloody Mary' seven times, until the scary Mary actually appears.

MDL: Rumour has it that L.P. Travers' inspiration for Mary Poppins was 'Bloody Mary'.

When she was five, she had held a candle up to her looking-glass and was told by a woman drenched in blood, who was standing by the fire-place in the reflection of her bedroom, "Close your mouth please, Pamela. You are not a codfish. Now spit spot, into bed, like a good little girl, and I might decide not to scratch your eyes out and steal your soul."

In 2016, Lewis Carroll's very own looking-glass was sold at Bonhams for £5,000. Were you tempted to buy it; or indeed, are you now its proud owner?

GM: I was not aware that Carroll's mirror was for sale, and wouldn't have paid that much for it anyway.

'... he wasn't there. There was no reflection of him...
He stepped up to the mirror, his heart beating in long, slow thumps. He touched it. Then he understood what he had done. He had killed his own reflection. He could never appear in a mirror again.' (p. 337)

MDL: I wonder... Would it be a curse or a blessing to never have to see your own reflection again?

GM: It was only some time after *Mirror* was published that I came across the poem *Mirror* by Sylvia Plath. This poem superbly sums up the curse and the blessing of mirrors and it is worth reading all of it. In some ways mirrors are a blessing because they alert us to how quickly time is passing and ensure that we are always encouraged to look our best. In other ways, as the last lines of Plath's poem show, they are a curse: *In me she has drowned a young girl, and in me an old woman | Rises toward her day after day, like a terrible fish.*

MDL: Then there's Paul Muldoon's poem about a malign mirror. I love the lines:

> *'I was afraid it would sneak*
> *down from the wall and swallow me up*
> *in one gulp in the middle of the night.'*

GM: Another strong influence on the writing of *Mirror* was Alfred, Lord Tennyson's *The Lady of Shalott*: *'The mirror crack'd from side to side; "The curse is come upon me," cried The Lady of Shalott.'*

(From *Mirror*): '"A curse on you for buying that mirror," said Mr. Capelli bitterly.
  "Yes," said Martin. "A curse on me."' (p. 336)

MDL: Waterhouse not only painted Tennyson's, *The Lady of Shalott*, but also *Mariana*; both poems about embowered young women. In the painting, Mariana is kneeling in front of a mirror – only her body from the waist up is reflected. I've often wondered, "What if her legs aren't there on the other side?" Her mirror self missing the lower half of her body like a dismembered ghost.
  What do you think ghosts see when they look in a mirror?

GM: I have no idea what ghosts see when they look in the mirror. You will have to ask one.

MDL: Well, it's funny you should say that...

Boofuls: Hello, Marc. I'm glad you enjoyed Graham's book about me.

MDL: It was a pleasure reading about you. Which version of you am I talking to?

B: I'm the Boofuls that was chopped up – the reflection who died and is now a ghost.

MDL: What do you see when you look in a mirror?

B: That depends.

MDL: Depends on what?

B: Which mirror I'm looking into.

MDL: Is there much of a difference?

B: Oh, yes – a great deal. For example, if it's one in which a serial killer shaves, I see their next victim's face staring into their own mirror on the day they are murdered.

MDL: How do you know it's on the day they are murdered?

B: Because no matter what the cause of death is, everyone looks into a mirror at least once on the day they die.

MDL: But what if they haven't? For example, they're in the wilderness camping, or ill in bed?

B: Then that is not the day they die.

MDL: So it's a 100 % full-proof way of avoiding death?

B: Sure is.

MDL: Thanks for the tip.

B: [smiling sweetly] You're welcome, Marc.

'... *supposing this is all true – supposing Mrs. Crossley killed Boofuls because she thought he was trying to bring back Satan – how do you think she found out about it? How do you think she found out what to do, to stop him? And where did she get hold of a sword blessed by God and the angel Michael?*' (p. 235)

MDL: Have you considered writing a prequel to *Mirror*? I'd love to read about his grandmother's emotional journey from taking care of him – to really taking care of him!

GM: Even though some of the supernatural premises of my novels are totally wacky, I always try to make them as believable as I can. Part of being believable is leaving questions unanswered, because life is like that.

I always like to progress and develop with my writing and so I have never been tempted to write prequels. I have been asked again and again by readers to bring back Harry Erskine from *The Manitou* or Jim Rook from *Garden of Evil* or Sissy Sawyer from *Touchy and Feely*, but there are new characters and new stories to be explored. When I did end a novel conclusively, such as *Unspeakable* (I won't spoil it for you by telling you what happens) I was met with a storm of protest and even messages saying that I had left my readers in a state of shock, with their mouths hanging open. So maybe it's better to leave them scratching their heads.

MDL: Did you plan to have the VORPAL sword made out of a long shard of Boofuls' broken mirror glass, or was it one of those wonderful – in the moment of writing it – ideas?

GM: That was planned, roughly, although I am not a great forward planner when it comes to novels because the characters as they develop can often change the course of a story quite radically. New characters will pop up that I never thought of when I was starting the book, and characters will say things or do things that later prove to be key to the way the story works out. It's a bit like being a clockmaker with cogs and springs and levers all lying on the workbench in front of you, and gradually they all come together.

MDL: In Shirley Temple's autobiography, *Child Star*, she describes several instances of sexual harassment at the hands of Hollywood studio heads. When writing *Mirror*, did you consider giving Boofuls a more sympathetic reason for wanting to destroy if not the world, then at least Hollywood?

GM: No, I didn't. When you read about the lives of most of these child stars, they were exploited relentlessly. A few of them survived the experience and either went on to become adult actors or lead a reasonably normal and happy life. But I have seen what fame can do to some people and it's no wonder that they become psychotic or alcoholic or drug-addicted.

"'... Nobody, but nobody, is going to want to make a picture about Boofuls. Why do you think that nobody's done it already?"

"Maybe nobody thought of it," suggested Martin. "Maybe somebody thought of it, but felt that it was too obvious. But it seems like a natural to me. The small golden-haired boy from Idaho state orphanage who became a worldwide star in less than three years."

"Oh, sure," Morris agreed. *"And then got himself chopped up into more pieces than a Colonel Sanders Party Bucket."* (p. 1)

MDL: Is there a reason why *Mirror* hasn't been adapted for the big or small screen?

GM: *Mirror* has been optioned three times for movies by major producers but for one reason or another has never made it. In fact, eleven of my books have been optioned including *Trauma* by Jonathan Mostow and *The Pariah* by Gold Circle and *Family Portrait* by Universal. Some of them have reached the point of having scripts written and talent arranged, but the problem is almost always the finance, especially with movies that are going to require a considerable amount of CGI. My friends Michael Halperin (who wrote episodes of **Masters of the Universe** and **Quincy**) has written a great script for *Spirit* and Fred Caruso (the producer of **The Godfather** and **Blue Velvet**) has written an equally terrific script for the Jim Rook thriller *Demon's Door*. At the moment I am writing a supernatural crime novel set in Reseda. I decided to set it somewhere which would be reasonably economic for any studio interested in filming it or using it as the basis for a TV series (see my later answer about movies and TV). My hero and heroine have just met at Miss Donuts on Sherman Way, which was the location for the bloody shoot-out in **Boogie Nights**.

MDL: Which of your new novels can we look forward to reading in the near future?

GM: At the moment, I am developing a series of new novels featuring two London detectives who, are assigned to solve supernatural crimes, Det. Sgt. Jamila Patel and Det. Jerry Pardoe. They first appeared in *Ghost Virus* and will appear in 2020 in *The Children God Forgot*. I have a new haunted house novel, *The House of a Hundred Whispers*, coming out in time for Hallowe'en this year. And very importantly, I have found a brilliantly talented co-author, Dawn G Harris, and we are writing short horror stories together. The first story, 'Stranglehold', will appear in *Cemetery Dance* magazine and the second, 'Cutting the Mustard', will appear in *The Horror Zine Book of Ghost Stories* anthology. Dawn is a young woman with one supernatural thriller to her name, *Diviner*, but for some reason our thinking and our styles fit seamlessly together. Those two stories have already appeared in magazines in Greece, Poland, Russia, Bulgaria and France.

MDL: I can't wait to review *The House of a Hundred Whispers* for *Phantasmagoria Magazine*.

Thank you for taking the time to answer my questions. I've been a fan of yours since I was ten years old, so this has been a great thrill for me.

GM: Thank *you* for your interesting questions, Marc. It's been a pleasure answering them.

(Dawn G Harris and Graham in a promotional picture for 'Stranglehold')

THE HOUSE OF A HUNDRED WHISPERS

The chilling return of the Master of Horror.
   Graham Masterton is one of the horror genre's most celebrated and popular writers. Now, after eight years writing crime fiction, he is back with this terrifying novel about a haunted house on Dartmoor.
   All Hallows Hall, a rambling Tudor mansion on the edge of the bleak, misty moor is not a place many would choose to live. Yet the former Governor of Dartmoor Prison did just that. Now he's dead, and his estranged family are set to inherit his estate.
   But when the dead man's family come to stay, the atmosphere of the moors seems to drift into every room. Floorboards creak, secret passageways echo, and wind whistles in the house's famous priest hole. And then, on the morning the family decide to leave All Hallows Hall once and for all, their young son Timmy goes missing…

The House of a Hundred Whispers will be published by Head of Zeus in October 2020.

WORLD EXCLUSIVE!

AN EXTRACT FROM GRAHAM MASTERTON'S *THE HOUSE OF A HUNDRED WHISPERS*

Before she had reached the door to the kitchen, it suddenly burst open, and Timmy came out. He stopped and looked at them all in bewilderment.

'What's up, Timmy?' asked Rob. 'You look like you've seen a ghost.'

'Who's that upstairs?'

'There's nobody upstairs, darling,' said Vicky. 'We're the only people here.'

'There had jolly well better not be anybody upstairs,' put in Martin, rising from his throne. 'The last thing we want is squatters.'

'You saw somebody?' said Rob. 'What did they look like?'

'I didn't see them. Only heard them.'

'Oh yes? And where were they?'

'In one of the rooms, right down at the end, by the coloured window.'

Martin turned around and said to the rest of them, loudly, 'He must mean the stained-glass window,' as if none of them could guess.

'I was looking through the different-coloured glass, so that the garden went red, and then it went blue, and then it went yellow.'

'And that's when you heard them? How did you know it was more than one? What – were they talking?'

Timmy nodded. Rob had rarely seen him look so serious, with his wide eyes and that little sprig of hair sticking up at the back of his head.

'Did you hear what they were saying?'

Timmy said, 'No. I couldn't. I pressed my ear up against the door, but they were whispering.'

Martin turned to Rob. 'Right! I think we'd better take a shufti, don't you, Rob. Can't have uninvited guests!'

***

Rob and Martin climbed the stairs to the first floor landing. Rob hadn't been up here since the day he left for art college, and he had forgotten how low the ceilings were, and how the floorboards creaked, and how strongly the corridors smelled of oak and wood-polish and dried-out horse-hair plaster.

Two corridors led off from the landing: one directly ahead of them, with three bedroom doors on the left-hand side and the large stained-glass window at the end. The other led off to the right, with another five bedroom doors and a door at the end to the bathroom.

'I still find it hard to believe that we'll never see Dad again,' said Rob, pausing at the top of the stairs. 'I keep thinking that at any minute I'm going to hear him shouting up at us to stop making so much bloody noise up here.'

'Well, let's go and see if we've got any unwelcome visitors, shall we?'

They walked along the corridor towards the stained glass window, and Martin opened each of the first two bedroom doors. There was nobody in either bedroom, only antique beds with faded cotton quilts, and bedside tables with dusty lamps on them.

'Ssh,' said Martin, cupping his hand to his ear. 'Do you hear any whispering?'

They waited in silence, their faces lit up by the harlequin patterns of coloured light that were shining through the stained glass.

The window depicted Walkham Valley under a dark blue sky, with a leat running through it. Beside the leat with his back turned and his arms spread wide was an impossibly tall man wearing a long black cloak with a high collar turned up. All around him, bristling black hounds were standing in a circle on their hind legs, their fangs bared and their red tongues hanging out.

According to the previous owner of All Hallows Hall, the man in the black cloak was Old Dewer, which was the Dartmoor name for the Devil. The story went that on certain nights of the year Old Dewer would mount a huge black horse and take his pack of ferocious hounds out hunting across the moor, searching for young women who hadn't been able to reach home before it grew dark.

Whether it was true or not, the window had apparently been installed to make Old Dewer believe that he was respected by the owners of this house, and so that he wouldn't come snuffling around it looking for souls to steal, especially the souls of their daughters.

'I'll bet you that it was the wind that Timmy heard,' said Martin. 'Or maybe the plumbing. The front and the back doors were both locked when we got here, and the burglar alarm was still on. I can't see how anybody could have got in.'

'Martin, there's no wind. And the plumbing has never sounded like whispering. It sounds more like somebody slaughtering a pig.'

Martin opened the last door. There was no bed in here, only an assortment of half-a-dozen spare chairs, some of them stacked on top of each other and a wine-table crowded with tarnished brass candlesticks and inkwells, all of which were draped with dusty spider-webs.

Under the window there was an oak window-seat, with a hinged lid covered in cracked green leather. Rob went over and lifted the lid up. It was full of nothing but legal documents, all rolled up and tied around with faded red ribbons.

'See? Nobody here. And it doesn't look as if Dad's been in here for years.'

'Oh, well. Maybe Timmy imagined it. He does have quite an imagination. He won a prize at school for a story he wrote about a bad egg that fell in love with a bullying centipede.'

Martin closed the door. But as soon as they started to walk back along the corridor, Rob heard what sounded like a man's voice, talking in an urgent whisper.

'Stop, Martin! No, stop! Can you hear that?'

Martin stopped, and listened.

'No. What?'

'It was definitely somebody whispering.'

Martin waited a few moments longer, but then he said, 'No. I can't hear anything.'

'Really. I'm sure it was somebody whispering.'

'Did you hear what they said?'

'No. They weren't speaking loud enough. But they sounded – I don't know – panicky.'

'Oh, come on, Rob. I think you and Timmy have both caught a dose of the creeps. You remember that old woman who used to live across at Wormold's Farm? She used to tell us this house could drive anybody who lived in it "maze as a brush."'

'You mean old Mrs Damerell. She was a couple of sausage rolls short of a picnic herself.'

Downstairs, they heard knocking at the front door.

'Come on,' said Martin. 'That'll be Dad's solicitor. Let's go down and find out who's inherited what.'

Rob followed him downstairs. 'Knowing my luck, it'll be the headless cherub.'

THE HOUSE OF A HUNDRED WHISPERS WILL BE RELEASED on 1st OCTOBER 2020...

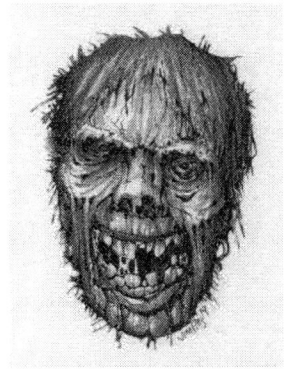

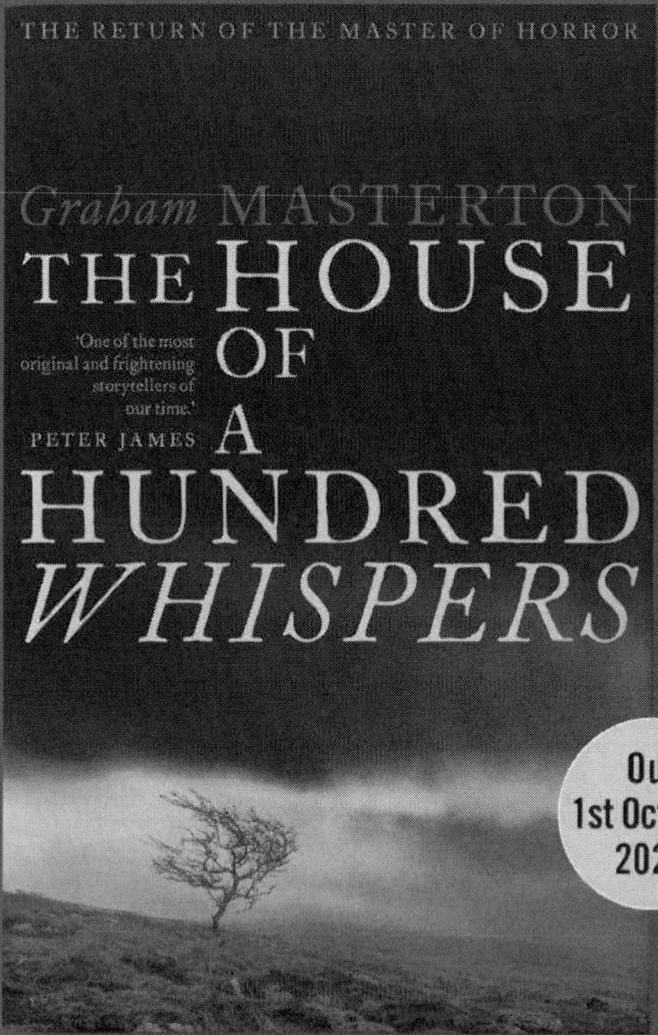

THE RETURN OF THE MASTER OF HORROR

'One of the most original and frightening storytellers of our time'
PETER JAMES

£18.99 hardback / 448pp / 9781789544244 • £4.99 ebook / 448pp / 9781789544237

 @HoZ_Books  headofzeus  @headofzeus headofzeus.com

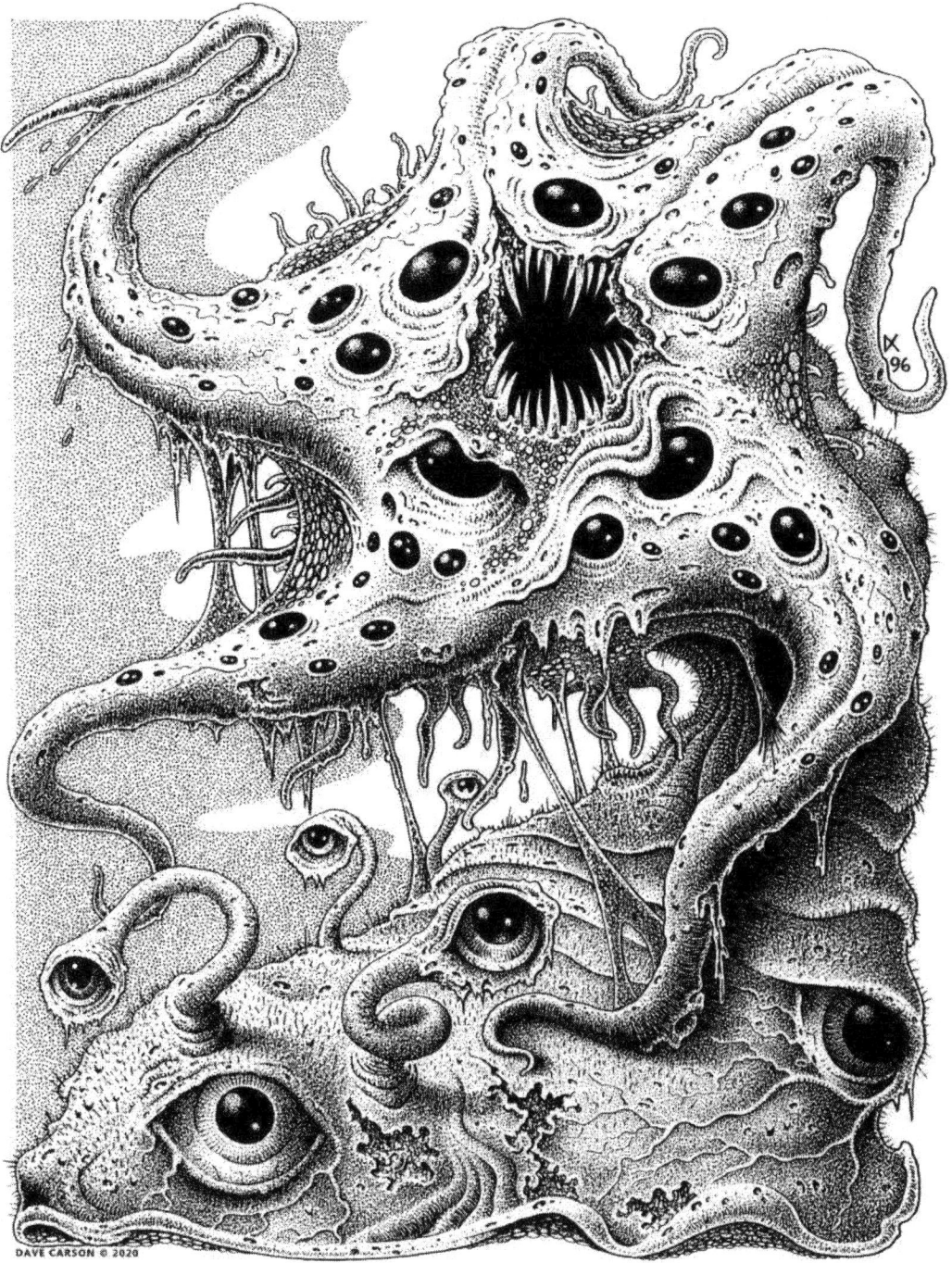

AIDAN CHAMBERS: MONASTIC LIVING, NATIONAL SERVICE, GHOST STORIES AND MORE!

*Trevor Kennedy chats to the multi award-winning **Aidan Chambers**, one of the great British ghost story authors, and a man who has also led a very varied and extraordinary life, which he discusses along with his latest release from PS Publishing.*

Trevor Kennedy: Aidan, it's a great pleasure to be chatting with you. You have a new book out, just released by PS Publishing and titled *Dead Trouble & Other Ghost Stories*, containing a large selection of your spooky tales over the years. How did the book first come about and what are your thoughts on it now that it is published?

Aidan Chambers: The book began as a passing thought. Steve [Jones] had contacted me about a book he was preparing. We talked about my ghost stories, and Steve suggested I put together some of my favourites and he would edit the book and look after its publication. He was a pleasure to work with. And the resulting book is the best produced of all my ghost books. I'm delighted.

TK: What makes for a good ghost story for you, both as a writer and reader?

AC: Sufficient scary events to keep me reading, but more to do with the reaction and thoughts of the observer than concentration on only the sensational frighteners; a style of writing that I can admire and has a personality of its own; and that it is short, ideally no more than ten pages. For me ghost stories are as much to do with the behaviour of human beings under stress than they are with the hauntings themselves.

TK: Do you think there will always be a place in the world for this type of tale? I certainly hope so.

AC: I do. Ghost stories were no doubt told round the fires in dark winter caves in prehistoric times, have been told ever since and still are. There is something deeply bedded in our human nature that both enjoys such stories and at the same time uses them to think about life, death, and what might or might not happen to us after death. Ghost stories raise fundamental questions about life and death – philosophical and religious questions – not in an academic way but by the power of dramatic entertainment. In a way they are meditations.

TK: Looking at your earlier life, you were born near Chester-le-Street in County Durham, later enlisting in the Royal Navy as part of your National Service. How were things for you growing up in the north of England and how tough was National Service? As a side note, my own grandfather also grew up in the mining village of Houghton-le-Spring in the same part of the world, along with serving in the Royal Navy as well.

AC: My grandfathers and other relatives worked in the coal mines. My father was a joiner who became an undertaker. He was a brilliant gardener and in his middle years took up river and sea fishing. My mother, my six aunts, and grandmothers were all wonderful housekeepers and cooks. What I inherited from them is a profound belief in the fundamental importance of skilled crafts people. They taught me to respect tools, the importance of preparation before getting down to a job, the discipline of everyday routine work, and a love of beautifully-made objects. Only one of them, my paternal grandmother, was a serious reader. My education up to the age of 11 was dire. I was eventually "saved" educationally and as a reader by a superb English teacher, P.J. Osborn (always known as Jim or Ozzy), at Darlington Queen Elizabeth Grammar School, where I was a pupil from the age of 14 till I left for two years compulsory service in the Navy in 1953.

At the time, I hated being conscripted. I wanted to get on with my chosen life. In fact, it was a godsend. I had never had to muck in with a crowd of other people before (I'm an only child brought up in the country). 150 young men double-bunked in a barrack room was a shock. As my father would say, it knocked the corners off me. I was in the Supply and Secretarial division. I was a clerk. The Navy called us "Writers", which amused me because my secret ambition was to be a writer. I was put to work in an office in Portsmouth for the 18 months after my training. There was a second-hand bookshop across the street. I spent most of my earnings and whatever other money I could scrape together buying books. I had plenty of spare time. I read, wrote, attended plays at the city theatre and concerts given by the Bournemouth Symphony Orchestra. Jim kept in touch. In my last year at school I'd been accepted by a teacher training college in London. They sent a reading list in preparation for starting there after the Navy. Looking back, I can see what a valuable two years it was.

TK: Other aspects of your career have included as a schoolteacher and as a monk in an Anglican monastery in Stroud. Could you tell us a bit more about these please and how challenging life was in the monastery?

AC: It was Jim who decided I should be a teacher and the college I should go to: Borough Road College, Isleworth. 300 students in two years. I loved it! The staff were excellent, I ran the Dramatic Society, directed and wrote plays, and discovered that, though my secret ambition was to be a literary writer, I also enjoyed teaching very much. In those days, you finished at training college not with a degree but with a teaching Diploma. We were trained for work in non-academic secondary schools. But by an oddity of fate, I was appointed to a post in a Grammar school as an English and Drama teacher at Westcliff High School for Boys, in Southend-on-Sea. I was very happy there.

I'd always been interested in religion and, though like most people then, I'd been baptised in the Church of England, I was not a believer and never went to church. On the staff at WHSB was a group of young men, almost all of them graduates of Oxbridge. Nine of them were practising Anglicans. We argued about belief and Christianity and religion in general, me all against and they all for. They drove me into an intellectual corner. How could I talk about belief and prayer and religion when I had never tried them? So, I agreed to attend the church of one of them, St. Margaret's Leigh-on-Sea. This was a high church, anglo-Catholic, with a devout priest one of whose sons I taught. Gradually, over a number of weeks I found myself very attracted to certain aspects: the drama and beauty of the Mass (which was conducted in a restrained, not over-fussy, very English way); the Elizabethan and Jacobean language of the Authorised Version of the Bible and the Book of Common Prayer (now of course ditched by the church, a huge mistake, in my opinion); and most of all by the increasing power I found in private, silent meditation.

To cut a long story short, I finally decided to go to what I considered the heart of the matter and find out whatever I could about the spiritual (as against the religious) life. Which seemed to me to mean becoming a monk. In 1960 I joined an Order which was dedicated to work with young people. This meant I could go on teaching, this time in a state school with the kind of non-academic teenagers I'd been trained for. I realised after a couple of years that, though I like the monastic life, I wasn't a true believer. But I kept on trying, until 1967, when I decided it was dishonest to remain, and left. Another reason for the decision was that I'd become a published writer of stories for and about teenagers of the kind I was teaching. And this faced me with the fact that my deepest compulsion – in fact, my true vocation – was as a writer, and that if I didn't devote myself to this, I'd never forgive myself. So I left and in 1968 became a freelance writer.

TK: You have received many awards and honours, including the Carnegie Medal, the Michael L. Printz Award, the Eleanor Farjeon Award, the Hans Christian Andersen Award and more. What have been some of your own personal highlights so far, however?

AC: It's always deeply satisfying to be recognised by awards. But they are always retrospective. They are given for work done. Whereas, perhaps like most writers, I am always tussling with what is being written now and thinking about what I must write in the future. It happens that I have a very fragile self-confidence. What awards do is encourage my confidence. But at least as important as this – in fact, to be honest, more important – is the response of ordinary readers, which used to come by letter, then by email, and these days by social media. (I can't stand social media and have nothing to do with it! So, now I don't hear as much from readers as I used to. No complaint: my choice.) As well as this, I've gained great pleasure from seeing my novels adapted as plays. In the end, though, all that matters is doing the work: facing the blank page every day, come what may, and whether I like what I've written on not. Looking back (I'm 85) I realise that since I was 15

I've been compulsively driven by three necessities: reading, writing, and teaching. Each serves and feeds the other. I can't teach any more. But, thank goodness, I am still able to read (even more than I ever have), and write (though now even slower than ever). For me, these are a form of meditation.

TK: You have written and edited many novels, collections, and educational books aimed at children and young adults, such as *Cycle Smash, Breaktime, Seal Secret, Dance on My Grave, Postcards from No Man's Land, This Is All, Dying to Know You, The Kissing Game, Ghosts Four* (as Malcolm Blacklin) and with your wife, Nancy, published the magazine *Signal*. You have also always been a strong advocate for literacy in children. What have been some of the barriers children have faced over the years concerning literacy and could you elaborate a bit more on your publications and how they have promoted this topic please?

AC: The barriers have been the same. You can't read without there being books to read. In my disastrous early schooling the only books in the school were nasty, boring booklets intended to teach you to read. Inexpensive books are essential. (Penguin Books were my saviour!). The free public library service is essential most especially for the least well-off and deprived of our people. The last few years, when many libraries have been closed, are a public and political disgrace. And we need teachers who are themselves readers and who know well not only a wide selection of the books published for the young but also how to introduce them to their pupils. Along with a rich provision of books, reading aloud to the young is essential. Reading is a cultural activity. As with all cultural activity, we learn it by imitation. Readers are made by readers; non-readers are made by non-readers. There is a lot more to it, but these are basic.

Nancy and I set up the publishing imprint The Thimble Press in 1969. This was really Nancy's work with me as an assistant when called on. Our aim was to help develop the standard and range of serious writing about children's and youth literature, and to produce articles and books dealing with the literature, education of the young as readers, and practical guides for teachers and librarians. We started our thrice yearly magazine *Signal* in 1970, and in the next thirty years published one hundred issues and 83 books and monographs. I'm immodest enough to believe the Press had a worthwhile influence and was a help to many teachers and librarians.

TK: Do you think children these days struggle even more so with literacy in this age of mobile phones and computer games? They don't really seem to pick up physical books as much as they used to, whilst libraries (at least here in Northern Ireland) seem to be constantly struggling and closing. What do you think are the best ways to address these issues?

AC: I'm not sure that things are worse than they used to be. You could argue that young people are reading and writing more now than they ever did. Think of the amount of time spent reading and writing texts on social media, for example. What people mean when they say young people are not reading as much as they used to is that they are not reading what these adults think they should read.

Certainly, when I think of the schools I was in between the ages of 5 and 14, and the teaching then, and compare them with what I see happening in most schools now, they are different worlds. Far better now than they were then. However, I do think that the interference in education by governments of both persuasions over the last twenty years has been ill-judged and badly informed. And the training of teachers is still not what it should be so far as serious reading – not just functional reading – is concerned. But that's too complicated a discussion to cover in a brief interview. So I'll bow out!

TK: Have you many more ghost stories and books lined up, Aidan?

AC: Not at the moment. Though Steve has made another suggestion, and having benefited from his persuasive ability, I'd better not say no!

TK: Thank you very much for speaking to us at *Phantasmagoria*, Aidan, and we wish you all the very best with *Dead Trouble & Other Ghost Stories* and your future projects.

DEAD TROUBLE & OTHER GHOST STORIES
by Aidan Chambers
(illustrated by Randy Broecker)

**Review by Trevor Kennedy
with exclusive illustrations from the book by Randy Broecker**

("Head Spot" copyright © Randy Broecker)

IN TODAY'S RATHER cynical world, much of the literature, film and television we are presented with is rather extreme in nature, both in fiction and non-fiction, it must be said. We just have to turn on our wide-screen, high definition, multi-platform television sets to be presented with a plethora of violence, gore, sex and swearing (or perhaps that's just the stuff I indulge in?!...). "Splatterpunk", no holds barred-style novels and anthologies are hugely popular. But so much of this lacks a certain subtlety and charm. Don't get me wrong, I believe there is a time and place for everything and try to embrace all aspects of the collective genre. I'm also hugely opposed to the censorship of art and would be quite the hypocrite if I attacked any of the aforementioned, but a lot of the time a little bit of restraint can go a long way and be so much more effective. A bit like *Dead Trouble & Other Ghost Stories* actually.

("Two Skulls" from "The Ghostly Skulls of Calgarth Hall"
copyright © Randy Broecker)

This bumper collection by Aidan Chambers of some of the favourite ghost stories he has penned over the years, for me, harks back to an era of classic spooky ghost storytelling, where the tales rely more on building atmosphere and tension, without falling back on shock tactics and gratuity. The type of stories perfect for reading out loud to friends and family in front of a warm blazing fire on a dark winter's or Halloween night (or any time of the year for that matter). I think children and young adults in particular will relish them, with their recountings of old haunted mansions, screaming skulls, angry poltergeists, spectres with a point to prove, and much more. Quite a few of them are also told in a matter of fact "real life case" manner, something I myself always had a fascination with as a boy.

One of my favourites would have to be the title story – "Dead Trouble" – a darkly humorous account of a bizarre workplace accident and the trials and tribulations a humble ghost must go through on a daily basis. "Last Respects", set in a funeral parlour, is an enjoyable and atmospheric yarn, as are "The Nameless Horror of Berkeley Square", "The Ghostly Skulls of Calgarth Hall", and the opener, "The Haunting of Ashley Hall". "The Mystery Ghost of Amherst, Nova Scotia", one of the longer contributions, is a romp told, in part, by an unreliable narrator looking to cash in on the case in question with his book on it. Other noteworthy tales are "Seeing is Believing" and "The Tower".

Whilst there is a lot of fun to be had with all of the stories contained, a couple of others really did stand out for me. "Nancy Tucker's Ghost" is an emotional, once again atmospheric, chiller of a lover spurned and a spectre looking for redemption from beyond the grave, whilst "Room 18" is a superbly creepy classic set in a Dublin hotel room with an M. R. James feel to it.

The wonderful interior illustrations by Randy Broecker add greatly to the overall spookiness factor.

I definitely recommend this collection by Aidan Chambers, although if you're looking for some of that hardcore gore and sex that I mentioned earlier, you won't get it in here, but what you will get is plenty of macabre chills told in something of an "old school", tongue-in-cheek manner, perfect for readers of all ages. A beautiful book (physically and in terms of content) that also contains a foreword by Stephen Jones, introduction by Aidan Chambers himself and cover painting by Les Edwards.

Dead Trouble & Other Ghost Stories is published by PS Publishing and is available to purchase from their website, Amazon and other outlets. For more details go to: https://www.pspublishing.co.uk

("Seeing is Believing" copyright © Randy Broecker)

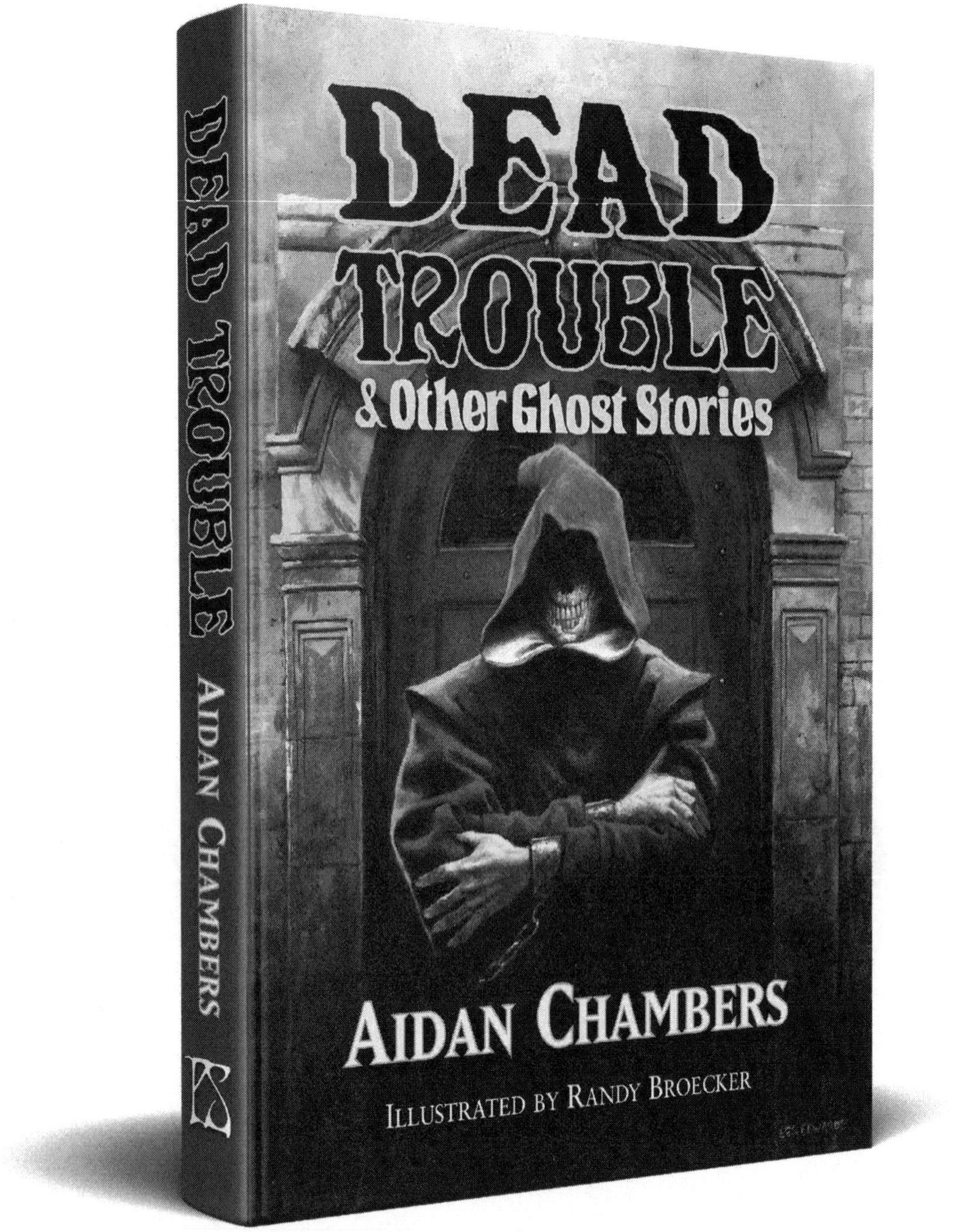
DEAD TROUBLE
& Other Ghost Stories
AIDAN CHAMBERS
ILLUSTRATED BY RANDY BROECKER
DEAD TROUBLE AIDAN CHAMBERS

IN HER OWN WORDS: "SCREAM QUEEN" LYNN LOWRY

Phantasmagoria's *David L. Tamarin recently caught up with an actress with an extraordinary resume, starring in a huge catalogue of horror and cult film classics over the years, including David Cronenberg's* Shivers *and George A. Romero's* The Crazies. *The one and only* **Lynn Lowry**.

David L. Tamarin: You are known for appearing in many horror films over the past fifty years, yet the last movie I saw you in was *Cynthia*, a horror comedy. What was it like to do a comedy role?

Lynn Lowry: Well, I've actually done a lot of comedy in my life. Before I started doing the horror movies that I have done over the past fifteen years I did a lot of stage work that was comedy. Neil Simon plays, and all kind of things like that. I'm real familiar with the comedy genre. The comedy-horror genre is a lot of fun, I enjoy it a lot. In England I think I've done about four comedy-horror films. Comedy is a lot of fun and especially fun if there's horror mixed in with it too. It makes it even more exciting. It was great too to see Sid Haig. I knew Sid, I had been to many shows with him. And although we didn't really get to act together a lot in the movie, he was the police officer who found my body in *Cynthia* and put me in a body bag – so in a way I got to work with him a little bit. He was such a great person.

DLT: I was shocked to hear of his death, it was terrible. I grew up watching him in *Spider Baby*.

LL: I think he was sick for quite a while. The last few times I saw him he looked like he was ill, so I wasn't surprised when I heard the news. I'm just sorry like everyone else, everyone just adored him.

DLT: One of your most famous roles is in George Romero's *The Crazies*. You have a small role in the remake, correct?

LL: Yes, I have a cameo in the remake.

DLT: What did you think of the remake, and remakes in general of old 1970s horror classics?

LL: The finished product was very entertaining, I enjoyed it. There were a lot of special effects and it was exciting and fun to watch it, but I don't think in forty-five years anyone will remember the remake, but everyone will remember the original because it's more real. It's earthier, darker, more political. There's something about it and something about the way George Romero directed it that I just think it's a film that will last over time. As far as working on the remake, it had a $21 million budget, and I enjoyed working with Breck Eisner, that was exciting, but they neglected to tell me that I needed to memorize a church hymn, so I had to learn it the night before we shot and I was really stressed out about it, trying to remember the song and the words. I had to ride a bicycle, which no one told me I was going to have to do. I had to do a lot of things that no one told me I was going to be required to do, which I thought was amazing considering it was a high budget film. The other thing about the remake is that everyone was professional and did their job and did it very well, but that's all it was, it was a job, whereas for the original, it was like a family and we were all there to make something special that would last forever and that was the kind of energy that George Romero had everyone feel when you worked with him, and that's the difference between the two.

DLT: There's something about the way George Romero directs, his films will definitely last. The remake was entertaining but I agree it won't be around for forty-five years.

LL: No, Breck Eisner even told me he had been asked if my original character was going to have the relationship with her father, like in the original, and he said "No, No, No, we can't do anything with incest." I thought, it's 2020 and you can't do anything with incest? Yet when George did it it was such a big part of the movie.

One of the things that makes the original film so memorable is when my father rapes me, and of course the death scene, and I can't tell you how many people have told me it is the most intense moment of the film, their favorite moment of the film.

DLT: It is intense, very intense.

LL: Thank you, thank you.

DLT: Do you feel the same way about a lot of these recent remakes that may be entertaining and won't hold up over time, like the remakes of *Last House on the Left* and *Texas Chainsaw Massacre*?

LL: Yes, I do. I think what happens is that people get caught up in having so much more money and they lose the essence of what the movie's really about. There's nothing more exciting as hands-on special effects. When you are right there on the set and they make the effect happen right there with you, that is so important and I think that's one of the reasons why these 1970s films and the 1980s films are so memorable. For *The Crazies* remake, they had five or six levels of make-up to make people look crazy, whereas in the original, George Romero would just say to us, in this scene you need to be crazier. We had to act. We had to pull this insanity and that darkness up from our instrument, not just have our faces painted. The remakes are slicker but they just don't have the depth that those originals do.

DLT: Do you prefer independent films to Hollywood?

LL: I do. I have done a few Hollywood films and they are just not very personal. It's a job. No one is very invested with their heart. You make good money and it's fun but it's not the same. Yeah, I love doing independent films and I love working with new directors that are just starting out and they have that wonderful, amazing desire to make something that will be remembered and is completing a dream that they have rather than somebody who saw *The Crazies* years ago and thinks it could be a commercial hit. It's just not the same.

DLT: It seems like you are acting now more than ever. Your IMDB page is quite amazing, you are in the middle of so many projects.

LL: Yeah, you know it's really amazing. When I started working in the early 1970s, I didn't really realize that there was this big independent horror movement – I don't even know if there was the way there is now. Those 1970s films were just kind of a fluke. I wasn't pursuing horror films. I just happened to get *I Drink Your Blood, The Crazies, Shivers*, and I never really pursued other horror films in that period. I did *Fighting Mad* with Jonathan Demme and *Cat People* with Paul Schrader and I was trying to warm up into Hollywood and get more work and I never pursued the lower budget films again until 2005, when I started back. At that time, everyone had seen those earlier films and knew who I was and I was sort of shocked because I didn't even know I had a fan base in 2005. Then all of a sudden people started asking me to work. I actually gave up the film business in 1995 and I took ten years off because I was just sick of trying to pursue it in Hollywood with all of those people. Then I came back in 2005 and that's when I started working so much.

DLT: There's a lot of movies like *Swimming with Sharks* that depict Hollywood as a really terrible place. And the sexual harassment is big news all over the world. Is it really that awful?

LL: When I was coming up in that period, in my twenties and thirties so many producers and casting people and photographers were always on the make. They were always telling you they would cast you if you went to bed with them. You had to deal with all of that kind of stuff which went on all the time. Then there was the whole thing when I did *Cat People* with Paul Schrader, he couldn't have cared less about how hurt I got on the set. No one helped me. I didn't have a stunt coordinator, I had to do everything myself. I was completely bruised, rug-burned, and bleeding and no one cared. That kind of insensitivity gives Hollywood a bad name unless you are a big star and you don't get treated that way. I'm sure Meryl Streep has never been treated that way.

DLT: I happen to think David Cronenberg is a genius and I am interested in him especially as you starred in his first feature film. What was it like working with Cronenberg on *Shivers*?

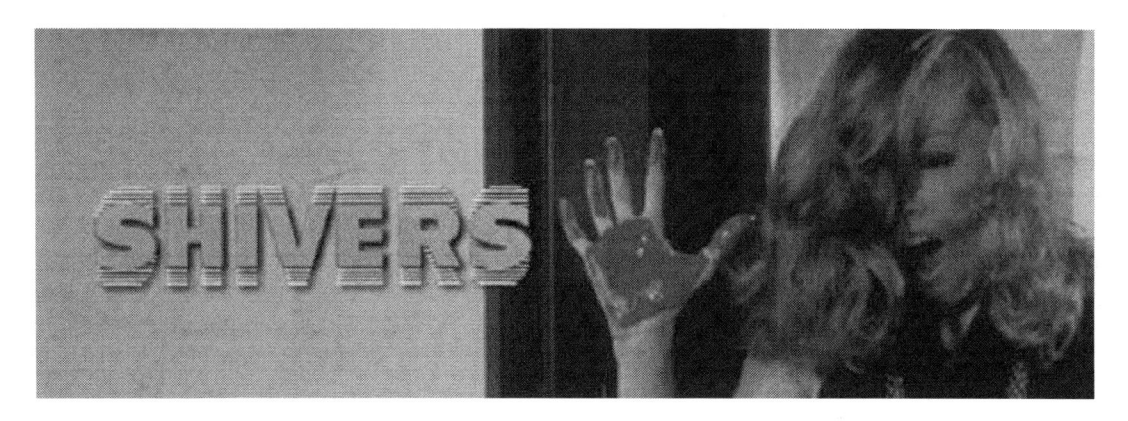

LL: When I knew David, it was his first feature film and I think the script that he wrote was pretty genius, because it had never been done before, with that kind of body horror. I think he was on the cutting edge by writing a script like that. *Shivers* is very smart.

As far as his directing ability, the film does hold up. I've seen it recently – it is scary, funny, shocking, and has all the right elements to make it successful, but I think a lot of what happened on the set was really just kind of luck. He was brand new, he had never done a feature, he was excited, he was hungry, he wanted to make it work. He didn't direct me hardly at all. I just came in and knew what they wanted and did what I thought was right for the character. He did work a lot with Paul Hampton because I don't think Paul was realizing for him what he was looking for. As far as his directing abilities at the point, I wouldn't have said that he was a genius or that he would become the remarkable director that he is today. But very, very nice and wonderful to work with and an incredible experience which I was very fortunate and lucky to have had.

DLT: Can you tell me about *The Whole Town's Sleeping*? Is that based on the Bradbury story with the same name?

LL: "The Whole Town's Sleeping" is a short story written by Ray Bradbury which I discovered when I was sixteen years old. There was something about the piece that really spoke to me and I just loved it and thought it was incredibly frightening. When I was 16 we did the whole story in The Reader's Theatre. There was a narrator and I played the main character, Lavinia. Later on in my life I was producing a Halloween show and I was looking for different things to put in the show and I remembered that piece, so I searched for it again and I found it and took the last three pages of the piece, which is just a woman walking home alone and I became the narrator and Lavinia and I changed my voice, and did the whole thing by myself. I have done it on stage a number of times, at a number of conventions, then we filmed it. J. T. Seaton directed it and we filmed it. It is one of the most frightening things I have ever done. You can literally feel the audience moving forward in their seats, and Bradbury's writing is just chilling and just builds and builds and she gets to the house and she can't get to the door and she can't get the key to work, and it is a continual build up until the very last moment and then there is a surprise ending which I won't say for people who haven't seen it but it is an excellent story. It was very challenging for me to do on the stage, because it is a twelve minute monologue. If you forget your lines or something like that you're really screwed because you're out there in front of the audience. It's a real emotional piece.

DLT: Do you like working on the stage?

LL: I love it. I haven't done it in quite a while, because I am always so busy now doing films and conventions and I just don't have the three month period you need to rehearse and perform a play. I have done many stage plays and won quite a few awards for my acting onstage. I did a lot of work onstage in New York and Los Angeles as well.

DLT: What are some of your drama awards?

LL: I won the Drama-Logue Award for *Finding Donis Anne* written by Hal Corley. I won The Best Actress Award for that. It's about a Southern woman whose teenage daughter has ran away and she is on the road with her emotionally disturbed nephew. It's basically the two of them on the road searching for her daughter and its such a wonderful play. I also won Best Ensemble for *Portrait of a Madonna* which is a Tennessee Williams play that I did in the Ensemble Theatre in Los Angeles. I have won thirteen awards for my acting, which is very exciting.

DLT: I noticed that you won several awards in a short time, for *Model Hunger* and *A Grim Becoming*, and several others as well.

LL: And *The Peripheral* too.

DLT: Congratulations!

LL: Thank you.

DLT: You mentioned your prefer independent films. Did you enjoy your role in the weird anthology horror film *The Theatre Bizarre*?

LL: I did. It was a fun role. David Gregory directed it and he was great, he was great to work with, and the crew was great, very professional, everyone respected David and there was so much love and camaraderie on the set. The role that I had, she's pretty outrageous, a pretty big character, she has this big energy about her. It took them what must have been two hours, just to work on my eyes. Just to get my eyes to look very goth. And the hair and everything. Yet it was great and I thought he did an excellent job on our segment "Sweets" and I also enjoyed the other directors' works as well. I would love to work with all of them.

I think the favorite low budget film I have ever done was *Model Hunger*, directed by Debbie Rochon. It was her directorial debut. I had the opportunity to take a character I had been working on since I was sixteen. A sort of Blanche DuBois/Tennessee Williams/Southern-type of character who is demented and schizophrenic. I do that kind of character really well because I have worked on it for so many years. I was able to take the basis of that particular type of character and turn her into a serial killer and a cannibal through the character from *Model Hunger* who turned out to be extremely funny, sexy, charming, and extremely lethal, and it was a great combination of things for me to play with that character, and again I loved working with Debbie and the crew and everyone. Just very exciting.

DLT: What was it like to work with so many scream queens in *Model Hunger*?

LL: Kaylee Williams was wonderful; she was a delight to work with and we keep in touch quite frequently and we've almost done a couple of films together but they didn't come to fruition, so I'm hoping to work with her again. And Tiffany Shepis, she's wonderful. I think she is excellent in the film. I was very excited to work with her during those two or three days we had together, she was great. All the actors were wonderful. I loved working with Brian Fortune, he was wonderful. I think I really did scare him, because after that scene where he is tied up and I was all over him and everything – I'm pretty scary in the scene, I think – he was all shook up.

DLT: Oh yeah, very scary.

LL: And he was pretty much shaking after the scene was over. I saw him on the porch trying to smoke a cigarette and his hands were shaking and I think I really got to him on that. I'm always very careful to make sure that I'm not hurting anyone but my intensity is pretty high when I'm working – there's always this little voice in my head that says, 'You're just acting, don't really cut his fingers off', that type of stuff. I had real garden shears and was coming real close to his fingers. You always have to remember what's really happening or else you have a problem.

DLT: I can imagine him being terrified. Can you tell me about the Lon Chaney Award for Excellence in Independent Horror?

LL: It was at the Fantastic Film Festival in San Francisco. It was really a great honor to have received that. I am very honored to have that.

DLT: Congratulations!

LL: Thank you. I also have a film that just came out, it's on the Full Moon Channel. Charles Band produced it, *Necropolis: Legion*. Augie Duke is in it, Christopher Alexander directed it, and I have a very nice role in that. You can see it on one of Charlie Band's stations.

DLT: Any other films?

LL: I'm excited about a film that I'm going to be doing in January called *Fang*. It is directed by Richard Burgin, and I play a women with Parkinson's disease. She's in stage four and she's pretty crazy and not a very nice person and she is driving her son absolutely mad and some pretty interesting things happen in the film and it's a very dark film and I think it could be quite artistic and quite well done and quite interesting, I'm very excited about that.

I was in a film that came out about a month ago called *Desk Clerk* that Gary Vincent directed. That's a comedy and I play a psychiatrist in it and it's fun. I have a web series named *Mindflip* that I'm in, and they're hoping to raise the budget to make that into a feature film. I also have a film called *Essence* which is a science fiction film that I shot last January that is almost finished, and there's quite a few other things I have coming out. I'm excited about the coming year. I have two or three other projects coming up that I'm looking forward to, and one of my favorite things, it's a short film, about twenty-five minutes long called *Ready for My Close Up*, based on my original idea. It's directed by Jason Read, produced by Stuart Morriss, written by Michael Haberfelner, and we shot it in England, and it is very funny. It's a horror-comedy and I play a Gloria Swanson-like B movie actress who has a taste for delivery boys, and it is just hysterical, so I'm very proud of that film.

DLT: That sounds great. Anything else?

LL: *The Peripheral* is excellent, it's a short film. I have won a lot of awards for that, it's very scary.

DLT: How can someone see your new web series, *Mindflip*?

LL: It's on: https://www.facebook.com/Mindflipmovie/. The prequel is available on YouTube.

I just want to say also that I'm so grateful to all the fans who have supported me and stayed with me for fifty years. Next years is *I Drink Your Blood*'s fiftieth anniversary and to have all these fans who saw me fifty years ago and all these new fans who have seen my movies and know me, it's such an exciting and wonderful experience. I'm so grateful for everyone who stayed with me.

DLT: Fifty years is amazing! Thank you so much!

The Alchemy Press

Available from Amazon
and other bookstores

THE MANY FACES OF FRANKENSTEIN...
AND HIS CREATIONS

John Gilbert

John Gilbert explores some of the many incarnations of Mary Shelley's Modern Prometheus and the creature he created.

IN NOVEMBER, 2019, the BBC included Mary Shelley's *Frankenstein* on its list of 100 Most Inspiring Novels: It was not always so.

As with the original Promethean gift of fire, the story of a man who presumed to be a god in creating life out of death was perceived as both dangerous and wonderful.

Published anonymously in 1818 – largely due to fears that it might appear unseemly for a woman to be the author of such a work – it has been both lauded and denigrated in just the same way. Critics were divided even at the time of its release. Novelist Walter Scott – most well known for *Ivanhoe* – praised the author's "original genius and happy power of expression" but at the same time was not convinced at the way in which the Creature so rapidly gained knowledge of language and of the world. Yet, when the author was revealed as the daughter of Lord Godwin, it did not take long for *The British Critic* to comment, "The writer of it is, we understand, a female; this is an aggravation of that which is the prevailing fault of the novel; but if our authoress can forget the gentleness of her sex, it is no reason why we should; and we shall therefore dismiss the novel without further comment." Parliamentarian and author John Wilson Croker simply described the novel as: "…a tissue of horrible and disgusting absurdity."

Time has, however, been kinder to both the author and her work. By the mid twentieth century, the book was seen as a seminal work of fiction with authors such as Harold Bloom praising its "aesthetic and moral relevance". It still, however, draws negative reactions, perhaps from unlikely sources, as Germaine Greer who described the novel as terrible due to its narrative defects. That has not, however, stopped other authors and media taking on the story of the scientist who broke natural laws by creating life out of death.

Chemical Creation

The first film adaptation of *Frankenstein* was a 16 minute silent short, shot in 1910 by director J. Searle Dawley with Augustus Phillips as Frankenstein and Charles Ogle as his creation. Unlike many more recent adaptations which use electricity as the conductor of life, the storyline kept close to the Shelley original with Frankenstein weaning his creation from a vat of chemicals. The creature haunts its creator until Frankenstein's wedding night when the spell of true love causes it to disappear.

This early adaptation is cloaked in mystery as the original print was for many years believed lost, but in 1980 a collector came forward claiming that he had purchased it in the '50s and had been unaware of its historical value.

Shortly after Dawley's version was released, a contemporary retelling of the tale went into production in 1915. *Life Without Soul* was directed by Joseph W. Smiley starred William W. Cohill as Dr. William Frawley, a science student who creates a "soulless man" who was played by Percy Standing. The actor gained much acclaim for the role as he, like Lon Chaney in his celebrated performance as the Phantom of the Opera, relied on body acting and facial expressions and little make-up to portray the creature. The film is now considered lost but it was shot in various US locations and concludes with Frawley waking up and realising that it had all been a nightmare brought on by reading Shelley's novel.

There was at least one European version of *Frankenstein* made before Universal made its groundbreaking first foray into the genre during 1920. *Il mostro di Frankenstein* (*The Monster of Frankenstein*) was released in 1921. Directed by Eugenio Testa and written by Giovanni Drivetti, *Il Monstro* had a creature played by Umberto Guarracino. Baron Frankenstein was played by the film's producer Luciano Albertini. It was one of the few Italian horror movies produced in the silent era as Mussolini had banned the genre, but it still suffered considerable censorship issues and was heavily cut before release – allegedly, down to just 39 minutes. It too is now considered a lost film. As an afternote, producer and star Albertini moved to America in 1924 and starred in a movie called *The Iron Man*. Shortly after, he moved back to Italy where he continued acting. Later in life he was confined to mental institution where he died in 1945.

"It's Alive, it's Alive!"

And so to the first talkie version of Mary Shelley's novel, directed for release in 1931 for Universal Pictures by James Whale and starring Colin Clive as Henry Frankenstein and a life-defining performance by Boris Karloff as "The Monster". In an unusual move to build up audience anticipation, the film was prefaced with a warning by Edward Van Sloane, who plays Doctor Waldman in the movie: "...It deals with the two great mysteries of creation: life and death. I think it will thrill you. It may shock you. It might even horrify you. So if any of you feel that you do not care to subject your nerves to such a strain, now is your chance to, uh... Well, we've warned you."

The audience was suitably hooked in that despite The Monster's apparent demise, a sequel was commissioned. Released in 1935, *The Bride of Frankenstein*, in which Karloff received top billing, proved equally as successful with Elsa Lanchester joining Whale and Karloff as The Monster's "love interest". Lanchester also played Mary Shelly in a scene towards the beginning of the movie whilst Colin Clive reprised his role as Henry Frankenstein and Ernest Thesiger as the insidious Doctor Septimus Pretorius who persuades Frankenstein, who is thoroughly cowed and dejected by his attempts to create life in the original film, to try again. This time, after receiving threats from Karloff's Monster, he decided to create a mate for his original creation but with equally devastating results.

Bride... is now thought by some critics to be one of the greatest sequels ever made, but its production and original release were dogged with problems. Preparation began shortly after the release of the original film but issues with the script delayed production. It was an immediate success with the public when finally released but had distribution and censorship issues in some American states which delayed its wider release. It is now, however, regarded as a masterpiece and, in 1998, was lauded by The Library of Congress and inducted into the National Film Registry as "culturally, historically or aesthetically significant".

Son of Sequels

Further sequels followed but only one of which starred Karloff as The Monster. *Son of Frankenstein* went into production in 1939 with director Rowland V. Lee at the helm, was written by Wyllis Cooper and starred Basil Rathbone as Baron Wolf von Frankenstein. They were joined by Bela Lugosi, fresh from his triumph in the title role of Universal's *Dracula*, as Ygor, the Baron's misshapen assistant and Lionel Atwill at the top of his form as the sinister Inspector Krogh. The movie introduced more of the Frankenstein family into the mix including Josephine Hutchinson and Donnie Dunagan as Elsa and Peter von Frankenstein.

The action begins when Wolf returns to the family home in the US with wife Elsa and son Peter. He is ostracised by the local community who remember the terror that his father had unleashed upon them. He is given a sealed briefcase which contains his father's scientific notes and learns from Ygor that the monster he had created is still alive but in a coma. Wolf's initial attempts to reanimate The Monster appear to have failed until his son reports having seen a giant man in the woods. Then a fresh cycle of killings begin and it appears that the curse of the Frankensteins is indeed alive.

As if *Son of Frankenstein* was not far enough off the original track, the next sequel, *The Ghost of Frankenstein* jumped firmly into B-movie territory. Released in 1942, it was directed by Erle C. Kenton, from a screenplay by Scott Darling and original story by Eric Taylor. It stars Cedric Hardwicke in a dual role as Ludwig Frankenstein and the ghost of Henry Frankenstein and Lon Chaney (Jr.) as The Monster. Bela Lugosi reprises his role as Ygor, who takes the injured Monster from the previous excursion to be looked after by Frankenstein family member Ludwig Frankenstein. It looks as if events could be on course for happy ending until Ludwig has the brilliant idea of replacing the creature's criminal brain with that of a normal person's. Due to the nefarious plotting of his co-conspirators, the brain swap doesn't go exactly to plan...

The Universal series continued on its B-movie path with *Frankenstein Meets the Wolfman* (1943), *House of Frankenstein* (1944), and *House of Dracula* (1945). Glenn Strange, who had taken over the monster's role in 1944, also appeared in *Abbott and Costello Meet Frankenstein* (1948), the first of a series of movies in which Lou and Bud meet members of the Universal monster gang. In this film, Wolfman (played by Lon Chaney (Jr.) warns the comic duo, who are playing baggage handlers, to be careful of a consignment which turns out to contain Dracula's coffin and the comatose body of the Frankenstein Monster.

This Charles Barton-directed escapade went down well with cinema audiences and despite its lightweight tone is largely regarded as another of the best Universal monster sequels. In 2000, The American Film Institute ranked it at 56th in its poll of *100 Years, 100 Laughs*.

Hammered

Whilst in the States Universal held sway with its monster movies and focused on The Monster as the central protagonist, in England a small film production house was readying its own slate of classic creatures. Amongst them was to be a series of Frankenstein stories, looser adaptations of the Mary Shelley original novella than the Universal films but with anti-hero Dr. Frankenstein played with Gothic zeal by Peter Cushing, at the centre rather than the creature.

Cushing's Frankenstein is a man driven by a desire to prove his theories no matter what the cost to his fellow human beings and even resorts to murder in order to get the brains required for his monsters. The results were, for the time in which they were first released, gorefests in which audiences were enraptured by the increasingly maniacal adventures of the doctor.

Hammer's first Frankenstein movie, *The Curse of Frankenstein* (1957) was directed by Terence Fisher and the screenplay developed by Jimmy Sangster. But who should play the iconic Monster? Height was an important attribute so Hammer originally considered Bernard Bresslaw for the role who stacked up an impressive 6' 7", but it was eventually suave sophisticated thespian Christopher Lee who was eventually cast despite being only 6' 5".

Script and cast in place, Hammer had one major obstacle to overcome. Boris Karloff's unique look, created by make-up artist Jack P. Pierce, in the American adaptation of *Frankenstein* had been trademarked by Universal which was intent on protecting its property with all the legal powers that it could muster. If the Hammer production showed any similarity to the Karloff version it would have been quickly shut down. Fortunately, artist Phil Leakey produced a new, unsettling, design for Lee.

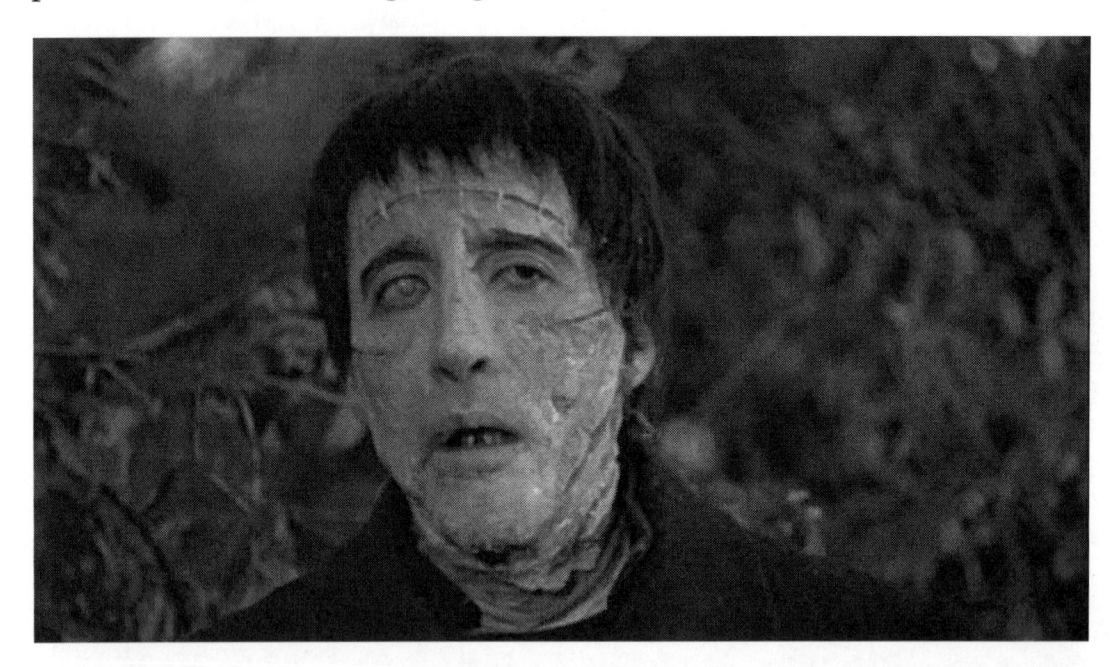

The movie was an instant success and led to several sequels, the majority of which featured Cushing as the evil doctor. They include *The Revenge of Frankenstein* (1958) in which Michael Gwynn played the main creation and Cushing the resurrected doctor, *The Evil of Frankenstein* (1964), featuring Kiwi Kingston, *Frankenstein Created Woman* (1967) starring Susan Denberg, *Frankenstein Must Be Destroyed* (1969), with Freddie Jones, *The Horror of Frankenstein* (1970) and *Frankenstein and the Monster From Hell*, both featuring Dave Prowse. Cushing played the Baron in all the films except for prequel *The Horror of Frankenstein* when the role of the young Victor was taken over by an earnest Ralph Bates.

Each of the movies in the series had a loose sense of continuity except for the first two and also *The Horror of Frankenstein* which was essentially a flashback to a time when a young Baron was just starting his experiments. Cushing played the Baron with a wide range of emotion: In some of the films he was kindly and caring whilst in others he was ruthless and prepared to stoop to murder in order to continue his experiments.

Universal Expansion

Hammer planned to expand its Frankenstein universe when in 1958 it produced a half hour pilot for a series called *Tales of Frankenstein*. To ensure a transatlantic audience, Hammer teamed up with Columbia Pictures in America. Directed by German-American author Curt (Kurt) Siodmak, it starred Anton Diffring as Baron Frankenstein and Don Megowan as The Monster. The series was, however, scrapped when it became apparent that Hammer wanted an emphasis on horror and Columbia wanted a "science gone wrong" show in the mould of *The Twilight Zone*. Frankenstein fans and completists will be pleased to hear that the single episode is still available on DVD (or YouTube).

Though, when examining the Frankenstein myth on film, the Universal and Hammer series are the most widely known, there have been several other stand out productions.

Singer and actor Sting took on the role of Charles Frankenstein, Clancy Brown The Monster, who in this version is named Viktor, and Jennifer Beals his female creation who develops a mind of her own, in Franc Roddam's *The Bride* (1985). Scripted by Lloyd Fonvielle, this UK/US co-production was given a glitzy launch but was generally panned by critics, making a paltry $3.6 million at the box office. Jennifer Beals earned a nomination in that year's Razzie awards for her performance in the movie, though, fortunately, the role did her career little lasting damage.

In 1994, fledgeling director Kenneth Branagh teamed up with Robert De Niro for *Mary Shelley's Frankenstein*. Branagh also played Victor Frankenstein whilst De Niro played The Creation, an innocent created from assembled body parts and reanimated in the time honoured manner with strong jolts of electricity. This creation begins life as a benign being but quickly descends into a maelstrom of violent rage when it realises that it will never be accepted as human. The strong cast also includes Helena Bonham Carter as Frankenstein's fiancee Elizabeth, Ian Holm as Victor's aged parent, John Cleese as his mentor and Aiden Quinn as the captain of the ship that picks up Frankenstein from a quest for The Creation in the Arctic Circle. Despite the high quality of the cast, the film received a critical mauling. Indeed, Frank Darabont, who wrote the original screenplay, lamented the movie as "the best script I ever wrote and the worst movie I have ever seen".

Undead Funny

Not all the filmic versions of *Frankenstein* have been played for gore or pathos. Though containing some of horror elements, Mel Brook's 1974 film *Young Frankenstein* played up the laughs with Gene Wilder taking the part of the doctor, Peter Boyle The Monster and Marty Feldman as Igor – who insists that his name should be pronounced "Eyegor".

Igor also stole the show in the 2015 American movie, *Victor Frankenstein*, in which Harry Potter actor Daniel Radcliffe took on the role of the hunchbacked assistant. James McAvoy played Victor with more than a thick slice of ham. Directed by Paul McGuigan and written by Max Landis it failed to win the support of critics and audiences and broke records for low opening weekend figures.

The year 2015 also saw a Bernard Rose adaptation, *Frankenstein*, in which he directed and scripted the storyline. Told from The Monster's perspective, it is set in contemporary Los Angeles where Danny Huston and Carrie-Anne Moss play Victor and his wife Elizabeth, a husband and wife team working on bringing artificial being Adam, played by Xavier Samuel, to life. Adam is "born" with a handsome, fully grown, body, but the mind of a child. As Adam matures, his body develops deformities. Victor decides to kill his creation with a lethal concoction of drugs but before he can finish the process Adam strangles the doctor and escapes into the forest beyond the lab where his adventures, and education in human cruelty, truly begin.

Frankenstein Futures

Recently, Universal Pictures has re-entered the fray with plans to resurrect its stable of monsters in all-new movie adaptations code-named "Dark Universe". A Bill Condon-directed remake of *The Bride of Frankenstein* was due to go into production in 2019 but was pulled from the schedule at the last minute, in part due to the abysmal box office performance of Tom Cruise's *The Mummy*.

Scripted by David Koepp, it was due to star Javier Bardem as the original Monster and Angelina Jolie pencilled in as The Bride. A spokesperson for Universal Studios has reassured fans that the movie will be made but commented: "None of us want to move too quickly to meet a release date when we know this special movie needs more time to come together. Bill is a director whose enormous talent has been proven time and again, and we all look forward to continuing to work on this film together."

From an inspired literary creation, through the golden age of horror movie-making and into the uncertain times of the present – where genre auteurs such as Guillermo del Torro continue to plan new adaptations of Mary Shelley's monstrous myth – *Frankenstein* has been brought to life again and again. The Monster shows no signs of vanishing into the shadows and, as long as the public continues to hunger for the dark meat of horror, it is likely that Colin Clive's cry of "It's alive, it's alive!" in the original Universal Pictures' masterpiece will ensure the crackle of electricity and the reanimation of mouldering flesh continues to pull audiences well into the future.

STEPHEN JONES'
THE BEST OF BEST NEW HORROR: VOLUME ONE

Feature/review by Trevor Kennedy

FOR OVER THIRTY years now, the annual Stephen Jones-edited (earlier editions were co-edited with Ramsey Campbell) *Best New Horror* series has been a staple of the highest quality genre literature around, unsurprisingly including work from the biggest names in the field and considered by many (myself included) as the most reliable go-to horror anthology in the world.

To celebrate PS Publishing's release of *The Best of Best New Horror* two volume set covering the first twenty years, *Phantasmagoria* will be taking an in-depth look at each of these bumper collections over the next two issues. First up (obviously), is *Volume One*:

The Best of Best New Horror: Volume One opens with an intense, gripping and unsettling tale from Brian Lumley, "No Sharks in the Med", a story which concerns a young newly-wed couple celebrating their honeymoon on a Greek island. Despite the reader knowing full well that something unpleasant is going to soon happen to the two, this in no way detracts from its power – or the uncomfortable feeling it exudes – when it inevitably does happen. And, as Ramsey Campbell correctly states in his Introduction to the overall book, there is just the slightest suggestion of the supernatural at the end, in what is an otherwise straight, albeit rather terrifying, thriller.

Michael Marshall Smith's "The Man Who Drew Cats" follows next. A stranger arrives in the small town of Kingston one day, a street artist of sorts, who creates the most vividly realistic drawings of animals imaginable. The man later finds himself caught up in the damaged lives of a young lad named Billy and his mother.

I actually reviewed this story just last year when it appeared in another anthology (*Terrifying Tales to Tell at Night*, also edited Stephen Jones) and at the time I stated that it is one of the greatest I have ever read. I stand by that statement. I also discovered for the first time in this book that this was the first story Marshall Smith ever wrote, a sign of serious quality if ever there was one.

This is followed by "The Same in Any Language" by Ramsey Campbell, about a young boy who is dragged away on a Mediterranean holiday by his rather brash father and his (the father's) new girlfriend to a resort close to a former leper colony.

Whilst the spooky stuff is indeed very effective (especially at the climax), what I really enjoyed most about this story was the beautifully observed exchanges between the kid (taken from his POV) and his cringe-worthy dad and partner. You really do feel for the lad and his plight.

The fourth story is "Norman Wisdom and the Angel of Death" by Christopher Fowler. Stanley Morrison is an official "Hospital Visiting Friend" in London. His private life consists mainly of obsessing unhealthily over post-war British comedians such as Charlie Drake, Hattie Jacques, Tony Hancock and, of course, Norman Wisdom, along with romanticising the era in which they were at their height. Incidentally, Stanley also just happens to be a serial killer, often quite literally boring his victims to death with intricate details of these much-loved entertainers' films and radio plays. When a young diabetic woman named Saskia is placed into Stanley's private care, things quickly take an unexpected turn for them both.

Quite frankly, this story by Fowler is truly mesmerizing and works on multiple levels. At first an extremely darkly humorous satire which had me genuinely laughing out loud in parts whilst shocking me at the same time, it then descends into a very tragic tale laden with pathos and a reminder that it is not always healthy to look back on the past with rose-tinted spectacles – the "good old days" is quite often a myth, as my own great-grandmother would often tell the members of my family. The real-life tragedies of troubled stars like Tony Hancock are testament to this. I grew up in the 1980s listening to the old radio plays of (Tony) *Hancock's Half Hour*, which my father owned on cassette, and watching TV repeats of the *Carry On...* films and *Dad's Army* etc (Norman Wisdom not so much, as I have never been into his slapstick comedy stylings), so this tale very much hit me on a personal level as well (in more ways than one, if I'm honest). An utterly sublime piece by Christopher Fowler that also touches on the mundanity of the lives and personalities of real serial killers like Dennis Nilsen and Peter Sutcliffe, despite the glamorisation of them by the media.

"Mefisto in Oynx" by the great Harlan Ellison is a modern classic dealing in no uncertain terms with the dark side of humanity, focusing in on the plight of two men: one a silver-tongued black man in his thirties with a special gift, the other a white guy of similar age on Death Row accused of dozens of brutal murders.

Written with more than a touch of class and genius, this is some profoundly powerful stuff from Ellison.

Next is "The Temptation of Dr. Stein" by Paul J. McAuley, a wonderfully atmospheric and Gothic take on the Frankenstein legend, set in in an alternate history Venice and featuring a version of Dr. Pretorious who appeared in *Bride of Frankenstein* (1935). There are shades of H. G. Wells' *The Island of Doctor Moreau* in there as well and, for me anyway, you just can't beat a mad scientist drunk on his own power with godlike delusions – it never ends well!

"Queen of Knives" by Neil Gaiman is a deeply puzzling – and beautifully brought to life – poem/story concerning a (very) possibly unreliable narrator revisiting memories of his grandparents and a stage magic act at a *Royal Variety*-style show. It may very well be intended to be read on face value (according to Gaiman himself in a quote before its publication in this book, it is "true in every detail"), but, like all great art, it is open to so many different interpretations, most, if not all, of them rather dark and bleak (at least in my mind anyway, although to be fair, this is a *horror* anthology!). For me, that makes it a magic trick in and of itself and one that I will ponder over for quite some time. I don't want to give the game away for those of you who haven't read it yet by sharing my own views on what happens, so all I will say is that you should read it for yourself, but make sure to pay close attention – there's some serious literary sleight of hand going on here!

In "The Break" by Terry Lamsley, a young boy named Danny goes on holiday with his grandparents to the British seaside town of Todley Bay, a resort that seems to be peopled mostly by old people. Danny is soon witness to some very odd happenings, including a "bear-like man" pushing a mysterious box along a jetty, a sinister seagull, and something rather unpleasant going on in the hotel where he is staying. What follows is an extremely intense, creepy, surreal experience that plays out like a vivid bad dream. A disorientating and atmospheric affair.

Caitlín R. Kiernan's "Emptiness Spoke Eloquent" is a sequel to Bram Stoker's *Dracula*, or more specifically the 1992 film version directed by Francis Ford Coppola and follows Mina Harker's life throughout the decades following the events of the original novel/film. In this dreamlike, finely weaved tale, we join Mina as she deals with the fate of her husband Jonathan and war-torn twentieth century Europe, whilst still haunted by the memory of her old friend Lucy Westenra.

The collection (at least in terms of stories) wraps up with the novella "Mr. Chubb and Mr. Cuff" by Peter Straub, set in New York and which details a thoroughly entertaining and bonkers, black humour-filled account of betrayal and revenge. A satire of sorts that really does "go there" at times in a deadpan, matter-of-fact manner that brought to mind the work of the Coen brothers fused with Brett Easton Ellis.

Also included is a Foreword by the Editor, an Introduction by Ramsey Campbell, a mini Foreword/Introduction to each story by Stephen Jones and the relevant author, and a fantastic front cover illustration by Norman Saunders.

There is an self-explanatory reason why this book is titled *The Best of Best New Horror* and it really does live up to this promise. A must for genre fans!

The Best of Best New Horror: Volume One (and *Volume Two*) *is* published by Drugstore Indian Press, an imprint of PS Publishing and is available to purchase from their website, Amazon and other outlets. For more details go to: https://www.pspublishing.co.uk

NEXT TIME: Trevor Kennedy takes a detailed look at
The Best of Best New Horror: Volume Two

JOHN STEWART:
A FORGOTTEN ARTIST OF FANTASY AND SUPERNATURAL HORROR

A tribute by James Doig

(Photograph of John Stewart from the back flap of Centipede Press's *John Stewart: A Portfolio.* Copyright © Centipede Press)

IN A LETTER to his Australian friend, the bibliographer and collector, Graeme Flanagan, dated 16 January 1989, John Stewart wrote that he and his wife, Anna, had recently been to the World Fantasy Convention, held in London in October 1988, "only to socialise and I freely admit that I was in the bar amidst dozens of bottles of beer, whiskey, Jack Daniels (Karl Wagner!), vodka and one bottle, nowhere near big enough, of homemade rum – that was wonderful." The day after the convention "somehow a great load of people turned up at our place... Karl Wagner cooked gumbo for about 20. Dave Carson was found curled up in a corner of the kitchen the following afternoon. It took John Carter three days to get back to Coventry via George Budge's collection of 'pure scotch malt – not a drop less than 12 years old.' He missed his wife's birthday!" And the following weekend "we had a fantasy wedding! Dennis Etchison who been looking for the 'right woman' ever since I have known him has finally got married to a girl from San Francisco whose name is Kristina... There were about a dozen of us at the actual ceremony, we then took a taxi back to Karl Wagner's hotel, opened several bottles of Champagne and around midday all the other people began to arrive – just another extension of the convention once again!" These quotes show that John was a well-known and well-liked artist who was at the top of his chosen profession at that time in the 1980s. He had illustrated the pages of important magazines such as *Amazing Stories*, *Whispers* and *Fantasy Tales* as well as a couple of books by important US fantasy publishers including Michael Shea's classic short story collection *Polyphemus* for Arkham House. However, these days there are few people who are aware of his work and it's almost impossible to find even basic information about him online.

Graeme Flanagan's correspondence with John began in 1984 when he wrote to John seeking illustrations for the bio-bibliography of Richard Matheson he was writing with Mark Rathbun. The booklet was published in 1984 and included art by Virgil Finlay (a reprint), Dave Carson, Stephen Fabian and Allen Koszowski, as well as an illustration by John Stewart of the spider scene in *The Shrinking Man*. Their correspondence lasted about five years and spanned two years when Graeme and his family lived and worked in Papua New Guinea; John was thrilled that Graeme was able to send him native artefacts in exchange for his illustrations. Their correspondence seems to have petered out around 1989, but Graeme kept John's letters, illustrations and the signed books he sent him which he had illustrated. When Graeme's collection of John Stewart illustrations was auctioned in 2019, almost all of the lots sold for under US$100 each (though a lot of five illustrations for *I Am Legend* sold for US$242), even though John's work rarely comes up for auction. The results were disappointing and indicate something of the neglect into which he has fallen in recent years.

Following John's premature death in 2006 at the age of 58, two of his friends and fellow artists have helped to keep his name alive, Jim Pitts, in an article for *Weird Fiction Review* that published for the first time John's art for H.P. Lovecraft's "The Cats of Ulthar," and in particular Andrew Smith, who was responsible for the huge Centipede Press portfolio volume of John's art, and who published an article on John in Centipede's *A Lovecraft Retrospective: Artists Inspired by H.P. Lovecraft.* Both volumes are hard to find and expensive to buy, so this article, based extensively on John's letters to Graeme Flanagan and on information provided by Andrew Smith, aims to make John Stewart's art accessible to a wider audience.

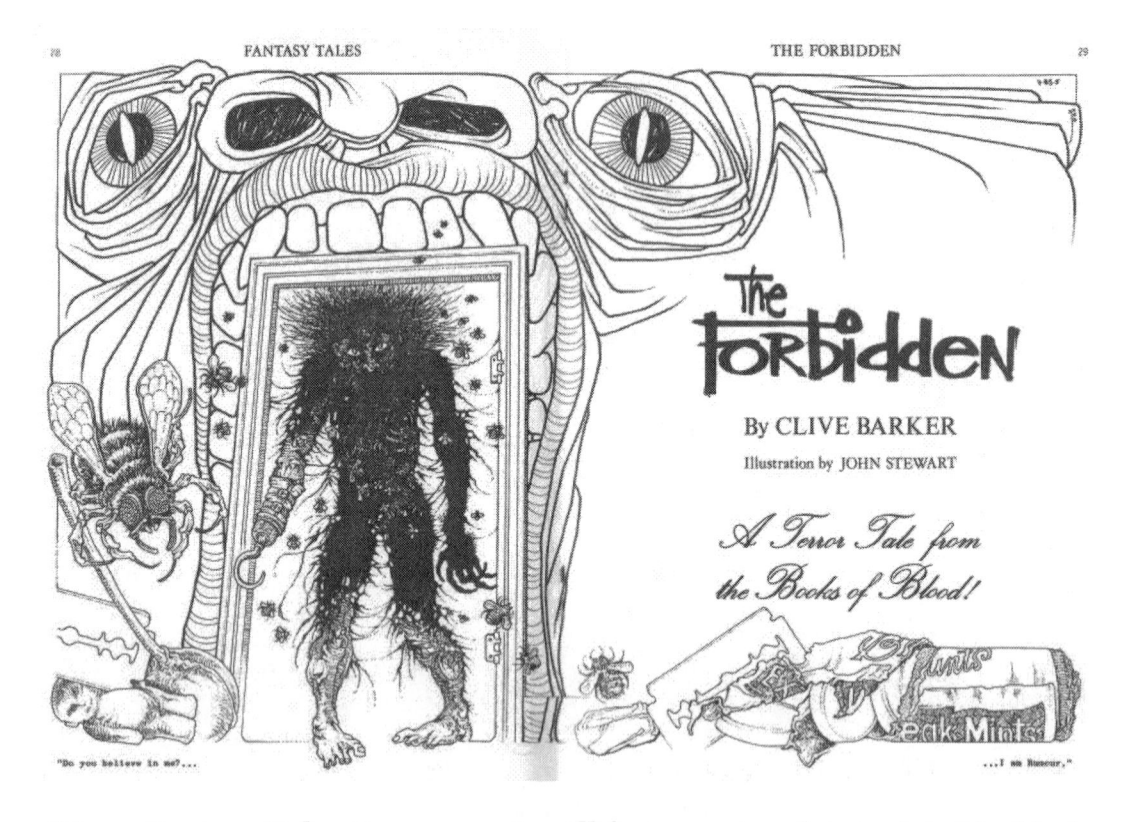

(From *Fantasy Tales*, Summer 1985. All feature artworks reprinted by kind permission of the Estate of John Stewart. They are also subject to the copyright © of the various publications they originally appeared in)

John William Stewart was born at St Neot's, Cambridgeshire, on 15 March 1947 to William, a Water Board Engineer, and Olive May Stewart. The family moved to South London when John was young and he continued to live in London for the rest of his life. Although neither of his parents were interested in art, John showed early talent and won a few local competitions, but the turning point in his life came when, at the age of 15, he visited Paris with a friend and worked as a pavement artist by day and sketched portraits in bars by night. The following year he left school to attend the Ravenswood

Arts College in South London, but soon left to take up an apprenticeship at a commercial art studio. Andrew Smith has pointed out that John was very much a child of the '60s, influenced by the freedom of expression and experimentation that burgeoned in the era, and which encouraged eclectic tastes and influences. Particular influences, which show through in his fantasy illustrations, were Aubrey Beardsley, W. Heath Robinson, Harry Clarke and Sydney Sime, as well as the work of Wallace Smith, especially his remarkable illustrations for Ben Hecht's novel, *Fantazius Mallare: A Mysterious Oath*. Contemporary fantasy and science fiction illustrators also had an enormous influence on John's development including Patrick Woodruffe, Ian Miller, and Bruce Pennington.

In 1966 John met his future wife, Anna Gedl, outside the National Gallery in Trafalgar Square. Anna, of Polish ancestry, was born in London in 1949, and the two were married in July 1974. The following year their daughter Niane (pronounced Nee-arn) was born. They were a very close, artistic family who, to John's irritation, were sometimes viewed as eccentrics by locals; in a letter to Graeme Flanagan, John wrote "Both Anna (my wife) and I are the local weird eccentrics. You have no idea of the things that we are supposed to get up to according to the local gossips... My attitude is that I like to be the local eccentric; if there is one thing that I cannot stand is people with closed minds. If you want to do something then providing that no one is going to get hurt, you should go ahead and do it."

John was a born collector. Andrew Smith notes that in the 1960s he was collecting pulp magazines, in particular copies of *Weird Tales* with Margaret Brundage covers. But the range of his collecting interests were much broader than that. In an article in *Fantasy Newsletter* about his visit to England in 1980, Karl Edward Wagner wrote, "John has enough edged weapons on his walls to withstand a Viking attack." In a letter to Graeme Flanagan, John wrote at length about his collecting interests, "Apart from my masses of old sf and fantasy books, pulps, illustrations, we also have a wall full of axes, clubs and maces, and a large collection of art deco porcelain from the 1920s and 30s. Luckily we started picking that up in junk shops when it was still cheap. Now most of what we would like to have is quite simply too expensive. My (no our) other great love is oriental rugs, carpets, tent hangings and primitive art. Well that is some of the things that we collect. I think that what it really boils down to is that we like to be surrounded by beautiful things, or what we think of as beautiful things."

Naturally, he also collected art when he could afford it: "I have over the years picked up several illustrations from 30s and 40s pulp mags. Also work by Hannes Bok, Lee Brown Coye and Clark Ashton Smith and quite a bit of contemporary work, most of which I have managed to get with a similar sort of arrangement that I have with you. One thing I have learnt. Hang on to it. Even if you get fed up with it, keep it. I can think of two Lee Coyes and four

Virgil Finlays that I no longer have and a Bok painting that I didn't buy. I could kick myself." He was particularly interested in primitive art and artefacts. In a letter dated 15 May 1985, he wrote to Graeme, by that time living in Papua New Guinea: "I am drooling! What you can lay your hands on, I am interested in just about all primitive art – small carvings – totems, fetishes, household protection spirits and erotic (I am trying to build up a small collection of the latter, but what I want is traditional stuff, not the sort of thing that is done specifically for tourists), weapons – axes and clubs and traditional clothing (before the missionaries got there)." His delight with the parcels Graeme sent him is clear from his letters: "Your parcel containing the mask, bone knife and pig tusks etc arrived about a week before Christmas. Graeme I just don't have the words to express my thanks and the sheer delight and pleasure of opening that package. The frog was wonderful, but the arm band and pig teeth necklace. These are exactly the sort of thing that I am after. I can only say thank you and that is absolutely nothing in return for what you have sent to me." His collecting reveals something of his interest in paganism and pre-Christian religions, and this is also evident in his art; for example his Christmas card for 1987 was an illustration of the Celtic cross at Glencolumbkille in Ireland, about which he wrote amusingly: "The stone pillar does actually exist, in southern Ireland. It was originally a huge penis, ten or twelve feet tall, what religious ceremonies were practised before it I leave to your imagination." He reused the image of the pillar a few times in his fantasy illustrations.

(Christmas card drawn by John Stewart)

Given his artistic influences, collecting interests and attraction to the bizarre, it is not surprising that John was drawn to illustrating tales of fantasy and supernatural horror, although he always felt this was just one part of his work as a commercial artist: "I am a commercial artist who is lucky enough to get a lot of illustration work, almost half of which is fantasy, horror & SF." He got jobs in advertising illustration ("which pays considerably more than book illustration") and other types of typesetting, paste up and keyline work. It was hard, time consuming work and he would easily get fed up with people who had a stereotypical view an artist: "They think I hop around on one leg and throw buckets of paint at a huge sheet of canvas and I am sure resent the 'fact' that I earn money for scribbling when the truth of the matter is that I earn money by standing at a desk with a ruler, set square and T square and paste up catalogues and brochures. Still that's people for you."

From the mid-1970s John was illustrating important small press magazines such as *Cross Plains, Phantasy Digest, Nyctalops,* and *Whispers*, and was quickly developing a reputation as a quality illustrator. In 1980 Karl Edward Wagner called John and Jim Pitts "two of the best of the new crop of British fantasy artists." In the early 1980s he started receiving lots of commissions for book illustrations from the German publisher Heyne Bücher for German translations of fantasy and science fiction titles by the likes of C.J. Cherryh, Richard Matheson (*I Am Legend*), Peter Straub (*Shadowland*) and Brian Aldiss (*Hothouse*). During this period he was often snowed under with work: "Between January 2nd and the end of March I had to turn out illustrations and covers for six books. The last one, "Dramocles" by Robert Sheckley was completed in six days (and a good percentage of six nights as well). Having got all that behind me I immediately received commissions for another two books by C.J. Cherryh, although thankfully I did not have to get them completed in some ridiculously short time." Andrew Smith estimates that John illustrated approximately 130 books, mainly from Dutch and German publishers in addition to the cover and interior art he produced for small press and professional magazines. Nevertheless, during his life he only received two book commissions from US publishers, from Whispers Press for Robert Bloch's *Strange Aeons* in 1978, and Arkham House for Michael Shea's collection *Polyphemus* in 1987, a book he was particularly proud of: "I enjoyed doing this one so much that I even did an extra illus., and I had them all finished three months before the deadline. Now that should tell you how much I enjoyed the job better than anything I could say or write." Although there were periods when his work was in demand, particularly in the UK, there were also times when he struggled to make ends meet; in a letter to Graeme Flanagan dated 15 May 1985 he wrote: "There is one other reason that I haven't written to you, and that was because I didn't (or rather could not afford) to pay the postage on a letter! Maybe you can't really appreciate that, but for the past six weeks I have been living on about £40-£50 a week (just for basics you need £100-£120 a week). So I have had to count every penny, but I have just received a decent size cheque so I don't have to worry about where my next meal is coming from for a while at least."

(Illustrations from the German edition of *I Am Legend* [1982])

John was always careful to protect his copyrights, largely a result of negative early experiences in the field. He wrote about this in a letter to Graeme Flanagan dated 9 August 1984 that is worth quoting at length:

...it has been my experience that anyone who is not in some way directly connected with publishing professionally is totally ignorant of these things. I was myself, and consequently lost quite a bit of money to a couple of American fanzine publishers who were among the first people to publish any of my work. One did not, I think, know anything about it himself and after losing a lot of money, sold my work to Arnie Fenner who used it without my permission or payment or anything. The other, who is still going strong, most certainly did know what he was up to and even claimed to own the copyright, something that I never sold to anyone. Once I found out just exactly what was what, I became very particular about who or where my work was published and as a general rule just forgot about any non-professional publications.

It some respects John was quite disparaging of his own work. In 1987 he wrote: "The fantasy illus. – there is maybe one in fifty that I consider good enough to want to keep." What brought out the best in him was his reaction to the book itself. A few times in his letters he mentioned the four or five books that he enjoyed illustrating most: "And the next book that I will be doing is a real gem – *Hothouse* by Brian Aldiss. I know when I am going to do a good job on a book and this one is so full of illustrations that my main problem will be what not to illustrate. I think that I have only had four books I like before, *Our Lady of Darkness* by Fritz Leiber, *Shadowland* by Peter Straub, *I Am Legend* and now *Hothouse* will certainly join their company."

(Front cover and illustration from the German edition of *Shadowland*)

For his illustrations John always used CSIO board or CSIO paper, the choice of surface depending on the commission. So, for the Arkham House commission for *Polyphemous*, "that was all drawn actual size on board because it was a really good collection of stories and something I have wanted to do for a long time." His approach, for example the size of the drawings, also depended on the importance of the commission or his own views of the work he was illustrating; in a letter discussing a German commission he wrote:

81

These illustrations are all half up in size (8 ¼" deep x 5" wide) and are drawn on paper. The reason that I have been working to this size is a combination of having more work to do in general and the publishing company still paying the same money as five years ago – but the news that I was doing work for people like Amazing Stories *and* Arkham House *and so I had to refuse a couple of books worked wonders! The money was increased and the schedule for the books put back three months. But by that time I had learned that working half up in size and using a more 'scribbling' technique, when the illus. were reduced to fit the book, there was no great difference in the appearance of each drawing and more important from my point of view, they took less time to draw. So now for the German books. I work to the larger size, on paper (considerably cheaper than CSIO board which is very expensive) each drawing takes less time to do and I get 20% more money. Possibly you may think that my attitude is mercenary, but as I always say to those who ask, I am not Toulouse Lautrec or Van Gogh, starving in an attic and buying paint before food.*

Although John is known mainly as a pen and ink illustrator, he worked in many different media. Andrew Smith writes of his early work: "As much as he enjoyed his work at the [commercial] studio, he still spent his free time drawing, painting, and creating models in ceramics or wax, and also making wood carvings." On a personal level he was drawn to natural subjects: "For myself I draw flowers, tree bark and naked women" – in particular the latter – "The nudes – I like all of them, but I am usually persuaded to give them to the ladies who actually posed for me." In a letter to Graeme Flanagan dated 27 March 1987 he wrote of his enthusiasm for a drawing of his wife, Anna: "Over the past week I have drawn a picture of Anna and I am very pleased with that as well. It is, I think, one of the best drawings that I have ever done. I intend to get some prints made of it and then to paint the original."

Throughout the letters John's love for his wife and daughter shines through. In 1989 Anna became very ill and John took her to Dorset to convalesce, leaving Niane with friends. John feared for her life, and his distress at the prospect of losing her is evident in his letters. Although Anna recovered, she was later to leave him as a result of his drug and alcohol addiction, which presumably had started in the sixties and was no doubt exacerbated by the trappings of success in the 1980s. Their separation coincided with a house fire that destroyed his personal belongings, artworks and equipment, and his life quickly spiralled out of control with a period of homelessness. From the mid-1990s he produced little new work as he grappled with his demons, and in October 2000 tragedy struck again when he was struck by a car while crossing the road. After a long convalescence it looked like he might resume work again, but by 2005 it was clear that drugs and alcohol had taken a serious toll on his health and he died at St. Thomas

Hospital, London on 18 January 2006. He was 58 years old.

John Stewart was a remarkable talent; his illustrations are unique and memorable, showing a consummate eye for detail and a thoroughly original eye for the bizarre and grotesque. Hopefully the small portfolio of his work here will open up his work to a new generation of fans.

(From *Shayol*, 4, 1980, illustration for Ramsey Campbell's "The Change")

Malachie du Marais, the wolf man of Sylaire

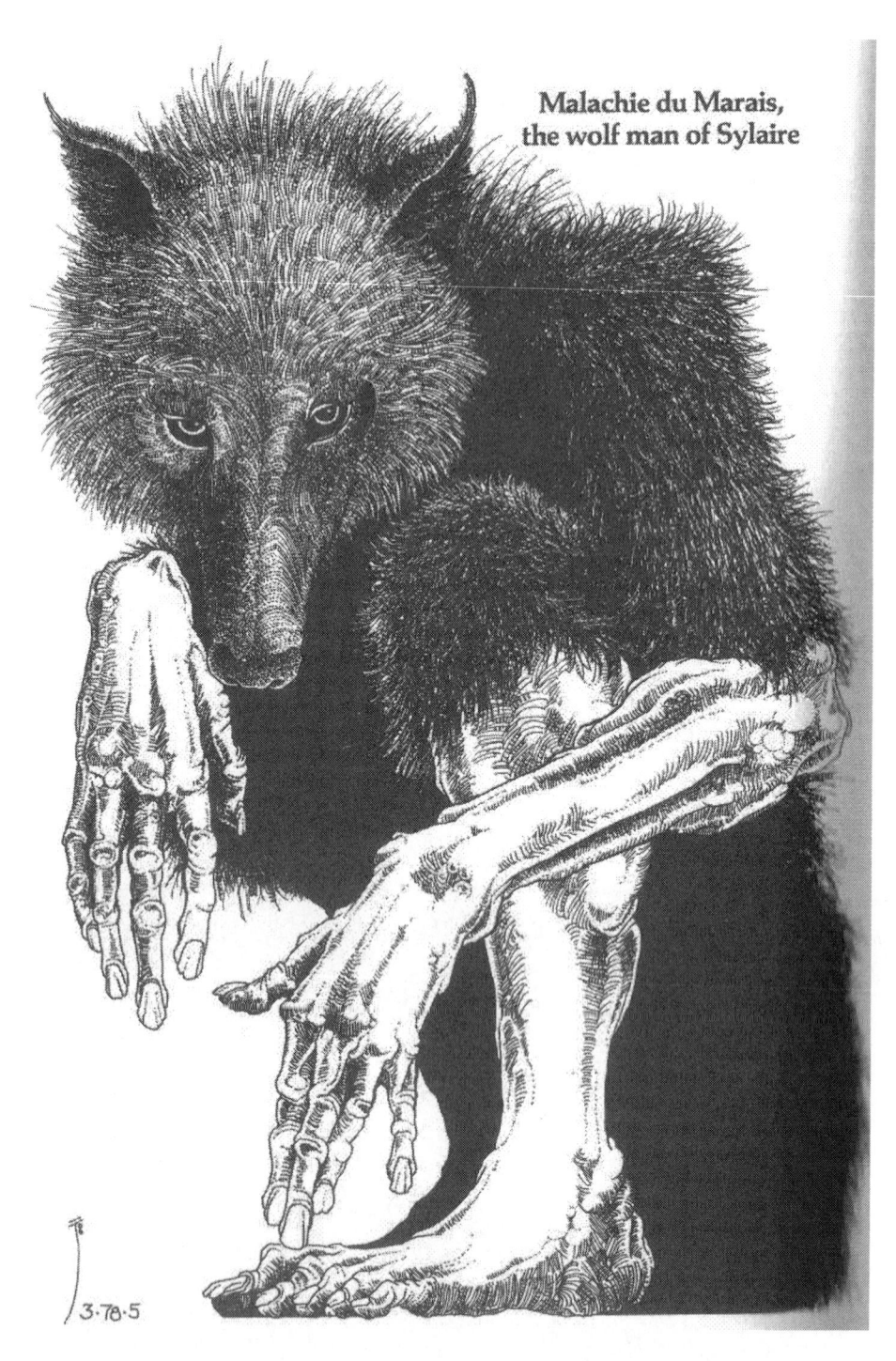

(From "Averoigne: A Folio", *Whispers* 11-12, 1978)

Moriamis the enchantress

(From "Averoigne: A Folio", *Whispers* 11-12, 1978)

(Illustrations from "Averoigne: A Folio", *Whispers* 11-12, 1978)

(Illustrations from the German edition of C.J. Cherryh's Morgaine trilogy and the German edition of *I Am Legend* [1982])

NOW AVAILABLE FROM CRYSTAL LAKE PUBLISHING, AMAZON AND OTHER OUTLETS...

IN CONVERSATION WITH LYNDA E. RUCKER

*Allison Weir gets to know the award-winning American-born, much travelled author, **Lynda E. Rucker**.*

Allison Weir: A great welcome to the *Phantasmagoria* fold, Lynda! How are you doing, all things considered?

Lynda E. Rucker: Not too badly, although like a lot of people, my productivity has certainly been affected by these apocalyptic times we're in!

AW: So you are a Georgia state girl, born and bred – what made you move over to Ireland and settle in Dublin?

LER: Well, I was actually born in Alabama, and then my family moved around the South a lot for a few years, but we did settle in Georgia when I was eight and I grew up and went to university there, so I definitely consider myself a Georgia native and a Southerner. But I've always had an intense love for travel and seeing new places. I took my first trip abroad on my own as a teenager, and I've never stopped except for some stretches when life got in the way. I've lived in several other countries—Nepal, Czech Republic—and I had actually lived in Ireland twice before I moved there again in 2012. My plan had always been to move away from the U.S. permanently. I never really felt like I belonged there and my values are much more aligned with European lifestyles and values. I feel at home over here in a way I never do in the U.S.

I actually moved away from Ireland a few years ago—not by choice, their visa policies changed—and have been living in Berlin for a while—and was in the middle of moving countries *again* (hopefully for the last time, but I needed to live someplace warmer!) when everything ground to a halt with this pandemic.

AW: When did you first realise you were a writer, when did that happen for you?

LER: I can't actually remember not writing. I've been trying to write down stories since I could hold a pencil and make letters, and I fell in love with the imagery of horror fiction and horror stories at a very young age as well although I didn't necessarily think I would end up being a horror writer. I grew up writing lots of poems and diaries but I was very bad about completing stories—it wasn't until I was in my mid-twenties that I started forcing myself to finish what I wrote.

It's only in the last decade that I've started to feel like a "real" writer though—I think after my first collection came out in 2012 and got a really positive response. I sold my first story in 1999, but I never got much attention for my writing until the collection. I'd like to say I didn't need any extrinsic recognition in order to feel like I belonged, as it were, but I'd be lying.

AW: Back in 2015 you won the Shirley Jackson Award for your short story "The Dying Season". Would you personally say that this is your best writing achievement or is there another project that you hold more pride over?

LER: It is certainly is one of the external rewards I'm most proud of. Here

I'm going to totally contradict what I said in my previous answer about needing extrinsic recognition and say that I am equally proud of a number of other stories I've written that didn't get that kind of recognition as well as both of my collections. However, yes, winning that award meant a lot to me. I know it's very fashionable to say you don't care about awards, but I had never been nominated for any award before (or since), so to be nominated for the one I hold in the highest esteem and then win it was amazing. I really didn't expect to win. I was actually spending the weekend in Whitstable and was sitting outside a pub on the beach having a beer when I remembered the ceremony must be on and I checked social media and Cate Gardner had posted that I'd won—I was totally shocked. It was a good night!

(A couple of the books Lynda's work appears in, including *Aickman's Heirs*, which features her Shirley Jackson Award-winning story)

AW: You have also worked alongside Stephen Jones and others on the intriguing *Lovecraft Squad* series. Could you tell us a little bit more about your contribution to this?

LER: So, the first thing I want to say about Steve is that I've known him a long time, ever since he picked my third published story out of essentially a slush pile of magazines and reprinted it in *Best New Horror*. He's been a real support for me since very early in my publishing career, when I felt like even the stuff I was managing to sell was just disappearing into a big black hole of indifference. I wouldn't have continued writing in the horror genre if not for Steve and a handful of other editors who really encouraged me in those early days.

Anyway, I was having lunch a few years ago with Steve and my partner, Sean Hogan, when the *Lovecraft Squad* series came up. From the very start, it was something Sean and I were going to work on together, and I was really pleased about that because I tend to work in a really intuitive way, kind of finding my way through the story. Sean's a screenwriter and so works in a very structured way, from an outline, and that's the approach that a project like that really needs since it has to fit into the book in a very specific way. Everyone had a different era, we got the 1970s and ended up doing a Lovecraftian take on Watergate and had an absolute blast doing it, each of us taking turns writing in the voices of a male and female FBI agent, respectively. Steve had told us to throw in as many pop culture references as possible, and as I was obsessed with the bionic woman as a kid, I essentially based my character off of Jaime Sommers. Steve is one of the best editors to work with as a writer, and it was just a real pleasure all around to get to be a part of the shared world he's created with that series.

AW: Have you ever written a screenplay or dabbled with something really out of your comfort zone in terms of genres, Lynda?

LER: In terms of form, it turns out I'm not one of those writers who is super comfortable at shifting away from prose, whether fiction and non fiction. A few years ago I wrote a short playlet as part of a larger anthology play by several writers that ran in London for a couple of weeks, and I also collaborated on a short piece for a horror comics anthology with Sean Hogan. In both cases, I was really happy about the final result but the writing requires entirely different skill sets, and it was pretty difficult. This makes it sound like I don't like to challenge myself, which isn't true—it's more that I don't think I'm particularly interested in developing the skills to write more in those mediums. If I did more of either, it would probably be trying to write for theatre again. I love comics and always had a little dream of maybe writing them, so I was actually surprised that I didn't particularly enjoy it. As for screenplays—I love film, but I have zero desire to write a screenplay!

AW: You have worked on many collections and anthologies, including *The Magazine of Fantasy & Science Fiction, The Mammoth Book of...* series and *Best New Horror*, so it seems evident that you write mainly within the horror, fantasy and science fiction genres, but if you had to perfect your writing in just one genre, which one would you be willing to focus more on and why?

LER: The vast majority of everything I write is horror, so I guess it would be that, but I honestly feel a bit panicky just thinking about this question! I really hate the idea of being constrained by any genre, so if, you know, someone held a gun to my head and told me to choose, I'd probably cheat and try to pass myself off as some kind of mainstream or literary writer and then just sneak genre into everything I wrote.

AW: Are there any genres you wouldn't touch with a barge pole?

LER: Ummmm, that's a good question. Honestly, there are no bad genres, just bad books!

AW: Now that we are all sort of adapting to a new life with that rotten COVID-19 on the warpath, have you found yourself busier with your writing?

LER: Not at all, unfortunately. It kind of paralyzed me for a while, just all the weirdness and uncertainty swirling around. I think I'm back on track now, which is good, as I'm a freelancer (obviously, I make the vast majority of money writing things other than fiction) and if I can't focus, I can't eat and keep a roof over my head!

AW: Have you been to many writing conventions recently, Lynda? I know Trevor was in the audience at a panel you were part of with Stephen Jones and others at last year's World Con in Dublin, which we also attended.

LER: I've been to a number over the past couple of decades—some World Horror and World Fantasy conventions, Fantasycons in the UK as often as I can. I tend to like smaller, book-oriented events. I've been to one EdgeLit run by Alex Davies in Derby and one of his winter events, which used to be SledgeLit but it was the Derby Ghost Story Festival last year when I went—I love those and would go to more if I could. I went to both Ghost Story Festivals run by Swan River Press in Dublin, and they were terrific; I'll go again if there are more in the future. I go to Octocon in Ireland sometimes too, their national science fiction convention, although it doesn't really have much in the way of horror programming, but it's a very social con for me and an excuse to get back to Ireland and see friends. I've got my eye on Necronomicon in Providence, Rhode Island. I really love cons; I love meeting new people and seeing old friends and talking about writing and stories all weekend. I stay up much too late, when they're closing down the bar every night, and get no sleep and have the time of my life. For about two or three days after the Dublin Worldcon, I actually had no voice left! I find UK cons in particular exceptionally friendly (the first one I went to in the UK was World Horror in 2010 and I didn't know anyone there and I met a ton of people and had an absolute blast). I would really recommend them to aspiring writers. I was gutted at the postponement of the UK StokerCon this year, and I was actually going to go to Eurocon in Croatia this October because I love Croatia, but it's going to be a "virtual" con now—I'm not sure we'll have any cons at all in 2020 at this point.

AW: Please share with us your favourite horror film, actor and the reasons behind your choosing.

LER: Oh gosh! That's an impossible question to answer. I don't have a single favourite horror film, but let's go with one that's not exactly obscure but that people might be less likely to have seen—the Korean film *A Tale of Two Sisters* from 2005. This is *one* of my absolute favourite horror movies, and I don't want to say too much about it, but while it's set in modern-day Korea, it draws on fairytale motifs to tell a poignant, melancholy ghost story. It's also genuinely terrifying—not many films scare me, so when they do, it's notable. I remember being scared to walk down the hallway to go to bed after watching this, and although it's been years since I've seen it, there are a couple of terrifying images from it that remain in my head.

Also, there have been some absolutely stunning horror films in the last few years, but I really have to single out the remake of *Suspiria* as probably the very best of them as far as I'm concerned, and one of the best horror films I've ever seen. And it's a film I love very much in the original, but I'm semi-obsessed with the remake. (I mean, *now* we finally know why the witches were running a dance school in the first place!) The denouement feels like the kind of witchy ritual I've been waiting my entire life to see in a horror film. What I love about both of these films as well is that they are both *about* something—*A Tale of Two Sisters* about grief, and families, and the *Suspiria* remake is about—well, a lot of things, with a profound political vein running through it as well. Seeing it while I was living in Berlin gave it a real resonance as well—here's where I nerdily have to point out that there's a U-Bahn station shown at the beginning that is one stop away from my station!

As for actors... that's a tough one for a different reason. I don't think I really have that intense love of any horror movie actor icons that a lot of horror fans do although Jamie Lee Curtis as Laurie in *Halloween* was certainly a heroine of mine when I was a kid. I'm a lot more interested in actors of any stripe who turn in great performances in horror films—Florence Pugh in *Midsommar*, for example.

But really, don't get me started on favorite horror films—we'll be here a very long time if I do!

AW: What does the future hold for you in terms of writing? Are you going to be exploring any new territory?

LER: I've been banging on about finishing a novel for so long I'm sure everyone is sick of hearing about it, but the fact is I've been dawdling over a novel for years without making much progress. Recently my brain has suddenly shifted into long-form mode; I can't really explain it, but after years of focusing mostly on short fiction I'm finding myself really craving that space and more leisurely pacing of a novel. It's a horror novel, but there are a lot of other things I want to write as far as new territory goes. I absolutely love crime fiction, and I've always had it in the back of my head that I'd write some novels in that genre. I also like historical fiction a lot, and although I've always been a bit intimidated about tackling any historical projects, I am feeling the urge more and more. There's also a few non fiction projects I've been mulling over for a while. The last three years or so have actually been kind of creatively fallow for me, for a lot of reasons, but it feels like time for a lot of new growth now, to extend that metaphor.

AW: Thanks for talking to us today, Lynda! Good luck in all your future endeavours!

OCCULT DETECTIVE MAGAZINE

"Rejuvenating weird fiction in the 21st Century"
Black Gate

Available in print now on Amazon

Cathaven Press
Occult Detective Magazine on FB

LIFE'S SILVER LININGS:
DOCTOR WHO'S SIMON FISHER-BECKER

Trevor Kennedy converses with stage and screen actor
***Simon Fisher-Becker**, whose impressive list of credits include*
Doctor Who *(as the unforgettable Dorium Maldovar),* Harry Potter and the Philosopher's Stone, Les Misérables, *and many more.*

Trevor Kennedy: Simon, it's a real pleasure to be chatting with you! Obviously with the current coronavirus situation going on throughout the world things are a little bit uncertain for all of us, but what are you currently working on?

Simon Fisher-Becker: Very strange times we're living in indeed. Isolating at home is not too much of an issue. As well as an actor, I write. Before coronavirus came along, if I was not on the road or filming, I'd be at home working in my office. My husband (Tony) works in his music room at the same time, so we keep our social distancing.

The lockdown has meant even more time at home. We have the luxury of a garden so we can sit outside when sunny and dry, so no cabin fever yet! Having all this time now means I have no excuses for missing deadlines for my writing projects. I'm currently working on the third part of my autobiographical trilogy – *Let Zygons be Zygons* – due to be published by Fantastic Books Publishing in November 2020. There's a deadline of mid-May to complete a new TV series – *Hello Lovely* – but that's all I can say on that for now.

I continue to record the audio series – *Hawk Chronicles* – a spoof sci-fi drama. I had a guest appearance as Agent Tony Simon in episode 103 and stayed on! I have just recorded Episode 137. It's available on: www.hawkchronicles.com.

TK: You have recently published the second volume in your autobiography series, this one titled *My Dalek Has Another Puncture*. In it, you discuss your life after *Doctor Who* and also bullying and how you will always stand up for your friends when they need it most, inspired by your grandmother. Could you tell us a bit more about these topics and the book as a whole please?

SF-B: *Doctor Who* fans are wonderful. Their interest in Dorium Maldovar and then in me has helped boost my confidence. For ten years now I'm constantly asked questions or to have a chat… about anything really. Initially there were the same questions: How did you get the role? What's it like working with Matt Smith? How much time did you spend in make-up? Gradually I noticed fans were asking if I have an autobiography.

Initially I developed a show based on the concept of a panel or Q & A session. I called it *My Dalek Has a Puncture*, telling my story up to the point when I was offered *Doctor Who*. More of a series of anecdotes than the usual format of an autobiography. There are useful tips for aspiring actors, talking about the tools of the trade, as well as the reality of working in show business. I also cover how I deal with obstructive utility companies and authorities. To my amazement I didn't realise how much the audiences empathised with the section when I talked about being bullied and my darkest times. I found that after the show many of the audience would meet me in the bar and talk about their similar experiences. One evening Dan Grubb from Fantastic Books Publishing approached me after a show and offered me a commission to put the show into book form. Hence the trilogy – *My Dalek Has a Puncture*, *My Dalek Has Another Puncture* and *Let Zygons Be Zygons*.

My Dalek Has Another Puncture is full of *Doctor Who* experiences as well as telling how things changed for me professionally after Dorium

Maldovar.

The first two books are available in paperback and eBook from Amazon.

Let Zygons Be Zygons addresses some of the issues fans have brought to my attention after seeing the show or reading the first two books. It is extraordinary how my anecdotes have meant so much to fans. Because of *Doctor Who* I've got involved with various charities and I cover the issues they deal with.

With our current times, coping with the COVID-19 and lockdowns, my focus in *Let Zygons Be Zygons* is to show people that all difficulties can be overcome. There may be life changing experiences but there is always a silver lining. You simply have to find it... there is always one.

TK: In *Doctor Who*, you appeared in several episodes as the truly unforgettable 52nd century black marketeer Dorium Maldovar, who was a bit of a futuristic Del Boy, your character even returning to the series after he was decapitated, as a literal talking head! But how was the role for you from an acting point of view? How did you approach it and what are some of your fondest memories of your time on the show? Although you have appeared in spin-off web series and such, do you think there is a possibility Dorium might one day return to the main show?

SF-B: The audition piece for Dorium was the scene with Dr. Song in series 5's 'The Pandorica Opens'. I was given this statement: *Setting, an homage to* Star Wars. *Dorium: Large blue man, think Sydney Greenstreet.* This gave me an idea of what the character was going to look like and as a huge fan of the film *Casablanca*, I knew Sydney Greenstreet, who played the black marketeer, Signor Ferrari. Physically large, he spoke very quickly but tended to be still. I knew exactly what Steven Moffat was looking for.

Originally it was the one scene with Dr. Song for Dorium. Naturally, I was excited to have a part in *Doctor Who*, but I was also very disappointed it was only one scene. My delight in being asked back for the episode 'A Good Man Goes to War' was thrilling, but to be asked back for 'The Wedding of River Song' was off the scale.

Each new script had something different about Dorium. Multi-layered like an onion. It was such a delight to have a complicated, complicated character to work with. Dubious, friend or foe, sinister but at times very funny. I shall also be ever grateful to Steven Moffat for giving me the honour and privilege of not only having the last line of 'The Wedding of River Song' episode, but the last line of series 6. The fans went into meltdown. If I had £1 for every fan project that has used the now famous line, I could easily retire!

In an early draft of one of the scripts there was a mention of Dorium's mother. She was a composer who wrote the 'Attack Prayer'. If Dorium's mother was a composer then was Dorium musical in anyway? I tried to visualise him playing a tuba or piccolo, but decided he would probably be a conductor.

There are so many fond memories – it's best if you read my books.

Every day I'm asked if Dorium is to return. In *The Eleventh Doctor Chronicles* from Big Finish Dorium returns. As for returning to the TV, that's up to the powers that be. I've let it be known I'd be more than happy to return. All I can definitely confirm is the fans want to see Dorium again.

TK: For me personally, the Matt Smith/Steven Moffat era was the strongest and most enjoyable in *Doctor Who*'s entire fifty-seven year run so far. You were very much a part of this, but what were Matt and Steven like to work with?

SF-B: It's very much a family on *Doctor Who*. The greeting I got from Matt Smith when there was the read through for 'A Good Man Goes to War' – he came up to me with open arms – "I knew you'd be back" and squeezed me tightly. All my inner child could think was – my God, the Doctor's hugging me!

TK: What do you think of *Doctor Who* in its current form, under Chris Chibnall and Jodie Whittaker?

SF-B: I think Jodie is excellent and I'm enjoying everything so far.

TK: I believe you often attend science fiction conventions across the world, sometimes in character as Dorium. How do you find these events and the fans at them?

SF-B: I've never attended a convention in costume. The irony is contractually I'm not allowed to. There are, however, many photographs of me sitting with Dorium cosplayers. The fans are wonderful, I love them all. The time and effort, let alone the money they have put into some of their costumes is extraordinary. The number of fans who tell me, "You are the reason I've come today" is humbling. Some come to me and say they took some advice I gave them a previous time and everything has worked out for them. I am also aware there are some fans who are socially awkward and/or in a dark place who say seeing me on TV and talking to me at conventions has helped pull themselves from a dark place. The idea that I can help people by them meeting me and it making their day means attending events is so much more than an enjoyable time.

TK: Looking at your other acting work, you have appeared in many television series, including *Vicious, Doctors, One Foot in the Grave* and *Hale and Pace*, and big Hollywood productions such as *Harry Potter and the Philosopher's Stone* and *Les Misérables*. How were your experiences on *Harry Potter* and *Les Mis*?

SF-B: *Harry Potter* was ten years before *Doctor Who*. At the time it was THE project to be associated with. Very exciting times. As well as filming there were interviews and publicity shoots as well as being photographed by Annie Leibovitz, and appearing in *The Observer* magazine and *Vanity Fair*. Plus, meeting so many established actors. It was very much a dream fantasy.

Les Mis was wonderful. My agent called to say they were looking for actors who can't sing or dance – and thought of me. They were looking for ensemble cast for the 'Master of the House' sequence. Although I consider myself as an actor who can hold a note, I accept I would never be cast in a West End production of *Les Mis*. So, I was very pleased to take part in the film. We had ear pieces fitted so we could hear the music banged out on a honky-tonk piano and we sang live on set. It was a two-week booking at Pinewood. Sacha Baron Cohen fell ill so we were put on hold for an additional week. With the additional payment I bought a new fridge!

TK: You are also a stalwart of stage and have done panto too. Do you prefer stage acting to film and TV?

SF-B: I started out – as most actors of my age – on stage. Live theatre will always be my first love. But I enjoy it all. I would perhaps add that the ideal job would be a stage job with film money!

TK: You are obviously very musically talented as well. I hear you can conduct a full symphony and choir?

SF-B: On paper I'm Grade 8 Clarinet and Piano but having not played either for years I would say I'm probably more Grade 5. Yes, I have conducted symphony orchestras and choirs and could comfortably do so if called upon. Perhaps a scene with Dorium conducting an orchestra would be a treat.

TK: As if all this isn't enough, you're also a motivational speaker with your one man shows. Could you give us more details about this please?

SF-B: As mentioned before, this has developed from my Dalek shows. A lot of physically large people come to my shows and speaking events, as do disabled. They are easy targets for bullies and seeing me, another large disabled person, getting out there doing my stuff regardless gives them encouragement and hope. This has not been deliberate on my part. It is something that's evolved. I rarely say to people "this is what you have to do". Life is more complicated than that. The same issue can be dealt with in different ways by different people – it all depends on their make-up. The media banging on about "fat people bankrupting the NHS" doesn't help. Especially as it's not true.

One unexpected and bizarre development (in my opinion) is some people just simply like the sound of my voice. Especially in USA. I have often been booked to simply talk – "We don't care what you talk about but please come and talk." These often turn into Q & A sessions. Fortunately, as those who know me will tell you, I can talk for hours, on a whole range of issues. I'm 59 this year and have a lot of experience in many fields so most of what I say comes from that experience which audiences can tell is authentic.

My message is from what my grandparents taught me. If you don't like the way things are, change them. If you can't change them, put up with them. And... find the silver lining, there is always one.

TK: You have many strings to your bow, Simon, but is there anything that you haven't tried your hand at yet that you would like to?

SF-B: Rally driver.

TK: What future works do you have lined up, both in the short and long terms?

SF-B: Every acting job I had lined up has come to a full stop. I'm always available for voice work. I have a working studio at home, so ready when producers are.
   There are talks about various projects but we're in a period of unknown. Not knowing when the current situation will come to an end is complicating everything. But as I've mentioned I'm writing and will have various things ready for when we can be released into the wild again.

TK: Thank you so much for speaking to us at *Phantasmagoria*, Simon. It's been great!

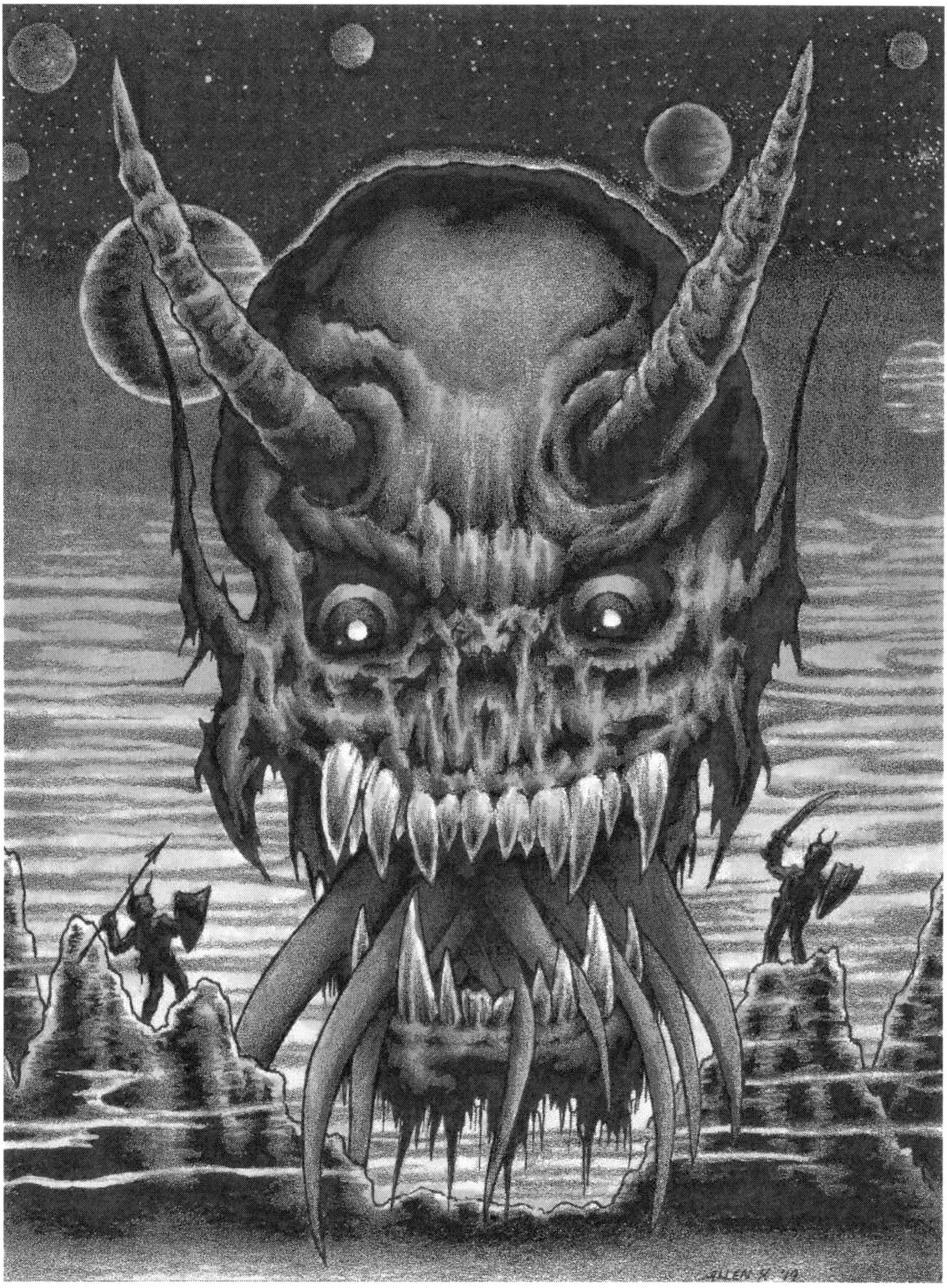

THE MANY WARS OF THE WORLDS

Raven Dane

"Ulla, Ulla, Ulla!
'The chances of anything coming from Mars are a million to one,' he said,
'The chances of anything coming from Mars are a million to one –
but still they come!'"

BET SOME OF you sang along with that!

The War of the Worlds has caught the imagination of people since H. G. Wells' iconic and highly influential SF novel emerged in hardcover by Heinemann in 1898. The world clearly had an appetite for the story. It had already been serialised in 1897 by *Pearson's Magazine* in the UK and by *Cosmopolitan* in the US. Fans of the book have always yearned for a faithful adaptation of it, one that has yet to happen. The wave of disappointment from SF fans after the recent BBC adaptation reverberated throughout the cyberverse.

Past adaptations include the notorious radio broadcast by Orson Wells, the one so frightening, many American listeners thought it was real. In 1938, the night before Halloween, the broadcast brilliantly sent out a series of news bulletins in real time, covering an invasion of New Jersey by Martians. It was so realistic it caused a mass panic across the states. Orson Wells heard reports of mass stampedes, of suicides and of angered listeners threatening to shoot him on sight.

"If I'd planned to wreck my career," he said at the time, "I couldn't have gone about it better."

Fortunately this did not happen, and on the back of the scandal, Orson Wells began his long, successful career as an actor and director.

The extraordinary reaction of the public is an excellent study into the continuing power of H. G. Wells' original story. An account of a sudden invasion beyond all accepted reality, an attack with no warning by an implacable and powerful enemy. A truly alien aggressor that cannot be reasoned with, that slaughters all with no mercy, no compassion. One that is impervious to all of mankind's defences. An enemy that is here to exterminate human life and seize the planet for themselves.

Attacks by such aliens have of course become a staple of SF and film. During America's Cold War, frightening aliens stood in for fear of a communist invasion as zombies have now for our fear of viral pandemics. Jokes and memes about a Zombie Apocalypse have already popped up again during our worldwide battle with Covid-19. A modern day Orson Wells can still cause pandemonium with a viral-based fake news broadcast. Most likely our litigious society would put people off such a venture. Are we too blasé to fall for such an event? The reaction to the BBC's spoof live broadcast *Ghostwatch*, aired on Halloween in 1992 and written by Stephen Volk, showed we are clearly not. The show caused a huge furore, resulting in an estimated 30,000 calls to the BBC's switchboard in a single hour! It has never been shown again on British national television.

Such is the power of H. G. Wells' original premise, directors have kept it for their own versions with considerable success critically and in the box office. There have been nine films, two TV series, fourteen radio adaptations and four adaptations to music, the most memorable, of course, being the enduringly popular Jeff Wayne musical version, first released in 1978 and the most faithful to H. G. Wells' original novel. There have also been seven video games based on *War of The Worlds*, the legacy is so enduring.

Two of the best film adaptations are George Pal's 1953 masterful version that remains chilling to this day. Based in contemporary America, the eerie arrival of the Martians and their ruthless destruction is wonderfully portrayed using the best special effects available at the time, that stand up well to modern viewers. Some of the most successful effects are the use of eerie, discordant sounds such as the Martian heat ray, which pulses and fires red sparking beams, all accompanied by thrumming and a high-pitched clattering shriek when the ray is used. *The Monthly Film Bulletin* of the UK called it "the best of the post war American science fiction films; the Martian machines have a quality of real terror, their sinister apparitions, prowlings and pulverisings are spectacularly well done, and the scenes of panic and destruction are staged with real flair".

Another excellent adaptation is the 2005 Steven Spielberg blockbuster starring Tom Cruise. Some of the early antipathy towards the film was caused by the unpopularity of the actor. Whatever his beliefs or private personality, Cruise put in another solid performance as the everyman protagonist Ray Ferrier. Despite the American modern setting, Wells' themes remained – enhanced by massive, grim and spectacular special effects – of the overwhelming power and cruel indifference to human suffering. There are scenes I still find unwatchable, such as the blood-red rain falling across the landscape and the discarded remains of humans harvested by the Martians. The feel-good ending was a both a relief for softies like me and a let-down for many after the grim struggle to survive for Ferrier and his family.

2019 brought two more versions to our TV screens. The BBC three-part drama series was eagerly awaited as it was set in Great Britain and supposedly at the correct time period. The first trailers forewarned that this was not exactly the case. The drama brought the setting to a later time, the Edwardian era. It also strayed from the novel in many ways and though it had its scary moments, the general consensus was it was not the much hoped for adaptation of H. G. Wells' work. *The Guardian* gave the series four stars, stating it as "solid and reliable" drama but had a "lack of urgency". Society's lack of preparation for such an overwhelming and destructive force that was too powerful to be defeated remained the same. Uneven pacing, the use of flash-forwards to a brutal post invasion world and concentrating on a frankly uninvolving central couple were the cause for most criticism.

It also alludes to the brutal effect of colonisation wrought by Western powers around the world. Wells had said that the plot arose from a discussion with his brother Frank Wells about the catastrophic effect on indigenous Tasmanians. Introduced diseases and persecution had led to the extinction of the Tasmanian race. What would happen, Wells wondered, if Martians did to Britain what the British did to the people of Tasmania?

All three of these versions ended the invasion in the same way, with the collapse of the Martian invaders, killed by their lack of resistance to Earth microbes. The might of the world's defences could not stop their conquest, but tiny specks of life proved fatal to the Martians. In the BBC series, the defeat of the Martians took longer and the world was left a contaminated wasteland, converted to a toxic red landscape to suit the invaders. A human scientist created a cocktail of different Earth virus types that finished off the Martians and killed their invasive red weed.

Which brings me to the latest TV offering, another modern adaptation in 2019 made by Fox and Canal, being shown on Fox TV with a second series currently under production. The central tenants of an adaptation of H. G. Wells' original story are there. A sudden and brutal attack that mankind is not expecting or prepared for, an enemy so unknown and powerful that humanity cannot defeat it by existing weaponry. This time the enemy does not come from Mars, no longer a believable home world for the aliens, thanks to modern science. It begins with the detection of curious signals coming to

Earth from deep space, well away from our solar system. The worldwide attacks from bomb-like alien craft and sonic weapons that kill most of the planet's population comes almost straight away and with a brutal and terrifying speed.

It is set in the present and filmed in London, Paris and the Alps. In my opinion it is the bleakest version by a long shot. In the tradition of *Game of Thrones* and *The Walking Dead*, no one is safe, however popular the character. This always makes for uneasy viewing. Some of the deaths are truly harrowing and unexpected. Being a good and heroic character means nothing to the yet unseen aliens, currently using devastating sonic attacks and rather primitive, but effective, walking droids to do the killing... so far. One episode in particular is so distressing, it still haunts me. It involves the killing of pregnant women by the droids, ripping out their unborn babies and a team of them removing all the newborns from a hospital nursery. This is a not a version for the faint-hearted! With a second season being filmed, maybe we will see what the aliens actually look like, find out what their plan is for the conquered remnants of mankind, and what will kill the invaders... if they are overcome.

With the basic theme working in any era, would a book-faithful version set in Surrey and London in 1898 still be enjoyable to the modern audience? One true to the text and not to a modern director's vision? With seeming no end to the popularity of Jeff Wayne's musical version, maybe a faithful, filmed adaptation of H. G. Wells' masterpiece is still waiting to be made.

"*Ulla, Ulla, Ulla!*"

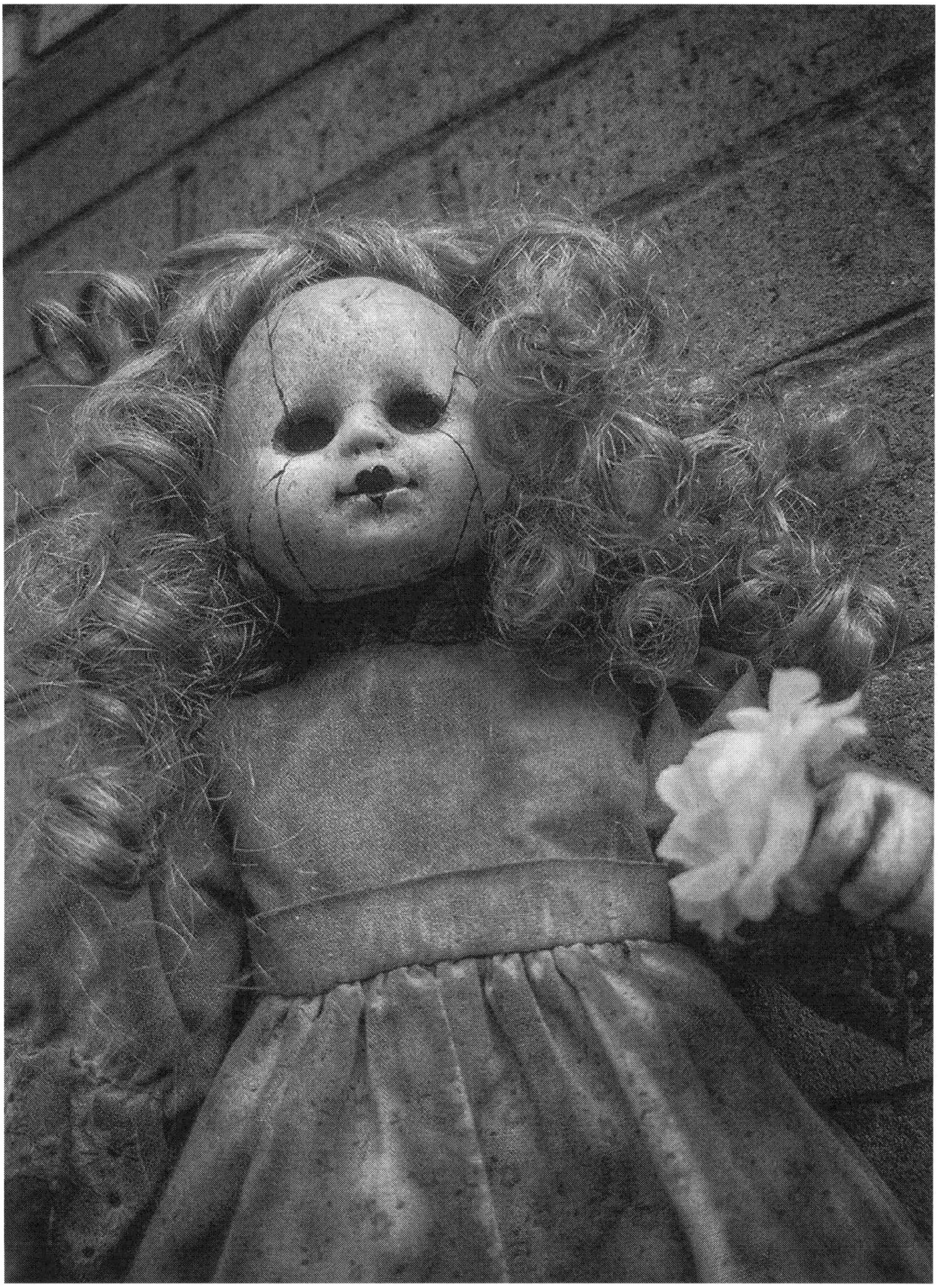

EVOLUTION OF A CLASSIC: THE STORY OF THE *PLANET OF THE APES* FILM FRANCHISE

Dave Jeffery

Part One: *Planet of the Apes* (1968)

PLANET OF THE Apes (POTA) has been part of my life for so long, I cannot remember the first time I ever saw it. What I do know is that it was one of the few movies from the 60s-70s franchise that I did not see on the cinema, with the other exception, *Conquest of the Planet of the Apes (1972)* as I was too young for the, as then, AA certificate (15 certificate in today's standards).

POTA's impact on the history of science fiction filmmaking is irrefutable. Its socio-political commentary is timeless, its message on the fragility of the human condition, as poignant as ever. Like many classics of the genre, it was a film ahead of its time, and in a league of its own.

This article takes as read these facts and focuses, instead, on how POTA came to be, exploring the origins and challenges in production and key creative decisions around the original 1968 film, and asking some questions as to just how much influence screenwriter Rod Sterling did, or didn't have, in the 'shape' of the final movie. This latter element is important as the esteemed creator of *The Twilight Zone* is credited with the lion's share of accolade when it comes to the final screenplay, but further research suggests that this may not be wholly justified.

Finally, we shall look at contributions made by creative make-up designer John Chambers and the principle cast, and some critical perspectives from the time of release.

In researching this article, I have looked at many sources and, of course, watched the original film several times. I can still say, it was no chore at all. Primary sources include the original script edits from Charles Eastman, Rod Serling and Michael Wilson (all available on the incredible POTA resource site: Hunter's Planet of the Apes Archives), J. W. Rinzler's *The Complete Making of Planet of the Apes* (HarperCollins), Paul A. Wood's 2001 *The Planet of the Apes Chronicles* (Plexus Publishing), and numerous websites, feature articles in the associated press and genre magazines.

The *Planet of the Apes* movie originates from the 1963 book, *La Planete des Singes* (*Planet of the Apes* in the US and *Monkey Planet* in the UK) by French novelist Pierre Boulle, famous for his previous work *The Bridge on the River Kwai*, released as a film in 1952.

Boulle's novel is told through a journal written by protagonist Ulysse Mérou. The record is found in a bottle by Jinn and Phyllis, two rich explorers who are travelling through space on a luxury yacht that is riding the solar winds. The journal tells of a group of scientists, including Professor Antelle and his protégé, Arthur, who travel to Betelgeuse and in doing so encounter a bend in time where, in the two years they have been in space, centuries have elapsed on the earth. They leave their ship in orbit and descend to a habitable planet in a shuttle where they meet a mute woman whom they christen Nova, and are initiated into her tribe of humans before she kills the pet chimpanzee the travellers have brought with them.

The crew are deprived of their clothing and their shuttle is wrecked by their brutal hosts. The following morning the tribe is ambushed by apes in a hunt and Arthur is killed. Ulysse is captured and housed in a behavioural centre for the study of humans. Professor Antelle is taken to a zoo where, over time, he regresses to a savage state. Ulysse is caged in the behavioural centre where his attempts to communicate using ape linguistics attract the attention of two chimpanzees – Zira and her mate, Cornelius. Ulysse learns the ape language, is given his freedom and allowed to mate with Nova who bears a child that can walk and talk within three months of being born. From Cornelius, an archaeologist, Ulysse learns of excavations and evidence of a human society that pre-dates ape culture, including talking human dolls.

Under threat of execution and experimental surgery from Dr. Zaius, the orangutan antagonist who realises their threat to ape society, Ulysse, Nova and their child escape on an experimental spacecraft originally intended to send humans as guinea pigs on the ape fledgling space programme. In orbit, Ulysse docks with his ship and they return to earth where, to their horror, when they land in Paris they are greeted by a gorilla in a jeep. In a final twist we discover the wealthy Jinn and Phyllis are chimpanzees who scoff at the idea of intelligent humans and discard the journal back into space.

The rights to the novel were procured by Arthur P. Jacobs in 1963 who was, at that time, looking for material 'something like *King Kong*'. Despite loving Boulle's concept, Jacobs had difficulty with studios buying into the idea that talking apes could not be anything other than ridiculous. Comedy film maker Blake Edwards (*Breakfast at Tiffany's*, *The Pink Panther*, *A Shot in the Dark*) was the original choice for director. While Edwards left at the development stage, he had the foresight to retain *Twilight Zone* creator Rod Serling to write the adapted script and help shaped the adaptation. Serling had already worked on a screen adaptation at the request of The King Brothers, a production company specialising in low budget movies, so was more than familiar with the piece.

The first screenplay pulls through Boulle's basic story structure while omitting the wraparound of Jinn and Phyllis, and the twist ending of the protagonist returning to earth to find it overrun by apes. Instead, Serling opted for a finale that was to become iconic, that of the last man on Earth bowed before a tarnished Statue of Liberty. In his 1972 interview with journalist, Dale Winogura, Serling admitted that the book-to-screenplay transition was a challenge: "I worked on the screenplay for well over a year, and 30 or 40 drafts came out of it. I could've taken the excess pages and made a TV series about it!"

From Boulle's source material, Serling was able to distil the plot structure, to include key events and characters. However, there were two important changes. Firstly, the astronauts become stranded on the planet due to damage to their ship on landing. The second was that, unlike Boulle's premise of a planet of apes, in Serling's version of events, unbeknown to the astronauts, they land on a future version of Earth destroyed by war. According to critics, this central conceit is what gave the film version its edge. Though there is often dispute over who came up with the original ending, most of the Serling's scripts feature the discovery of some Earth icon to demonstrate to the protagonist he is back home. His final script certainly features the Statue of Liberty image at its conclusion. One element that Serling was keen to retain was the ethos of the apes living in a more modern-day society, with technology and machinery.

The script was submitted to Arthur P. Jacobs & Associates Company (APJAC) Productions in March 1965. Along with Serling's screenplay, Jacobs had concept sketches drawn up and set about co-ordinating a studio pitch.

But even with this and illustration ideas, the major studios remained reluctant. Attracting a major star like Charlton Heston, who in turn, brought his *The War Lord* director Franklin J. Schaffner to the project, still could not change the minds of studio executives. It was at this point that Jacobs adjusted his approach, opting for a visual pitch. Using Heston and legendary actor Edward G. Robinson, a screen test was shot, taking a portion of Serling's script and directed by Schaffner. Jacobs' wife Natalie Trundy would make her first appearance in the franchise, this time playing an early rendition of beneficent chimpanzee psychologist Dr. Zira. Although the make-up was crude, the scene demonstrated to reluctant studio heads, especially Richard Zanuck at 20th Century Fox, that the concept of a planet ruled by apes was not a whimsy, but an intriguing slice of science fiction. Under Zanuck, Fox greenlit film production in 1965.

Jacobs handed the script over firstly to Charles Eastman who took the story leftfield (his treatment had the astronauts still on the ship after twenty-seven pages) and was promptly replaced by Michael Wilson. The introduction of Wilson is poignant in that he also co-wrote another Boulle screen adaptation, *Bridge on the River Kwai*, directed by David Lean in 1957. Wilson was blacklisted for suspected communist leanings by the Un-American Activities Committee and was, at that time, living in Paris, therefore his name was uncredited as screenwriter.

There has been much debate as to who wrote the shooting script attributed to Wilson, and the ultimate tone of the final movie we watch and enjoy today. Much of the contention is around dialogue and the 'dumbing down' of the original adaptation of Boulle's book. For purists, the film would have been better served by Serling's script. This is, of course, a subjective view, but the evidence available demonstrates that only thirteen sentences from Serling's 157-page final draft remain in the shooting script. Serling himself had long since left the project once submitting his final draft in early 1965. In the 1972 interview with Dale Winogura, Serling clarifies the contribution of both screenwriters: "The scene breakdown, the concept, and the thrust of the piece was mine. But the actual dialogue was Michael Wilson's."

The fledgling production lost Edward G. Robinson as Dr. Zauis early on, the actor finding even the rudimentary make-up of the screen test a challenge. Another casualty was Serling's script, with name changes to all characters save for Nova, and Schaffner culling the premise of ape society being at least equal to ours in terms of technology, opting instead for a society that was not as developed, aided by surreal, prefabricated buildings that gave the franchise its trademark production design. It also, of course, helped trim the production budget, allowing for development of John Chamber's ground-breaking make-up effects.

Already an established make-up artist for NBC TV network and 20th Century Fox, Chambers learned his craft providing prosthetic appliances for injured servicemen returning from conflicts in World War II, afterwards working for government departments before moving to Hollywood. His work has featured in many 1950s and 1960s science-fiction shows, including *The Munsters*, *The Outer Limits*, *Lost in Space*, and Ron Serling's *Night Gallery*. He is also known for creating the earpieces for sci-fi icon Mr. Spock from the *Star Trek* franchise.

As noted by Chambers in an interview with Jack Hirshberg in 1967, the challenges of the ape make-up for production were significant: "We had to handle several problems – including voice projection so that the actors could properly enunciate their lines and speak them clearly enough for sound recording. The actors' own lips had to synchronise with the outer lips – the ape lips – so that when any given word was spoken the ape lips would properly form this sound visually."

Chambers was involved in the development of the apes' appliances six months before shooting began, developing new techniques, and pushing the boundaries of make-up design. He was also insistent that he be on set throughout the entire shoot, overseeing his incredible creations. He would later receive an honorary Academy Award for his work in 1969, and his techniques became industry standard for the next few decades.

Charlton Heston bought heavily into the project from an early stage, based primarily on Serling's original script. As noted by Heston's son in J. W. Rinzler's remarkable book *The Complete Making of Planet of the Apes* (HarperCollins, 2018): "Dad often put in twelve-hour days on set, plus another hour back at the Fox lot, watching the dailies …"

Heston was an inspired choice. Astronaut Taylor was both adventurer and cynic, but it was unusual for the larger-than-life actor to be placed in so many vulnerable and demeaning situations in a film. The construct of all-American hero was pushed to the limits, challenged and demeaned, and Heston's portrayal of the isolated hero made more potent. The final scene, the cowed Taylor on his knees before a ruined Statue of Liberty, is perhaps the ultimate statement of America in the '60s – unsure and vulnerable, browbeaten into change by extremes.

Roddy McDowall has become synonymous with the POTA franchise. He starred in four of the original movies (apart from *Beneath the Planet of the Apes* due to shooting schedule conflicts) and the subsequent TV series. A long-standing actor in Hollywood, McDowall had already starred in Serling's *The Twilight Zone* episode 'People are Alike All Over' (1960) based on a short story by Paul W. Fairman. McDowall's considered approach gave the character of Cornelius a blend of cynicism and kindness that endeared him to fans. A classically trained character actor, McDowall spent months studying the facial expressions of chimpanzees and incorporated these into his performance.

Kim Hunter was a distinguished actress who had already a Best Supporting Actress Golden Globe and an Academy Award for her performance in the 1951 film adaptation of Tennessee Williams' *A Streetcar Named Desire*. Like McDowall, Hunter had also featured in Serling-written productions, this time for *Playhouse 90*, including 'Requiem for a Heavyweight' (1957) and 'The Comedian' (1957). Her portrayal of Dr. Zira is considered by many to be POTA's beating heart, allowing the audience's sense of humanity to be personified on screen.

Maurice Evans was already a Shakespearean and theatre actor of great renown. He also had an association with both Heston and Schaffner through his role as a priest in *The War Lord*. His portrayal of orangutan Dr. Zauis, Minister of Science and Defender of the Faith, has significant presence in the film, working through the contentions between scientific discovery and maintaining theological status quo. His speech when tied up by Taylor on the beach (during the "Beware the beast Man" scene and one of few pieces of dialogue remaining from Serling's original script) is beautifully delivered and sums up the character's ambiguity throughout the film.

Linda Harrison was, at that time, a model and under contract with Fox. By her own admission she was also dating studio executive Richard Zanuck who suggested she audition for the role as it did not require her to speak. With limited acting experience, she adopted the concept of Nova as an animal, focusing on physical movement rather than performance. She quickly found out that this was in harmony with Schaffner's view of the character. Harrison brings a sense of animalistic innocence that gradually softens as her interactions with Taylor continue. Her confused expression at Taylor's angst as she stares up at the Statue of Liberty is the harrowing moment before cinema history is made on the screen.

When POTA premiered in New York on February 8th 1968, few could have envisioned the impact the film would have on cinema. When it went on general release April, 1968 the audience reaction was affirming of its ability to entertain and ask moralistic questions of present day society. In the years that followed, the final few moments have been parodied countless times, on countless populist shows and movies. Unsurprisingly, critical reaction at the time was generally favourable:

> "*Planet of the Apes* is that rare film that will transcend all age and social groupings." – John Mahony, *The Hollywood Reporter*.

> "This is one of the most entertaining science fiction fantasies ever to come out of Hollywood." – Pauline Kael, *The New Yorker*.

But some found issues with the allegory-heavy aspects of the script:

> "A promising idea, and yet ultimately too cute: it is a one-to-one allegory, and this much of the film is spent exploring this not very rewarding vein." – Richard Round, *The Guardian*.

What is without dispute is that *Planet of the Apes* had the special ingredients that make classic movies, a perfect storm of passion and production that ultimately created a masterpiece of sci-fi cinema. Great pacing and direction, a wonderful screenplay, unique sets and production design, Academy Award-nominated music and costume design, and Academy Award-winning make-up effects. To look at the film today, it is timeless, a remarkable feat given a movie that is over half a century old.

In 2001 POTA was inducted into the National Film Registry by the US Library of Congress for being "culturally, historically, or aesthetically significant" – testament, it seems, to its influence on modern day art and culture.

In the words of Dr. Zaius, "And deservedly so."

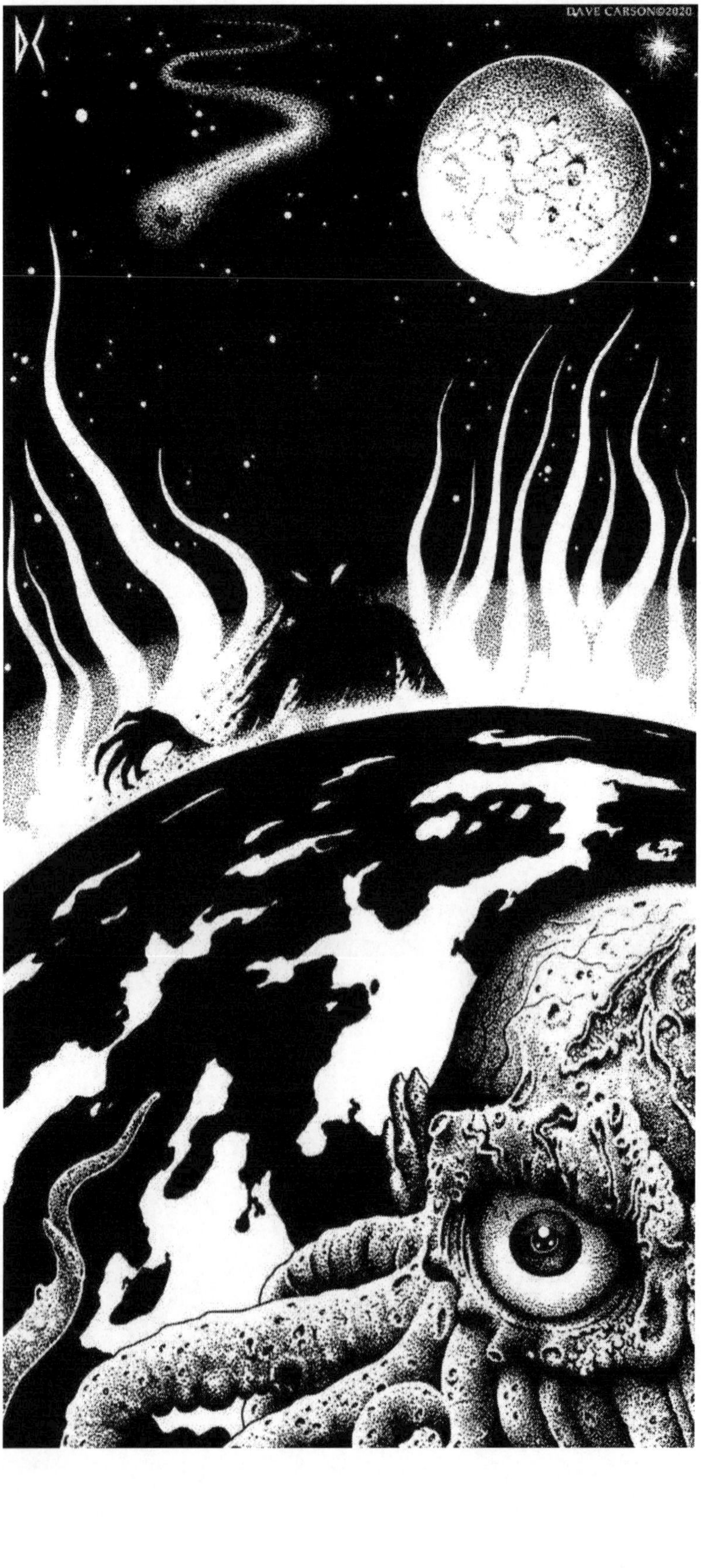
DAVE CARSON©2020

THIS FILM HAS NOT YET BEEN RATED PODCAST

Genre films past and present discussed in detail!

All episodes available from:
https://podbay.fm/podcast/1480146959

PHANTASMAGORIA FANS' EUPHORIA

(READERS' COMMENTS AND FEEDBACK)

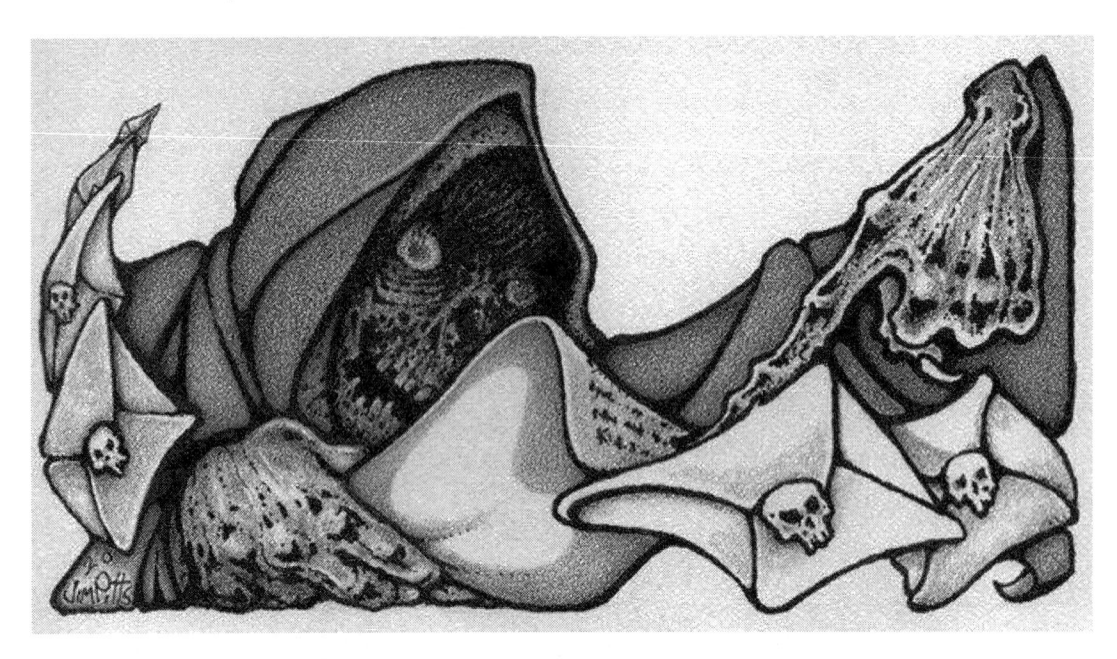

(Phantasmagoria Magazine) is great value as a magazine and each issue is packed with great stories, articles, interviews, reviews on all aspects of horror, fantasy and science fiction, plus some fabulous artwork, both on the covers and inside.
(David A. Riley via Facebook)

Thoroughly enjoyed devouring the Phantasmagoria Special Edition *on R. Chetwynd-Hayes. Great work.*
(Rob Talbot via Twitter)

Packed to the brim with awesomeness. A fantastic read, full of great stories and useful information. Worth every penny.
(Christopher Fielden, 5 star Amazon review)

Well penned! Fantastic read!
(Forever Changes, 5 star Amazon review)

A further short horror story sent in to us by 15-year-old schoolboy **Ethan Horner** from Belfast. Horror fan Ethan also belongs to a community drama group and sings in his school choir.

DEATH OF A GLADIATOR by Ethan Horner

I AM A normal 15-year-old boy and also a big fan of scary horror-type things, so I was sitting at home when I decided to hop on my Xbox. As I was on what was possibly my fourth round of Xbox, and just before I logged into the game again, an annotation came up on the screen asking me to come to an address.

When I got to the place that was given, I found it was surrounded by a very dense forest. I had come alone, so I swallowed my fear and started walking through it where I soon saw a very muscular giant who was foaming at the mouth. I looked to my left where I saw a sign which read: ***Battle the gladiator in the pit to get out of the forest in one piece***.

As I ran towards the giant, I had a flashback to when my little brother and I would fight for fun and as I came back to the present, the giant upper-cutted me. I did a full backflip but quickly got back onto my feet and hit him with a few good punches, but he knocked me to the ground, grabbed my ankle and chucked me to the side of the pit where I saw a piece of bone. I ran towards it, but the giant went to trip me up. I flipped over his leg and picked up the bone and beat him in the face with it until he was unrecognisable. I straightened up my back and stumbled away with my knees weak, soon passing out just outside of the forest.

I woke up in a morgue and when I did the workers there freaked out. I shouted, "What the hell?!" They told me I had a six inch stab wound in my shoulder and also an injury to my abdomen. I had temporarily stopped breathing, so they had thought I was dead.

I got out of there as soon as possible and ran home.

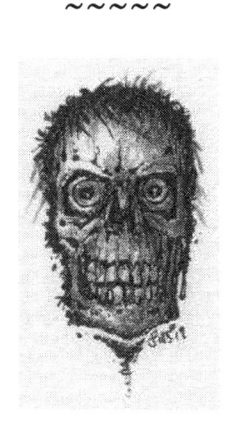

~~~~~

If you would like to contact us at *Phantasmagoria Magazine* with feedback or suggestions we are available through the following channels:

Email: tkboss@hotmail.com

Facebook: https://www.facebook.com/PhantasmagoriaMagazine/

Twitter: https://twitter.com/TKBossPhantasm

Instagram: https://www.instagram.com/tk_pulp_phantasmagoria/

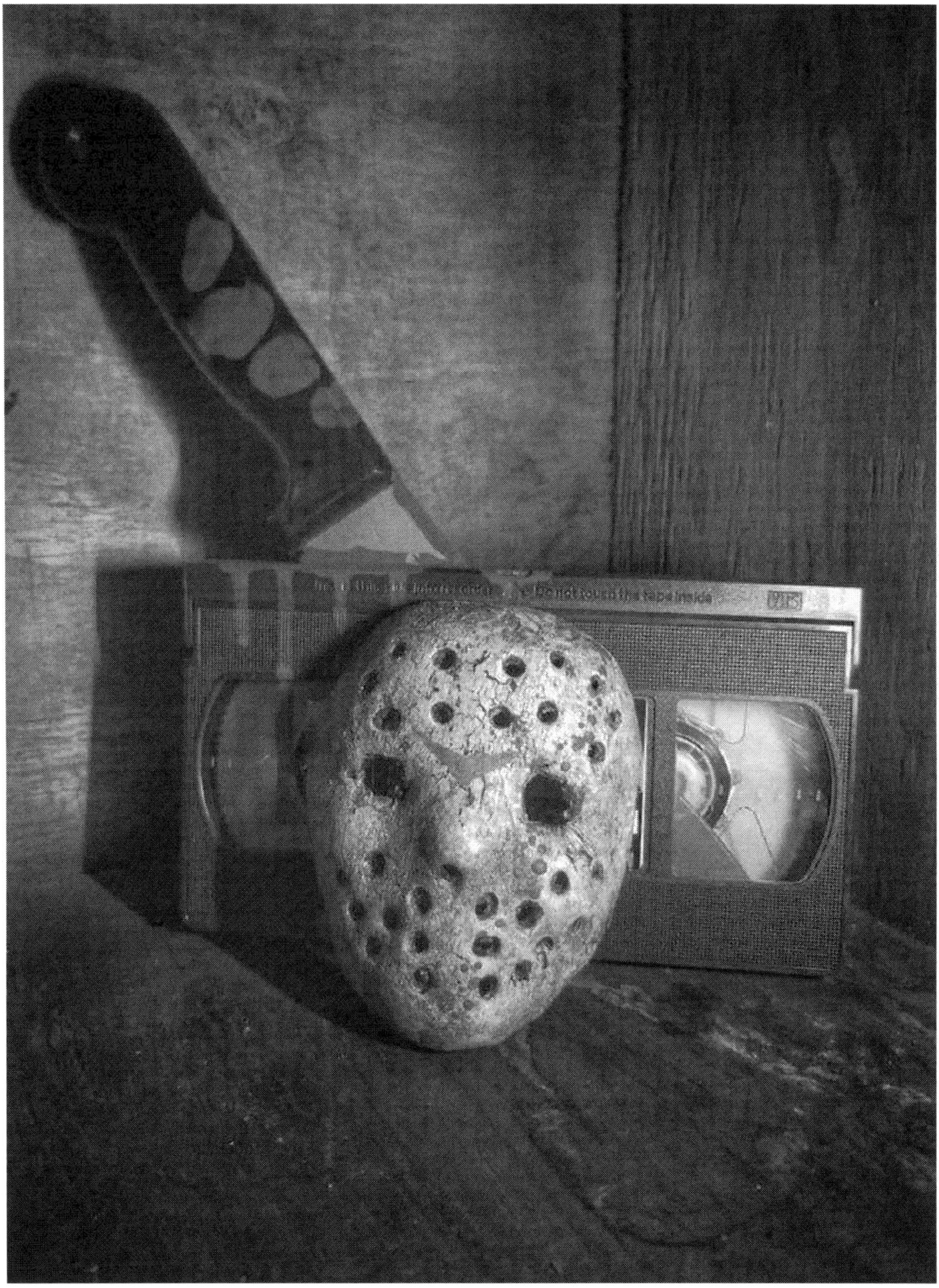

PHANTASMAGORIA FICTION

Page 127: **The Fragile Mask On His Face** by David A. Riley

Page 145: **Fair Dues** by Mike Chinn

Page 151: **The Amazing Xandra Lee vs Ned Swann** by Adrian Baldwin

Page 160: **Prey** by Joe X. Young

Page 163: **A Place For Junkmen** by Connor Leggat

Page 180: **Greasehead** by Conor Reid

Page 183: **My Pillow is a Ship** by Marc Damian Lawler

Page 185: **I Should Not Be** by Richard Bell

Page 187: **As Silver Dusk Suffuses Red** by David A. Riley

Page 188: **Byron's Burning Bones** by Emerson Firebird

THE FRAGILE MASK ON HIS FACE

David A. Riley

IT HAD BEEN a long night and Helen was glad to get away when the class finally ended. She neatly stacked her notes together, then slid them inside her briefcase.

"Do you fancy going for a drink on the way home?" Joyce asked, her own notes rolled in a rubber band and stuffed into her coat pocket.

Helen wasn't sure. It was Thursday and it was a normal workday tomorrow.

"One drink won't make you ill," Joyce insisted, almost mind-reading the reasons for Helen's indecision. "And don't tell me, after tonight's session, you don't feel like having something to help you unwind."

"I had thought of a cup of hot chocolate," Helen said, but she could feel herself giving way. Joyce's bouncy enthusiasm was almost irresistible and a sure tonic for any tiredness she might have felt a few moments before.

"One round. That's all. No more than two anyway," Joyce said, flashing a smile. "Besides, it's so cold tonight, you need something to warm you up."

The Potter's Wheel was only just off the town centre and reassuringly busy midweek. Just the usual suspects, Helen thought as she took a seat at one of the tables by the wall, while Joyce strode over to the bar. A boisterous group of old men occupied one window table, itself crowded out with full and half full pints of beer. Throughout the rest of the pub there was a dense scattering of singletons, quietly drinking their chosen solace, while a group of pool players were shouting and laughing in the next room.

"Do you think they picked this particular shade of brown so you couldn't see the nicotine stains?" Joyce asked as she deposited their drinks on the table, then shed her heavy coat. Beneath she wore a thick jumper that could have out-rivalled Joseph's coat of many colours.

"Could you not find anything more startling?" Helen asked, pretending that her eyes were being dazzled. "It was distracting enough in class."

"I'll have you know my mum made this for me and she has impeccable taste."

They broke out in laughter, then sipped their drinks, a lager for Joyce and a gin and tonic for Helen.

"Oh, oh, there's Goggle Eyes giving you the once over again."

Although, with a break from college over Christmas, it was nearly a month since they last came into the Potter's Wheel, Helen still remembered the pale young man with the goatee beard, a worn corduroy jacket and dark, curly hair, whose eyes always seemed to keep glancing their way, though he had never made any other indication of noticing their presence as he sat, slowly drinking his glass of cider.

"That's cruel," Helen said.

"You're joking. If they're not the closest things you've ever seen to goggle eyes on a man..."

Helen shook her head, though she had to admit it was an accurate description.

"I just hope he never hears you."

Joyce grinned and took another sip of her drink. "Fat chance of that with those old guys over there. They make more noise than a pack of unruly school kids."

Laughing and shouting and arguing with each other with the boisterous camaraderie born of decades of familiarity, the old men were as much a part of the pub as its outdated décor.

"Anyway, I don't think it's a good idea to make fun of him, even between ourselves. There's no saying how much he might pick up, even without hearing us."

Joyce snorted. "You're a real little scaredy cat, Helen. Anyway, he's as far through as a tram ticket, even if he did get upset."

Helen felt like saying that this wasn't the point, but it would have been wasted on Joyce, who would only be encouraged to make even more outrageous comments about him if she persisted.

"I'm surprised Tony wasn't here to meet you after class," Helen said, to change the subject.

"Tony's history now, Helen. History." There was a sneer that jarred with her humour a moment before, and Helen wondered just how historical Tony was.

"You've argued?"

"You could put it like that." Joyce pulled out a slightly crumpled pack of cigarettes and lit one. "See this? See the state of it? I've tried to give up half a dozen times since I told him to fuck off. I've fished this pack out of the bin three times already." She glanced around at the young man in the corduroy jacket. "Seen enough?" she snapped at him irritably.

"Joyce!" Helen admonished. "Keep your voice down."

There was already a lull amongst the old men, and Helen felt as if every eye in the pub was on them.

"I think I'll settle with just one drink," she said, taking a quick gulp of her gin and tonic, and tried not to cough as the harsh liquid caught in her throat.

"Helen, I'm sorry." Joyce touched her wrist. "It's just that I'm still a bit raw about the bastard."

"That's all right. But you shouldn't let your feelings about him make you lash out at other people."

Joyce nodded. "I know. I said I'm sorry." She smiled wryly. "Am I forgiven?"

For a moment Helen wondered. Joyce's mood swings tonight were catching her off balance and she really didn't feel up to it. The accountancy lesson had already taken its toll on her, what with that and worrying about the exams looming ahead of her at Easter and all the revision she would have to do, listening to Joyce's outbursts were too much just now.

"You're forgiven," she said. "Of course you are. Though there's really nothing to forgive in the first place. But I really am tired."

"One more drink," Joyce insisted. "I'll get it. Just one. Then we'll go to the bus station together. It'll be safer that way."

Which was true. There had been too many attacks against women walking the streets at night by themselves, even in built-up areas, for her to feel easy about heading for the bus station from here on her own.

"Another gin and tonic?" Joyce asked.

Helen nodded. It would help her relax, if nothing else, she thought, as the effects of her first drink began to flow through her. She glanced over at "Goggle Eyes", feeling guilty as the nickname Joyce had bestowed on him automatically came to mind, especially when she caught him looking towards her. His large, round, slightly protuberant eyes instantly turned downwards to stare at his drink, and she wondered if she caught a faint trace of a blush on his pallid cheeks. He reminded her of a very young, lightly bearded Peter Lorre; his strange eyes, far from being repellent, were oddly exotic.

"Here we are," Joyce announced, perhaps a trifle too cheerfully as she once more deposited drinks on their table.

As they talked Helen suspected that, given the chance, Joyce wanted to linger even longer in the pub, but it was nearly ten and Helen had a twenty-minute ride ahead of her even after they reached the bus station. As soon as she had finished her gin and tonic she told Joyce that she really had to be going now.

Joyce reluctantly placed her own emptied glass on the table.

"You sure?" she asked, but Helen was already putting on her coat.

Outside, the cold had become even more bitter than before, and Helen knew that winter had well and truly arrived.

"Hope it doesn't snow again," Joyce moaned as they ducked their heads into the wind. "Perhaps we should have rung for a taxi."

"I can't afford taxis. Besides, it's only five minutes to the bus station."

Joyce suddenly stopped. "Bugger and damnation!"

"What's the matter?" Helen turned her back to the wind to face her.

"I must have left my notes from tonight in the pub."

"Are you certain?"

"Positive. They were in my coat pocket. They must have fallen out while I was putting it on." An extra strong gust of wind howled around them, bringing icy cold through every gap in their clothing.

"I'll nip back for them. I'll only be a few minutes. I'll catch you up on the way to the bus station."

Helen looked down the long, deserted street, with its closed shops, sheltering behind galvanised steel shutters daubed with graffiti. Flakes of snow were beginning to spin across the road, adding to the brown smear of slush spread across it.

"I can come back with you," Helen offered. But Joyce shook her head. "I'll run and catch you up."

With that she began to hurry back to the pub, its windows beckoning with their comforting glow against the darkness.

Turning back into the wind, Helen again ducked her head against it.

Typical of Joyce to desert her like this, she decided. It wouldn't have surprised her if her friend still had her notes on her and was using their alleged loss as an excuse to get back to the pub for another drink and to order a taxi, never mind that this left Helen out here on her own. Feeling angry, Helen strode on faster, determined to reach the bus station well ahead of Joyce, even if she did intend to try and catch up and it wasn't all a lie.

She had almost reached the bus station when the car passed her. The snow had become heavier in the last few minutes and was sticking to the ground. Slush from beneath the car's tyres hissed through the air, striking her legs in icy lumps. She stopped, gasping at the shock of it. Bloody fool, she thought, angry at the driver for speeding past so close to the kerb. She looked up at it. And thought she saw Joyce's face pressed to the rear windscreen, looking back at her. But most of the glass was already covered in snow and she could have been mistaken. It wasn't even a taxi and she could think of no reason why Joyce should have got a lift in someone's car, especially from the Potter's Wheel, where they were hardly even on nodding terms with any of the regulars.

Next Thursday, though, Helen was disturbed when Joyce failed to turn up at night school. This was a crucial time for both of them, with only a couple of months to go before their exams. When the lesson had finished she asked Henry Hanshaw, their tutor, a stiff, thin-haired academic with a perpetually miserable expression on his face, if Joyce had rung in, but he told her he had no idea why Joyce hadn't come here tonight. Ringing in wasn't a requirement. They weren't schoolchildren. They or their employers had paid for this course and as far as Henry Hanshaw was concerned it was up to them if they came or not.

Stifling her irritation at his infuriating manner, Helen took out her mobile and rang Joyce's number, but there was no answer. Instead she was diverted to Joyce's answer phone facility. She left a brief message.

"Hope you are okay. Missed you tonight. If you need any help with this week's lesson, give me a ring."

She put her phone away and strode out of the austere college building. Last week's snow still lay on the ground in glaciated rucks, with ominously glistening patches of ice, which Helen gingerly avoided.

The Potter's Wheel was only a few minutes out of her way to the bus station and, though she knew Joyce was unlikely to be there, for some reason Helen felt the need for a drink before going home.

As she settled in the pub's comforting warmth, Helen remembered that she let Joyce borrow her mobile to ring her boyfriend, Tony, a few weeks ago, the battery of her own phone having gone flat. Helen looked up her record of dialled calls and scrolled down them till she found the one that was probably his. Suspecting that there may have been a reconciliation between them, which could account for Joyce's absence tonight, Helen rang Tony's number. A few seconds later she heard his familiar voice.

"Tony Farr."

"Hi, Tony, it's Helen Taylor. I'm trying to get hold of Joyce. You haven't seen her lately, have you?"

"Joyce?" Tony hesitated, as if embarrassed. "I haven't been in touch with Joyce for over a week. She's not answering her phone. She has it on divert, which I think is her way of telling me that she doesn't want to talk things over." If embarrassed to start with, his voice had very quickly adopted a tone of being aggrieved.

Ignoring this, Helen said: "She should have been at our accountancy class tonight, but she didn't turn up. That's why I'm ringing. I wondered if you guys might have made up or something."

"Fat chance of that," Tony responded petulantly.

"I'm sorry you've had an argument. I know it's none of my business, but I was sad to hear about it."

"Thanks."

"I'm beginning to get worried about Joyce. She didn't need to put her phone on divert to avoid talking to you. She could just cancel your calls when she sees who they're from. Anyway, she's not responded yet to the message I left half an hour ago."

Tony paused for a moment, probably collecting his thoughts, she supposed.

"I don't know what to suggest. I did go round to her place earlier this week, but she wasn't in. Or, if she was, she wouldn't answer her door. Though there weren't any lights on."

Helen could imagine him standing there, minute after minute, ringing the doorbell, then banging on its panels. Patience had never been one of Tony's virtues from what she knew about him.

"Perhaps she's staying with her mother," Helen suggested finally.

"Perhaps," he replied. "But I tried there as well. And, unless she's got her mother to lie for her, she's not there either."

All of which was beginning to make Helen feel distinctly uneasy. She remembered the face she glimpsed in the back of the car that doused her with slush a week ago on her way to the station. Had it been Joyce's face she saw in the back of it after all, she wondered. She preferred not to dwell too much on the expression she seemed to remember on the woman's face. As she looked back on it now she could not understand how she had failed to recognise the fear and panic that had stared back at her.

"What are you going to do now?" Tony asked. For the first time there wasn't a trace of anger, resentment or self justification in his voice. Just worry.

"I'll ring her mum myself. I don't think she would have lied for Joyce. But even if she did, she wouldn't have any reason to lie to me."

"Will you ring me back when you've spoken?" Tony asked.

Helen smiled, despite her fears. "Okay."

After Tony had given her the number for Joyce's mother she rang off and called it.

"Mrs. Wainwright? It's Helen Taylor. Joyce's friend."

The woman who answered sounded cautious, though that was probably because of the lateness of the hour. Only now did Helen realise it was nearly ten o'clock.

"Is anything wrong? Joyce hasn't had an accident, has she?"

"Not so far as I know. That's why I'm ringing. She missed her lesson at college tonight and isn't answering her phone, so I thought she might be staying with you."

"She's not staying with me, dear. In fact, I haven't heard from her for over a week. I was starting to get worried. She usually rings every day or so to see how I am."

After promising to get Joyce to phone her mum the moment she got in touch with her, Helen sat pensively for a short while, then finished her drink. She remembered that she had promised to ring Tony back, and decided that she would get another drink, then call him. At the bar she asked the landlord if he remembered her friend calling back into the pub again last week because she'd lost some papers.

The landlord scratched one ear for a moment in thought. "Curly red hair, wearing a very, *very* colourful jumper?" he asked.

Helen said that was her.

"I remember her, yes. She came back here all right. All in a-flutter, she was. Found her papers, though. They were on the floor right where you'd been sitting."

"Did she leave again straight away?"

"Probably. But I can't remember, sweetheart. There were a few people leaving about that time. Something good must have been coming on telly that night. Regular little exodus, it was."

"I don't suppose it's any good asking if you remember if she left by herself?"

The landlord beamed. "'Fraid not, my love. I was too busy with that gang over there." He nodded to the old men sat by the window. "They were ordering in another round about that time and it was all hands to the pumps, if you get my drift."

Collecting her drink, Helen returned to her table. "Goggle Eyes" was here again, drinking his cider, the glass nearly full. Though he never seemed to finish it, from what she could recall. Just took small sips, as if he didn't really care for it at all and only had it because you had to have a drink of some sort to be here, she pondered, before her thoughts inevitably returned to Joyce.

She took out her mobile and called Tony. He answered straight away as if he had been waiting. Which he probably had been, Helen thought.

"Any news?" he asked.

"Her mum's not heard from her for over a week. She's worried herself, as Joyce normally keeps in regular touch with her."

"Oh, God," Tony moaned, and she wondered if he was feeling guilty now about whatever it was that made them row. "Do you think we should contact the police?" he asked.

"I don't know," Helen said. "Would they take any notice after only a week?"

"I'll ring her office in the morning," Tony said. "If she's not been to work and hasn't rung in sick, then I think we should go to the police anyway."

Helen agreed. "Till then I don't suppose there's much more we can do."

Afterwards she stared for a few minutes at her drink, wondering if perhaps Joyce had met someone else on the rebound and was spending time with them. From what she knew of her, there was always a possibility of that. A very distinct possibility, she thought, which was one reason why she was reluctant to involve the police just yet.

"Excuse me, is your friend not going to be with you tonight?"

Helen looked up, startled. It was "Goggle Eyes". He had risen from his table and was stood next to her, contrary to her thoughts a few moments ago, having actually drained his pint. Holding the empty glass in one hand, he was on his way to the bar.

"I'm afraid not," Helen said after a pause that seemed to go on a little too long as she tried to collect her thoughts.

The young man nodded, as if absorbing the information, then took a step further towards the bar, paused, and said: "I couldn't get you a drink, could I? I see you've nearly finished."

Flustered at the unexpected offer, Helen said: "I wouldn't say no," though she regretted accepting almost at once. But it was too late. By then "Goggle Eyes" was already at the bar.

"I asked Bob for the same drink you had last time – gin and tonic, he said – if that's all right," the young man told her a few moments later when he returned.

"You really shouldn't have," Helen said.

"No problem. You look as if you're worried about something. Perhaps this will help cheer you up."

"Thank you, but I don't think it will, really. I'm worried about my friend. She's gone missing and no one seems to know where she is."

"That's bad," the young man said. He held out one hand. "My name's Mat Denton."

Helen took his hand lightly. It felt cold and soft. "Helen. Helen Taylor."

He smiled, looking slightly embarrassed.

"I hope you don't think I'm being presumptive, offering you a drink like that. But I feel like I almost know you, with you and your friend coming in here every week or so over the past year."

"I suppose we have become sort of familiar faces here," Helen admitted, uncertainly.

"Sort of." Mat took a tiny sip of his cider. "This friend of yours...?"

"Joyce."

"When was the last time you saw her?"

"In here. Last Thursday. We were on our way to the bus station when she remembered leaving something here and returned. She said she would catch me up a few minutes later, but she didn't."

"I was in here last Thursday," Mat said, though Helen already remembered this. She also remembered Joyce being unnecessarily rude to him.

"You don't know if she spoke to anyone when she returned, do you?"

Mat thought for a moment. "It was very busy just then. The old Grudgers, that lot over there," he added, indicating the old men, "were ordering a fresh round of drinks, and that always causes bedlam. And a few people were leaving about then, though I don't know why."

"The landlord thinks it was because something was starting on TV in a short while."

"Could have been, though I wouldn't know. I never watch television myself."

Helen added one more item to her list of oddities about him. He was the only man she could remember meeting who actually claimed that he never watched TV. What an odd thing to claim, she thought, unless he spent most of his nights here in the Potter's Wheel taking minuscule sips of his cider.

Somehow Helen managed to pass the next ten minutes in a disjointed form of conversation with Mat, till she finished her drink.

"Would you like another," Mat asked, but Helen was prepared and said: "No. I really must be on my way." She reached for her briefcase. "I have work tomorrow and it will take me at least an hour to get home."

Outside it was cold, miserable and quiet, her footsteps echoing back at her as she headed through the town centre to the bus station. She was barely halfway there, though, when she heard her mobile chime, telling her that she had just received a text message. For a moment she was undecided whether to wait till she reached the bus station before checking out what it was, but ahead was the lit doorway of Marks and Spencer, and she decided to stand there for a moment to read it.

She was surprised to see the message was from Joyce.

hi. sorry u r worrying about me. i'm ok. meet you in a few minutes. i'll pick you up in my car. i'll explain all then. joyce.

Meet you in a few minutes? Helen looked up and down the street. There were several cars moving, but which was hers? In fact, Helen hadn't been aware till now that Joyce even had one. It was something she had never mentioned before and had always gone home from college by bus. Anyway, Helen thought, how does she know where I'll be? Or had she been watching the Potter's Wheel? Which hardly made sense.

Undecided, Helen wondered whether to ignore the message and continue on her way to the bus station. So long as Joyce was all right that was all she was really bothered about. She wasn't interested in meeting her, certainly not at this time of night, when she was more concerned in getting home to her flat and a relaxing warm drink curled up in front of the fire, with perhaps an hour or so of watching TV to unwind, before going to bed. Why should she want to meet Joyce now to hear why she had not been to college tonight?

A large, dark car pulled up alongside her. Its passenger door swung open. Inside she could just make out Joyce's face at the steering wheel. She looked pale, almost peaky, though that could have been because of the gloominess of the car, lit only by a small white light that came on above the windscreen when the door opened.

"Come on. Jump in," Joyce barked, her voice harsh as if she had a sore throat.

When Helen hesitated, Joyce added: "It's getting cold in here. Please hurry. I'll drive you home while we talk."

An icy gust of wind, billowing down the high street and striking deep through Helen's coat, decided her, and she ducked her head beneath the door frame and let herself fall back onto the passenger seat, her briefcase on her lap. Almost immediately, as soon as Helen closed the door behind her, Joyce accelerated away from the kerb, driving quickly through town.

It was only then that Helen realised there was someone slumped on the seat behind her. She looked round as much as she could. In the intermittent light cast into the car she was surprised to see Tony Farr. His mouth jerked into a sort of smile when he saw her look at him.

"Have you guys' made up?" Helen asked, disturbed at the silence that had fallen over everyone in the car.

"Later," Joyce said.

Helen stared at her as the car turned onto a road that would take them up onto the moors above the town. Darkness loomed ahead of the car as the streetlights petered out along the winding road to become randomly intermittent.

"Which way are we heading?" she asked Joyce. "Is this a short cut?"

A large farmhouse rose in silhouette against the pale, snow-laden clouds that dominated the sky. Joyce drove down a rough path that branched off the road towards it, drawing up a moment later on a snow-streaked cobblestone yard.

"What is this place?" Helen demanded. "And why have we stopped here?"

Joyce ignored her as she opened her door and climbed out of the car. Behind her, Helen heard Tony heave himself out onto the yard too, standing beside the car like an indistinct shadow.

For a moment Helen hesitated. Though she had known Joyce long enough to trust her – and had even grown to like Tony from what she had seen of him – there was something about the two of them now that disturbed her. Tony looked ill. He looked worse than ill. He looked like he seriously needed to see a doctor. His face had the grey pallor of someone with an ominously critical heart condition. Indeed, as the wind buffeted him, he rested against the side of the car as if it was too much effort to stand unaided.

"This way," Joyce said, and she led them towards the main door into the farmhouse. It swung open as she pushed it. "Inside," she went on, leading the way. A light came on in the hallway; Helen stared into the large, unfurnished room. Opposite, a flight of stairs rose into darkness. The walls were covered in old, patterned paper, stained with huge patches of damp; much of it looked like fungus. There was an overpoweringly dense smell of mould, dry rot and vermin, and Helen felt sure she would be sick if she was forced to stand inside. But Tony had moved up even closer now, pressing against her, and she stumbled forwards, up the worn flagstone steps and into the hallway, almost gagging on the smell.

Joyce, though, seemed unaffected by it. Or was she? Helen seemed to detect a change in her friend's face as she strode across the threadbare, old-fashioned carpet that only partially covered the floorboards, her heels thudding across them. She turned and faced Helen and Tony. There was a mark around the edge of her face that Helen had not noticed before, like a ragged line. Their eyes met. Joyce's looked strange, almost milky, old and oddly shrivelled. She felt suddenly squeamish as Joyce reached up to touch the line. A fingernail seemed to catch beneath it. Then slowly, deliberately she began to peal the skin from her face. It came away with disgusting ease.

"Joyce!" Helen called out, sickened at the sight of her friend's face clutched like a flimsy, cheap Halloween mask in her fingers, till she realised that the face underneath wasn't the disfigured remnants of Joyce's at all, but the blood-blotched face of Mat Denton.

For a moment she felt utter revulsion, then everything seemed to swim before her eyes. Her sense of balance deserted her, and she was aware suddenly of falling forwards, of reaching out to protect herself as the floor seemed to tip towards her.

And the cold, hard, snow-covered paving stones jarred against her arms and knees and made her cry out in pain as she slithered across them.

"Are you all right, lass?"

She looked up. Speckles of light danced in front of everything as an intense feeling of nausea washed through her and she felt the urge to be sick.

"Did you slip on the ice?"

The man's voice sounded friendly enough. An old man's voice. She looked up as he carefully took hold of one arm and helped her to her feet. The light from the window display in the Marks and Spencer store next to them looked comfortingly normal, as Helen looked around herself in disbelief. The old man held a walking stick in one hand as he gripped on to her arm with the other, a look of concern on his face.

"You took a right tumble then, lass. Have you hurt yourself?"

"I think I'm all right," Helen said, though her voice still sounded distant and she had a strange feeling of disorientation.

Just then her mobile rang. Clumsily, the palms of her hands scuffed raw by the paving stones, she fumbled through her pockets as the old man stood back and watched her with concern.

She saw before she answered her phone that the call was from Tony Farr. An image of him, grey-faced and mute, stood outside the semi-derelict farmhouse, came to mind, of the strange dream or hallucination that had come over her when she fell.

"Hello, Tony," she murmured, still feeling shaken.

"Are you all right, Helen?" His voice sounded concerned, even nervous.

"I think so. Why? What made you ask?"

There was a pause. "I don't know. I just had the oddest experience. I thought you were in danger. Sounds stupid, I know."

"Did you have some kind of a waking dream?" she asked.

The pause this time was even longer. The old man who had helped her nodded, then started to walk away, carefully shuffling his feet across the icy pavement.

"How did you know?" Tony asked.

It was a question Helen could barely understand herself. Why should he have had a dream? What made her ask? And what made him ring? The more she thought about it the less sense it made.

"I just fell," she told him. "Slipped on the ice, I suppose. And had a bizarre dream about Joyce."

"That she came for you in a car?"

For a moment Helen wondered if the dream had really ended, if this was still a part of it, if she had not woken up at all. But the pain in her hands and knees was enough to convince her that this was real. Even if she was asleep this would have been enough in itself to waken her.

"What's happened to her, Tony?"

"Where are you?" he asked. "I'll come and meet you."

Feeling that this was some weird kind of deja vu, with Tony replacing

Joyce this time, she told him where she was.

"Stay there," he said. "I'll be with you in less than ten minutes."

He drew up even before the first five minutes had passed, his car screeching to a standstill on the gritted road. He looked tussled and edgy when he came round to help her across the pavement to the passenger door, concerned at the scuffs on her hands and knees.

"I'll take you home as soon as we've finished," he said. "But I'd like to take a diversion first."

"Up onto the moors?" Helen asked, her voice quiet. "To the farmhouse?"

"If it exists," Tony said flatly. "This sounds nuts to me. But the dream seemed so real. So oddly real."

"Our dream, you mean," Helen said.

"That's even more stupid." Even though they had not discussed their dream in detail, they both knew they had experienced the same, impossible though they knew this was.

Tony drove carefully. The moorland road had not been gritted for days and shone with a menacingly black glossiness in the headlamps. Farmhouses up here were widely scattered and lonely, grim-looking buildings, surrounded by lines of dry-stone walls and snow-covered hedgerows.

"There it is," Helen said, no trace of excitement or enthusiasm in her voice. She had been hoping against hope that they would find nothing here, that their nightmare had been nothing more than a dream. But there was no mistaking the dark, isolated, box-like building.

Tony nodded in recognition, then carefully drove down the side road towards it. He flipped open the glove compartment and took out a torch. "Are you game?" he asked. "Or would you prefer to wait in the car?"

Helen did not hesitate. "I'd be more scared waiting for you by myself."

He smiled, briefly, then climbed out. They approached the farmhouse gingerly. The icy cobblestone yard in front of it was hazard enough, even without the strong winds that buffeted them. But it was more than just this that made them walk slowly. There was an ominous presence about the unlit building, an aura that disquietened both of them, and Helen wondered if it would not have been better to have left this till daylight, perhaps after ringing the police. Although how they could explain their interest in this place without mentioning their dream she was not sure. And just how that would go down with the police she could well imagine.

At the door Tony hesitated, then he rapped on it. The sound seemed to echo through the hollow emptiness of the building. When there was no response, he rapped once more, then tried the handle.

"Locked."

With a grunt, he strode over to the nearest window and shone his torch inside. Satisfied that the place was empty, he returned to the door, took a step back, then kicked it hard with the flat sole of his foot immediately below the lock. The door thudded open explosively, bouncing against its overtaxed hinges.

The musty mixture of mould, decay and rat droppings was unmistakeable.

"How can it be so similar?" Helen murmured, as Tony shone his torch into the unlit interior. There was the staircase and the damp-raddled wallpaper, with its patches of evil-looking fungi, and the worn-out scraps of carpet that barely covered the old floorboards. It was not just similar to what they had seen in their dream, it was identical. The only element missing was Joyce.

Tony led the way inside, his footsteps hollow on the floorboards. Helen shivered. Apart from the wind, it was virtually as cold inside the farmhouse as outside on the moors.

"No one lives here," she murmured, dispiritedly, wishing she was home. "Look at the ice on the walls. There's been no heating in this place all winter."

Tony nodded. "Let's explore. If we find nothing, what have we lost?"

Though she was uneasy about this, Helen nevertheless fell in step behind him as he moved to the nearest door. It opened stiffly; its hinges frozen. Like the hallway, this room was empty apart from cobwebs, dust, patches of mould and the inevitable scattering of rat droppings. Once started, though, they continued to move about the house, going from room to room on the ground floor, including the kitchen, with its stone sink half full of green slime and broken crockery, and cupboards littered with mouldering packets of food, abandoned here when the last inhabitants moved out what must have been years ago.

"We're wasting our time," Helen grumbled, feeling the cold numbing her hands and feet.

"Then why did we dream about it?" Tony insisted, gritting his teeth. "There must be some reason. There must."

Returning to the hallway, he started up the stairs. The landing above wavered in the torchlight; its banister rails cast elongated shadows across the high ceiling.

"Are you sure?" Helen asked. The steps creaked beneath her feet and she was sure she could smell dry rot in the air. If the floor gave way beneath them and they were badly injured they would be dead from exposure long before anyone found them here. But Tony climbed the stairs with a determination she could only attempt at mimicking. On the landing Tony paused just long enough to scan the line of doors facing them. Some were partially open, revealing rooms just as empty as those downstairs. One at the end, though, was different. It was the main bedroom at the front of the house. The door was shut fast and had a large, inverted cross painted on its varnished panels in bright red. Tony turned to Helen; his face grim. It was almost too obvious, and Helen was tempted to urge him to wait, but Tony's eyes were full of rage as he looked again at the door, its crudely painted symbol taunting him.

Abruptly he suddenly levelled the torch and marched down the landing so quickly that Helen had to run to catch up.

He gripped the handle and thrust the door violently open.

The large, gloomy, dank room beyond seemed to change shape and size as the torch beam darted about it, picking out the strange symbols painted all over the bare floorboards and about its walls. Hundreds of partially used candles were littered about the edge of the room, surrounded by hardened rivulets of melted wax. But dominating the floor was an immense five-pointed star painted inside a crudely outlined chalk circle. Within the pentacle lay the body of a woman, her ankles and wrists bound with rope to metal rings fixed to the floorboards.

Tony grunted with horror as if he was about to be sick.

Dried blood had soaked into the floorboards around the woman's head. Her face, which had been savagely cut away, was an unrecognisable horror of darkened, decaying flesh, sinews, cartilage and sliced blood vessels that lay exposed across the front of the skull. Beyond the pentacle, heaped against the wall, was a pile of discarded clothes, amongst them a dirtied, brightly coloured jumper. By then, though, Helen had already recognised the curly red hair of her friend, spread amongst the dried blood surrounding the disfigured head.

This time, when reaction swept in, Helen was violently sick. Her stomach heaved again and again till there was nothing left but bile, and her throat felt scoured by stomach acids.

"The bloody, fucking, murderous bastard!" Tony grated in a voice stretched taut by emotion.

He stepped into the room. From within it, as if moving out from behind an invisible barrier, a figure emerged on the other side of the pentacle, though Helen would have sworn that a moment before there was no one there. She gasped with horror as she recognised Joyce's face, stretched like a very old waxen mask across that of the man, whose dark, distinctive corduroy jacket she recognised at once – as she did the swollen, glittering eyes that gazed out at her from between the eyelids of her friend's dead face.

Tony crouched as the figure moved towards him, too late to avoid the hammer in Mat Denton's fist. Helen watched as Denton raised it high into the air, high enough for the torchlight to pick out the matted strands of hair that were stuck to its head. Then it swung down, swiftly, bounced off Tony's upraised arm with a crack which she knew was a bone breaking, and Tony cried out in pain.

"Oh, my God!" Helen whimpered, too shocked to move.

From somewhere close she seemed to hear a voice call to her:

"But I warned you. *I warned you!*"

Mat Denton, the dead face wrinkling across his own hidden face as his mouth twisted in a snarl, moved in on Tony as he swung the hammer down again. And again. With savage, resounding blows that beat down the weak defence of Tony's arms, then pummelled his head.

"Joyce!" Helen cried out, though she did not know why – except for the voice that had sounded so much like her friend's. "*Joyce!*"

It was then that another figure seemed to flicker within the room. Mat Denton, distracted, looked round, the fragile mask on his face becoming even more wrinkled, becoming even less like that of Joyce as he suddenly started to back away from Tony. The raw-faced apparition took a step towards him and Mat took a further step away from it. Which was when Helen heard the floorboards give way as the smell of dry rot became more intense. Mat lost his balance as his feet crashed through the weakened wood. Dust motes rose into the air around him, grey with fungus. The translucent, faceless female figure reached out towards him, and it was as if its added weight, if such a thing had any weight at all, was enough to destroy what solidity the floorboards still had. Mat Denton cried out as, with a resounding crash, he fell through the floorboards, and through the fragile plaster and ceiling paper beneath. His arms reached out in a desperate attempt to stay his fall, but it was too late, and Helen watched in stunned silence as he gazed towards her before disappearing into the room below.

Helen was on her feet in an instant. She rushed to Tony to pull him back away from the hole and onto the safety of the landing. He was barely conscious; blood streamed down his face from where the hammer had hit him, but he was still breathing.

"We have to get out of here," she whispered to him. There was no certainty that the fall into the room below would have been enough to hurt Mat Denton seriously enough to make him harmless, and she half expected to see his plaster-covered figure return up the stairs towards them. Which was when she heard the scream. The seemingly endless, high-pitched scream of unutterable agony and terror.

Helen gripped Tony's shoulders and began to drag him with desperation along the landing towards the stairs. They had to get out of here. Get back to his car. Get out of this place completely.

At the stairs she halted. All was silent now apart from Tony's stertorous breathing.

How she managed to manhandle Tony's body down the stairs, step by step, without injuring him worse than he already was, she was afterwards unable to recall properly. Most of her consciousness was concentrated too much on listening for Mat Denton. But, eventually, what seemed like hours later, she reached the hallway. The door into the next room was still open. Lying there, amidst the debris, was Mat Denton's body.

Whether it was rage or fear that he might come round while she was still struggling to get Tony to the car across the frozen cobblestone yard outside, Helen knew she had to make sure that Denton was either dead or too badly injured to threaten them again.

It was only after she had seen him that the full horror of it all hit her. Mat Denton was all but dead. But she doubted that his fall from the room above had been what killed him, though she had no intention of staying there long enough to find out. Somehow she managed to get Tony back into his car, driving off as quickly as she could away from the farm and the moors and on into town, where she headed for the hospital. Fortunately, the blows on Tony's head had been enough to blur his memories of that night's events, and she was able to fabricate a story of him being attacked in town by a gang of thugs.

She never returned to the farmhouse. And it was months before anyone ventured there and found what remained of Mat Denton's body: by then, time, decay and the ravenous appetites of the local vermin had done much to remove the full horror of what she saw that night. Of how his face had been ripped away from his head by what she knew must have been human nails; leaving only a red, raw ruin around his staring, barely living eyes – eyes which stared up in stark, paralysed terror, even in the daytime.

NOTE: This story was first published in *Dark Discoveries* (USA).

David A. Riley is a writer specialising mainly in horror, fantasy and SF stories. In 1995, along with his wife, Linden, he edited and published a fantasy/SF magazine, *Beyond*. His first professionally published story was in the *11th Pan Book of Horror* in 1970. This was reprinted in 2012 in *The Century's Best Horror Fiction* edited by John Pelan of *Cemetery Dance*. He has had numerous stories published by Doubleday, DAW, Corgi, Sphere, Roc, Playboy Paperbacks, Robinsons, etc., and in magazines such as *Aboriginal Science Fiction, Dark Discoveries, FEAR, Whispers*, and *Fantasy Tales*.

His first collection of stories (four long stories and a novelette) was published by Hazardous Press in 2012, *His Own Mad Demons*.

A Lovecraftian novel, *The Return*, was published by Blood Bound Books in the USA in 2013.

A second collection of his stories, all of which were professionally published prior to 2000, *The Lurkers in the Abyss & Other Tales of Terror*, was launched at the World Fantasy Convention in 2013 by Shadow Publishing. Hazardous Press published his third short story collection, *Their Cramped Dark World and Other Tales*, in 2015. Both Hazardous Press collections have now been reprinted, with brand new covers, by Parallel Universe Publications.

A fantasy novel, *Goblin Mire*, and a horror novel, *Moloch's Children*, were both published in 2015. He and his wife recently relaunched Parallel

Universe Publications, which originally published *Beyond*. Parallel Universe published twelve books in 2015, including an anthology of new stories, *Kitchen Sink Gothic*, edited by David A. Riley and Linden Riley.

David Riley's stories have been translated into Italian, German, Spanish and Russian.

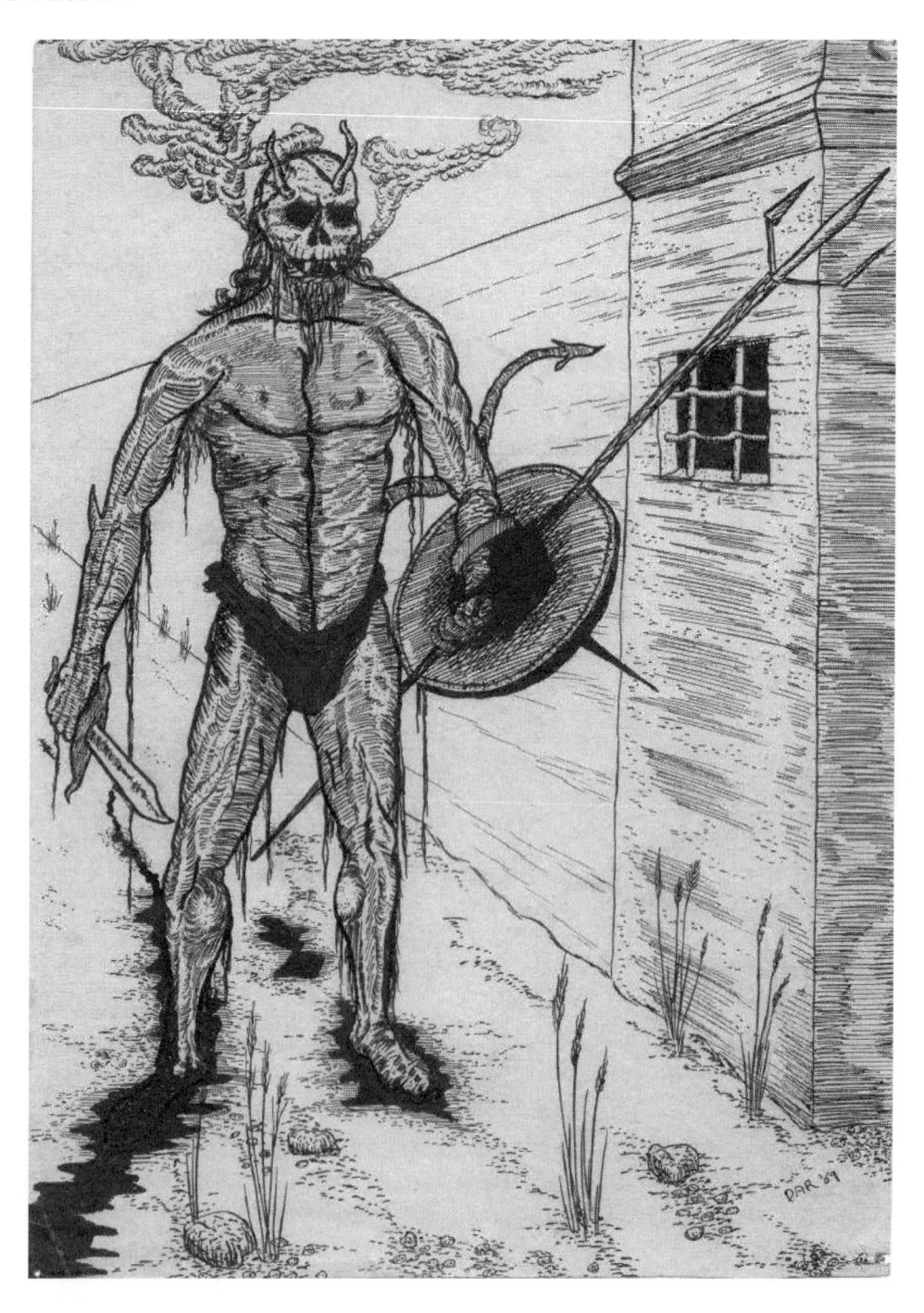

FAIR DUES

Mike Chinn

"SUCH POOR DEFENCES. I'm surprised you have managed to live this long."

The words, spoken in a sibilant voice, spun the wizard Falobane away from his work. A wide sleeve of his gaudy robe fluttered, catching an elaborate piece of glassware. It fell to the hard floor, shattering. "Kathis-Rann!" he muttered in alarm. "Are you insane? What if someone saw?"

A tall, vaguely humanoid lizard wriggled comfortably through the workshop's embrasure, his tail snapping, black eyes glittering. Disconcertingly, he managed to look amused at the wizard's discomfort. His long skull swung left and right as he took in Falobane's untidy cell.

"*K'th'sss-Rr'nnn*," he corrected the wizard's poor pronunciation. "And no one saw me, soft-skin – that is my trade. Besides, your city's guards are fat and incompetent. If our two races ever came to war, I know which side I would favour."

"It will never come to that," mumbled Falobane, stooping to clear away the shattered debris. "Men and lizards occupy differing environments – you the hot plains, we the cooler high plateaus. Neither offers a threat."

Kathis-Rann hissed, his black eyes sardonic. "The world is drying up, its resources dissolving. How long do you think our two species can co-exist under such straitened conditions?"

Falobane drew himself up with obvious effort. He tossed the fragments of glass out of the window the lizard had so easily entered. "Are lizards such cynics, then?"

"Cynics, no," replied Kathis-Rann, flinging his scaley frame into a chair. Despite being designed for human use, he seemed to find it comfortable enough. "We are realists. Unlike humans, we are not governed by emotions or distracted by needs. Our females come into season but once a year, and when they do the courtship is practical – although sometimes a little violent, I grant you." Again he seemed to be enjoying a private joke. "We may go for many weeks without food – and then gorge ourselves close to exploding." The lizard hissed again. It was, Falobane realised, a form of laugh. "Do not make the mistake of thinking us men who have simply sprouted scales and a tail, sorcerer. Our glands do not rule us."

"You have glands then?" Falobane asked, genuinely interested.

Kathis-Rann shrugged – a peculiar gesture in a creature with no perceptible shoulders. "We have never looked. Curiosity is also an uncommon trait among us."

"Have you no emotions?"

The lizard raised its long head, eyes unreadable. "Salin Thur knows."

Falobane had heard that expression before, from other lizards. Salin Thur seemed to be some kind of myth figure – both god and demon. Anything a lizard failed to understand – or wanted another to believe it could not understand – was consigned to Salin Thur's eminence. Falobane had tried to determine whether this being had ever existed, but met with no success. Such replies he had received were always ambiguous. One lizard even claimed Salin Thur lived still, eternal, in the remote sky-supporting peaks of Khan-Da. Even a cold, practical species seemed to need its mysteries.

"I am waiting," prompted Kathis-Rann, cutting through Falobane's musing. The human nodded, as though his thoughts hadn't been half a world away.

"Gatharyne, from the city of Burnharnh."

"I know the name," admitted Kathis-Rann.

Falobane reached through his cluttered paraphernalia and produced a heavy purse. He flipped it abruptly towards the lizard. Kathis-Rann caught it with a faster than human response.

"Lizards are not averse to gold, then?" Falobane sniggered.

Kathis-Rann tucked the purse inside his tunic and waved a claw in a gesture the wizard failed to interpret. "Some have found a use for it." His scaly, frozen grin seemed to broaden, although that should have been impossible.

Flustered for reasons he could not define, Falobane turned back to his apparatus. "See you carry out your task, then!"

Kathis-Rann rose fluidly from the chair. "I always do what I'm paid for, soft-skin. And I never fail."

With serpentine grace, he slid back out through the window.

**

Kathis-Rann was more cautious in his arrival at Gatharyne's chaotic tower-cell. Slithering through the embrasure, the lizard assassin crouched on the floor and surveyed the workshop carefully. Empty of humans, it was crammed with even more arcane apparatus than Falobane's untidy den. A bleached equaar skull lay atop a towering jumble of bones: random pieces from every species still clinging to existence on the parched, dying Earth. An overwhelming clutter of glass tubes, bottles, flasks and alembics, fused from the sand of endless deserts, dripped a rainbow of distillates. A tanned lizard hide was nailed to the low wooden ceiling. Kathis-Rann noted it without enmity. Perhaps one day he could return the favour to some luckless soft-skin.

The cell's wooden door swung open and a slight figure shuffled in the cell. With inhuman grace and speed, Kathis-Rann was across the floor, grabbing the newcomer by the throat. Before the human could react, the assassin flung him across the room, scattering bones and splintering glass randomly. His flight was brought to a premature end by the far wall.

He opened pale green eyes. Kathis-Rann was already standing over him, a short blade at the human's throat.

"What do you want?" the small man stuttered. He wiped at his face, smearing the fine traceries of blood seeping from a score of tiny cuts.

"You, Gatharyne," replied the lizard. "Your life."

"Falobane sent you!" Gatharyne tried to sit up, but the lizard's motionless sword point kept him in place. "Whatever he paid you, I can double it. Treble it! Kill him instead!"

"What a treacherous breed," said Kathis-Rann, not without humour. "How have you avoided mutual self-destruction for so long?"

Several bags – each the match of the one snuggled inside the lizard's tunic – drifted across the workshop, to drop at his feet. "Take them," urged Gatharyne. "Tell him you've slain me – then take his life instead."

Kathis-Rann hissed in disappointment. "You humans will persist in trying to define my species by your own, narrow terms. I am an assassin, wizard: I do not bargain. And I never fail!"

He drove the point of his sword through Gatharyne's throat before the wizard could say another word. Choking on his own blood, drowning in it, Gatharyne sagged across the ruins of his laboratory.

Kathis-Rann scooped up the purses, sheathed his sword, and turned to leave. But something odd distracted him. More blood than he would have expected was pouring from Gatharyne's punctured throat – and pooling in peculiar ways. Instead of draining to the lowest point, much of it was running uphill, nudging up against the scattered bone and glass. Rapidly the debris was engulfed, drawn together, becoming a single, amorphous red mass.

Then it stood up.

It was obviously meant to resemble the slain wizard, but the unique assembly of bones and broken equipment left it looking more like a caricature sculpted by an imbecile. The equaar skull had become the left foot, curved lengths of glass tubing formed the ribs, the limbs condensed from nonsensical groupings of bones and an assortment of vessels both whole and splintered. Kathis-Rann noted with some amusement that the thing's face had formed out of countless knuckle-bones, their constant writhing a failed attempt at expression.

It stepped towards the lizard. Had he been human, Kathis-Rann had no doubt the sight would have momentarily frozen him. But he was a reptile: his blood already ran cold. The supernatural held no terror for him.

He retreated towards the open window, not taking his eyes off the congealed shape which limped after him. He halted when his tail was hanging through the embrasure, and groped inside his tunic for two innocuous vials. Holding one in each claw, he waited for the mess of bone, blood and glass to be just beyond what he judged to be the reach of his sword. Then he hurled both vials at the floor under its mismatched feet. An instant later he was back-flipping through the window – ahead of the explosion by a heartbeat. Shards of bone and splintered glass – along with chunks of Gatharyne's tower – scattered over half of Burnharnh.

In the ensuing chaos, no one noticed the figure of a lone lizard slink away into the desert.

***

"He is truly dead?" Falobane asked for the fourth time, pacing excitedly around his workshop.

"I told you: I never fail," said Kathis-Rann. He drew his sword, the wizard too distracted to notice. "And I also told you I always finish what I'm paid for."

With a practiced flick, he hurled the sword unerringly at Falobane. It drove through his heart, pinning him to his own door like a choice specimen. Kathis-Rann stepped up to the body, twisting the bloodied blade free.

"My heartiest congratulations, K'th'sss-Rr'nnn," came a disembodied voice, speaking the lizard's own, sibilant tongue. Kathis-Rann wiped his sword clean on Falobane's robe and turned to face a glowing square that was forming itself out of the cell's air. A lizard's head was framed in it, one crowned by a bony frill which grew back from its long skull, and short horns jutting above eyes that flickered with their own, dancing light.

"Your estimations have proven correct, my lord Ss'll'nn Th'rrr," replied the assassin. "Both human wizards acted as predicted."

"Leaving me as Earth's only sorcerer," said Salin Thur, the one a deceased Falobane had dismissed as a myth. *"They paid in gold?"*

"Aye – more than I imagined." Kathis-Rann pulled eight purses from his tunic and held them up. Salin Thur's arm reached from the flickering square, and the assassin placed the purses in an outstretched palm. "Tell me, what use do you find for it?"

Salin Thur's arm withdrew. His glowing eyes were sardonic. *"There is a strange, gaseous race living on an obscure Tier of the Internection who finds this yellow metal a rare culinary delicacy. In return for it, they are prepared to reveal portions of their vast occult knowledge to me."*

"I see," said the assassin, although in truth he did not. Occult knowledge was as worthless as gold, it seemed to him. More, it smacked of human. "And our bargain?"

"In the eastern foothills of the Fl'rr'd'nn Heights is a band of females.

Within the lunar cycle, all will be in season. Would you like my assistance in reaching the spot in time?"

Kathis-Rann bowed humbly. "If I might impose on your generosity, my lord—"

"Think nothing—" There was a moment of disorientation, the coolness of the workshop replaced by the furnace blast of the desert *"—of it."*

Kathis-Rann found himself within sight of the great rocky shelf of the Fl'rr'd'nn Heights, rising far above the Tlantykh Plain. Salin Thur's portal still glowed beside him.

"Good breeding, K'th'sss-Rr'nnn," came the wizard's voice, his image beginning to fade. *"Many males – ready for our coming struggle..."*

The assassin bowed, although the glowing square had already gone. Many males? Perhaps. He began to walk towards the distant, towering cliffs.

Salin Thur knows.

("Salin Thur")

NOTE: This story was first published in the British Fantasy Society's *Dark Horizons* #33 in 1992.

Mike Chinn has edited three volumes of *The Alchemy Press Book of Pulp Heroes* and *Swords Against the Millennium* for The Alchemy Press. His first Damian Paladin collection, *The Paladin Mandates*, was short-listed for the British Fantasy Award in 1999; and an expanded edition is due out from Pro Se Press in 2020. Pro Se published a second Paladin collection, *Walkers In Shadow*, in 2017. He sent Sherlock Holmes to the Moon in *Vallis Timoris* (2015, Fringeworks), and has two short story collections in print: *Give Me These Moments Back* (The Alchemy Press, 2015) and *Radix Omnium Malum* (Parallel Universe Publications, 2017). In 2018 Pro Se published his first Western: *Revenge is a Cold Pistol*.

Next up, an exclusive short story originally published in
Gruesome Grotesques Volume 5: The Outer Zone, currently retailing from
Amazon and Forbidden Planet Belfast…

THE AMAZING XANDRA LEE vs NED SWANN

Adrian Baldwin

THE CHAIR IS wooden, the kind you'd expect to see a gypsy fortune-teller sitting on; the table small, round, and covered in a red, patterned cloth – a crystal ball, pack of Tarot cards and set of old runes wait patiently upon the table's surface. Other than the tools of the trade there's also a teapot, sugar bowl and two bone china cups on matching rose-patterned saucers.

Beyond the tent's entrance, people of all ages, height and circumstance walk by, take in the signs, and generally mill around: well-to-do toffs in Sunday best; street urchins in rags; the middleclass masses; an occasional uniform – each and every one a Victorian.

The Amazing Xandra Lee straightens her headscarf then checks her pocket watch … any minute now.

He had no qualms about it; he was going to kill The Amazing Fucking Xandra and no mistake. Not with the small, loaded revolver in the left-hand pocket of his long black coat (that would be too loud; the gun – a Webley "British Bull Dog" – was just for emergencies); no, the butcher knife in the right-hand pocket had her name on it – and she'd suffer all ten inches of it before the afternoon was done or his name wasn't Ned Swann. Everything she'd predicted at last year's carnival had come true; all of it bad – including the six months hard labour in Wormwood Scrubs. If he hadn't wandered into Xandra's booth last year half-stewed on cheap ale and been sweet-talked into wasting a halfpenny on fucking palmistry and bleeding cards, none of that shitty bollocks would have happened, none of it! Why couldn't the witch have predicted something helpful, something handy, like stumbling upon a swell's dropped wallet, overhearing a piece of juicy tittle-tattle ripe for a measure of blackmail, or one of his dollymops soft-soaping a landed gent into dallying on a more regular basis?

Why couldn't the witch have predicted something else?! That's right, Ned wasn't just a shrewd and black-hearted opportunist, a street-wise villain well-versed in the ways of thuggery and pimping, he was also as dumb as the proverbial rock.

Xandra swills the teapot, re-agitates the leaves.

'Come in, dear, don't be shy – I've been expecting you.'

'Yeah, of course you have; like you don't say that to every punter that strays into your tent.' Ned's accent is pure East End; cockney to the core. Xandra's is harder to place; London, sure, but with a strong hint, possibly affected, of eastern Europe – Romania maybe.

'Have a seat.'

A broad-shouldered man with a disposition akin to a crafty workhouse rat and hair the colour of coal soot, Ned sits opposite, heavy, sullen and primed. He stares hard into the fortune-teller's face. She replies with a smile, untroubled and composed, sugars her tea – three heaped spoonfuls – and stirs.

'Like it sweet, do you?'

'My weakness I'm afraid.'

'Business must be good,' remarks Ned before sizing up the tent's interior.

'Well, I'm not called the Amazing Xandra, medium, clairvoyant and fortune-teller extraordinaire for nothing.'

After another smile she takes several sips and then places the cup back on its saucer.

'Now, dear, what's it to be?'

'Don't recognise me, do you? Perhaps you don't see backwards as well as you do forwards.'

'I never forget a face, dear; especially one as ... *distinct* ... as yours.'

'Here, I hope that's not a sly dig at my rash?'

'Not at all, dear; typhus is no—'

'S'not typhus, it's just a rash.'

'Of course it is – and anyway, I was referring to those striking black eyes of yours.'

'What about them?'

'Darker than the night, blacker than the—'

'What's your point?'

'They've been around, that's all I'm saying: back alleys, workhouses, the docks, public houses ...'

'So?'

'The deeds they must have witnessed.'

Ned weighs up the fortune-teller.

'You see a lot, woman.'

'Comes with the territory.'

'But you don't see everything.'

'The past, as with the future, can be a little hazy; it's difficult to be exact with these things.'

'Yeah, well you pretty much nailed it with your last great bloody vision,' sneers Ned. His eyebrows lift and the pair stare at each other for a moment – eventually Xandra nods.

'I see; and you blame me for events transpiring as I'd correctly foretold?' she asks sweetly.

'Well, if you'd seen something else, perhaps things might have turned out different. Maybe that old git in The Ten Bells pub *wouldn't* have got beaten up and thrown in the Thames, and I wouldn't have got nicked by the coppers for it. I'd hardly mind but it wasn't even me,' he winks, 'just some bloke who happened to have the same ugly mug, no doubt.'

Xandra sucks on a tooth, picks out a tea leaf.

'*No doubt,*' she echoes.

'Bloody coppers.'

'You know he died,' remarks Xandra after a moment.

Ned shrugs; seems he either didn't know or doesn't care.

'A couple of weeks back.'

'Yeah, well they can't blame me for *that.*'

'Coroner said he probably died of a blood clot in the brain – the likely delayed effects of bashing his head as he floated down the Thames.'

'Probably?' sneers Ned. 'Likely?' he grins. 'Mere *speculation* as they say. Trust me: murder or manslaughter, they'd have pinned it on me if they could. Bad enough I did six months hard labour for that boss-eyed old toe-rag just for a fight – even though, like I said, it wasn't me.'

'How do you know he was boss-eyed if it wasn't you in The Ten Bells that night?'

'Might have *seen* him in there; that don't mean nothing – I'm in there regular like. Besides, the story was in all the papers,' smirks Ned. 'A quack, wasn't he?'

'A doctor, yes.'

Outside, the carnival crowd shuffles around to the loud sounds emanating from a steam organ that chimes and whistles its way through a composition clearly designed for gaiety and jollification.

Chattering voices express 'Hello's, 'Afternoon's and 'How-Do-You-Do's from all corners of the fair – no doubt you can easily picture the smiles exchanged in passing.

Pushy, loud-mouthed booth barkers invite punters to roll up, roll up, Hook a Duck, Dart a Card or Roll a Penny; to come inside and witness the Bearded Lady, Wolf Boy, and Siamese Twins.

Leaned back on his chair, Ned has been listening to the calls without.

'The sword-swallower's something to see but the knife-thrower ain't nothing special.'

'You should try the snake-charmer, The Great Zadie, she's very good.'

'Whatever; where were we?'

'This time you wish for a more *favourable* prediction?'

'That's it – a *better f*uture.'

'And if that is not what's foreseen?'

Ned feels the weight of the knife in his pocket. 'Well then,' he sneers, 'that's just too bad – for one of us.'

'Whether the palm or the cards, our destinies can only be—'

'Who says I want either of those?'

'It's a free choice, dear, and yours to make. So, what *is* your fancy this time? The crystal ball? The runes?'

'Don't you know?'

'Oh, I think I do,' smiles Xandra.

Ned scoffs at that.

'But better you say.'

'How about you read my tea leaves?'

'Whatever you wish, my dear, whatever you wish.'

Xandra lifts the pot and swirls it several times. 'Need to get those leaves moving again,' she smiles.

'Did you see anything in your own?'

'Oh, I never read my own.'

'Just as well,' mutters Ned.

'Sorry?'

Xandra slides the unused cup across the tablecloth.

'Nothing,' replies Ned as his tea is poured. 'Okay if I help myself to sugar?'

'Yes, dear, it won't affect the result.'

Ned plonks in four big spoonfuls of sugar and stirs in a loud, heavy-handed manner.

'Think about any specific question you might have as you drink your tea; otherwise, contemplate your life generally as you imbibe. Be careful not to ingest the leaves, mind. I'll need those for the reading. Just leave a little liquid if you can.'

'Yeah, I know,' carps Ned. 'I might be a mutcher but I ain't no-one's charlie.'

Xandra blows her nose and then waits patiently as Ned drinks his tea. After a minute or so he resets his not-quite-empty cup on its saucer.

'All done?'

Ned nods and the fortune-teller takes possession, sliding the cup before her.

'How was it?'

'Not nearly as strong as I normally have it—'

Xandra slowly swirls the cup around then turns it upside down on the saucer to drain.

'—but sweet enough.'

Placing the cup back on the saucer the right way up, Xandra now turns the cup around, three times, clockwise then peers into it.

As she studies the shapes formed by the leaves, Ned's hand slips inside the pocket of his coat and he fingers the handle of the butcher knife.

Xandra's eyes rise to meet Ned's gaze.

'So what do you see?'

'An anchor.'

'Oh yeah? Maybe I'm going sailing; taking a boat to New York – disappearing for a while – start a new life away from these filthy shores.'

'Well, an anchor can mean good fortune—'

Ned mops his suddenly overly sweaty brow with a ratty kerchief fished from a trouser pocket.

'—but this one appears blurred, cloudy, so it probably means the opposite.'

Xandra again looks up, studies Ned's face.

'Is that a fact?' he asks, one eye twitching. 'What else do you see?'

Xandra revisits the leaves ...

'A goat and clouds; clouds usually portend significant difficulties.'

Ned scoffs at that. 'And a goat?'

'A goat often indicates an encounter with an enemy.'

'Sounds about right.'

'And what's this?' Xandra squints deeper into the cup. 'Yes, I see it now ... an hourglass.'

Ned raises a quizzical eyebrow.

'The hourglass shape commonly suggests upcoming danger. Perhaps *serious* danger.'

'Death?' sneers Ned.

Xandra frowns. 'Could be.'

'Oh, it *definitely* could be.' Ned's sneer ends abruptly as a muscle in the side of his neck spasms markedly and he clutches at it.

'What's the matter, Ned; cramps?'

'Don't worry about me—' Ned leans forward, straining from a stomach convulsion, his skin now turned a funny colour. 'What else is in there?' he barks.

'Let's see … is that … a sword? Yes, a sword.'

Xandra's eyes meet Ned's.

'This symbol can signify an argument.'

'Sword, eh?' An excess of saliva drools from Ned's drooping mouth. 'And what about a butcher knife?' he asks knowingly. 'Do you see one of those?'

'See a knife? No; cyanide.'

'Come again?' puffs Ned.

Before Xandra can reply, an abrupt seizure arches the full length of Ned's backbone and stiffens his legs; the limbs shoot out like ramrods and kick the table – the crystal ball unseats from its little wooden base and rolls across the table top.

'Relax, I'm just teasing. It's not really cyanide.' Xandra grabs the rolling crystal ball and sets it on her lap. 'Well, maybe a little,' she continues, 'mixed in with some strychnine and arsenic for good measure; actually, quite a large measure.'

Ned's body loosens but immediately spasms again, a flailing arm almost knocks over the sugar bowl. Xandra quickly relocates it nearer to her.

'Poison!?' gasps Ned. He slumps and his wide eyed gaze rests upon the sugar bowl. 'What, in the sugar? But it can't be; you had—'

'Oh no, not in the sugar, dear; in the tea – it was already in the pot. And not just a few spoonfuls; I'm afraid it was actually more toxins than tea.'

Xandra picks up the pot and empties the remaining poisoned tea onto the grass beside the table.

'See, I did know you were coming,' she smiles, 'and what you had in mind.'

Ned gasps for air, the very act of breathing now a struggle.

'Wait, what's that, spirit voice?' blurts Xandra dramatically. 'Yes, I'm here; what is it? I'm listening.'

She cocks an ear as if to the next world.

'Oh, he says he knows you, Ned; says he's the old git from The Ten Bells – you know, the one you beat up and dumped in the Thames.'

Ned can find no words but after much effort he manages to sit up.

'Oh, this is interesting: he says he recognises your symptoms, what with him being a retired quack and everything. You want to say hello, Ned?'

Ned's face is blank.

'No? Fair enough. Yes, Xandra's here; what is it, dear? ... Oh, I'm sure Ned would *love* to know; he's not very responsive right now but please, carry on.'

A rough, throaty, rasping noise escapes Ned's slack mouth as he toils to slide a leaden hand into his pocket.

Xandra has been listening to the air. 'I understand,' she nods.

She turns to Ned.

'He says: *Death by asphyxiation due to paralysis of the neural pathways that control the lungs.* Does that sound right to you?'

Ned can little more than blink and does so.

'Yes, I think he understands, Uncle Jack – thank you.' She turns back to Ned who's now wearing a deep frown. 'Oh sorry, I should have said; yes, Dr Lee was my uncle – on my mother's side.'

After no more than a final heartbeat or two, Ned's sickly face keels forward, the cups jumping on their saucers as his dead head hits the table.

'Well, all pretty much as I'd predicted,' crows the fortune-teller. 'The Amazing Xandra strikes again – good to know I've still got it.'

But Xandra can't hear the spoken words for the high-pitched ringing that chokes her ears and squeezes her brain. Son of a bitch, when did that start?! *Since Ned's dead head hit the table, that's when!* Yes, that's right; she realises she'd thought the percussive thud overly loud at the time. And what's this? Xandra has become abruptly aware of a warm, wet sensation around her left thigh, her petticoats and skirt growing heavier, and more ... something seeping under her backside as well as trickling down her leg. *Blood*; and a lot of it – the toe-rag must have got off a shot somehow!

'A death spasm,' confirms Uncle Jack's voice, loud enough to overcome the noise, now a shrill drone, in her ears, '—a twitch to the trigger finger. I fear the little shit had a snub-nose pistol in his pocket.'

'Hells Bells,' gripes Xandra. 'But ... *so much blood*?'

'Femoral artery,' advises the ghostly ex-quack. He sighs. 'Anywhere else and you'd have been fine. Just a lucky shot, I'm afraid.'

'*Lucky?*'

'Well, you know – a fluke.'

'The jammy bastard,' winces Xandra. 'So, it's serious then?' she asks.

'Death within a few minutes,' states Uncle Jack's voice.

'Oh, piss,' laments Xandra. She sighs deeply. And with that, the soon-to-be late fortune-teller's eyes close and her head slowly droops forward.

'Didn't predict that, did you?' laughs Ned from the great beyond. 'Not so blooming *Amazing*, after all.'

Copyright © Adrian Baldwin 2019

All characters and situations in this book are entirely imaginary and any resemblance to actual events or real persons – living or dead – is purely coincidental.

The right of Adrian Baldwin to be identified as the Author of this Work has been asserted by him in accordance with the Copyright, Designs and Patents Act, 1988.

All rights reserved.

No part of this publication may be reproduced, copied, stored in a retrieval system or transmitted, in any form or by any means, without the prior written consent of the copyright holder, nor be otherwise circulated in any form of binding or cover other than that in which it is published and without a similar condition being imposed on the subsequent purchaser.

A CIP catalogue record for this title is available from the British Library.

Adrian Baldwin is a Mancunian now living and working in Wales. Back in the Nineties, he wrote for various TV shows/personalities: Smith & Jones, Clive Anderson, Brian Conley, Paul McKenna, Hale & Pace, Rory Bremner (and a few others). Wooo, get him.

Since then, he has written three screenplays, one of which received generous financial backing from the Film Agency for Wales. Then along came the global recession to kick the UK Film industry in the nuts. What a bummer!

Not to be outdone, he turned to novel writing – which had always been his real dream – and, in particular, a genre he feels is often overlooked; a genre he has always been a fan of: Dark Comedy (sometimes referred to as Horror's weird cousin).

Barnacle Brat (a dark comedy for grown-ups), his first novel won Indie Novel of the Year 2016 award (see above) – his second novel *Stanley McCloud Must Die!* (more dark comedy for grown-ups) published in 2016, and his third novel: *The Snowman and the Scarecrow* (another dark comedy for grown-ups) published in 2018.

Adrian Baldwin has also written and published a number of dark comedy short stories. For more information on the award-winning author, check out: adrianbaldwin.info (*You can read the beginnings of all his works there.)

Adrian cites his major influences as Kurt Vonnegut, Monty Python, Stephen King, David Bowie, Christopher Moore, David Mitchell, Robert Rankin, Galton & Simpson, Colin Bateman, Bruce Robinson and Irvine Welsh.

THREE NOVELS COUNTLESS VICTIMS!

BARNACLE BRAT

STANLEY McCLOUD MUST DIE!!

THE SNOWMAN & THE SCARECROW

Starring **LEON BLANK** **STANLEY McCLOUD** **HEAD HONCHO**

Written & Directed by **ADRIAN BALDWIN**

PREY

Joe X. Young

SHE THE ECCENTRIC, her style was very 'Strawberry Shortcake', yet she was certainly not a moppet as no amount of carefully applied make-up could conceal the sagging and wrinkles of a woman who could only look at her retirement in a rear-view mirror through extremely powerful binoculars.

You could bless her little cotton socks, except there would be some doubt that they were in fact cotton as her entire ensemble was either knitted, tatted or embroidered in a rainbow confection which somehow seemed to be exactly her. The entire outfit looked cute, and would have been more so were it on a four-year-old girl who was playing dress up. Regardless, she, the eccentric, wore it with abandon. The woollen hat, striped like a 1970s tea cosy flopped on her head, the knitted framework clinging on either side down to her jawline, serving as a fitting barrier for the cold and muffling any sound which may disrupt her perfect mood. She had no geriatric struggle, no wince of pain as she strolled carefree and unaided, headed who knows where for who knows what, to a destination without incident.

He, in contrast, wore cheap black trainers and white socks, black tracksuit top and bottom flanked either side with a single thin white stripe, his hood obscuring the part of his head not hidden behind mirrored sunglasses and the grinning Skeleton Jaw bandanna which covered his face from the nose down as he sat idly on his bike. He watched her disappear behind the buildings at the T-junction, the right pedal creaked as his foot forced down on it, propelling it forward. His bike lurched and wobbled as he placed his other foot on the left pedal. No rush, no traffic, he would easily catch her up.

The destination was rarely the same but the journey was for the most part reliable, he knew each course, the forward and the backward, each pathway and side road and point of escape. She would reach the main road soon, a turn to the left and a shopping trip with possibly a stop for coffee and cake on the way – it was 'pension day' and she liked the occasional treat. The turn to the right was homeward bound, a few neighbourly visit options but generally home, off the beaten track. Ideal.

On cold days the light is different, clean somehow, and everything it touches looks fresh and new. It made her jewellery look more valuable as the rays bounced off the large gold rings which were seemingly adhered to her now bony fingers by nothing more than the memory of flesh. The diamonds seemed just that little bit brighter, that little bit more real. He hoped that was the case, that he wasn't going to be going through all of this for costume jewellery, and that she would turn toward home where he could do a better job of robbing her. The slow rotation of his pedals timed for stealth, with mindful distance being kept as she, sauntering in a world of her own, would remain oblivious to his presence just long enough to reach seclusion. A little farther and she would make his decision for him.

Go to the right, straight home, make it easy.

She reached the junction, the step to the left made his heart race, his firm push on the pedal propelling him faster, but then she hesitated. He couldn't pull on his brakes in case they squealed and so he banked around in a circle to maintain distance as she turned to her right and headed off homeward. Beneath the grinning skull on the polyester bandanna his true mouth grinned, he followed knowing he would have to head off down the road when she turned into the lane leading to her house – the gravel and potholes were a klaxon for bicycles and he had no idea if she could hear properly. A single-pass in each direction, a minute either way, she would be far enough down the path to be his for the taking, but her home was where his jackpot waited.

She crossed the road, reached the lane, he cycled on unseen, mentally counting to 100 before turning and heading in the other direction with a count of 200 to put him returning to the lane. Once there his front tyre crunched on gravel, he held his breath as if it would make a difference and dismounted. Lifting the bike up he carried it to the hedge at the side of the lane and rested it there. He could continue quickly enough on foot and his getaway wouldn't have to be quick. She would be in no condition to call for help.

He crossed over, watching out for her. She was so far ahead as to be hidden by the trees which lined the lane beyond the curves. He quickened his pace, careful to catch up but not too much, eking his way forward.

The end of the lane splayed out, her home was a delicate chocolate box cottage affair, a white picket border her only nod toward a fence, no gate to make for an uninviting home. From unmown grass the glazed eyes of myriad garden gnomes watched her as she walked down the path, and then stared beyond her at the stranger crossing in shadows. He saw her grab the door handle; she didn't use a key, how very remiss of her! Not locking when she was out made for a great indicator of not locking behind her, which made things a lot easier for him. He followed down the path, ignoring the garden gnomes and took the steps to her door. He stood still for a few heartbeats, listening out for any sign that she was nearby. All quiet. He eased the latch, slowly slid the door open just enough to get inside and gently closed it behind him. He bowed his head, looking over the rim of his sunglasses. His eyes tried to adjust to the dim light of the hallway as he saw her there, motionless, staring at him. It took him a moment to realise who it was, her woollen garb removed, hat on a peg on the wall, coat beside it. She was impossibly thin.

He reached into the pocket of his tracksuit and pulled out a lock-knife, thumbing it open with practised ease.

"I'll take them chains and rings – and I want everything else, jewellery, family silver, the money your sort keeps under your mattress for a rainy day – the fucking lo…"

The distance between them closed before he could finish speaking. He barely had time to register his wrist fracturing before the knife plunged deep into his ear. He opened his mouth to scream, only to feel his teeth leaving their sockets as her skeletal hand pushed into his mouth and reached down his throat, her razor sharp fingernails slicing meat and cartilage as she gripped his spine from within and yanked it forward. She withdrew, allowing him to drop to the floor. Paralysed and dying he looked up at her and watched as she extended thin leathery wings behind her and moved in for her feast.

Joe X. Young is a freelance writer, illustrator and Englishman living in Frankfurt, Germany with a very understanding fiancée. He is a member of the Horror Writers Association and his short fiction and/or artwork is in such publications as *Dark Places Evil Faces 2* (for which he wrote a story and provided thirty-three illustrations), *Something Remains: Joel Lane and Friends, Night of the Living Cure, Carnival of Horror, Morpheus Tales, The Journal of the British Fantasy Society*, the Serling award winning *Another Dimension* anthology and many more. He loves his job to a ridiculous degree and is always up for new challenges. His contact details are as follows:

https://www.amazon.com/Joe-X.-Young/e/B07H6HNJJT/ref=dp_byline_cont_ebooks_21
https://twitter.com/THE_Joe_Young
https://www.facebook.com/MrJoeYoung
joereviews2015@yahoo.com.

A PLACE FOR JUNKMEN

Connor Leggat

MACREA STOOD BY the graveside and wasn't sure what to say. He had known Jon Cyprus well enough, they had shared beers together now and again. But, he didn't know the man *that* well.

They were standing in a young graveyard. The trees were nearly all sproutlings, still slim and scrawny, tied to tall planks of wood to help them grow. The sunlight glinted off the giant dome overhead. It almost seemed healthy in the oxygen-rich graveyard. The local church leader was there. He was one of those new types who didn't hold with the old myths. He wore a smart, black, open collar shirt offset with long hair and an untamed beard. He'd just asked Macrea to say some words over the departed. It felt weird. Jon Cyprus had been burnt down to ash and was now only a tiny capsule – the size of a mint – dangling over a crypt that could have been dug with a toothpick.

"Um..." he said and let that nugget of wisdom hang in the air.

Four people attended Jon Cyprus's funeral, that was if you included his delirious mother and her carer. They were off to the side while the old crone demanded her medication, hurling shrill abuse at the carer when she was denied. The carer was older, about Macrea's age. He'd smiled at her when she arrived, thinking he'd try his luck, but she sneered at him as if he were a shit she'd recently stepped in.

"Jon was a good guy," Macrea began, hoping the words would pour out of him if he only started speaking. "We had a few laughs, and a few beers together... yeah."

The church leader nodded solemnly at that, eyes glistening with reluctant tears.

"Um, so yeah. See you around, Cyprus."

"Beautiful," the church leader said, gripping Macrea momentarily by the arm. "We once came from the Earth, now return to the Earth, Brother Jon." The little capsule, that was now Jon Cyprus, dropped into the crypt. It made no sound.

The church leader got to his knees and filled in the grave with two handfuls of dirt. He took his time about it, sprinkling the soil in then patting it down. Once that was done he leaned forward, kissed the fresh mound and whispered, "Thank you," before rising.

"Is that us?" Macrea asked.

"You're free to go, Mr. Macrea."

The church man shook his hand and wished him peace.

And that was it.

Macrea returned to the office before heading for home. No one there had stopped. Mr. Carmichael came out to ask how the funeral had gone, then asked Macrea to pick up some overtime in Jon's old unit. Macrea made out as if it was a big imposition but agreed anyway. His days off consisted of drinking, watching TV, or wanking himself into near oblivion, so he was hardly missing much.

That night Macrea stared at the ceiling, the roof fan humming above him. He stared up and thought about the stars as he drifted off to dreamless sleep.

***

Macrea caught the tram to work. The old, hovering carriages rattled horribly, always sounding like they were going to fall right out of the sky. The alternative approach, however, was to walk through the streets. There was a reason humanity had taken to burning its garbage up in the closest star. Pollution and crime were rife in the lower city. Macrea attempted to take no notice of that though, it was nothing to do with him.

The tram left him one walkway from the Great Space Elevator. It had been built in the middle of the twenty-first century and was starting to show its age. The elevator looked like a giant tree, but instead of green moss it was patched with copper rust, and instead of branches it was bare, and barren. At its apex, up in the thin atmosphere above the Earth, were the hangers where they launched the ships from. It was there that humanity reached out to colonise the solar system and then, with childlike wonder, to begin voyaging out amongst the stars. Nothing was ever that easy. The science fiction of the last two centuries was just that: fiction.

The elevator dwarfed all the towering skyscrapers around it. Although most of the buildings now gazed out over the city with derelict, vacant windows. As if someone had come along and plucked out their eyes. The space elevator remained a constant buzz of lights and activity.

Macrea stood in the personnel lift, sandwiched in with a hundred other strangers. No one ever spoke on the high-speed system that ascended and descended the giant tower day in and day out. Sometimes people mumbled into wrist-worn comm-units, but for the most part everyone mirrored Macrea. They all looked dead ahead, their eyes out of focus, until the bell alerting them to get off at their floor pulled them from their daze. Macrea rode the elevator to the top. He was flying out today. Five days into the Long Black.

***

Macrea flew garbage. That was his full-time job, his hobby, his wife, kids, dog and everything else. It wasn't that he loved it, there was just nothing else left.

He flew a rig called: *TheDandyHighwayman* which he referred to as *Jerry*. All the garbage rigs were bought on the cheap and second hand, re-writing the ships V.I. – even to change a name – was nigh on impossible. Jon Cyprus had flown *Carol and Jane's Dream Boat*, an old honeymoon wagon that he'd called *Betty*. Macrea hadn't flown another rig since he'd started hauling at seventeen. Each one was unique, with their own ticks and problems that you had to work out for yourself.

Betty was an old Starcamper. They'd been designed to emulate the Volkswagen campers from Earth circa 1950, except these ones could break atmo and haul tonnes. They were rare now as groups of young idealists had flown them out past the boundaries of Sol, looking for somewhere to start anew. They never returned.

Betty was a giant, much larger than Macrea's *Jerry*. She looked as if she'd been white in a past life but was now splattered with a planet's worth of people's refuse. The rigs hauled everything, from food stuffs, to nuclear waste, to what you'd flushed down the bog that morning (after they'd siphoned off the water, of course). They dragged it up and out of atmo, drifting out into the centre of the solar system where they chucked it into the sun's orbit. Couldn't have half a solar system of waste floating about in the Long Black – not with the speed ships moved.

Betty did look like one of the old campers though. She had the colour slash on the side, though it was faded by the sun. Even the windows along the ship's flank mimicked the old style. Though *Betty* could probably fit around twenty original Volkswagens inside her cargo hold. A close inspection showed that the VW symbol had been there, long ago.

Macrea got one of the engineers to show him how to get inside the thing after much shouting in broken English and even more broken Boli. Inside *Betty* was weirdly clean for a junk rig. Macrea didn't see himself as a slob, but he never thought to clean out *Jerry*. The ship constantly smelt like garbage and that hot, metallic smell from the fusion drive. He didn't see the point. *Betty* on the other hand, had a gleam to all her white surfaces. Up in the cockpit the windows were well kept, no marks or grime build up like Macrea's rig. The seat, however, was the main attraction. The pilot's chair was a huge, black, leather throne. There was an indent that Jon's arse had left on the seat but Macrea was sure he could soon squash that out. He hadn't even flown *Betty* yet, but he'd already sworn to harass Carmichael until he got switched over to the ship permanently.

The ship handled well. Surprising for how chunky it was. It lifted Macrea up and out of the dock and propelled him into space in moments. They broke through the final thin layers of atmosphere and drifted while Macrea set the co-ordinates. Behind him he hauled five carriages of garbage from Earth. Each one weighing around ten thousand tonnes. It was a light load today. He programmed in the usual coordinates for a 'drop' and lay back in his new captain's chair to await arrival. That was pretty much it for the junkmen. They spent most of their time drifting through space, only paying attention if something went wrong. But, when you moved the speed a rig moved, there was a much higher chance if something went wrong, you'd never know about it. *What was the last thing to go through the fly's head when it hit the windscreen?* You know.

Most of the time, Macrea entertained himself by playing puzzle games on his tablet. Other times he'd just crack into the chiller of beers he took starward and get a buzz on. Today, however, he went snooping into Jon's old log journal. Log journals were usually a dull affair. Co-ordinates, any issues with the ship etcetera, etcetera. Every now and then a junkman would compose poetry to a pretty prostitute he'd slept with on one of the asteroid mines. Or they'd be writing their *magnum opus*, often about a dashing junkman whose ship gets overrun by aliens, pirates, or shadowy government characters. It was genuinely surprising how many junkman novels could be dug out of old logs and how similar the storylines all were.

A standard log would have six or seven entries per trip, there and back again. When Macrea opened Jon's, there were hundreds.

"My, my, Jon. That's a lot of poems for a lot of ladies," Macrea laughed, and he clicked into the final entry. It was titled, 'Song of the Sun'.

Static began to hiss through the speakers of the rig. There was nothing but the static. Macrea at first checked all the connections to the log journal to make sure it was broadcasting. Everything looked set up. Then there was a scream, Jon's scream.

"Can you hear it? Please tell me you can hear it?" the dead man's voice crackled through the speakers. His speech was thick and slurred, as if he'd been crying. "Oh, she sings, she sings, she sings to me. Listen..." Again, nothing but static followed. Macrea's hairs all began to stand on his arms and his neck. His heart seemed to beat at the base of his gullet.

"Oh, the sun is singing. Jon, Jon can you hear it? Can you hear her? I can hear her."

The static continued as Jon moaned to himself. The speakers were ship-wide and the disembodied voice crept up behind Macrea, like a ghost.

He reached out and switched the log off. The entire ship fell into silence. Space was empty and black beyond.

"What the fuck was that?"

He flicked back through the logs from Jon's final voyage and saw they were all named something similar. He didn't dare to click into another one of them. He cracked a beer to cool his nerves and locked the cockpit door, shutting the rest of the ship out.

Then, Macrea got drunk. So drunk that he nearly forgot to dump the cargo. Your job as a junkman wouldn't last long if you rocked up, three days after you set off, still towing all the crap you'd been sent up to get rid of.

Hauling junk wasn't cheap, but it was that, or drown planetside in the stuff. *Betty* ditched her garbage load and Macrea turned the ship for home. By the time he set down in port he'd rationalised the logs away to himself.

"Jon died of something," he'd told the empty cockpit often and loudly during his return. "No doubt went gaga in his last few weeks. Tumour the size of a baseball or something." Macrea was feeling pretty good as he walked down the ramp of *Betty*, back onto solid land...

"Well, Mac, how'd she handle?" Carmichael asked him.

...And *Betty* was a great ship.

"Like a beaut. I was wondering if I could be changed over to the old girl, full-time?"

"I don't see why not."

Macrea went to leave. He stopped, hesitant. "Hey, Mr. Carmichael, you wouldn't have one of the tech lads scrub the log journal for me?"

"Jon's tale of the junkman warrior not worth keeping then?"

"Yeah, something like that."

"I'll get someone on it."

***

The Truck Stop was a bar near the base of the space elevator. It lingered on the semi-lawless cusp of the lower city. The junkmen all drank there. It stank like they stank, they'd hold your keys behind the bar, and they didn't mind much if you passed out on the stools. Most of the time they'd just let you lie there until you woke up and started drinking again, or they'd buzz you awake for the start of a shift. Girls came by looking for johns, boys too. The whole macho bullshit still pervaded – there was a definite reek of sweat and testosterone – but no one was going to give you grief for where you slung your rope. They all trucked the shit, day by day; they all drifted out into the Long Black. Sometimes you needed to fuck someone, sometimes you needed someone to fuck you, sometimes you just needed someone. Whatever helped. The Truck Stop frowned on fighting, and you paid your tab, or they'd gun you down, but short of that – anything goes.

"Hey, you land *Betty* today?"

The girl jabbed a finger into Macrea's gut. She was young, but haggard around the eyes. She had the same spaced-out, rough look all the sex workers had. Every one of them itching for their next hit of whatever.

"I ain't interested lady," Macrea grunted and returned to his beer and the TV screen. He'd put a bit of money down on the races.

"Well I ain't sayin' I'm interested in nothin' or you. But, you *diiiiid* land *Betty*, yeah?"

"Yeah. And what? Bug off, kid. Find someone who's into that shit."

"Mister, if you assume I'm gonna suck your dick one more time, I'll cut it off."

Macrea's horse went down on a hurdle. The close-up camera zoned in as the marshal came out carrying the old, shell-slugger shotgun. There was a loud cheer as the mule's head exploded. It thrashed about a little longer, spilling the contents of its brain everywhere.

Macrea thumped down on the table.

"Girl, if you don't get away from me I'm gonna ugly you up."

"Try it big guy and it'll be the last thing you do."

She was fierce. There was a savagery in her eyes. She was snarling, like she was halfway feral. Macrea glared back and finished off the tail end of his beer. A new one was placed in front of him before his empty glass reached the bar-top.

"What'd you want?"

"I just wanna know where Jon is?"

"Jon who?"

"Cyprus."

"Jon Cyprus is dead, doll. We planted him last week. Your invite get lost in the mail?" Macrea smiled as the girl's face fell.

"Motherfucker owes me money."

"Yeah well, good luck with that. Last time I saw Jon he was the size of a bean."

The girl cursed again and Macrea chuckled into his beer. You met all sorts at the Stop.

The girl began chopping up a line next to him. She got down to the bar top and snorted – hard – a weird green powder, hoovered up with crisp crumbs and the salt off peanuts.

"Well thanks for nothing fat-arse," she muttered before heading off.

Macrea's hand shot out before he even realised he was doing it. It moved faster than he thought he could and snagged the girl by the wrist. She tugged away from him, but she was so scrawny, he could've broken her arm with two fingers and a thumb.

"What's the big idea, dick?"

"That shit you're snorting, what is it?"

She gave her arm a few more half-hearted tugs before giving up. "This?" The pouch she produced was substantial. Inside the mashed crystals glowed luminous in the trippy lights. "They call it Dream Dust."

Macrea bit. He bought himself a gram of the stuff after she let him sample it. It was good. Made him a little woozy at first but once it kicked in, it felt like his brain was on a roller coaster, like he could feel a breeze brushing against it. The girl called herself Pip, and she was indeed a prostitute, doubling up as a prettyish face to sell her Matron's product.

"Where does it come from?" Macrea asked, rubbing viciously at his nose.

"Man, how would I know? I ain't got no sciences. S'good though. Get me a beer will yah?"

"Are you even old enough to drink?"

"We've been snorting green dope off the table for the last half hour, I think I can risk a beer, dick."

Macrea wasn't going to fight that logic. He ordered two more and they pounded them. After that, everything got fuzzy.

He woke up in his cabin. Pip was snoring softly next to him. His head felt like someone had beat him with a bar stool. Though that was just the hangover; the Dream Dust hadn't left much of an impression. *Bonus,* he thought.

He got up, pissed, took an icy shower and came back to the room. Pip was sitting up at that point, slipping back into her clothes.

"Did we...?"

"Well we didn't split a cab home."

Macrea nodded. He felt fat suddenly, *really fat*. The girl was a rake, he could see her ribs pressed right up against the skin. He was standing there, bollock naked, all lard and hair.

"Um, how much?" he asked, checking the wallet implant on his wrist.

"Listen, Mac. Let's call this one even. For the beers. Not to mention I ripped you off something vicious on the Dream Dust."

Macrea's head snapped up at that, sending his dehydrated brain thumping like a gong.

"I'm taking the piss... dick." She held up her arm and the little blue wallet read:

RECENT CREDIT

Macrea didn't ask how much. He smiled, sadly. She really did look young in the daylight.

"Maybe I'll see you around?"

"Yeah," she replied. "Later 'gator."

The booze was still slurring around his system as he showed up for his overtime. He stopped one of the engineers working nearby.

"You clear out that log?" he asked.

"No English."

"Egghead! The log, did you clean... out... the log?"

"Yesyes. Sure. Whatever."

Macrea wasn't sure he believed him, but he was having a hard-enough time shouting at people in English, never mind trying to establish whatever the engineer spoke and then garbling at him in whatever bastardised form of *that* Macrea knew.

Moments later Macrea was blasting out of atmo and drifting off for the long voyage to the sun. He'd settled for re-purposed water with nettles in it rather than beer this time. The hair o' the dog might literally kill him at this point.

The cabin door was unlocked, and he went to the front windows to gaze out into the Long Black. He found himself, after a few hypnotised moments, humming a tune. It made him melancholic, he thought of an old Earth, in a time before the junkmen and the Stop. A time before, when kids like Pip weren't selling themselves to fat wash-ups like him and when people went into the ground with a bit of dignity. He wondered if a time like that had ever existed and the song seemed to promise it was so.

Macrea slipped into a hazy sleep full of dark and depressing dreams.

***

Awake. Hangover free at last. There was some protein paste in a mini fridge he'd had humped over from *Jerry*. He lathered the grey pulp onto some stale bread and washed it down with the nettle water. He fired up the log journal to make sure the eggheads had wiped it properly and what he saw caused him to choke on the bite he'd just taken.

His entire body went cold, as if the roof had been torn off the ship and he was immediately exposed to the vacuum of space. There was a single log, from Jon. By itself, nothing to worry about, something the techs missed. What scared Macrea was that it was dated today. All the hairs on his arms were stood to attention. A thin sheet of cold sweat was spreading across his body. Behind him, somewhere in the ship he heard a hollow *thunk* of metal. A miserable little scream escaped his throat. The artificial air pushed a breeze into the room behind him and all at once the metal of the ship groaned.

RELEASE PAYLOAD!

...the ship's V.I. warned him.

"Fuck!" Macrea went into autopilot and dumped the trash. He had to physically wrench the ship out of the steadily building gravity of the sun. Even as far out from it as he was. The glaring white light blinded him through the safety glass of *Betty*.

He saw for an instant the slowly orbiting fields of trash – year after year of it – working slowly into the fiery point in the distance.

The ship protested loudly as Macrea turned back towards Earth. Eventually the pull began to subside and Macrea's jets began to carry him safely away.

Free from the danger the eerie message remained on the screen. Macrea went to the door of the cabin and locked it tight. He sat himself back down in the chair and didn't dare turn it around. He really wished he'd taken beer.

***

Betty landed roughly and Macrea stormed out of the door, hauling his mouldy bomber jacket on.

"Good trip," Carmichael called from the plateau of his office.

"Tell your fucking eggheads to wind their necks in! That message in the journal wasn't funny."

Silence fell in the hanger. The whirl of power tools instantly stilled as Macrea's voice echoed deeper into the colossal workstation. He was acutely aware that everyone was just staring. Carmichael glared down at him from the office door. A harsh, florescent light was eclipsed by his head, darkening his features. But the air of menace was unmissable.

"It wasn't very professional," Macrea added weakly.

Carmichael beckoned with his finger and disappeared through the office door.

The silence continued. All work had stilled. Even the bots who helped with the heavy lifting had all stopped and were staring with hollow, lit up eyes.

"Ooooh, shit," one of the roughhands laughed.

Macrea looked around for the perpetrator but everyone dropped their heads back down. The din of the hanger rose like the swell of a wave as the whirl of tools and the wordless mumble of chatter began anew.

Macrea wasn't sure what he expected to find in the office. He reckoned Carmichael would be manically anal about cleanliness. Organised to the extent of obsession. The man wore a suit to a refuse hanger every day! But no, Carmichael's office was as cluttered as any other. The single bulb that lit the room buzzed and flickered like everywhere else. Carmichael sat behind a rough, cheap-looking desk in a chair that appeared as though he'd fished it out of one of the skips. He looked sternly at Macrea, his fingers steepled with his chin resting on top of them.

"Take a seat, Mr. Macrea."

He did so.

"How was your trip?" Carmichael asked, not taking his eyes from him.

"Same as." Macrea shrugged.

"A wee bit of an outburst there, Mac. Want to tell me what that was about?"

"Just eggheads thinking they run the place."

"The engineers *do* run this place. You'd go trundling off into the sun without their good work."

"Aye, and they'd drown in their own shite without mine…"

Carmichael raised up his hand, silencing Macrea. "I get it, I get it. Everyone does their bit."

"Aye," Macrea grunted.

"I'm getting reports of some of the pilots hearing voices. Have you heard anything about this?"

Macrea began to sweat. "No, nothing like that."

"Very well. We think it might be caused by the radiation," Carmichael muttered, as if to himself. He continued, "Each of the rigs are being examined. *Betty*'s come up for inspection this week. Why don't you take this week off? Relax, calm your nerves a little."

Macrae's heart began to pound. Panic filled his throat choking like vomit. "Mister Carmichael, I need this job..."

"And your job will still be here for you in a week. This is a routine inspection."

"I'll fly *Jerry*!" Macrea was nearly hanging over the desk now. A small smirk appeared on Carmichael's face as he nonchalantly looked at a clipboard.

"*TheDandyHighwayman* is up for review as well I'm afraid."

"I'll fly another rig, sir. Please."

"Calm yourself, Mr. Macrea. I'll not have my riggers bubbling like wee lassies. You *are* taking this week's reprieve. It's already decided." There was a long pause between them. "Unpaid, of course."

Macrea hung his head, he didn't respond. There was nothing else to say.

"Off you go, Mr. Macrea. Enjoy your week off. And do let me know if you get whiff of any of your compatriots going do-lally."

Carmichael brushed Macrea out of his office with a disinterested waft of his hand. His attention had already moved to a bright tablet that lay on his desk. Macrea got up and left, scurrying in case he lost another week by looking too dour. To live was to work as Macrea saw it. Practically everyone who'd got the sack before had ended up in the lower city or had opted for taking an unsuited spacewalk from the hanger doors.

***

That night Macrea ended up back in the Stop. He pounded some beers with the chest-beating Neanderthals there and challenged a few folks to arm wrestles for stupid sums of money, desperate to coax some edge back on his nerves. None of it worked. Eventually he lumbered to a dark spot on the bar and hunched over his beer. He knew exactly what he needed. And as if, like a descending angel, the Old Gods had answered his prayer, he spotted Pip's slim figure, sliding through the crowd.

"Alright, dick?" she greeted him. "Gimmie a sup of your beer."

"No foreplay?" he asked. There was an odd sensation in his chest. A swell of joy, as if he was happy to see the little junkie again. It was probably just the Dust.

"Can you afford foreplay?"

He slid his pint down the bar towards her, the red liquid inside sloshing, dangerously close to spilling out. The glass came to rest neatly in her open hand.

"Pretty smooth," she said, taking a drink. "Good start. Not what I meant, but a good start."

They drank together again. All on Macrea's dime, but he didn't mind. The company was... refreshing. Afterwards they stumbled into a cab and jetted back to Macrea's cabin where they fell drunkenly onto his cot. The sex was short and clumsy. They snorted Dream Dust from the bedside table and rubbed it onto one another's gums.

When they finished Macrea was drenched in sweat. He could barely catch his breath. Pip rolled into the crook of his arm and closed her eyes. And even while the drugs ran riot through their systems – making it feel like there was a window open on a cold crisp day, and not that they were crammed into a box with no windows to keep the smog out – they both fell asleep.

The next day Macrea wasn't really sure what to do with himself. He couldn't remember the last proper day off he'd had. He functioned on a cycle of work, drink, sleep, repeat. Now, sitting up in bed at noon, it made him feel nervous, guilty even. Pip decided to stay which he didn't dislike. She'd also decided to keep them both supplied with Dust.

"Hey, Mac! Where'd you grow up?" Pip was perched on the bed, drowned in one of Macrea's tee shirts, eating beans from the tin.

Macrea looked at her, stern for a moment. "Why d'you care?"

"Just curious. That a crime?"

"Grew up here on Earth. Like everyone else."

"Nuhuh! I met a Jon once. He grew up on Titan."

Macrea just shrugged his shoulders and ignored her. He wasn't totally sure where Titan was, but he was pretty sure that was bullshit.

"So, where'd you dream of going as a kid?" she asked.

"I didn't."

"I used to dream of going to Venus, they say it's a tropical paradise. You ever dream of going to Venus?"

"What's with all the questions? You think I'm some kind of weepy faggot?"

Pip frowned. She looked at him curiously, sadly. "No, you dick. I think you're some kind of person."

That made him feel dumb, then it made him feel angry. He wasn't used to this. Wasn't used to people.

"Venus is a shithole, just like everywhere else."

"How'd you know? You've never even been?" she snapped.

"Don't have t'ave been. Just know. Ain't nowhere decent anymore."

Pip rolled her eyes and spoke through a mouthful of beans.

"You junkmen are a dour lot. Almost as bad as roughhands 'cept they're all half-mad."

"Don't call me that," Macrea said. He wasn't even sure what had annoyed him. He knew people called them junkmen, just like the mechanics were roughhands and the engineers eggheads.

"What? Junkman?"

"I said quit!"

She rolled her eyes again and huffed. They sat in the awkward silence.

Pip set down the tin. "Listen, I know what it's like to be labelled by people, as if they know you. Especially with a name you don't like."

Macrea didn't say anything. He just nodded to the skinny, young woman on his bed and they both silently understood.

Pip stayed for the week. She would leave in the evenings and sometimes she would return that night and sometimes she wouldn't. But, every morning she was there, with Macrea. She'd crawl into his bed and into the crook of his arm. He became used to her presence. Just by being there he felt better about himself, his work, even the shitheap city they both lived in. He'd sit awake and smoke, listening to the soft rattle of her breath. Her small lungs damaged by years of tobacco and who-knows-what-else abuse. Perhaps he was falling in love, like some wuss on the TV or perhaps it was the drugs. Because what Pip returned with every night was a small bag full of luminous green Dream Dust.

There was a peace between them. A comfort. But Macrea would soon return to work and the little bags were getting smaller and smaller. In the back of his mind he heard a hum.

***

The week passed in a haze. Soon Macrea was back in *Betty*, being pressed back into his chair as he jettisoned into space. The voyage was anything but smooth. He was only one day into his journey to the sun when the shakes started. He'd brought the customary chiller of beer to try and keep *some* kind of buzz going and he'd figured some time off the Dust would do him good. He thought wrong.

Day three was when he started to think he'd really cracked. He drank all the beer like a man dying of thirst, and the hum in his mind had started to take form into something lucid. He'd catch himself whistling it, other times it just reverberated his skull to the beat of a drum. When he opened the log journal, desperate for distraction, the ghost of Jon Cyprus had been updating it every day.

"Aww Jon," Macrea slurred, "Help me through this."

He pressed play. That's when he heard it.

It was only for a moment, the entire cabin boomed with the song. It scared Macrea so bad he was hurled back in his chair like he was getting malleted by lift-off gees. His ears thumped with pain, even after the song died down into a silent whisper, a suggestion at the back of his mind. There were tears freely flowing down his face.

"You heard it that time."

Macrea looked up, mouth hanging lamely open. In the doorway to the cockpit stood Jon Cyprus. He was tall and hunched, slim as if starved. His skin was saggy and grey. When he smiled Macrea could see that all his teeth were black or missing. He wore his trademark green windbreaker and red trucker cap.

"What is it Jon?" Macrea sobbed.

"Hell, Mac, it's the *Song of the Sun*."

"I can't hear it anymore."

Macrea was on all fours at this point, curling up, like he was preforming agonising yoga.

"Well you need more of the dust, Mac. You know that's what you need. Head back home. Make that little bitch give you some."

Macrea groaned. Jon's mouth moved while he spoke, but the voice emitted from the speakers all over the ship. It sounded as if a hundred Jons all spoke at once. Then something cut through the voice. The warning of the alarm.

"Oops, better drop that payload, Mac."

Jon started to cackle, shrill and unfriendly. The alarm became louder and louder. Macrea began to drag himself off the floor, sniffing back the tears he'd shed. Back in the seat he looked out towards the sun. The red warning text from the V.I. blaring on the screen. He wondered if it might be easier, just to drift off into space and never come back. Let the sun's gravity suck him in and her flames eat him alive.

Then he crashed his hammy fist down on the eject and dumped the garbage he carried. Macrea wasn't ready to go. Not yet.

***

The ship came in a little rough but landed safely. The egghead scowled at Macrea as he stumbled down the ramp of *Betty* and into the harsh light of the hanger. He didn't take any notice. It was like the autopilot he'd used to guide his course back to Earth was now leading him onward. The song had faded so badly he could barely hear it anymore. It made him want to hurl himself on the ground, screaming and crying as if he were a child. He felt like pulling his hair out at the roots just to vent out some of the rage that bubbled up inside him.

The lift down the space elevator was nearly empty at this time of night. A woman in a filthy jumpsuit gave Macrea a wide berth. He didn't know why. He hadn't noticed he was twitching.

His footsteps took him through the high levels of the city. Even here the pollution rose up and clawed at the walkways. People pressed masks over their noses and mouths, fleeing between one safe spot and another. A man passed him in an expensive suit, wearing a gasmask, with an oxygen tank on his back. The handgun he carried slapped against his lapels in time with his step.

His journey took him deeper and deeper through the city. The lights began to fade and the people out and about this late began to teeter off. The stench got worse. Until at last, he reached his destination. The neon lights of the Stop buzzed before him. He'd had enough of seeing the world this way.

Macrea took a seat in a darkened corner and fidgeted, waiting for the next night worker to come in. He'd approach any of the scantly-clad dealers to get the Dust. He needed to numb himself. He checked his funds on the little implant on his wrist. It was looking pretty dicey. For a brief moment he considered caving a dealer's head in, just to get the Dust. A shapeless whisper in the back of his mind did not dissuade him.

"You look like you could use this."

Pip tossed a heavily depleted bag of Dream Dust onto the bar. Macrea launched on it like a bird of prey. Greedily, he opened it, lifted a little crystal on his manky fingernail and huffed it. He went back in for round two and filled his second nostril. As he dipped for a third volley Pip snatched it back from him.

"There's not much left!" she snapped, baring her teeth like a dog.

Macrea glared at her for a long while, his top lip quivering with rage. Then he forced it into a smile.

"Not like I give a fuck."

She smiled as well, warily. Then lifted his beer and gulped at it while maintaining eye contact. She planted the half empty pint down again and belched.

"Can I see you tonight?" he asked.

"If you can afford it."

He nodded.

"Get us another beer and I'll think about it."

Macrea had no problem with that and he listened to the girl moan about the johns she'd dealt with since they'd last seen one another, and how her Matron was running low on Dream Dust. Her boss claimed the talent was stealing it, but it wasn't Pip's fault if the stuff sold like fire spreads. Macrea nursed his beer and nodded along.

As soon as the final dregs of lager disappeared down Pip's thin throat Macrea stood up.

"Another?" she asked, hopeful.

"No."

"Oh, I see. Long voyages away from home. Many years since you've seen a woman."

"Don't be fucking cute."

"Right." Her eyes downcast, she slipped off the slightly too tall stool she'd sat on.

They didn't talk in the cab ride back. Macrea had the window low and even through the smog of pollution that hung around the city he could hear the stars up in the sky. They were calling to him. The humming started again. The Dream Dust was taking a hold now. It seemed like the tune was coming from somewhere at the back of his brain. The tune coming out like a pulse. He was so close to hearing the song in earnest. Each time he tried to focus in on it, it just slipped away. He needed more. A final hit would have the 'Song of the Sun' blasting out like a brass band. He'd know what it was like, before the smog, before the junk, before the radiation burns from the trips to and fro, to and fro; up and back, up and back.

He shoved Pip slightly as they walked through the door. He felt his cool slipping as the song faded in his mind.

"Hey! I'm fuckin' back ain't I? You can wait five fuckin' minutes to get your dick sucked."

"What?" he said, recoiling from the vulgarity.

"What's going on in your head?" she snapped.

"Nothing." He felt abashed for a short moment, ashamed. He lowered his head and the humming started up again.

"What's that tune you're singing?" she asked.

He looked up at her.

"Jon used to hum it... before, you know."

"It's the 'Song of the Sun'," Macrea said.

Pip's eyes went wide with panic as she stared into the long black of Macrea's gaze. She'd been brought back by a shell and she was in so much danger. She screamed – too little, too late.

Macrea smashed her with all his bulk into the door to the bedroom. The door blew off its hinges and shattered around the room. Pip's back cracked loudly. She was hurled across the room and her neck snapped against the side of the bed. Macrea lorded over her, breathing deeply. The song was getting louder and louder, his blood pounded in his temples to the beat and his eyes felt like they'd burst due to the uproar.

He got down on his knees and started to search Pip's pockets. He had assumed she was dead, so he screamed when her arm came around and grabbed his wrist. She was gurgling in her throat, staring blankly at her own navel, unable to move her head. But, there was a power of life and rage in her grip. Macrea found himself again and wrapped a giant, meaty hand around the girl's throat and crushed the life out of her.

Through the open door the sharp winds blew in and brought with it the stench of decay from all around the city. Macrea left Pip inside, the stench as her body breaking down would simply meld with the world around it.

Macrea used his key to lift a little powder out and snorted it. The smell of the city faded away and a cool, fresh breeze caressed his brain. He was *fucking* out of here.

After grinding away on the junk rigs all his life Macrea had accumulated a level of trust and authority, minute though it may be, it granted him enough leeway to board *Betty* and be waved out of the hanger by a tired egghead. Before he knew it, he was breaking atmo and heading, once again, back towards the great star. That bubbling, boiling mash of elements, breaking down and changing in near endless fire. Somewhere, deep in his heart, maybe even beyond that, in his soul, he knew he'd hear the song best from there.

The trip there was a blur. Each time Macrea felt the song slipping into deeper obscurity he would take more Dream Dust, then the song would return, and he'd laugh and smile. He imaged this is what it must have felt like. Kicking it down a dirt road, the clean country breeze in your hair, up your nose. The smell of trees and teeming life. This was it. This was the world they lost.

He went into the log journal, one last time. Unsurprisingly it was full of log entries by Jon Cyprus. Thousands and thousands of them. When Macrea loaded one up his old friend's voice crackled on the ship-wide speakers.

"Far out, Macrea, you found us. Not long now, brother. Not long now."

He heard the song a little clearer this time. In the distance. Just too far from it to hear the words, but he got the tune. It plucked at his heart strings while it filled every cell in his body with nostalgia and pleasure. He was crying and then he was laughing, and Jon was crying down the speakers and saying, again and again, "Right on, man. Right on. Not long now."

The song reached ear-bursting volume and Macrea closed his eyes and lay back in the chair. The ship's V.I. flashed messages across the screen, unnoticed.

RELEASE PAYLOAD.

RELEASE PAYLOAD, IMMEDIATELY.

**SHIP UNABLE TO SUSTAIN GRAVITATIONAL PULL.
RE-PLOT COURSE.**

DANGER! DANGER! CATASTROPHIC COLLISION IMMINENT.

Macrea dipped his head back. He couldn't hear the alarm over the sound of the song and Jon's wailing and laughing. He felt salt tears evaporate on his cheeks and as the heat pooled into his cockpit, he wished he'd brought some beer. The last particles of Dream Dust drifted up his nostril and he knew he was going somewhere better.

Connor Leggat is a fantasy and sci-fi author based in Northern Ireland. After graduating with a degree in English with Creative Writing he worked with Scottish Opera as Librettist on the "The Cello Player". Shortly after he was commissioned by Aberdeen Preforming Arts to write short stories. He has a been published a few times for his poetry and a few times less for his prose (and mainly online). Currently he writes in Omagh with his incredibly patient partner and their dog called Pig.

GREASEHEAD

Conor Reid

GETTING HIS HAIR cut was always an unpleasant experience for Patrick Smith. It was somewhat a problem of trust, as Mr. Smith did not trust many people, let alone those who repeatedly placed sharp blades near his neck and also his haircuts were so sporadic and unplanned that he often did not wash beforehand. Not a crime by any measure, but a condition that always left him feeling self-conscious in his barber shop. He had developed the habit of looking around while in his chair, desperate to look at anything other than his greasy, matted hair.

On the afternoon of September 18th, 2017, Patrick sat in his usual chair in his usual barber shop, on its usual street and avoided the usual possibility for conversation with his hair-care professional. Mr. Smith's chair sat equal distance between two parallel walls, in front of him was a mirror, and behind him was a door Patrick always assumed led to a kind of staff room. On this afternoon, Patrick noted all the usual things during his haircut; a freshly sharpened razor, a pair shiny of scissors, a folded and pressed white towel, and a pile of loose hair swept into the corner of the room that resembled a mound of fuzzy autumn leaves. He also noticed in the mirror's reflection that the staff door behind him was slightly ajar. A small crack was all that could be seen through, and as Mr. Smith's eyes scanned it from top to bottom, sating his need to distract himself, he felt a sudden jolt of cold rip through his spine as his gaze crossed with another's. Inside the crack in the door was an eye poking through the surrounding darkness, staring back at him, itself a mere three feet from the ground. The eye shook slightly, and its inside was full of thick red veins and a cloudy white filling, a single dot of blue in the middle focused at Patrick. Mr. Smith then heard the sounds of licking, which drove him to look only ahead for the rest of his haircut.

That night, Patrick Smith lay in his bed, unable to sleep. He thought from the height of the being behind the door that it may have been small, a child maybe, and began to feel sick when he imagined what horror it would need to live in to have such a harsh, battered stare.

Over the next month, Patrick tried to tell as many people as he could about what he had seen. He tried to argue to his friends, "I told you, I saw it, a child, behind the door! It can't have been anything else!" but nobody cared. He begged for the police to look, but they told him a child in a barber's shop was nothing unusual. Patrick thought this was no ordinary kid, that no kid would have the manic eyes he saw and not be in trouble.

Patrick may have been self-conscious on occasion, but he did believe that underneath his edifice of inadequacy there was a braver, more virtuous man. All he needed was the right incentive, to pull this braver man out, and what better motivation than a child in danger. When the time came for his next haircut, Patrick would be ready to prove his suspicions, and he started to plan. He would sit again in his usual chair and watch for the boy behind the staff door, awaiting any confirmation of his worries. He prepared for the reality that he could do nothing while he was there, that maybe the barber was in on it, so he would go back after they close. He needed to learn to pick a lock, and spent a week researching before buying a kit online, and when his hair finally grew long enough, he set a day for this incurious; October 25th.

The day had come, and he entered the shop. This haircut proved to be unique torture for Patrick. His eyes were trained hard at the reflection of the staff door, his forehead sweating and his palms and fingers being rung in and around each other underneath the cover that caught his falling hairs; greasy, again. However, no eye emerged this time. No piercing gaze or sense of quivering dread or sounds of licking came forward at all. Before he knew it, his haircut was over, and he found himself wondering that maybe he was crazy. Or maybe, he thought, now was the time to really follow through. When the police turned a blind eye weeks ago, Patrick knew it would come down to breaking the law.

Later, now deep into the night of October 25th, Patrick Smith was at his usual barbershop, on its usual street, standing at its usual door in a very unusual manner, hunched forward and nervous as hell. The shop was old, and thankfully old-fashioned, not much coaxing with needed for the front door to click open, with no alarm or sound beyond the door's squeaking, rusty hinges.

Patrick reached for the light switch, which clicked, and lit up nothing. No matter, he thought, he knew the layout of the shop from memory and started to feel his way through. Railing, railing, chair, railing, counter, counter, usual chair, and now the usual mirror. He drew a long breath as his fingers touched the cold glass before him, his own reflection obfuscated by darkness. He took a cautious step backward, turned, and faced the staff door. He reached for the door handle, slowly pressing down with his palm, fingers clenched and knuckles protruding. It was unlocked. He opened the door and there was a dripping sound. He reached for the light switch and felt a chilly air meet his face. There were sounds of slopping and sloshing now. The light clicked on and the room became visible. Not a staff room at all. Staff rooms don't have unpainted, grey brick walls, a single uncovered light, a stench or rot and a full, steaming bucket of waste in the corner, but this room did. A cell, and in the middle was a mattress-sized pile of hair, arranged in a mound, with a child nestled on top of it. A child, no older than ten sat there, in a knee-high treasure trove of bristly hair, hunched, looking barely alive, wearing a stained pillow-case over his torso, eyes manic and dotted with piercing blue pupils, and unkempt hair that smelled of the droll of the long-since-dead. The child's face was covered in hairs, glued to his cheeks and mouth with thick pastes of saliva, and more hair came to his face as the boy began to heap handful after handful of hair from his nest-pile into his dripping mouth. Thick clumps were clenched in between his bony fingers as the boy shoved them harshly again and again past his lips, his bulbous lumpy tongue lapping and swishing hungrily at the strands.

Patrick stood still, watching as the boy took a bushel of clipped, shimmering hair; greasy hair. The boy squealed in joy and Patrick felt ill. Patrick saw hairs of various colours stuck between the boy's teeth like popcorn kernels, and now the boy brought forth a clump of shimmering greasy hairs and began to suck down hard on them. The slackened hairs were like straws in a cup with just a bit of delicious nectar left teasingly at the bottom, the boy's inhaling sounding like a slimed-up vacuum cleaner. Patrick could feel invisible bristles in his mouth just from staring, and upon thinking these hairs the boy was eating were his own from earlier that day. He ran, screaming in to the night.

To this day, Patrick Smith has refused to get his hair cut. It now hangs low, to the back of his knees, and is easily messed and hard to manage, often becoming tangled and tatted. He began to lose sleep and lost his job over an argument about his workplace appearance. Similarly, his friends could not stand to be around him, complaining of his greasy stench, and so now his life is sedentary.

But Patrick does not dare entertain the idea of cutting his hair on his own, not ever, especially in his own home. He fears that allowing his hair to fall to the ground will call the boy back, allow him in somehow, and while Patrick Smith lays in bed at night he may feel the phantom bristles in his mouth again, hear the sounds of licking...

Because somewhere out of sight, the boy may be there, suckling hungrily on his clipped greasy hair.

Conor Reid is a Belfast-based writer of fiction, articles, and blogs. He enjoys horror, sci-fi and fantasy fiction, and his aim is to excite and provoke his readers.

"It is a strange, often horrific world we live in, and providing that strangeness and horror in a digestible context is one of the greatest joys I can experience. I am available for freelance work, and open to collaboration. You can contact me at conor.reidwrites@gmail.com for any inquiries. I hope you enjoy."

MY PILLOW IS A SHIP

Marc Damian Lawler

My pillow is a ship...
I sail through the night.
My pillow is a ship...
I sail out of sight.

My eyes are world weary...
this dream will light the way.
My eyes are world weary...
this dream will shape today.

Mighty waves of self-doubt
crash hard against my soul.
Mighty waves of self-doubt
have failed to take their toll.

All troubles washed away...
it is now time to rise.
All troubles washed away...
I see the morning's prize.

But the sun fiercely shines
upon my land-locked mind.
But the sun fiercely shines
and slowly turns me blind.

Come fast the night again...
I need to sail the sea.
Come fast the night again...
I need to search for Me.

Island hut, or in a
cavern underwater...
I have settled somewhere
without bricks and mortar.

I will join myself there...
and sink my ship offshore.

> I will join myself there...
> and sleep for evermore.

NOTE: This poem won 1st Place in the Wordsworth Poetry Competition, Dove Cottage, Grasmere, in 2006.

Marc Damian Lawler grew up in Bracknell, Berkshire, but was born in Liverpool. He now lives on the Wirral. He has a BA (Hons.) degree in English Language and Literature; but would gladly swap it for a one day tutorial from Edgar Allan Poe. His favourite modern day horror writers are: Richard Matheson, Stephen King, James Herbert, Graham Masterton, and Britain's Prince of Chill, R. Chetwynd-Hayes.

I SHOULD NOT BE

Richard Bell

Rumours glide on phantom draughts
Flickered flame on spattered mantle
Casting shadows thick with fears
This mansion echoes haunted years
Move on tiptoes, creep like cats
Feel the dread in throttled creaks
Mirrors keep the eyes of hosts
I should not be among the ghosts

Crusted toys are curios
Cobweb blankets waft like sails
Taxidermy startled snarls
Gardens overgrown to gnarls
In the cursing growling gut
All imagined terrors lurk
Their legends are a tall tale's boast
I should not be among the ghosts

Climb the stairs as Nosferatu
A puppet's prance on unseen strings
This place weeps fright from blackened sutures
Wide-eyed fright awaits trespassers
Atop the stairs each candle nipped
By slipstream of unearthly hearse
I'm chilled as fog that shrouds the coast
I should not be among the ghosts

A breath, a wreath of mourning flowers
Another yet the air is still
Like tyres rolling over gravel
The words thumped hard like judge's gavel
"Get thee from our realm beyond
Begone your curiosity
To look upon us life is lost
You should not be among the ghosts"

I sprinted three by three the stairs

A hurtle with no self regard
I left with them my boy's bravado
Inside ghost hunters El Dorado
A welcome sunrise shone through me
My body broken in the hall
The truth of afterlife exposed
And me, with them, among the ghosts.

Richard Bell is a poet and writer with a passion for the horror genre, especially the supernatural. He has had work published by Weasel Press, Carmen Online Theatre, *Night Gallery*, *The Horrorzine* and the *Fragments of Fear* series on YouTube (under the name Rick Nightmare). He lives in a sleepy hamlet in Northern England with his family and cheese-induced insomnia.

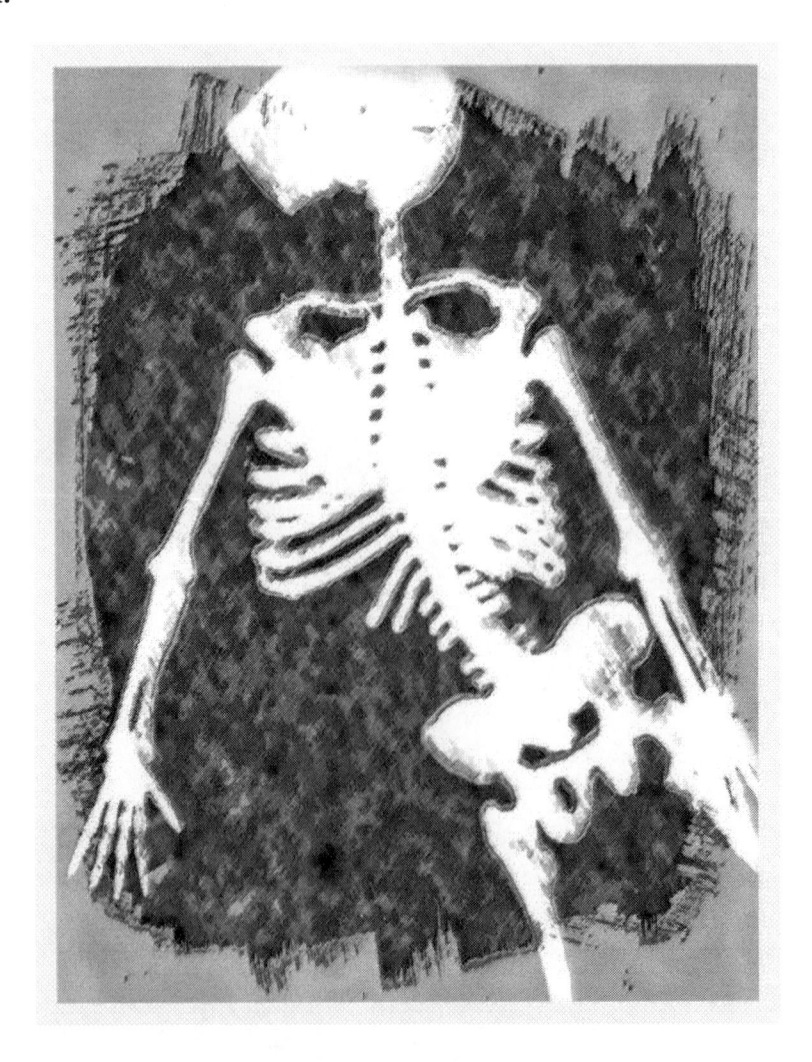

AS SILVER DUSK SUFFUSES RED

David A. Riley

As silver dusk suffuses red
And eastern skies dull mauve,
Frail laughter comes out through the gloom,
From every bush and grove.
The sound of movement, gay and brisk,
Bursts through the night's warm mist,
And, as the sky harvests its stars
Vague forms leap up, moon-kissed,
Each writhing, with wide open mouths,
Each eye bright as a bird's,
Whilst through the woods come further shapes,
Sprites in a thousand herds.
Blossoming flames from fires reach up
And strive to dye the moon.
The dancing, singing hurries on,
For dawn will come so soon!

BYRON'S BURNING BONES

Emerson Firebird

Fill me up with insubstantial stuff that dies.
Take my bones away and laugh at them forever.
Nothing to return for.
Fading diamonds fill the skies.

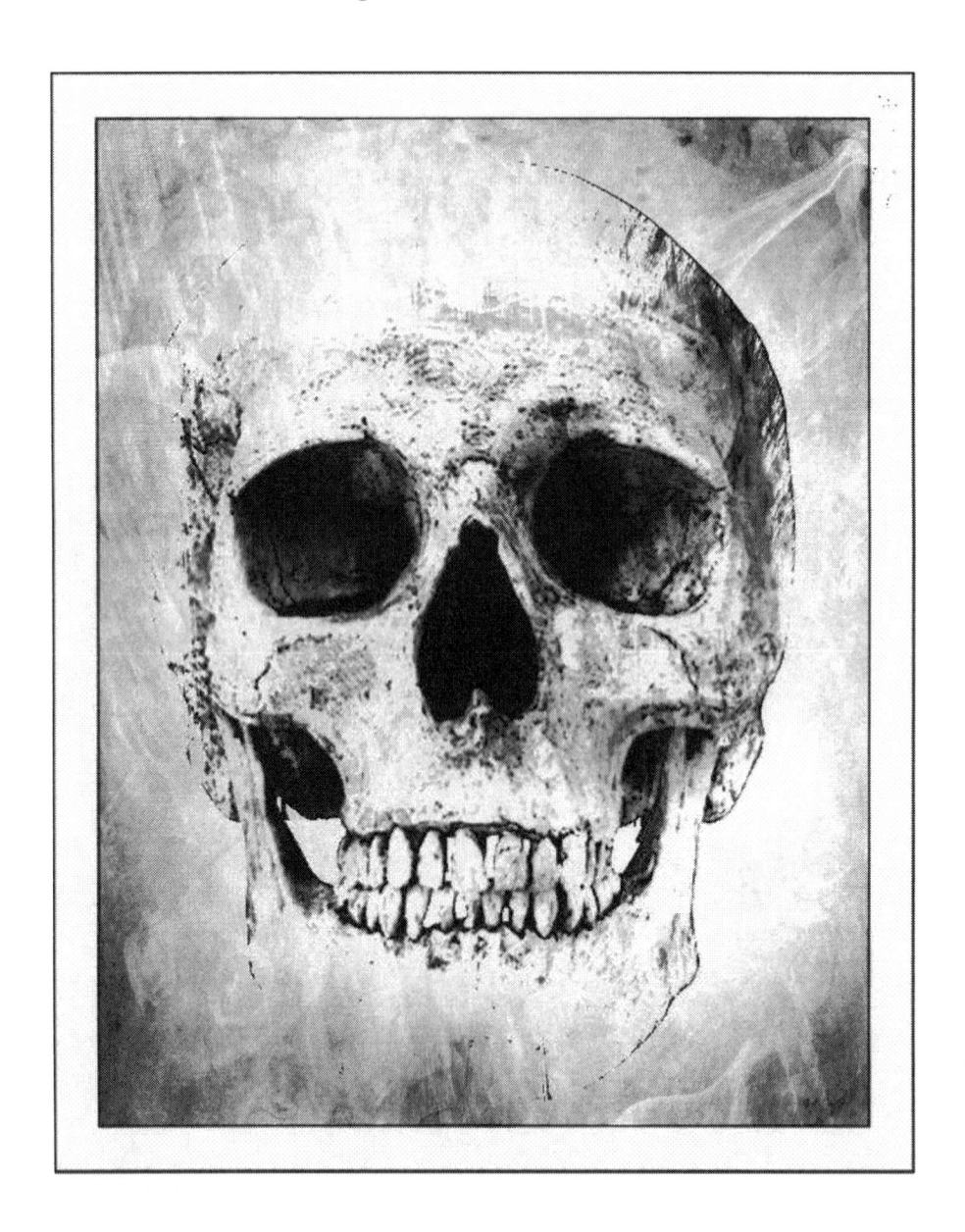

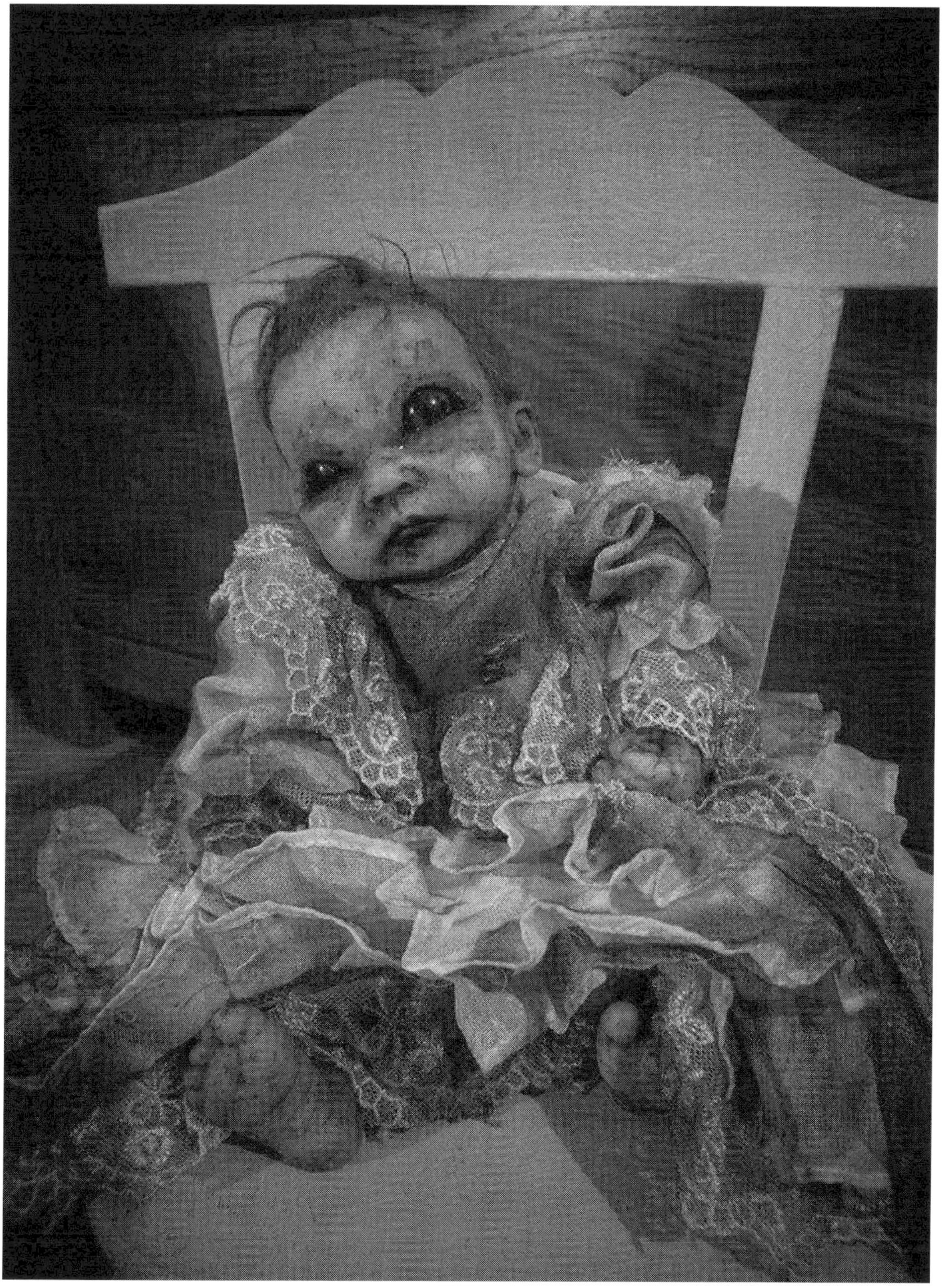

BATMAN TRIUMPHANT:
HOW THE DARK KNIGHT ROSE
FROM THE ASHES TO BEGIN AGAIN

Nathan Waring

BY 1997, THE Batman film franchise had come to a crashing halt due to the release of the critically panned and fan-hated debacle that was the fourth entry in the Batman film series: *Batman & Robin* (1997). The film series had once been the crown jewel of Warner Brothers and DC's film output, beginning in 1989 with Tim Burton's seminal *Batman*.

Batman was a dark and brutal visualisation of the Caped Crusader, a far cry from what the society of the time would have envisioned for Batman as the character was considered the height of camp due to the Adam West-starring television series of the 1960s. And, despite the enormous success of the *Superman* film series (1978-2006), the superhero genre was not the box office behemoth that it is today, meaning that studios were reluctant to put money down for an expensive superhero film, especially one as dark and, potentially, corporate sponsor-upsetting as what Burton envisioned for Batman's blockbuster debut. Therefore, when *Batman* was released to enormous success, both critically and financially, it proved beyond a shadow of a doubt that superheroes, whether they be light-hearted or dark, were an impressive box office draw when done right. In the immediate aftermath we saw other studios trying to replicate *Batman's* success with the release of *Teenage Mutant Ninja Turtles* (1990) and *Captain America* (1990). Burton began work on a sequel immediately, which was released in 1992 as *Batman Returns,* a film that was both darker and more violent than its predecessor. The sequel fared well critically and performed well at the box office, but still came in at over $100 million less than the original. What frightened Warner Bros. most, however, was the response from the corporate sponsors. Due to the film's violence and sexual themes, McDonald's withdrew their support for the movie, which included a lucrative "Happy Meal" toy deal. Complaints about the film's adult tone meant that the studio decided to take the Batman franchise in a more family-friendly direction, meaning that although Burton had already began work on the next Batman film, he would be replaced as director by Joel Schumacher. Schumacher's film, titled *Batman Forever* (1995), would retain some of the actors and sets from Burton's films, but ultimately change the style and tone of the series to fit more in line with the studio's family-orientated mandate. Gone was Burton's dark, gothic architecture of Gotham City, to be replaced with the MTV-style bright neon of Schumacher's depiction, bringing with it a Batman with a more West-esque demeanour and shinier Batsuit. Despite a mixed critical reception, *Batman Forever* was a roaring success at the box office, becoming the second-highest grossing film of 1995 (second only to *Toy Story),* and convincing Warner Bros. to double down on the franchise's new direction for the next sequel.

Shortly following the release of *Forever,* Schumacher began work on a sequel. His original idea was to bring the franchise back to its darker roots, and he had discussions with the studio about doing an adaptation of Frank Miller's masterpiece, *Batman: Year One* (1987-1988), as a prequel to the previous films. Warner Bros. turned down this idea and instructed Schumacher to make a film more in line with *Forever,* and, more importantly, a film from which they could sell plenty of merchandise and toys. The result was arguably the worst superhero film ever made, and perhaps even one of the worst films ever. *Batman & Robin* was deservedly bashed upon release by the critics, who all remarked how far the franchise had fallen since the glory days of Burton and that the cheesy camp spectacle of the film had set the Batman character back over thirty years to how he was perceived during the West era. Financially the film fared no better, becoming (even to this day) the lowest grossing entry in the film series. And with the Batman fans, the film is seen as a black mark in the history of their beloved character. The failure of *Batman & Robin* would force the franchise into a hibernation that would last eight years, during which time Warner Bros.' scrambled to figure out what to do with the character. After going through several directors, screenwriters, scripts and concepts, the studio settled on visionary director Christopher Nolan, a decision that has left a legacy still felt within the cinematic landscape to this day. But the journey from the lows of *Batman & Robin* to the heights of Nolan's *Batman Begins* (2005) and his "Dark Knight Trilogy" (2005-2012) was a long one, with many twists and turns, with more than a few interesting sequel ideas lost along the way.

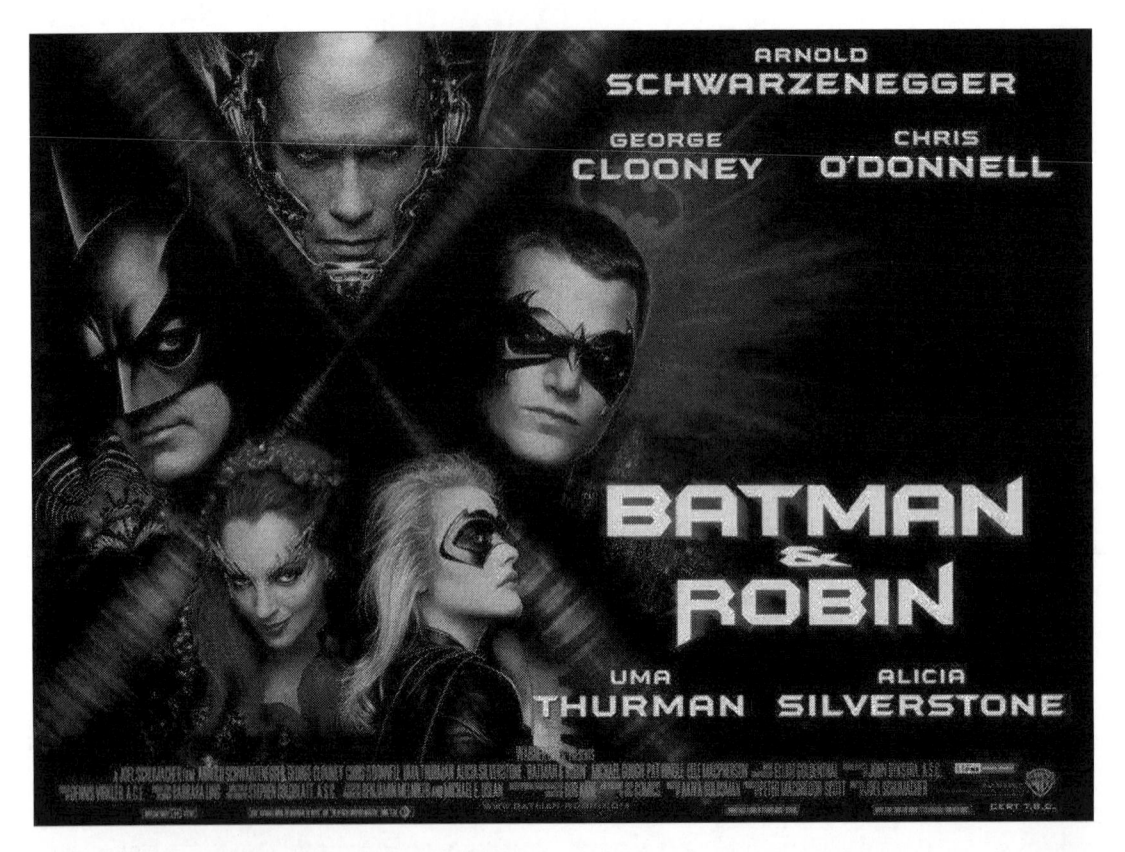

Before *Batman & Robin*'s release, Schumacher had begun work on a fifth film, tentatively titled *Batman Unchained* (or *Batman Triumphant*), with the script being written by screenwriter Mark Protosevich. The cast from the previous films were signed on to return, including George Clooney as Batman and Chris O'Donnell as Robin, along with rapper Coolio as villain The Scarecrow (although Schumacher had given some consideration to replacing him with Nicolas Cage), and both Madonna and Courtney Love reached out to about playing Harley Quinn. Having given in to studio demands to make his last two Batman films more kid-friendly, Schumacher now fully intended to have his next Batman adventure be more in line with the depiction of the Batman character both in the comics and in Burton's films, as he had "envisioned a psychologically complex take on the character, something he said he wanted to do with his *Batman Forever* follow-up before getting push back from the studio" (*The Hollywood Reporter*, 2015). The main theme of Protosevich's script dealt with Batman learning to conquer his fear and confronting the demons of his past. The film's main villains, Harley and Scarecrow, each hated a different aspect of the title hero, as Harley hated Batman as he killed her father, The Joker, in the first film, while Scarecrow hated Bruce Wayne. The two villains would join forces against the Dark Knight. They would drive him insane, sending him to Arkham Asylum, culminating in "an ambitious, all-star sequence that would have seen a hallucinating Batman face the demons of his past, where he is put on trial by the franchise's previous villains" (*The Hollywood Reporter*, 2015). The studio wanted cameos from Danny DeVito as The Penguin, Michelle Pfeiffer as Catwoman, Tommy Lee Jones as Two-Face and Jim Carrey as The Riddler, with these appearances "all leading to a final confrontation with the man himself: Jack Nicholson's Joker" (Protovesich, *The Hollywood Reporter*, 2015), a sequence which would have undoubtedly been the most expensive aspect of the entire movie, as well tying the entire franchise together by having characters from both Burton and Schumacher's tenures as director appear. However, despite how intriguing Schumacher and Protvesich's vision for the film was, it was never meant to be, as the enormous failure of *Batman & Robin* meant that once again Warner Bros. was searching for a new direction in which to take the franchise as the "Joel Schumacher-driven Batman train was taken off the rails" (Protovesich, *The Hollywood Reporter*, 2015).

Warner Bros. passed the project on to screenwriters Lee Shapiro and Stephen Wise, whose story treatment, titled *Batman: DarKnight,* was envisioned as a continuation of the Burton / Schumacher series, with both Clooney and O'Donnell still tapped to reprise their roles. Speaking in 2015, Shapiro remarked that his script was "a direct answer to the last movie. Everything we were doing was 'What did they do? Let's not do that'" (*The Hollywood Reporter*, 2015). The story was very horror-themed, with a lot more gruesome violence than in the previous films. Robin would become the central character of the story, as Batman had spent years living as a recluse following a tragedy in Gotham City. While in college, Robin would meet Jonathan Crane (The Scarecrow) who suffers from a skin disease that stops him from feeling physical pain. Shapiro would further elaborate on his characterisation of Crane, saying that his "sense of touch is off, so it's heightened his other senses, and it's made him like a living scarecrow. He gets physically scarred during a confrontation with Man-Bat, and that scarring of his face becomes his mask... His face becomes the Scarecrow mask" (*The Hollywood Reporter*, 2015). Crane would kidnap Robin and conduct horrific experiments on him at Arkham Asylum, causing Batman to re-emerge in order to save his friend. Man-Bat would also serve as a secondary villain. The film was also seen as the beginning of a new Batman trilogy, as the script included many Easter eggs that were planted to set up future sequels. This included a scene during a riot in Arkham in which the psychiatrist Harleen Quinzel becomes injured, beginning a transformation into Harley Quinn that would be explored in the second film. Plans for the third film included Robin's transition into the solo vigilante Nightwing, while filling the role of the film's villains would be Killer Croc and Clayface. Although the script was finished relatively quickly, it would sit at the studio for two years, during which time Shapiro and Wise would attempt to entice the studio by sending them figurines of Man-Bat and Scarecrow. This would all be in vain, however, as when Jeff Robinov took over control of the Batman franchise in 2001 he decided against moving forward with not only the script, but with the idea of making a continuation of the Burton / Schumacher series. As Wise would later state: "That was where the term 'reboot' came from. They basically wanted to start over" (*The Hollywood Reporter*, 2015).

The first filmmaker that Robinov sought after for his reinvention of Batman was acclaimed director Darren Aronofsky, who had just shot to success with *Requiem for a Dream*. Aronofsky, like Schumacher had before him, wished to make an adaptation of Miller's *Batman: Year One*. However, his ideas for the story were quite different to the source material, which Miller elaborated on by saying that he "really had specific ideas about the character and which way to take it. I was surprised at the time, because I tend to be the more radical of any team that I'm on, but it was Darren who was more radical than I was. I said 'Darren, would you be willing to be more faithful to the comics?' and he was ready to rip the eyes out of them. We just had a wonderful time bashing around the story every which way and developing these characters" (*The Hollywood Reporter*, 2015). In Aronofsky's script, Bruce Wayne would reject his inheritance, not wanting to claim it until he had proven himself, as he wanted to "live on the streets he was going to defend" (Miller, *The Hollywood Reporter*, 2015). After this self-imposed exile, Wayne would then use his fortune to travel the world, honing his crime-fighting and detective skills, before returning to Gotham and taking the mantle of The Batman. Like *Year One,* the story would also revolve around the character of Commissioner James Gordon, who juggles his family life with his fight against the corruption in the Gotham City Police Department. As in the comic, when Batman saves Gordon's son from Gotham's top crime boss, Don Carmine Falcone, they form an alliance to defend Gotham. The screenplay that Miller and Aronofsky turned in to the studio was powerful, violent and, most importantly, R-rated. This was a far cry from what Warner Bros. was looking for, as they wished for the franchise to remain as family-friendly as possible. Miller recalls the negative reaction that the script got from the studio, claiming that he "heard a shriek of terror at first. They were shocked at how bold it was..." (*The Hollywood Reporter*, 2015). The studio rejected the script and looked at other ideas for the franchise.

While Batman, and DC superheroes in general, were languishing at the cinema, they were having great success on television through the various properties of the "DC Animated Universe" (1992-2006), a collection of interconnected animated programs that began in 1992 with the Bruce Timm's seminal *Batman: The Animated Series* (1992-1995). Of all these programs, perhaps the most interesting was *Batman Beyond* (1999-2002), a show set in the not-too-distant future that followed an elderly Bruce Wayne as he trained and guided the new Batman, Terry McGinnis. Paul Dini, who had worked on the various series in the DCAU, was brought in to work on a script for a film adaptation of *Beyond,* along with screenwriter Alan Burnett. Speaking about the script, Dini remarked that it "didn't quite have the fantastic, futuristic edge. It was a little bit of an amalgam of the animated show and traditional Batman comics. There was a little bit of *The Dark Knight,* there was a little bit of contemporary comics" (*The Hollywood Reporter*, 2015). Unfortunately, the script failed to garner much interest from the studio, and they decided to focus on another high concept idea for the next film.

While Batman and Superman had crossed paths many times over the decades in the comics and in animation, they had never met face-to-face on the big screen. The Superman franchise had been stagnant since 1987, after the release of *Superman IV: The Quest for Peace,* which, much like *Batman & Robin,* was met with universal scorn from critics and fans alike. Although there were plans for Christopher Reeve to return as Superman as late as 1990, it never came to be, and the Superman franchise would remain in development hell for the better part of two decades, with one of the most infamous attempts to restart the series coming in the form of Tim Burton's unmade *Superman Lives,* which would have starred Nicolas Cage as Superman. With both franchises on ice, Warner Bros. made plans to combine the two in a project tentatively titled *Batman Vs. Superman. Se7en* writer Andrew Kevin Walker was brought in to write the script, alongside Akiva Goldsman, while Wolfgang Petersen, fresh off his success with *The Perfect Storm* (1999), was offered the director's chair. The script would later be leaked online in full, giving as the chance to see what the story for this ambitious crossover would have entailed. The story opened at the wedding of Bruce Wayne – with Clark Kent as his best man – having been retired as Batman for five years. Wayne's wife is killed while they are on honeymoon, with the presumed dead Joker as the prime suspect behind it. Lois Lane has divorced Clark, leading him to return to his home town of Smallville to rekindle his romance with high school sweetheart Lana Lang. Batman storms through the criminal underworld in search of Joker, and discovers the Joker has been working with Lex Luthor the entire time, even hiring an actress to play his wife. Their plan brings Batman and Superman into conflict with each other, and the two comic titans would battle to a stalemate, before inevitably teaming up to take down the two villains. The main theme of the film would explore the dual identity of the superhero, and that superheroes use alter-egos so that they can separate themselves from the acts that they commit as vigilantes. Sam Dickerman, who headed Petersen's production company, urged Walker to consider the material seriously, as Walker would later divulge that Dickerman "said 'lets write this to be a movie that gets considered for an Academy Award.' It's not supposed to be some kind of disposable pop culture. We wanted to take the characters seriously" (*The Hollywood Reporter*, 2015). When the events of September 11th 2001 took place it effected the film's development, as it was felt that society needed a role model like Superman more than ever. It also meant that some changes had to be made to the script as there "was a terrorist event in the screenplay that took on an entirely different timbre", and it also effected how the filmmakers perceived the characters of Batman and Superman as "before 9/11, Batman was always the cooler, cynical Dark Knight character and Superman, to a certain extent, was regarded as a little more wholesome, a little more old fashioned and at certain points wasn't as admired as a character. Post 9/11, Superman became much more what people really wanted and needed in a big way" (Walker, *The Hollywood Reporter*, 2015). While the film was ambitious in both its scope and themes, Warner Bros. ultimately decided it best to keep their Batman and Superman franchises separate for the time being, and the two icons would not meet on the silver screen until 2016 in Zack Snyder's *Batman v Superman: Dawn of Justice.*

In 2003, Warner Bros. hired Christopher Nolan, who had risen to fame following his acclaimed film *Memento* (2000), to develop their Batman reboot. Nolan would work on the script with David S. Goyer, a renowned comic book writer that had recently completed work on Marvel's *Blade* trilogy (1998-2004). Speaking on why he decided to take the project, Nolan stated that he wanted to do the "origins of the character, which is a story that's never been told before", further elaborating that "the world of Batman is that of grounded reality. It is a recognisable, contemporary reality against which an extraordinary heroic figure rises" (Nolan, *Wikipedia*). Nolan saw the Burton / Schumacher films as "exercises in style rather than drama" (Nolan, *Wikipedia*), and he instead decided to look to Richard Donner's iconic *Superman* (1978) for inspiration, such as its use of an all-star cast to lend the film credibility. Nolan and Goyer saw Batman as a romantic character, and envisioned their film as an epic akin to *Lawrence of Arabia* (1962). They also used various comic book source materials for inspiration, such as *The Man Who Falls,* which depicted Bruce's training and travels around the world, as well as *The Long Halloween* and *Year One,* from which they used the ideas of Gotham's criminal underworld and corruption. For the tone and pacing for the movie, Nolan looked to the 1933 classic *King Kong,* which slowly builds up to the appearance of the film's titular character, much like how Nolan masterfully builds up to Bruce Wayne's first appearance as Batman. The look of the film would also be a drastic departure from the looks of both Burton and Schumacher's films, as Nolan's Gotham used location shooting in Chicago and New York City to give Gotham a modern, realistic look, with Nolan saying that his main inspiration for Gotham's design came from Ridley Scott's 1982 masterpiece, *Blade Runner*. Adding to all of this was the masterful score produced by Hans Zimmer and James Newton Howard, with Zimmer doing the Batman themes while Howard covered the themes for Bruce Wayne. To avoid comparisons to Elfman's iconic scores for the Burton films, Zimmer used a mixture of orchestra and electronic music, creating a soundtrack that now rivals Elfman's as the definitive Batman theme. Adding to this was the film's ensemble cast, which included Christian Bale as Batman, Michael Caine as Alfred Pennyworth, Morgan Freeman as Lucius Fox, Liam Neeson as Ra's al Ghul, Gary Oldman as Commissioner Gordon and Cillian Murphy as The Scarecrow, all of which give stellar performances.

All of these elements combined to create *Batman Begins* (2005), a film that not only brought Batman back to the big screen in explosive fashion, but also changed how both Hollywood and society viewed superhero cinema. Critics and fans alike lavished the film with praise, including famed critic Roger Ebert who remarked in his review of the film that it was the "Batman movie I've been waiting for, more correctly, this is the movie I did not realise I was waiting for" (Ebert, 2005). Almost immediately, critics and analysts began to discuss the themes of the film. Comic book writer Danny Fingeroth argued that one of the film's strongest themes is Wayne's search for a strong father figure, musing that "Alfred is a good father figure that Bruce comes to depend on. Bruce's real father died before Bruce could establish an adult relationship, and Liam Neeson's Ducard is stern and demanding, didactic and challenging, but not a father figure with any sympathy. Morgan Freeman's Lucius is cool and imperturbable, another steady anchor in Bruce's life. If Bruce is anyone's son, he is Alfred's" (Fingeroth, *Wikipedia*). Blogger Mark Fisher would reiterate Fingeroth's ideas, saying that Bruce's search for justice requires him to learn from a father figure, and that Thomas Wayne and Ra's al Ghul were the counterpoints to this idea. Fear was also said to be a very important theme in the movie, seen most obviously through the character of Scarecrow, who uses fear as a weapon against his enemies. Nolan has described the film as the story of "a person who would confront his innermost fears and attempt to become it" (Nolan, *Wikipedia*), as Wayne uses his fear of bats to create his Batman persona. The theme of fear is also further intensified by Zimmer's score, which often "eschews traditional heroic themes" (*Wikipedia*). These themes would give the film a sense of intellectual importance, and established the superhero genre as one that could discuss ideas and concepts about our society – a far cry from the camp, cheese-fest of 1997.

The impact that *Batman Begins* had on both the superhero genre and cinema itself cannot be understated. It introduced the notion of a reboot, which is the idea that a franchise or series can be started over from scratch when a change is needed, which has become somewhat of an overused Hollywood trope over the last decade and a half, often with the property being rebooted given a dark and gritty makeover, such as *The Amazing Spider-man* (2012) and *Robocop* (2014). Many filmmakers have been quoted as claiming Nolan and *Batman Begins* as their inspiration, such as Jon Favreau, who began the box-office juggernaut Marvel Cinematic Universe in 2008 with the fantastic *Iron Man*. Head of Marvel Studios Kevin Feige would even say that "Chris Nolan's Batman is the greatest thing that happened to superhero films because it bolstered everything" (*Wikipedia*). When Warner Bros. rebooted the Superman franchise in 2013 with Zack Snyder's *Man of Steel,* Nolan was brought on as producer and creative consultant, and the film would adhere very closely to the aesthetic and ideals Nolan had used for Batman, with Snyder going on to create his own version of Batman for the film's sequel, *Batman v Superman: Dawn of Justice,* one which is even darker and more violent than Nolan's own interpretation. The film was also the inspiration for many films outside of the superhero genre, such as Damon Lindelof's 2009 *Star Trek* reboot, Sam Mendes' James Bond epic *Skyfall* (2012), Gareth Edwards' 2014 *Godzilla* remake and even the video game *God of War* (2018).

This leads me to the conclusion that despite the fact that 1997's *Batman & Robin* derailed the Batman franchise and set back the superhero film genre quite a few years, its place in cinematic history is of immense importance. Without that film's enormous failure, Warner Bros. may not have decided to take the Batman franchise down a different path, and the massive influence that Nolan's *Batman Begins* has had on both cinema and pop culture may not have happened. I don't know what everyone else may feel, but as a fan, I'll gladly take that exchange.

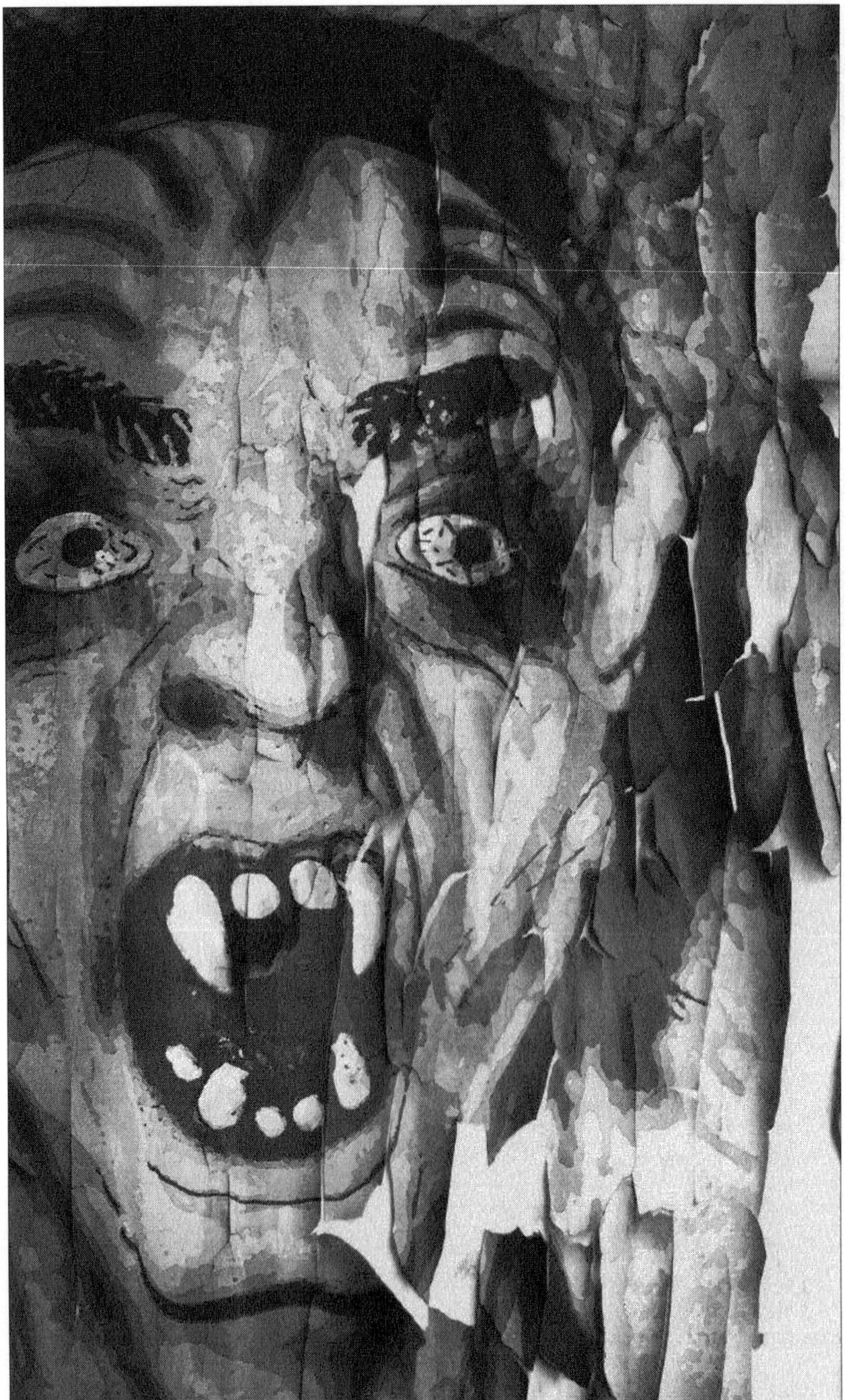

AVPR: ALIENS VS PREDATOR – REQUIEM: THE MOST UNDERRATED MOVIE OF THEM ALL

Owen Quinn

SO HERE WE go again in the ongoing debate between me and my buddy as to what is good and not so good in this sci-fi and horror world we love so much.

We both love the *Aliens* and *Predator* franchises (mostly, yes I'm looking at you *Covenant* and *The Predator*) but the much anticipated crossovers are not held in the high regard they should be. I like the first one because anything with Lance Henriksen in it I love anyway but the second is usually dismissed as not very good. For the purposes of this article that's the politest language I can use but the words of my buddy haunt me as I type those prophetic words. You know who you are you close-minded heathens.

But I disagree completely. It's a great movie!

AVP – Requiem is by far the most realistic, gritty and terrifying of all the movies featuring our beloved Xenomorphs and Predators. Everything about these creatures, especially the Xenomorphs, is based on nightmares and

Requiem takes full advantage of this. The bottom line is the question, what would happen if the Aliens reached Earth? The Predators are not a threat anywhere in the same league as the Xenomorphs because they operate on a hunter's code of honour. Needless killing is not in their nature; the hunt is everything. The Xenomorphs are a different kettle of fish. There is no reasoning with them. They are driven by one instinct and one instinct only; to take as many hosts as possible to breed for their Queen. They have no conscience, no morals, no reasoning except to kill and gather hosts. They are stealthy and formidable enemies, which is one of the reasons the Predators chose them to hunt. Earth had been used as a breeding ground by the Predators in the past and kept a Queen and her eggs in stasis in controlled environments for the purpose of controlled hunts. The one scene that does stand out for me in the first movie is the one where hundreds of the Xenomorphs swarm from a pyramid temple. Even the Predators knew this was a doomsday situation and choose to detonate one of their nukes to stop the infestation. That very scene gripped the fanboy in me because even in *Aliens* we didn't see so many of these creatures in a mass attack. Right there I wondered what would happen if they arrived on modern day Earth.

Shane Salemo obviously thought the same thing because *Requiem* was born.

The greatest enemy is the one you don't know exists, so if these creatures got a hold on Earth, the consequences would be devastating. We know the company has wanted embryos for biological warfare and we also know Ripley managed to stop the Aliens getting to Earth at the climax of *Alien: Resurrection*, so the very thought of these things walking our streets is the very stuff nightmares are made of.

This is what makes *Requiem* absolutely riveting stuff. The writer has taken the fear factor that is the Xenomorphs and amplified it tenfold against the background of the town of Gunnison.

The first clever thing they did was cast no big names. Well, I had never heard or seen any of them, which added to the realism of it for me. Nobody ran about muscle bound or armed to the teeth with every gadget the military had to give. There were no prisoners fuelled by killer instincts or cloned hybrids fighting alongside mercenaries.

Every last person is an ordinary citizen, a cast of everyday Joe and Josephine Bloggs that we would know in our own lives. The waitress, the bad boy, the fighting brothers, old friends you no longer connect with, cute kids, and the homeless people you walk by in the streets. There is nobody with super powers or special skills that will help them kill monsters. The biggest struggle these people face is paying the bills and keeping a roof over their family's heads.

When the waitress, Carrie, is pinned by the Predalien and impregnated it is heartbreaking, especially when her body is found. Real life murder of someone as innocent and harmless as Carrie would be a shock to the system if you heard it reported on the news, but her death here is much more tragic because of the nature of it.

Aside from a few instances, the people have normal names we are again familiar with in real life. We meet Kelly, Robert, David, Molly, Carrie, Tom and Johnny, to name but a few. I personally know people with these names, some of them friends of mine. On a psychological level this is where the movie connects with us. Some of us have been waiters or waitresses. There are no jobs here out of the ordinary and no spaceships to work on. Everything is relatable to the audience consciously and subconsciously.

Even the Predators have underestimated the immensity of the threat the Xenomorphs pose to this town, which is a great tragedy. They have bred faster than expected and now literally control the town.

Right from the get-go this movie has balls and capitalises on part of the human psyche we preach in real life. A huge part of a town's populace consists of children. We saw Newt stay alive despite a Xenomorph infestation in *Aliens*. In a deleted scene we see her brother Timmy with a facehugger wrapped around him, but it doesn't follow through to the chest-bursting part. In *Requiem* there is no such shying away from the reality of an alien invasion. Kids are very much at the forefront of the horror here, in scenes I never thought they would be brave enough to do.

There are so many nightmare scenes that have stayed with me to this day. Salemo goes for it to show what would happen, warts and all, if Aliens infested a town. Even if the Aliens landed in a city it would have made no difference. The same things would have happened. Within minutes of the movie starting we have a little boy not only see his father's arm fall off in an acid burn, but attacked by a facehugger. The scene is beautifully done and brimming with tension with that little sound the kid makes as the hugger wraps round his face hitting your senses like a hammer. It is subtle but there is no adult watching this scene did not instinctively want to help the kid.

As a parent you see your own child which kicks our protective natures into full throttle. But worse is to come as the kid gains consciousness only to see his father die as his chest explodes. Moments later the little boy suffers the same fate and again it is all in the reaction of the child actor. The second he clutches his chest we know what is coming, and again that sticks in our heads because we picture our own kids in danger.

But it just escalates from there. Most movies that feature a kid dying under a supernatural or unnatural threat will end it there but not *Requiem*.

We tell our kids that there are no such things as monsters. We check under the bed and in the closet to prove to them there is no scary monster there before they will even think of going to sleep. It's a double-edged sword because as parents we fear something happening to our children. One of the most vulnerable times for all of us is when we are asleep. We lock the doors and windows, double checking until we feel comfortable to go to sleep. That's why we leave the door to our children's rooms ajar, so we can hear them in distress and leap straight away to protect them. Our homes are our castles and nothing should ever break that.

In the next shocking scene that is literally the stuff of nightmares, little Molly O'Brien's bedroom is invaded when a Xenomorph smashes through her window and kills her father. So much for the assurance that there is no such thing as monsters. Molly manages to survive the apocalyptic ending along with her mother Kelly. God knows what those images of her father dying, the monster smashing its way into her room and the mass slaughter will do to her as the years pass. It's a nice touch, because just because the movie ends for us doesn't mean those characters end. Ripley herself is a good example of this.

What all great horror movies do is take what we consider as normality and twist it into something abhorrent and terrifying to the point we will never look at it the same way again. The swimming pool scene comes to mind. How many times as children did we think that there might be a shark or monster under the water? As a parent I often played at monster going underwater and grabbing my kid in mock scares. It's a scare that ends in laughter and good memories. In *Requiem* it ends in a chlorine-soaked death.

We all see hospitals as places of safety where usually our loved ones go to heal. Even if they do die in hospital they are treated with respect and dignity. However Salemo screws this completely in a way I again never saw coming.

The sight of multiple Xenomorphs swarming all over the hospital exterior is a shocker. But the most shocking scene for me and the one that has stuck with me all these years more than any other horror movie is the maternity ward.

I remember very clearly the moment the Predalien enters the room full of mothers in labour. I thought that when it had seen this it would withdraw and leave this sacred happy moment. But when it begins to attack and impregnate every last one of them my jaw hit the floor. Being a father and having gone through the labour process with my wife, it really struck a cord with me. I said at the start of this that nothing was sacred and this movie has balls to go all the way with the horrors of Xenomorphs. This epitomises it for me. My morals and sense of reasoning double stepped me here because I thought it would have shown mercy like a Predator would do, but to be kicked in the balls like that should have told me that this is not going to end well. At that point I would have happily kicked the crap out of the first smiling extraterrestrial I met on the way out of the cinema.

If anything, this movie shows that no matter what there is hope too, as humans will prevail somehow against the odds and fight to live another day through the characters of Kelly, Molly, Ricky and Dallas. They are the lone survivors of the massacre. Gunnison's last remaining citizens are tricked to go to the town centre and die at the hands of the government's final solution. In reality the government killing its own citizens is unbelievable but in this situation understandable. Add to that this is not the first time we have seen this in movies, for example *Outbreak* and *The Crazies* remake. It is a desperate final solution but there is no other option. It does follow the pattern of all the other movies with the entire cast, bar a few, dead at the hands of either Aliens or Predators.

Requiem gives us the most realistic view of a Xenomorph infestation. There is no happy ending and everyone, from the young to the old, is a potential host for the embryos. It speaks to our most basic instincts as humans and more importantly as parents on levels that shock us with images that stick with you. I have no doubt that even if you hate the movie and send me gifs with *Simpsons* characters typing "Worst movie ever", those images pop into your mind when you think of *AVP – Requiem*.

So with all this in mind, the next time you happen to come across the movie on a night you have nothing else to watch, give it a second chance. You just might find it's a much richer and layered movie than you first thought.

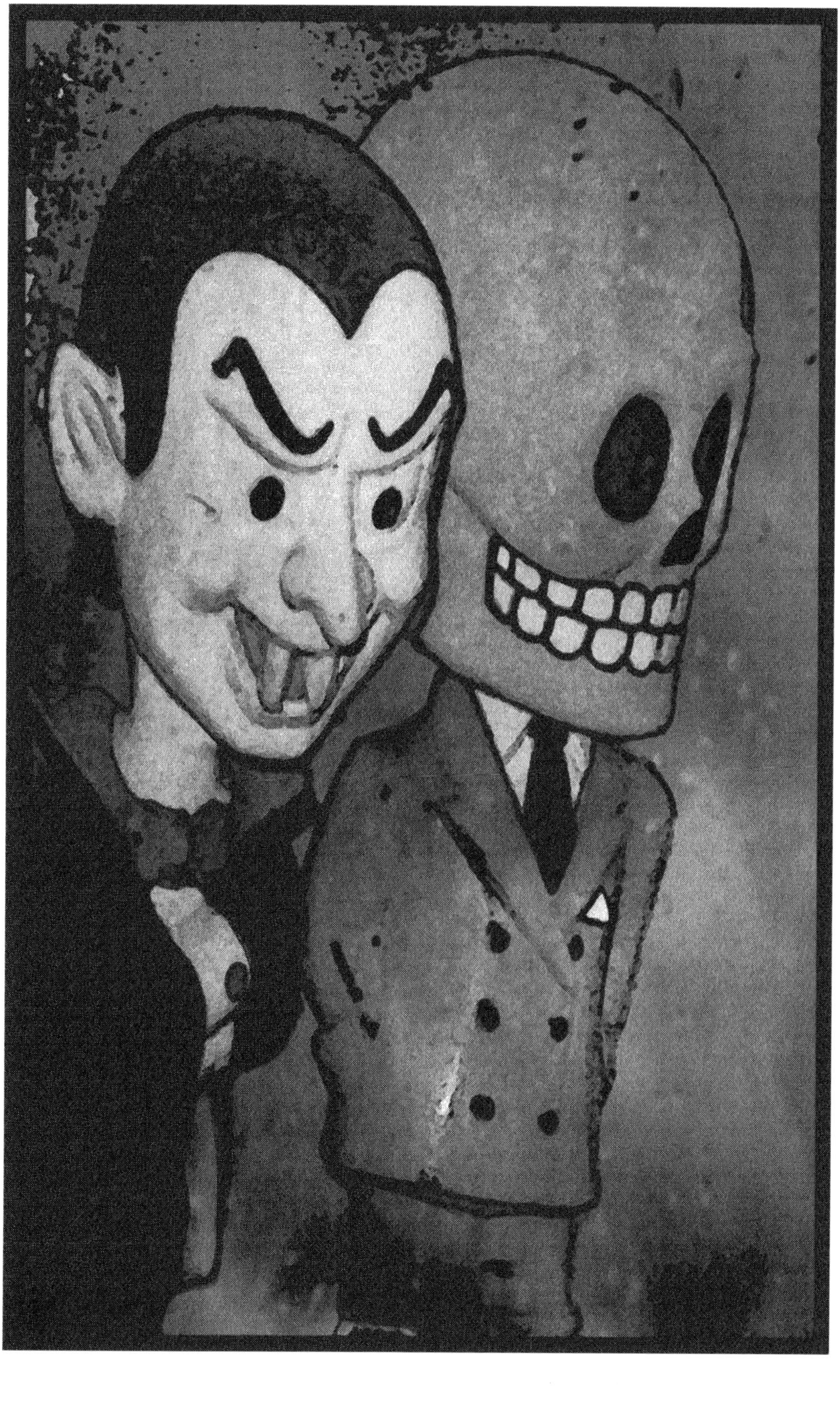

THE FAMILY ARE NOT WHAT THEY SEEM: A LOOK AT THE DOMESTIC HORROR OF *TWIN PEAKS: FIRE WALK WITH ME* (1992)

Michael Campbell

*** Warning: Contains major spoilers for both *Twin Peaks* and *Twin Peaks: Fire Walk With Me* ***

THOSE OF US who encountered David Lynch and Mark Frost's *Twin Peaks* many years ago, were introduced into a world of coffee, pie, murder and surrealism the likes of which few had ever encountered before in episodic television. A small-town drama with a murder-mystery occurring at the centre, *Twin Peaks* was launched in 1990, running until the following year, and its second season. It would spawn a 1992 movie prequel, and a third series memorably in 2017. Initially, the ABC show was equal measures teen romance and investigative crime drama, melded with an off-kilter soap opera sensibility. That cocktail alone is either a recommendation or a warning, depending on individual taste!

It's difficult to quickly emphasise its impact. This wasn't just a TV broadcast that broke the mould, it was a cultural phenomenon and an unlikely favourite within the conciousness of the general public. Today, "event" television that provides networks' much desired "water-cooler" talk is commonplace, be it through creative and brilliantly realised drama such as *The Sopranos*, or shows like *Game of Thrones*, which managed to enter into the everyday imagination of casual audiences, these dramatic shows are churned out a remarkable rate, sometimes to a stunning standard. Indeed, the advent of Netflix and other streaming platforms, has in recent years increased the appeal of this format for not just audiences, but for filmmakers.

In its day however, the notion that an Oscar-nominated director the calibre of Lynch would then switch to television work to fulfil his artistic ambitions, was incredibly unusual. Upon considering the impact it had too, the fact that a programme about a father (Leland Palmer, played by Ray Wise) murdering his daughter in astonishing circumstances became so beloved, was just as bizarre.

Twin Peaks was a revelation that has been adored over the years, so much so that the 2017 third season, "The Return", proved a troublesome experience for some. While lauded by the majority, its stubborn aesthetic was entirely a thing onto itself, that sometimes looked back upon the familiar *Twin Peaks* but more often felt uncomfortably different.

Fire Walk With Me, directed by Lynch and released in 1992, remains an even rougher ride. Famously booed in loutish fashion by sections of the Cannes press, it is nonetheless quintessential Lynch. Over the years, whatever tale or characters he has turned his eye to depicting have been bathed in similar ingredients. *FWWM* stands apart as the dark side of *Twin Peaks*' mythology, and is perhaps the most nightmarish of all the director's works, but it's far from his only effort to bring the horror home.

Trial By Fire

Even for fans of the TV show, a series that opened with the focal point of Laura Palmer's (Sheryl Lee) corpse being discovered, the film has proven to be a difficult experience. Shorn of the comedy that proliferates throughout the series and the luxury of enjoying the idiosyncrasies of its likeable cast, *Fire Walk With Me* is a much more downbeat experience. There's also a natural disconnect, as the demands of a serial production that requires certain concessions in terms of pacing and story, ensured more a tangible structure than with this movie. For many viewers, *Fire Walk With Me* is a struggle. Obtuse, bizarre, and outright impenetrable at points. There are visions of angels, white horses, masked children, symbolic FBI codes in the form of dance routines, sleazy, repugnant nudity, and of course, David Bowie. Even in relation to the show, that's a lot of weird in one place. The viewer's attention being diverted for just a moment could lead to all sorts of confusion. It's lengthy, it's suffocating... it's hostile. It's also an entirely different experience for those versed in the *Twin Peaks* universe and those encountering it for the first time.

There is a linear story at play within the film, even if it is shrouded in bizarre imagery, horrifying sounds, and baffling incident. Understanding the various motifs and nods to the series' mythology certainly requires further knowledge beyond the self-contained running time. However, these aspects are not a requirement in order to be terrified by the actual plot and the film's central thrust.

It is a very different experience for the series' fans, and one no less oppressive. All the comforts of creamy coffee and sumptuous pie, of the wholesome faces and sense of community are ripped away. At one point we literally descend into a similar town (Deer Meadow), which is like an evil clone of Twin Peaks. Perhaps it has a less rank layer underneath, but on the surface, it's cold and unappealing. The unfriendly diner staff are complimented by their gross clientèle, and police force whose manner FBI agent Dale Cooper (Kyle McLachlan) would be traumatised by. It's terrifying, and brilliant. But it isn't frightening just because of the upsetting sound design in the filthy nightclub scenes, or the haunting, brilliantly realised visions that Laura has. It isn't even the supernatural aspects of the Bob spirit possessing Leland, which is explicitly realised. What makes *FWWM* very much a blistering, raw horror film, is in the depiction of child abuse.

The real companion piece to the movie, is Jennifer Chamber Lynch's gob-smacking novel, *The Secret Diary of Laura Palmer*. It is consistently unpleasant and yet dream-like. It's immediate and absorbing, offering an unfiltered view into the psyche of the show's entire heart. It's heartbreaking watching a girl self-destruct in her own words, especially as she appears unaware of the nature of what will come, but increasingly gives the impression of being aware that something bad is impending. It's this sense of dread that lends both the book, and *Fire Walk With Me*, nauseating momentum.

One of the most powerful moments in the entire *Twin Peaks* repertoire, occurs during *FWWM* when Laura flees her own house, cowering in the garden. Having entered her bedroom, she is confronted by her abuser, Bob, lurking in plain sight, behind the dresser. Following a horrific, guttural scream, she launches herself straight out of the house and hides. While cowering in terror, she witnesses a figure leaving – her abuser... her father, Leland.

"No... not him...no no... it's not him, it's not him..." she repeats to herself... panic-stricken.

Towards the end of the film, the image of Leland stomping through the night is vivid and deeply disturbing, harking back to the traumatic episode of the show in which he was revealed as the killer. Dragging Laura through the woods alongside another unfortunate victim, Leland is freakishly imposing, physically even – arguably for the first time – as he's illuminated in sinister fashion by a stark light from the moon.

This is very similar in effect to the horrific murder of Laura's older cousin Maddy from season two, which simultaneously revealed the mystery, and killed off a key character. Maddy runs out of the frame, seemingly to meet her doom off-camera, before a scrap leads to Leland dragging her back into the picture. She is then cornered in the living room, and the spinning camera is positioned in a manner that traps the viewer with her. It's one of the most horrendous moments in television history. It's also one of the most cinematic in the show's deck, occurring in the episode "Lonely Souls". Directed by Lynch himself, it's a searing reminder of the ugly side of both his output, and the show itself. His taking the reigns for one of the most aesthetically accomplished moments in the show cannot be considered a coincidence, nor can the scene's similarities to many that it echoes in the film.

Interestingly, the deaths of Laura and Maddy are both similar in effect, but Laura's occurs in a grimy, abandoned train boxcar, whereas her cousin is butchered in the Palmer family home. Maddy's death hits hard in the series, not just because she was (as played by Sheryl Lee who also played Laura) an endearing pseudo-resurrection of the Laura character, but also because the circumstances revealed that it was indeed Leland who was the perpetrator. The horror coming home is because Leland has been a vessel for evil to enter into his household. With *FWWM*, regardless of evil spirits, or any other supernatural connotations, the horror is so close because of his relationship with his daughter. The movie depicts Leland attempting to construct a sordid orgy involving young girls – but he only baulks because he realises one of the number will be Laura. In the moments in which he is possessed by Bob, that restraint and control is no longer there. However, the outcome is the same either way, he is still a father committing inconceivably unforgivable acts.

Removed from the context of the show, *FWWM*'s depiction of Bob can be taken in a much less supernatural vein than with those in the series, despite the numerous references made. The existence of Bob could be perceived as a coping mechanism rather than a literal possession within the context of the movie. Even the hallucinatory imagery could be explained as part of the drug abuse. Remember, Laura isn't just abused by her father, but by her boyfriend – who facilitates her hard-drug use – and by the other scumbags she encounters, who encourage her to sell her body, her looks, and enable her to succumb to all of her combined vices.

Leland's rage comes across in the film as all too real, and Bob could also be seen as a literal, horrible manifestation of his dark side, or a multiple personality of Leland. Within any interpretation though, it's genuinely horrible, uncomfortable stuff, regardless of one's familiarity with the material, which is what makes it one of the most effective and disturbing horror movies in memory.

Obviously, *Fire Walk With Me* depicts abuse and home-bound horrors in a much more graphic, extreme fashion than the television show, in a manner that places it alongside Lynch's later *Lost Highway*. The sleaze and vile aura that infiltrates an otherwise sleepy town isn't limited to Leland and Laura Palmer however. Within the show, one of the central storylines is the abusive relationship that Shelly (Madchen Amick) suffers at the hands her of husband, Leo (Eric Da Re). Shelly herself is having an affair with Bobby (Dana Ashbrook) – understandable, given the circumstances, but a secret nonetheless. Bobby himself is a drug dealer, which shatters the ideal family set-up as the son of Garland Briggs, a upstanding Air Force Major. Laura's mother meanwhile, eventually harbours an alcohol addiction – another coping mechanism – (though is also initially being drugged by Leland), while as we see in Jennifer Lynch's novel, her cousin Maddy is a key figure in the very notion of concealment becoming a daily part of Laura's duel personality.

Even in the more likeable characters, there's a hidden layer. One of the most immediately sympathetic figures, Ed Hurley (Everett McGill), is having an affair with Norma (the late, great Peggy Lipton), behind the back of his wife Nadine (Wendy Robie), whose eye he accidentally shot out on their honeymoon!

The Night He Came Home

This overwhelming sense of a poison infiltrating a wholesome exterior is absolutely a vital part of David Lynch's extraordinary body of work. Domestic horror is nothing new to him, and prior to *Fire Walk With Me*, it was always something that bubbled under the surface, exploding in terrible incidents.

1986's *Blue Velvet* famously found the director focusing on a suburban murder-mystery that exposed the considerable cracks beneath a seemingly perfect, picket fence-lined surface. A body part found in a pristine-lawn paradise causes wide-eyed young people to be exposed to unfathomably seedy characters in a deeply uncomfortable but stunning psycho-sexual noir. Grimy undercurrents have never been more literal in Lynch's oeuvre, than in the opening moments in which his camera literally plunges through a grassy surface into a writhing mass of bugs underneath.

Lynch himself said in an interview last year, *"I don't like going out anyway. I like to stay at home."* But despite clinging to that safety net and finding comfort in the home, he has also clearly demonstrated that he finds more terrifying than anything else, the invasion of that sanctuary.

In 1997, Lynch delivered his closest relation to *FWWM*, in the guise of *Lost Highway*. Horrifyingly, the impetus for the majority of the film is a dysfunctional relationship between a married couple which eventually leads to the husband murdering his wife. In a popular theory as to the film's second half, said husband, Fred (Bill Pullman), succumbs to madness in prison, and conceives a different life for himself in his head. Even more intriguingly, the film's events unfold following the arrival of a video tape, recording the couple as they sleep, delivered to their door. In this instance, the home is invaded by a documentation of the environment itself. It's as if any surface idealism that their relationship is positive is at risk because someone has literally peeked behind the curtain to expose their reality. In concept and consequence it's perversely haunting. *Lost Highway* then explicitly delves into the realm of dreams in order to escape "real horror", much in the manner that 2001's *Mulholland Drive* does. Popular interpretations of the latter believe that it also taps into a similar stream of thought, again indulging in fantastical escapes from reality. If this theory is to be applied to and work for this film, the vast majority of its running time must then be considered an escapist fantasy, from the horror of failure, of falling between Hollywood's cracks.

Even *The Elephant Man* (1980) portrayed someone abandoned and driven from having a home due to physical imperfection. Prior to that, Lynch's feature film début, the bleak masterpiece *Eraserhead*, occurs almost entirely within the lead character Henry's apartment. But his issues with repression and outside fears seem to result in his dwelling being anything but a "home", least of all for his girlfriend, who flees, leaving him to contend with their deformed baby.

Lynch has never been shy when it comes to uncovering hidden evils. Clearly, the inherent dark side of humans is something that inspires the very fundamentals of his output. Home is his safety net, it's where he can work, he takes the elements of the outside as and when he sees fit. The thought of that being compromised is among his greatest fears. Maybe even in this controlled environment, he's tasted enough evil and unsavoury behaviour seeping through to know that it's something that can never be kept on the outside indefinitely.

The world of *Twin Peaks* is the perfect demonstration of these obsessions – it's a place full of hidden secrets, and evil characteristics. In his cinematic deep dive into that world, Lynch unearthed a horror that few understood at the time, and which continues to alienate many still. Ultimately though, it's Lynch's most brutal, searingly powerful meditation on the underbelly of suburban life to this day.

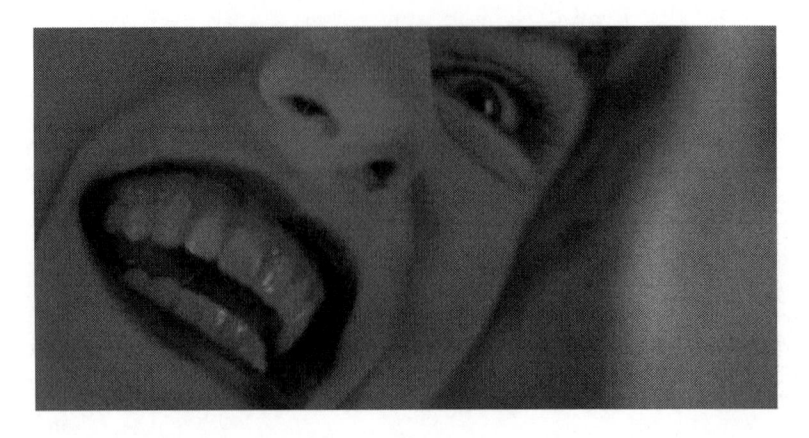

TWIN PEAKS: FIRE WALK WITH ME-INSPIRED ARTWORK

Franki Beddows

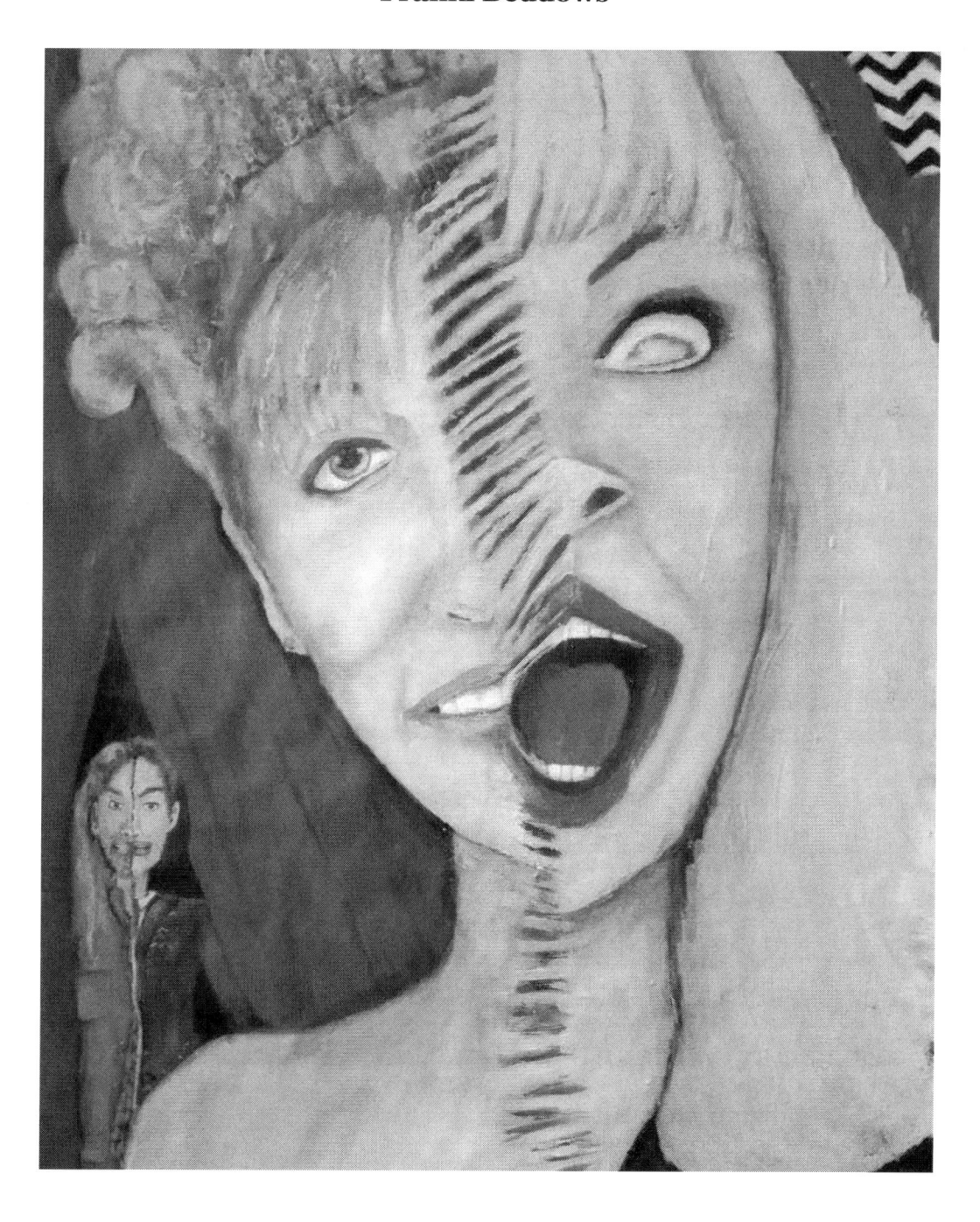

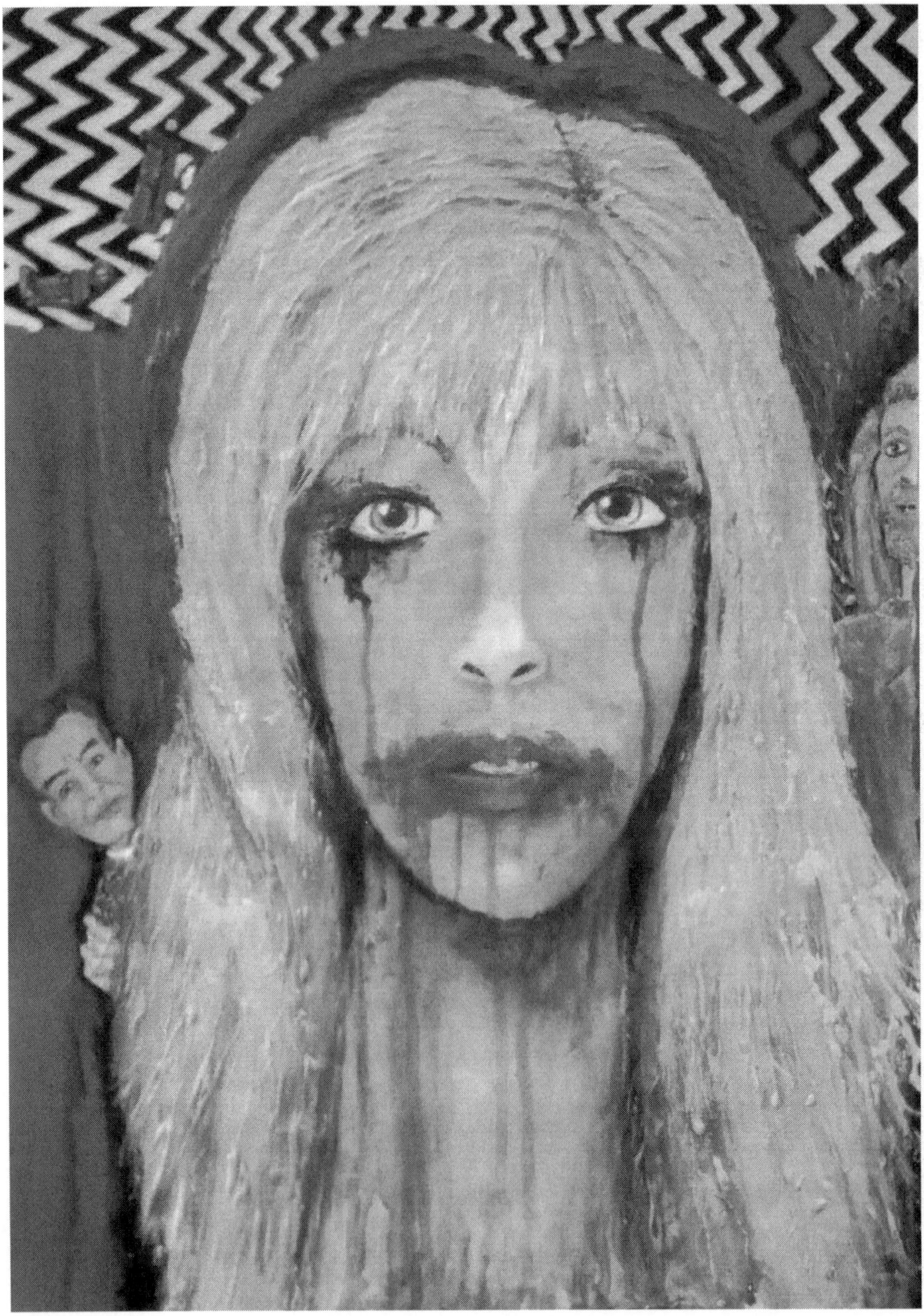

BYDDI LEE ON NOVEL WRITING, TRAVELLING, THEATRE AND MORE!

*Trevor Kennedy chats to **Byddi Lee**, an Armagh woman who has lived throughout the world and whose credits include as an author, playwright and editor.*

Trevor Kennedy: Byddi, it's great to be chatting to you during these very strange times. Are you finding yourself writing more from home during the current coronavirus quarantine?

Byddi Lee: Hi, Trevor. Thanks for chatting with me. Strange times indeed, but on a day-to-day level, little has changed. I usually write from home, but concentrating is more of a challenge these days. Writing is always a battle of self-discipline and never more so than now. I'm finding that I'll make any excuse to do something else. I garden. The weather has been particularly beautiful for April in Ireland, so I disappear into the veggie plot when I know I should be getting words down. I'm weeding and deadheading when I know I ought to be editing and paring out words instead. In the first few weeks of the lockdown, the stress levels were as much a pandemic as the virus, I reckon. Since then, I feel like I've adjusted to the situation, and that feeling of anxiety has abated. This week I've turned back to my writing, and I've rediscovered how much of an escape it can be. I'm grateful to have that.

TK: You grew up in Armagh, but have also lived in Belfast, South Africa, Canada, the USA and France. Was all this worldwide travelling something you'd always wanted to do and in what ways does it fuel your writing? Have you any other countries lined up on your "to do" list?

BL: I always wanted to travel. I was especially obsessed with the Amazon (the river, not the online bookseller – but the irony doesn't escape me!). When I was ten years old, I read *Amazon Adventure* by Willard Price. It was one of a series of adventure books, about two brothers who travelled the world collecting animals for their father's zoo. In hindsight, they were really not very PC, and the science was all wrong, but they did instil in me the desire to study Biology and the natural world. I was determined to visit the Amazon (which I did in 1999.) As a teenager in the middle of the Troubles in the North of Ireland, the David Attenborough nature programs really inspired me. While my friends had pictures of Duran Duran on their bedroom walls, I had posters of elephants and lions on the Savannah and jaguars in the Amazon jungle on my walls. I daydreamed hard in those days.

I studied Environmental Biology at Queen's University Belfast, worked as a research associate and then went on to get a teaching qualification and taught biology. In 2002, I had the opportunity to travel to South Africa to study dolphins, and that kick-started a two year long round-the-world trip.

In those days, there was no social media, but I kept in touch with my friends by writing long emails. Travel really helped me to write. There's a mindfulness that accompanies travelling, or at least it did in those days when you weren't able to be online other than when you were at an internet cafe. I'd sit on a bus or train with the world spooling out beyond the windowpane and let it ignite my creativity. I always kept a notebook and many of those scribblings made their way into published work.

As for a "to do" list for travel – I used to think in terms of visiting countries, but now, with the lockdown, I think when I can travel, I'll be focusing of visiting people (in Ireland and in other countries.) That's the short answer. The long answer is a list that may never end... but I'll start with ... nope can't do it. I can't just name one place because a catalogue of destinations builds in my head.

TK: Your "Rejuvenation Trilogy" is currently being published by Castrum Press, the first book of which is on sale from Amazon and other outlets. Amongst other things, it is set in a world where Earth's surface has been destroyed and a mysterious disease is afflicting people. Given the current climate, that actually sounds pretty prophetic. Could you give us some more details on it please? What exactly is the "Melter War" and who are the

"Rejuvenees"?

BL: The "Melter War" was so named when the Earth was attacked by high-energy beams from an unknown alien entity in space, and all the ice caps were rapidly melted. The resultant devastation was exacerbated by these "Melters" attacking Earth's major population and economic hubs with the same energy blasts, creating inhabitable scorch zones over large regions.

Rejuvenation is told from the point of view of Dr. Bobbie Chan, a geriatrician who obeys the rules and upholds the status quo in a post "Melter War" society, a couple of decades after the war when Earth has united under the governance of a giant corporation. Bobbie is one of the first to notice a strange new disease emerging which seems to target and initially kill the elderly. A group of her patients, including her grandmother show symptoms of the new disease, but mysteriously continue to grow younger and become the "Rejuvenees".

TK: With the first book in the series now published, what plans do you have for the following two and when will we see them?

BL: Books two and three are written, and Castrum Press is planning to release them over the coming months.

TK: You published your first novel, *March to November*, back in 2014. What's it about?

BL: *March to November* is set in contemporary Belfast and tells the story of five people whose lives intertwine with devastating consequences during these nine months.

Tracey has escaped the grip of a violent boyfriend and wants a normal life with a loving man. When Tracey's sister-in-law introduces her to her cousin Tommy, Tracey is afraid that she's not good enough for him. Tracey and Tommy's lives are thrown together when Tracey's brother leaves his wife, Tommy's cousin, for another woman. Despite falling for one another, their conflicting loyalties drive Tracey and Tommy apart, further complicated by the actions of a violent stalker from Tracey's past. Tracey and Tommy's relationship navigates the devastating fallout from the lives of those around them.

TK: Which authors inspired you growing up and which do now?

BL: I am a voracious reader and have a wide range in taste, so this could turn into a long list! Regardless of genre – if a story is well told, I'll enjoy it. I've already mentioned Willard Price. I was also really inspired by the Narnia books by C. S. Lewis. Walter Macken's historical fiction broke my heart in my late teens. As a young woman, I gobbled up Maeve Binchy because I could relate to the Irish setting of her stories. I've read Margaret Mitchell's *Gone with the Wind* dozens of times. I've always enjoyed being scared by Stephen King's books and thought *The Stand* was brilliant. More recently, I've discovered Blake Crouch and particularly love his book *Dark Matter*.

TK: You have also co-written the play *Impact*, which concerns the tragic real-life Armagh rail disaster in 1889 where over eighty people lost their lives. How was this experience for you? I'm sure it was quite harrowing considering the subject matter.

BL: I was working with a great team. Yes, the subject matter was very tragic, especially with it being a local story and the finished product was incredibly emotive. It was a fabulous experience to write the play alongside the other two writers. The Armagh Theatre Group was simply amazing. There was a lot of camaraderie, and we shared a lot of laughter, probably as a coping mechanism to deal with the immense burden of the sadness in the story.

TK: Does scriptwriting come to you just as easy as the penning of prose in short story and novel forms? Which format do you prefer and are more at home with?

BL: I've been told that I write dialogue well and I reckon that helped when scriptwriting. I find prose easier because I can unpack what is in a character's head more directly. That's trickier with scriptwriting and involves more subtext and showing. I'm much more at home with novels, in particular. I like the "at home" feeling I have with the characters in my books, and I grow pretty attached to them. Short stories feel like fleeting relationships, and if I become attached to the characters, I find myself plotting out a novel-length story for them.

TK: On the subject of short stories, you are one of the founders of the spoken word event Flash Fiction Armagh and also co-edited *The Bramley – An Anthology of Flash Fiction Armagh*. Could you tell us a bit more about both of these please?

BL: Flash Fiction Armagh is a spoken word event inspired by Flash Fiction

Forum San Jose. Its purpose is to build community among local writers and between writers and readers. Writers submit their stories, and we curate a selection to be read out by the writer at the event and then publish the pieces in *The Bramley – An Anthology of Flash Fiction Armagh*. Our second volume is due out this summer.

TK: Aside from the next two books in your "Rejuvenation Trilogy", what other future works do you have in the pipeline, Byddi?

BL: I'm working on a new novel that has been inspired by my first job as a Research Associate in Dendrochronology (tree ring analysis). We have been able to identify in the tree ring chronology cataclysmic climatic events that happened thousands of years ago. My imagination has ventured into the heads of possible Neolithic characters who witnessed those events in real-time. There is a lot of research to be done for this one, but my characters already feel like they are real, so that's a good start.

TK: Byddi, it's been a pleasure. Thank you for taking the time to chat to us here at *Phantasmagoria*.

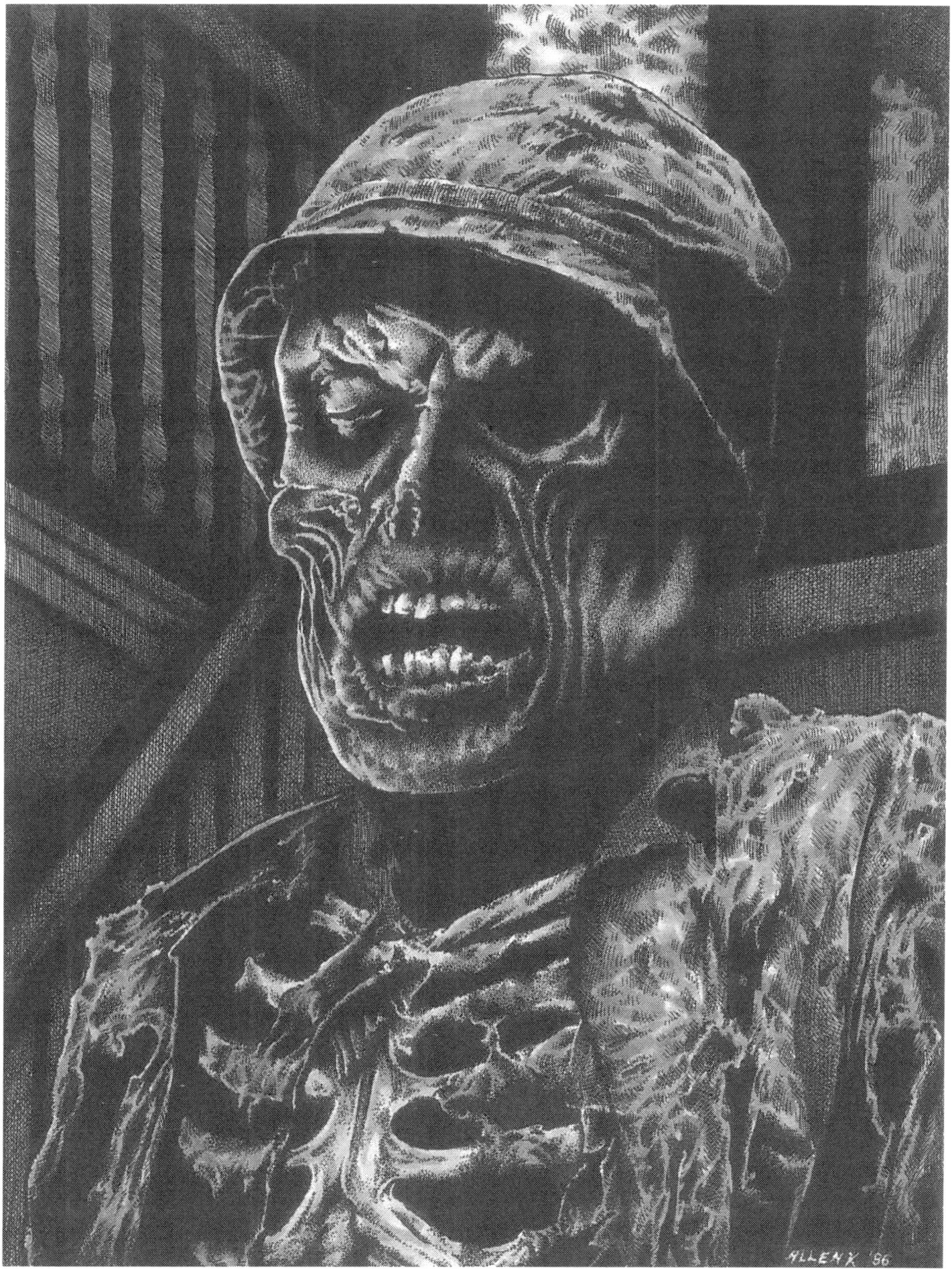
ALLEN X '86

OWEN QUINN AND THE TIME WARRIORS ARCHIVES: CASEY BIGGS

Phantasmagoria *continues its series of taking a look at some of the interviews* **Owen Quinn** *originally featured on his* The Time Warriors *website. For this issue, it's* Star Trek: Deep Space Nine's **Casey Biggs**, *whose other roles include in* The X Files, The Equalizer, ER, Melrose Place, The Pelican Brief *(1993),* Broken Arrow *(1996), and many more.*

Owen Quinn: How did you first become interested in acting and what made you decide to do it as a career?

Casey Biggs: I could always sing and in high school. We did big musicals and I was in them. I realized that I liked being on the stage more than I liked football!

OQ: What defines acting for you?

CB: As an actor you are a storyteller and your ability to do that defines you. It is a craft that you must train like an athlete to master.

OQ: What do you look for in a script before accepting a role?

CB: I look for challenges. Emotionally and physically.

OQ: What was your first breakthrough role?

CB: On stage it was in the musical *Elmer Gantry*. I feel I have yet to have one in film.

OQ: Was your first day on a television set everything you expected or not at all?

CB: My first day on set was for a TV film called *The Great Wallendas*, about a high wire circus family. We shot in Florida. I was a bit nervous but I had a blast.

OQ: How do you approach every new character you play? Do you stick to the script or do you have the leeway to add your own twist to the character?

CB: I was trained as a classical actor so I have high regard for the author. I feel we have a responsibility to honor their work. It's your job to make the words come alive. You don't say to Shakespeare, "Who wrote this crap?!"

OQ: Were you a fan of *Star Trek* before you got the role of Damar?

CB: Only the first series. I didn't know DS9 at all.

OQ: How did you land the role and did you know what a Cardassian was?

CB: I had no idea who or what a Cardassian was. After the audition I thought, "They could get an extra to play this, why am I here?" I didn't know they had such big plans for Damar.

OQ: What was the original character breakdown given to you and did you know he was intended to be a long-running character?

CB: I thought it was going to be one day's work. I had five lines. "They're in range, sir." I ended up on the show for five years and became the leader of the Empire!

OQ: Is it hard coming into an established group of actors on a show like DS9 or does having so many actors in prosthetics make it easier to bond?

CB: DS9 was full of classically trained actors who really knew what they were doing. It was a great bunch who had great respect for the work. Everyone was very open and helpful.

OQ: Had you had much experience in the way of prosthetics and how did you find having to wear them?

CB: Never. It was fun for the first few years, then it got tiresome. 4am for three hours!

OQ: You and Marc Alaimo had a fantastic on screen chemistry. How much does that play into your enjoying of a role?

CB: It is terrific when you get along with the actors you work with. Marc and I had great respect for each other coming from the stage.

OQ: Damar had a lovely streak of sarcasm and came out with some great one-liners (the one about Leeta's breasts that comes to mind). Was that something you were able to ad lib?

CB: There was no ad libbing. The writers were very strict, as they should be, in my opinion. They were very good at picking up on your strengths as well and wrote to them.

OQ: On a show like *Deep Space Nine*, how much collaboration is there between the writers and the actor about their characters?

CB: The writers watch you develop and then write for you. For example, they liked the way I looked in Quark's bar, so I ended up an alcoholic for two seasons!

OQ: Were you pleased when Damar became the saviour of Cardassia? No one could have seen that coming.

CB: It was great to play. I got to stop drinking that horrible Kanar! Damar had a great arc.

OQ: What, for you, defined Deep Space Nine?

CB: The quality of the writers and actors. Especially Ira Behr.

OQ: What is the legacy of Damar you're most proud of?

CB: He died to save his people.

OQ: You also appeared on *Star Trek: Enterprise* as an alien captain. There always seems to be a buzz when an actor from one *Trek* show appears on another. Did you find that?

CB: A bit. They offered me the part saying it was a new race that was going to figure in the story. Not!

OQ: Were those prosthetics easier than Damar's?

CB: Yes. Probably because they were saving money. I wasn't very fond of the look.

OQ: What was attending your first convention like? Did you know what to expect?

CB: It was a blast. I had great fun and have a great respect for the fans. They pay so much to come and I think they deserve your attention.

OQ: How have these events changed your perception of fandom in general?

CB: I am a big fan of fans. For the most part they are smart, interested, and caring. Rarely do I think, as Shatner said, "Get a life!"

OQ: You are a part of history now because of your portrayal of Damar. What has been your greatest lesson about acting from playing the role?

CB: Grace and respect.

OQ: Can you tell us about the Enterprise Blues Band?

CB: It Vaughn Armstrong's idea. He wrote some songs and got some of us who are musicians as well to do them. It was great fun and it gave the fans another look at who we were. We have a large European fan base and love playing there. In fact, we would love to come and play for you all!

OQ: You now teach acting and directing. How vital is it for an actor to have more than one string to their bow?

CB: An actor needs to be a jack of all trades. I have played aliens, lawyers, elephant tamers and the Devil. Actors are the most interesting people I know. You must become an expert in whatever field you are playing so you always have a wide range of knowledge. Studying the craft of acting will make you better at whatever you choose to do, even if you never set foot on a stage.

OQ: What is the greatest lesson you could teach someone about acting, or is an ever-evolving craft?

CB: To be present in your life. No matter whatever it is.

OQ: Have you a message for your Irish fans?

CB: I AM IRISH!!! I want to come see you all!!

**Some titles by Owen Quinn
currently available from Amazon…**

RETROSPECTIVE
THE HORROR FILM YEARS: 1960s

David Brilliance

Phantasmagoria's resident historian of all things weird and wonderful continues his series chronicling the history of horror films throughout the decades.

THE 1960s WAS a decade where film companies specialising in horror films seemed to spring up like cases of Covid-19: Hammer and Amicus in Britain were joined by Tigon, while AIP branched out from cheap and tacky SF flicks to colour, more up-market horrors. Looking at some examples of the genre, year by year, *Black Sunday* (1960) is an impressive Italian horror, directed by Mario Bava, the Italian equivalent of Terence Fisher. It stars Barbara Steele (sorry, Steele-Lovers – I could never see the attraction myself!) as a sinister witch who gets a mask of spikes hammered into her face, in a very famous sequence. *City of the Dead*, also in 1960, was the first Amicus horror (though it was called Vulcan then), and has Christopher Lee as the head of a sinister cult of witches in the titular... city? It's not big enough to be a village, from what we see of it! A great film, with an eerie cameo from Valentine Dyall, better known to radio listeners as "The Man in Black" at this point.

The Fall of the House of Usher (1960) was the first of the lavish Poe adaptations from AIP and set the standard for the other seven to follow. *Village of the Damned* (1960) is a British SF yarn based on *The Midwich Cuckoos* by John Wyndham and features sinister alien children attempting to take over the world via a small village and only George Sanders can stop them. *Curse of the Werewolf*, in 1961, is a stand-out Hammer horror from that period – Ollie Reed's werewolf make-up has never been surpassed, and the reason Hammer didn't dabble any more with that particular subject was because the film flopped at the box office.

The Innocents (1961) is a slightly overrated, but still good, nineteenth century ghost story, with Deborah Kerr playing a governess to two odd kids in a large country house, and it turns out they are both possessed. I remember seeing this on BBC2 on Christmas Eve, 1985 and being chilled by a scene where Kerr is saying goodnight to the kids and, as the lights are turned off, the boy starts talking in a decidedly adult tone!

Night Tide (1961) is a disappointing love story involving Dennis Hopper and a mermaid. *Night of the Eagle* (1962) is an enjoyable witchcraft yarn starring Peter Wyngarde – I remember this being shown on a Friday afternoon on Tyne Tees in 1982 (ah, the good old days, where ITV regions would screen old films on Monday and Friday afternoons!). *The Birds* (1963) is Hitchcock's masterpiece, far better than *Psycho*, and presents a terrifying vision of the beginning of the end of the world. *Black Zoo* (1963) has Michael Gough killing folk using animals from his own private zoo, and *The Old Dark*

House (1963) is an oddly atypical Hammer black comedy, loosely based on the 1932 film, which was based on a play called *Benighted*.

Twice-Told Tales (1963) is a Price-starring anthology but it's no *Tales of Terror* – the stories are too long by half and the second story (with scientist Price giving his daughter the ability to kill with a touch) looks like a Hollywood musical! *The Black Torment* (1964) is a very nice British specimen, with John Turner going round the bend as he gets blamed for a series of rapes, pillages and murders carried out by his psycho twin brother!

Devil Doll (1964) is another UK film with pock-marked star Bryant Haliday as a ventriloquist who is controlled by his sinister dummy. It's a good little film this, and unlike the similar story in 1945's *Dead of Night*, there's no doubt as to the supernatural element of the story. *Kwaidan* (1964) is a lengthy Japanese anthology and although it's not as great as many more pretentious critics claim, it still hits the spot.

The Last Man on Earth from 1964 is a nice little Vincent Price starrer in which he is seemingly the only human alive in a world of vampires. This film often gets a bad press but it's not bad at all, just not great. *Witchcraft*, on the other hand, is a bit crap. This 1964 British film has a sauced-up Lon Chaney Jr. attempting to resurrect an ancestor who was a witch. Chaney Jr. doesn't get enough screen time in this one and it's quite slow. *Curse of the Fly* (1964) is average and has Brian Donlevy carrying out matter transmission experiments, one of which is quite revolting, with two people 'fused' together!

Dr. Terror's House of Horrors (1965) was the first of the seven Amicus anthologies and it's also the weakest, simply because the other films are even better. The "Werewolf", "Voodoo" and "Disembodied Hand" segments are the best, the "Vampire" story the weakest, though it has a nice punchline. *The Skull* from the same year and same company is an excellent full-length story based around the skull of de Sade. *Planet of the Vampires* (1965), is an eerie SF masterpiece from Mario Bava, and is a film I always wanted to see after I read that it featured the most frightening and impressive depiction of an alien world ever seen on screen! *Face of Fu Manchu* in 1965 kicked off a series of average films with Chris Lee in oriental make-up as the sinister Chinese villain, a role he'd sort of played earlier in Hammer's *Terror of the Tongs* in 1962.

Chamber of Horrors (1966) was the first American TV movie and is an average affair with Patrick O'Neal as Jason, a murderer at large in the nineteenth century. The film features a weird gimmick whereby the screen flashes and a honking horn sounds to warn the viewer that something grisly is about to happen on screen, but because this is a '60s TV movie, nothing much really does. *The Deadly Bees* from the same year is an Amicus "Bee" movie and has Frank Finlay siccing his black and yellow pets on various folk on an island. *The Plague of the Zombies* and *The Reptile* (both 1966) are two Hammer films shot back-to-back and both set in nineteenth century

Cornwall, the former involving a squire using zombies to work in his tin mine, the latter with Jacqueline Pearce transforming into a curvaceous snake woman.

It! (1966) is a disappointingly slow-paced British film with Roddy McDowall getting control of the clay creature the Golem. Some nice moments, and a touch of *Psycho*, with McDowall keeping his mother's corpse in his front room, but the film drags too much. *Dance of the Vampires* (1967) is a lavishly-filmed horror comedy. It's not actually very funny but is above average generally. *The Sorcerers* (1967) and *Curse of the Crimson Altar* (1968) are two Tigon films with Boris Karloff, of which the second is the best. *The Blood Beast Terror* in 1967 is another Tigon film, one generally panned, even by its star, the great Peter Cushing. I've always liked the film though and surely a woman transforming into a giant moth is no more far-fetched than stuff seen in countless other horror films?? Transplanting a person's soul using nineteenth century technology springs to mind with *Frankenstein Created Woman*, from the same year. *Corruption* (1968) has the Gentleman of Horror playing a plastic surgeon who gets involved in several bloody murders, as he attempts to repair his wife's sizzled face.

The Devil Rides Out (1968) is one of the top five Hammer films, a fantastic adaptation of a reportedly very boring novel. Rosemary's Baby from the same year is an enjoyable, but not very scary, film about Mia Farrow getting impregnated with the Devil's child. *Witchfinder General* (1968) is a Tigon cult classic and stars a camp-free Vincent Price as the infamous witch-hunting Matthew Hopkins. The film has a nice revenge theme and contains some nicely gory moments, ending with the villain getting hacked up into chopped liver and his henchman getting his eye kicked out!

Targets (1968) has Boris Karloff playing himself (sort of), in a very strange film in which his ageing horror star confronts a killer, based on an actual murderer, and who has been randomly shooting motorists. *Frankenstein Must Be Destroyed* (1969) brings this most eventful of decades (734 horror films in the '60s, compared to 304 in the '50s) to an excellent close, with the best of the Hammer Frankenstein films, one in which Peter Cushing's brain-obsessed Baron is the monster.

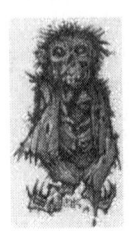

PHANTASMAGORIA SPECIAL EDITION SERIES
#1: R. CHETWYND-HAYES CENTENARY

Retailing from Amazon, Forbidden Planet London Megastore, Forbidden Planet Belfast and Coffee & Heroes (Belfast)

(Cover artwork by Les Edwards, www.lesedwards.com. Cover design by Adrian Baldwin, www.adrianbaldwin.info)

READING R. CHETWYND-HAYES

Marc Damian Lawler

Continuing his series following on from Phantasmagoria Special Edition Series #1: R. Chetwynd-Hayes Centenary, *Marc Damian Lawler dissects another classic story by the author.*

'THE UNDERGROUND'

First published in *After Midnight Stories*, Selected / Edited by Amy Myers, William Kimber & Co., London, England, 1985 (hc)

'As a child Laura Munro had been terrified of the underground railway, for did not the red trains which came running out of the black-mouthed tunnel, bear an uncanny resemblance to her conception of a fire-breathing dragon?'

Right off the bat, I sympathise with her. The first time I stood on an underground platform (Northern Line [south] at Tottenham Court Rd.), I remember almost shitting in my shorts as the train rocketed into view out of the darkness.

'On reaching early adulthood, such imaginative flights were remembered with amusement, but at least a ghost of the fear still lingered. She had a tendency to lose herself in the labyrinth of passages and all those coloured, lighted signs confused rather than helped. Then she could never dismiss the doubtlessly silly thought as to what would happen if all the lights went out. Creeping along these passages in total darkness, until she fell off the edge of a platform.'

That's nothing compared to what that poor passenger suffered in *An American Werewolf in London*.

'In fact the entire business of travelling by the underground railway is fraught with danger. Stand on the edge of the platform in the rush hour, take up an "I'm going to be the first in and get a seat" stance, and over you go. Loss of balance – an inopportune fainting spell – a slip – a push. The merest flick of a folded umbrella. At the very best, eternity is but one step away.'

Twenty-first century tube travellers would think themselves lucky if all they had to worry about was a 'push' or the 'flick of a folded umbrella'... since the 2005 terrorist attacks, the fear of being in close proximity to a passenger wearing a rucksack has taken commonplace commuter anxiety and mutated it into wide-spread justifiable paranoia.

'Laura first saw the young man standing on the Charing Cross underground station... He was attired in what she later knew to be a battle dress, covered by a thick khaki overcoat, equipped with shining brass buttons. Green canvas gaiters overlapped thick-soled, highly polished boots... For the space of perhaps two complete minutes he stood framed in the window, his grey eyes staring directly into Laura's own, and never before had she seen such an expression of baffled, unadulterated misery on a young face. Then the doors closed with a long drawn out sigh, the train moved and the young soldier slid out of view. It was not until some while later that Laura realised she was trembling.'

Later that day, she mentions the young man to her father.

"*Damn disgraceful. Kids going around in the uniform we were proud to wear...*"
    "*Wasn't he a proper soldier?*" Laura asked.
    Her father snorted. "*They don't wear battle dress for walking out these days. Not fancy enough...*"
    "*... he had a greenish kind of satchel slung on a broad strap over one*

shoulder." Richard Munro nodded. "Gas mask. We all had to wear them during the war years. The one you saw was probably crammed with drugs..."'

During the late '60s / early '70s, military jackets were worn – most famously by the Fab Four on the album cover of *Sgt. Pepper's Lonely Heart's Club Band* – as mock nostalgia for an empire in decline.

Her father's reaction reminds me of the time Jimi Hendrix, himself a former soldier, famously purchased an antique hussar's uniform, that dated back to the 1850s (Hendrix's most iconic photographs have him wearing it, bare-chested beneath; a universe away from the upright officer who must have originally worn it) and was told to take it off and roughed up by two policemen (bully boys in blue) outside his flat in London.

'It was a full month before Laura saw her young soldier again. He was leaning against the end door, the one which, when opened, gives access to the next carriage ... Laura toyed with the idea of actually getting up, easing her way through the strap-hangers and starting a conversation with the young stranger. "How crowded! Most tiring," sort of thing, then she killed the notion with self-mockery. It would be very like cradle snatching. The boy could not be more than twenty, whereas she was pushing forty-five. Well on her way to confirmed spinsterhood. A fine thing to pick up a young soldier at such an advanced age, always supposing he didn't run for his life the moment she opened her mouth.'

This happened to me once. I was approached by a middle-aged woman with a soppy look on her face. Had I not been waiting in a queue to meet Deee-Lite's Lady Miss Kier, I would have bolted down the nearest underground entrance like a frightened rabbit! As it was, she turned out to be an old friend of the family who hadn't seen me since I was three and had posed for a Polaroid – sporting a *Six Million Dollar Man* T-shirt – on the bonnet of her car. She even went so far as to pat me on the head and say, "It's a shame, ducky, your hair doesn't curl anymore." As I'm sure you can imagine, that went down splendidly with those nearest to me in the queue.

'What was it that made him something more than a young man dressed in a world war uniform? ...Well, he did not seem to move about much. No turning of the head to look at the platform, no fidgeting, shuffling of feet, seeking what comfort that could be obtained from leaning against a metal and glass door. Neither – when Laura came to examine his face more intently – did he blink, nor move his face muscles. She thought it could have been a corpse propped up there – and wished she hadn't.

… She closed her eyes and tried to dismiss the wretched boy from her mind, while hoping that by the time she opened them again he would have gone away.

But when she looked, he was standing a scarce yard away; just beyond the glass partition, wedged in the corner… his grey eyes were looking directly into hers!

Loneliness and despair, frozen by time, blazed an icy trail across her mind and she screamed a silent protest, like a recluse threatened with the burden of a stranger's problems.

Then he disappeared, left an empty space that might never have been occupied, and Laura felt her heart beat faster as shock demanded its due, even while pity fought an even battle with fear.'

This 'when she looked again the apparition had moved closer' nightmare scenario reminds me of a true ghost story that's been talked about in my family for over a hundred years. In the year 1910, my maternal grandmother's cousin, Winifred Graham, was…

'travelling from Hampton Court to Waterloo one morning, and was lucky enough to find an empty carriage at Hampton Court. At Thames Ditton, the next stop, quite an ordinary-looking man got into the carriage and sat down at the far end of me. We took no notice of each other, and in the ordinary course of events I should have continued reading my newspaper without giving him a thought. But suddenly I had the most dreadful feeling about him, in fact, it was so strong that I could hardly support his presence, and something seemed to say "Take in every detail of that man's appearance, because you will have to identify him again."… Without appearing to observe him, I registered in my mind his face and figure, the colour of his clothes, and especially, a little pile of four books, fastened neatly together with straps.

'So uncomfortable and nervous did I feel that I was ready to jump out of the train at the next station. But, rather to my amusement, before I had time to rise to my feet when the train drew in at Surbiton, my fellow traveller calmly took his books under his arm, stepped out and marched off. "So much for intuition," thought I, and telling myself I was very silly, I dismissed the incident from my mind.

'Surbiton is always a busy station in the morning, and a minute later some other people got into my carriage, and the train proceeded on its journey. I closed my eyes for a while… and opened them at Vauxhall to see which station we had arrived at, when to my unutterable horror, I saw the very same man seated in front of me! On his knee were the four books in their straps, and he sat very still, gazing quite calmly and normally at me.

'… I got out and ran the whole length of the train, desirous of nothing except to put distance between us. Then I jumped, panting, into a compartment, terrified lest I should meet him again at Waterloo.

'Alas, this ghost story has no sequel; this experience was the beginning and the end of my phantom man, and I shall never be able to explain it to myself, or cease regretting my folly in doing a bolt. How often have I longed to know what would have happened had I asked the 'ghost' the time... or waited to see whether he would vanish when we reached our destination.' — *True Ghost Stories*, compiled by Marchioness Townsend & Maud Ffoulkes, Hutchinson, 1936.

Unlike Winifred Graham, Laura Munro is destined to know all about her 'phantom man'.

She is approached by a fellow passenger.

'"You saw him, didn't you? I expect you know there's quite a few of his kind wandering around down here. Get trapped, see. 'Ope you don't mind me talking to you like this. But a word of warning – be careful. Don't encourage it. I say 'it' because they're only bits and pieces left behind. If one gets drawn into your aura, it can be a nuisance. Follow you. Start hanging around the house. If you get my meaning. Hope I haven't upset you. Mean well."

And after raising his bowler hat, he disappeared into the crowd, which was surging onto the down escalator. Laura never saw him again, but what he had said set up home in her brain...

Who – what – how was it possible?

Could a momentary flash of pity form a line of communication?

If so – with what result?'

Never mind all that... check your purse is still in your handbag!

'"You're getting as thin as a beanstalk," her father remarked, "and it don't become you. No wonder we haven't seen much of Harold Smithers lately. What with the way you look and the way you've been treating him, I'd be surprised if he hasn't taken to looking in another direction. It's the shelf for you, my girl, and no mistake about it. Still, I suppose when I'm gone, with what the house will fetch, plus the bit I've managed to put away, you'll just about manage."

"You're a selfish old man who never wanted me to marry. Not while you live. Oh, yes, I believe your conscience is troubling you now, when you remember those you drove away... By innuendo, fits of temper, ridicule, anything to ensure you were not left alone to cope for yourself. I pray to God I never grow old, not really old, for advanced age means selfishness. I suppose it is the dread of loneliness that does it."

"You're cracked, woman," her father whispered. "God knows who you

take after."

She looked down at him with something akin to a sneer. "I wouldn't know. After forty years you're still a stranger, and my mother... I can't take after her. After all, she had enough love for at least two."'

Aha... I was wondering if Mrs. Munro was going to play a part in the story.

'*Harold was waiting for her at the entrance to the underground...*

"Fancy running into you! Well, I never! I had to come into this part of the world today, but never dreamed that I'd..."

"We'd better move on," Laura said. "Otherwise, we'll be pushed off the steps."

... Down they went through that curved, domed tunnel and into the network of passages... a stream of humanity robbed them of individuality, temporarily transformed them into mere units of a multi-head, scurrying-legged creature that was born every evening at about five p.m. and died some ninety minutes later. This creature was constantly dividing, then sub-dividing itself into segments, that flowed onto platforms, squeezed into carriages, there to send out a mass of undisciplined seething thoughts.

... "Can't think why you've been dodging me lately. Worried me no end, that I can tell you."

... "I've just been busy."

... "Tell you what – let's let my mother cook one of her special meals. Roast beef, crumbly roast potatoes, boiled sprouts and mouth-watering batter puddings. She loves to watch people she likes eat. Father used to say, "Mother" – he always called her mother – "Mother, you'll feed me to death." And I'm not so sure she didn't. He was eighteen stone when he died. I always say the way to a man's heart is through..."

He was back. The soldier boy. Standing a scarce two feet away, looking straight at Laura... his grey eyes filled with the sadness of one who has suffered a recent bereavement. She wanted to reach out and place her hands on those narrow shoulders and gently pull him towards her, but bodies – parts of the creature – pressed so tightly her arms were imprisoned and her ear was held captive...

"Pity about your mother. Mother told me all about it. How she ran off with that Canadian... Wonder he didn't go mad, particularly when she fell under the train. On this line too. One wonders if she really fell or... I mean when one remembers what was on her mind. I say, I haven't put my foot in it again, have I? It all happened such a long time ago, but the association of ideas – your mother and mine – brought it all to mind. You did know about it... didn't you?"

The sad young man's eyes stared at her forlornly – and she knew. The pale, unlined face was stone waiting for time to etch lines of experience, suffering – guilt. She whispered: "I know now. Please go."

The apparition went and was replaced by a tall, thin man with rimless glasses who smiled faintly and said: "Sorry if I bumped into you"...

She fled the moment the doors slid open at the next station, leaving an enraged Harold, who shouted after her: "Go to hell, you silly stuck-up bitch," and there was no room in her mind for pity or regret. She got a taxi the rest of the way home...

Her father was seated in front of the artificial log electric fire... she stood watching him with intense interest. From being a plain, ordinary and rather boring man, he had been transformed into someone extraordinary. In fact, he was possibly one of the most unique persons alive.

...There was no time or desire for a tactful approach to a bizarre subject, so she asked simply: "Did you follow my mother on to the underground station, or see her there quite by accident?"

He jerked his head round and she had a glimpse of the young soldier peeping out from the frightened eyes. "What are you talking about?"

She explained without pity or rancour. "I'm talking about the day you murdered my mother. Pushed her in front of a tube train. I've often thought how easy it would be in the rush hour and wondered how many times it had been done. Now I know – you did it."

He groaned and covered his face with shaking hands... Laura heard her voice revealing the truth – as she knew it. "I do not know if she deserved to die, or not. Leaving a serving soldier and an infant child during a war must be regarded as despicable, but I have never had to experience the temptations she had to contend with. But if everyone was killed for surrendering to temptation, the world would be sparsely populated."

"She just left," the old man whispered. "Not so much as a note. I was half mad with grief. Then when I saw her in the underground, my temptation was too strong to be resisted."

Laura nodded. "I can understand. But the great tragedy was born of the second murder. By killing your wife – my mother – you at the same time slaughtered your own youth. The young soldier who loved, worshipped and staked all on one person. You left his ghost behind in the underground, and there he is to this day. A pathetic something that cannot die."

... "You won't tell? No one has ever suspected. They must never do so. Never."

... "Do you understand? An extension of you walks the underground looking for the love you lost."

He ignored the statement. Perhaps he did not hear or understand, and Laura did not pursue the matter further. The young soldier was standing by the window watching her with a look of pathetic expectation. Unwittingly,

she had led him up to the light of day.
   "I haven't pity to spare for both of you," she whispered.'

As 'skeletons in the closet' go, that's got to be as big and as sad and as shocking a revelation as they come.

One of the criticisms aimed at Chetwynd-Hayes is that his stories are sometimes anti-female (a criticism not entirely unfounded)... Well, in this story that's certainly not the case. Laura is a highly sympathetic character; whom, ultimately, decides not to settle for a safe future married to a terrible bore (by the way, it's my belief that Harold Smithers died soon after their break-up when he fell – or was he pushed? – in front of the 'six minutes past seven' Northern Line train to High Barnet. A woman fitting the description of his former girlfriend was seen on the platform as it happened, but nothing was proven in a court of law), and confronts her miserable murderer of a dad... and, I might add, still holding her shit together when she finds out her 'ghost dad' has followed her home.

Rating: 4/5. This story got me wondering where exactly I might have left my ghostly double... the most likely candidate is Room 2 of my secondary school's Science Block... where – back in the late '80s – I chucked up my packed lunch in front of the whole damn class... and cried inwardly as my playground credibility collapsed to the floor and died in front of me.

PS Publishing's edition includes 16 tales of terror & the supernatural, plus:

- A rare novella reprint

- Two tales that have never been reprinted

- A vampire novella in print for the first time

- An interview with R. Chetwynd-Hayes by Stephen Jones & Jo Fletcher

- A detailed Working Bibliography by Stephen Jones and Marc Damian Lawler

- A full-colour artwork portfolio by Les Edwards

- A rare photo gallery of R. Chetwynd-Hayes

- Endpapers by John Bolton and Graham Humphreys

- And a painting by Walter Velez, all inspired by The Monster Club

Available in 3 states:

- A regular trade jacketed hardcover

- A signed and slipcased limited edition

- A strictly limited deluxe edition that will include a holographic or carbon page from one of the author's original manuscripts

Order Now at www.pspublishing.co.uk

New from Shadow Publishing

To celebrate the centenary of
R. Chetwynd-Hayes, new tales of
The Monster Club, Clavering Grange,
Temptations Unlimited, Madam Orloff,
vampires, ghosts and of course Shadmocks!

Edited by Dave Brzeski, with stories by Fred Adams, Simon Clark, Adrian Cole, Cardinal Cox, Theresa Derwin, Pauline Dungate, John Grant, Stephen Laws, William Meikle, Marion Pitman, John L. Probert, Tina Rath, Josh Reynolds, I.A. Watson, and R. Chetwynd-Hayes. Plus an arteicle on 'The Fontana Book of Great Ghost Stories' by Robert Pohle
Cover wrap by Jim Pitts

Available now from Amazon & other booksellers
or direct from the publisher www.shadowpublishing.net

BOYS 'N' GHOULS
FILM REVIEW PODCAST

EVERY MONDAYS & WEDNESDAYS AT WITCH HOUR (MIDNIGHT)!!!
AVAILABLE WORLDWIDE ON:

ANCHOR.FM/BOYSNGHOULSFILMREVIEW

FEATURING: SPECIAL GUESTS, FILM REVIEWS, SPECIAL OFFERS, UPDATES, EVENTS AND MUCH, MUCH MORE...

VENOM of VORTAN

A new book from Mark Lain

Cover art by Mike Tenebrae
Internal art by Gary Ward

destiny's role

Coming to **KICKSTARTER**
8pm (GMT) 1st May 2020

PHANTASMAGORIA REVIEWS

LITERATURE

THE WISE FRIEND by Ramsey Campbell

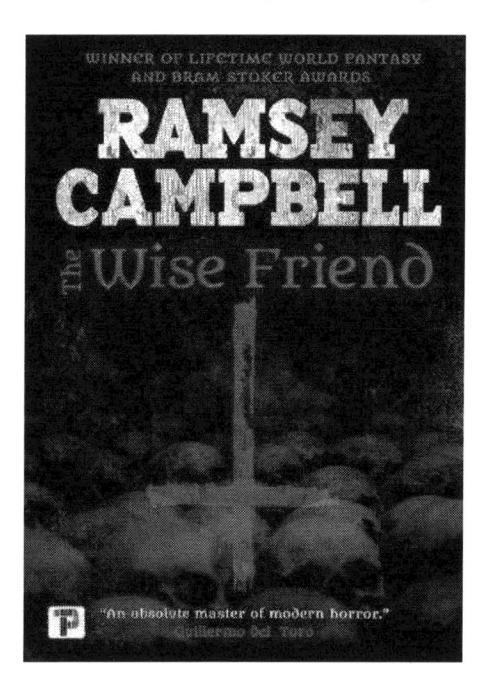

Warning: Review contains potential spoilers

Set mainly in the general Liverpool area, *The Wise Friend* follows Patrick in contemporary times as he recounts the days of his childhood when he stayed with his aunt Thelma, whom he was quite close to, before she died in tragic circumstances after falling to her death from the top of a block of high rise flats. Thelma was a renowned artist and painter, but in the later years of her career, she began a relationship with a somewhat odd man and her work took on a very different tone, one that suggests she was dabbling in occult practices that may well be connected to the woods beside where she lived.

Back in the present day, Patrick's teenage son Roy has developed a bit of a keen interest in the life and work of Thelma, just like his father before him. Although seemingly innocuous at first, things soon take a turn for the strange and dark when Roy begins dating a girl named Bella with similar artistic interests and the couple begin to investigate Thelma's work in deeper detail, based on one of the artist's journals and the sites she used to visit for inspiration…

As with the other Ramsey Campbell works that I have read, there is a lot going on here in terms of themes explored. For example, the author is highly adept at portraying family dynamics and their complex relationships. The consequences – for "good" and "bad" – of experimenting with mood-altering substances is looked upon too, bringing to my mind the religion/belief system of Pantheism and the writings/thinking of Terence McKenna, in essence the mechanisms of the universe and reality itself (is it all really "magic" or just nature doing its thing?). The sometimes ambiguous nature of our memories is hinted at as well.

Art, in its varying forms, and how any good work of art is always open to multiple interpretations and meanings is a running thread, which actually serves to make this novel in and of itself rather meta in nature, due to it working on several levels as well. This is backed up to a degree in the final chapter.

Other themes addressed are obsessive behaviours, parental fears as their offspring get older and begin to bring home girlfriends/boyfriends, and growing old itself.

The horror elements are more subtle, especially in the first half of the book, slowly building in tension and atmosphere, and when they do happen – or when they are suggested – they are indeed chilling and unsettling, especially the stuff pertaining to what lurks within the woods and that faceless figure which often pops up in Thelma's paintings. As is the character of Bella. Enough said.

The circumstances surrounding Thelma's death at the high rise also strongly brought back to me the details of a real-life case from my youth where a young woman from Belfast, who had taken hallucinatory drugs, jumped from the window of her flat after believing she saw the face of "The Devil".

The Wise Friend is very much recommended for those of us who like our horror delivered in a more subtle, creeping and mature manner, and yet another fine addition to the extremely impressive bibliography of a man once described as "perhaps the finest living exponent of the British weird fiction tradition". It is an intriguing, expertly penned folk horror novel for the twenty-first century.

The Wise Friend is published by Flame Tree Press and is available to purchase from Amazon and other retailers.

Trevor Kennedy

WARTS AND ALL by Mark Morris

In 1990, issue 23 of *FEAR* magazine contained 'Warts and All', the first published short story from new author Mark Morris. It wasn't his first professional sale – he had already sold another story to an American magazine and was preparing for the publication of his first novel, *Toady* – but I am glad that we made the decision to publish rather than perhaps wait to see how well the novel sold.

At the age of 58, I have seen the development of many writers who were starting out when I began my career in literary and film journalism, but it is with particular delight that I have seen Mark progress as an author and editor, sometimes against great odds. In the beginning, he decided to concentrate on his great love, writing, and secured an arts grant that allowed him to complete *Toady*. Since then he has, at my last count, published some sixteen novels, four novellas, three short story collections, four film novelisations, five audio plays and a plethora of magazine features and contributions to non-fiction books. Quite a career.

There is, however, no way that I can claim to be Mark's oldest friend in the 'community of writers'. That honour belongs to Nicholas Royle, an author and editor in his own right, who first met Mark at the start of their careers and has provided the Introduction to this volume. In 'Never Mind the Stories, Here's the Introduction', Royle describes their meeting in 1986, how their friendship developed and, through a brief examination of the short stories in the new volume, how Mark's career progressed.

This introductory piece is followed by the title story 'Warts And All', a slow burn but an insidious tale of body horror that gets under the skin that, though written in his early years as a professional author, shows Mark's propensity for the unsettling and grotesque anchored in gritty, real life settings with 'every person' protagonists who are, as in life, not always heroes. He, like many horror writers, also likes a good sting in the tale.

Of the thirty tales, published between 1990 and 2019 and representing a life so far in writing, my current favourites, which also include the title story, are: 'Against the Skin', about a poacher, a fateful meeting and a fog-bound bus ride towards an unexpected fate; 'The Other One', a tale of paranoia and home invasion; 'Down to Earth' in which a dream house and attached garden shed come with more than the new tenants could have ever imagined; 'Coming Home', with an expectant mother whose waking nightmares are anything but the result of 'raging hormones'; 'Nothing Prepares You', about loss, grieving and its consequences, and which struck a very personal note for me; 'Fallen Boys', a ghost story set in a school; 'We Who Sing Beneath the Ground', set in a Cornwall village where a teacher's concerns about one of her pupils lead her to a nightmarish discovery; in 'Holiday Romance' the rose-tinted glasses Skelton wears on his return to a childhood seaside haunt are soon smashed; and, 'Sigils', a novella of folk horror to round off the collection with a definite nod towards M. R. James.

Though I do have my favourites, each story within this collection represents top class storytelling anchored in gritty location detail and finely drawn characters, slices of life with supernatural scarring. The book is beautifully put together, a hallmark of the no expense spared quality exhibited by all PS Publishing productions. No fan of Mark Morris's work will want to be without this collection and those who do not yet know him will find it to be a comprehensive introduction.

Warts and All is published by PS Publishing and is available to purchase from their website, Amazon and other retailers. For more details go to: https://www.pspublishing.co.uk

John Gilbert

A SMALL THING FOR YOLANDA by Jan Edwards

The Paris Metro murder of May 1937 remains an unsolved real-life locked-room mystery and it seems papers relating to the investigation are sealed by the French authorities until 2038.

Laetitia Toureaux, a young Italian widow, was seen boarding a first class Metro carriage at Porte de Charenton station and, ninety seconds later, at Porte Doree, she was found alone and dying, with the knife that killed her protruding from her torso. Laetitia was the widow of a well-to-do young Frenchman who, snubbed by his snobbish family, was forced to work in a factory. By night she was said variously to be a bar hostess in the Montmartre district; that she was planted in the club district to spy on the notorious La

Cagoule (a far-right anti-communist terror group that operated in France between the wars) for the French security services; that she worked for a detective agency; that she spied for the Italians and made many clandestine trips to their embassy.

Any or all of those rumours may well have some basis in fact. The investigation into her death did point toward La Cagoule, yet, at the outset of WW2, the case was set aside as a 'crime passionnel'. And after the war ended the case file was 'sealed' by the French authorities and remains unsolved.

Jan Edwards takes this fascinating true-life mystery and provides us with a both a solution and a stand-out tale of occult fiction. Taking the rumoured double life of Letitia as a take-off point, she introduces us to Yolanda, Mme Toureaux's alter-ego, an elegant Mata Hari figure, skilled in the art of seduction and the craft of espionage. A freelance operative with private investigation agency, L'Agence Rouss, Youlanda is engaged by two clients, Fortier and Le Carreau, themselves obviously with the security services (although reluctant to specify which branch), to use her charms to get close to Etienne Plourde, a man whose involvement with far-right terror groups has brought him to the authorities' attention. Plourde falls quickly for Yolanda and their first tryst ends literally with a bang, after an explosion in his apartment, in which she has seen evidence of the presence of disturbing and unnatural creatures and is puzzled as to the presence of a box of silver bullets.

It becomes apparent that Yolanda was the target of the detonation and a further encounter with a horrific monstrosity in Pere Lachaise cemetery, while visiting her late husband's grave, confirms that there are dark forces at play that mean her harm. Yolanda, however, is not without resources and allies of her own and discovers that the enigmatic Le Carreau may know something about the mysterious ailment that killed her husband. The denouement, of course, takes place in a Metro carriage and does not disappoint.

This is a superb novella and Jan Edwards packs a multitude of delights into its eighty-six pages. The sense of place is brilliantly done, evoking both the glamour and the intrigue of the Parisian *entre-deux-guerres* epoch, while still retaining a wry contemporary sensibility. Letitia/Yolanda is an appealing and fascinating creation and her double life nicely sets the tone for a tale where most of the other characters have alter egos and/or hidden agendas. The shift from the world of espionage, political unrest and the emerging struggle between fascists and communists, towards a hidden conflict between occult forces and creatures is tensely and subtly done and while the experienced horror reader may predict a certain direction when Yolanda finds a box of silver bullets, Edwards is too well versed in the supernatural to confine her tale to lycanthropy alone, although, fittingly for a tale set in France, the legend of the Loup-garou does indeed feature.

For a novella, an impressive range of topics are raised, from the art of seduction, to the rise of the far-right in inter-war France (foreshadowing the Vichy regime), to Nazi spies (Herr Tildmann, an associate of Etienne Plourde), is a memorably monstrous creation) and the Third Reich's fascination with the occult and quite a few mysteries are resolved, including the tragic and unexplained death of the late Msr. Toureaux. The petty snobbery and thinly veiled racism and sexism of the 1930s is subtly evoked by the various characters treatment of and attitude towards Laetitia/Yolanda, whose liberated sensibilities and independent nature cause her to both rise above it and view it with a cynical detachment. Of course, being a horror tale, there is gore and scares aplenty too, during Yolanda's visits to Claude's apartment, Pere Lachaise and in the Metro.

Overall, this is a rich and rewarding read and one wishes that it were longer, as the welter of detail could easily carry a full novel; failing this, one hopes that Jan Edwards will choose to set more tales in the supernatural Parisian milieu she has created so evocatively (and this is added to even more by the amazing cover, courtesy of Peter Coleborn). While we only have eighteen more years to wait until the French authorities release details of the investigation into the murder of the real Mde. Toureaux, these will have to be sensational indeed to match the ingenious solution contained in *A Small Thing For Yolanda*.

Jan Edwards is an editor of anthologies for The Alchemy Press, the British Fantasy Society, Fox Spirit and others. Her short fiction has appeared in many crime, horror and fantasy anthologies. Some of those tales have been collected in *Leinster Gardens and Other Subtleties*, and *Fables and Fabrications*. Her novels include *Sussex Tales*, *Winter Downs* (Bunch Courtney book one, and winner of the Arnold Bennett Book Prize), *In Her Defence*, and *Listed Dead*.

A Small Thing For Yolanda is published by The Alchemy Press and is available to purchase from their website, Amazon and other outlets. For more details go to: https://alchemypress.wordpress.com

Con Connolly

THE CURSE OF THE FLEERS by Basil Copper

Warning: Review contains mild plot spoilers

In Victorian times, Captain Guy Hammond is recovering in London after being injured whilst serving for Her Majesty's forces in Afghanistan. During his convalescence period, he is contacted by an old Army friend, Cedric Fleer, who pleas for his help in a mystery surrounding his stately family home in

Dorset, which, it seems, is driving his father, Sir John Fleer, insane.

Hammond soon decides to travel to the Fleer home to aid his friend and his family in their troubles, finding himself embroiled in an enigmatic case involving a bitter historical feud dating back to Cromwellian times, a phantom figure stalking the walls of the Fleer mansion at night, and a long-lost buried treasure.

As the bodies begin to mount up, and with the assistance of a local police detective named Cobbett, the dashing Captain Hammond goes in hot pursuit of his quarry, while at the same time dealing with matters of the heart relating to a beautiful young woman called Claire Anstey.

I must admit, I was largely unfamiliar with the works of Basil Copper beforehand, but I'm certainly glad to have now read this Victorian Gothic novel by him.

A slow burner at first, Copper sets the scene nicely in picturesque Dorset, vividly capturing the stunning scenery and placing the reader right there in the midst of the action. There is a certain very British "Sunday evening period drama" feel to things – and I mean that in the best possible way – with the finely detailed countryside surrounding the Fleer house, the seaside town of

Sar Malna, the handsome, brave hero, and the classy, beautiful young ladies on horseback.

When the real story kicks into gear – that of the Fleer "curse", and which involves murders, spooky happenings in the middle of the night, a music hall-style entertainer known as The Great Waldo and a strange private zoo – we are treated to some enjoyable Gothic high jinks, very much in the vein of Conan Doyle and his contemporaries.

Although I'm no expert on the classics and my main experiences with them would be through the likes of Stoker and Shelley, I believe that readers of *The Curse of the Fleers* may very well associate it with other greats such as Agatha Christie and perhaps even the Bronte sisters. And any story with spooky castles (the Fleer home is a former fort), dark, treacherous history, charming ladies and hidden treasure is always going to have an instant appeal to me. I have to confess I also fell for the red herring.

This work by Basil Copper is the perfect companion for a nice, quiet relaxing weekend at home, where you can just sit back and immerse yourself in some quirky, more traditional, escapist fun from a bygone age. One that also comes with an Introduction by Stephen Jones, cover artwork by Stephen E. Fabian and, fascinatingly, the in-depth original notes by the author, offering a wonderful insight into the mind of a man described by August Derleth as "An outstanding British writer in the genre".

As a side note, this is the recently discovered long-lost and most complete version of *The Curse of the Fleers*, as Basil Copper originally intended it, after a heavily revised publication of it was released in the 1970s.

The Curse of the Fleers is published by Drugstore Indian Press, an imprint of PS Publishing, and is available to purchase from their website, Amazon and other retailers. For more details go to: https://www.pspublishing.co.uk

Trevor Kennedy

TALKING TO STRANGERS AND OTHER WARNINGS by Tina Rath

When people try to ridicule the horror and fantasy genres as lightweight and frothy or gory and gratuitous puff, I just point them in the direction of authors such as Tina Rath.

Dr. Rath is truly a renaissance woman; an academic with a fascination for supernatural literature and folklore, an actress, Queen Victoria impersonator, poet, and librarian; she has a formidable intellect and ferocious wit. Oh, and according to Gail Nina-Anderson's 'Introduction' to *Talking to Strangers*, Tina's latest short story collection, she is a part-time vampire.

The twenty-nine supernatural tales in her brand new 'best of' collection range from the dark and forbidding to the gently humorous, many of them distilling a sense of unease from everyday items in contemporary settings with a hefty sting in the tale.

The best stories in the collection demonstrate Dr. Rath's deep knowledge of classic and contemporary supernatural fiction. Alien encounters is the theme of 'Talking to Strangers in Finsbury Park'; 'A Visit to Blastings Manor' is a superb Christmas ghost story; in 'This is How It Happened', a classic fairy tale is given a modern setting. A young cleaner gives a hospital ward an unusually deep clean in 'Ilona' and in 'A Beautiful Boy', a handsome young man appears to bring out the best and youthfulness renewed in an old folks' home.

A newcomer at St Walburga's school shows herself as no geek and no pushover for the bullies in 'Scruffy The Vampire Slayer' and a lodger proves more difficult to get rid of than originally anticipated in 'Sitting Tenant'. 'Diversion' takes bus passengers on anything but a magical mystery tour whilst 'A Trick of The Dark' poses the fateful question, "What kind of job finishes just at sun-set?". '"It's White and It Follows Me"' is a ghostly lament; 'The Fetch' in a tale of a ghostly guest first published last year in a collection to commemorate the life of R. Chetwynd-Hayes; in 'The Bus', Mrs Fortescue waits for eternity and in the 'Fifth Sense' the author engages in some clever lycanthropic olfaction (the lengths to which I go in order to hide spoilers).

Packed full of supernatural fun and surprises, *Talking to Strangers*... demonstrates the great breadth and depth of Tina Rath's talent as a writer of supernatural fiction, collecting together the very best of her output during thirty-seven very productive years and four stories which were specially written for this book. Entertaining, dark, perplexing and humorous, the stories will keep horror fans enthralled during many a day in lockdown and beyond.

Talking to Strangers and Other Warnings is published by The Alchemy Press and is available to purchase from their website, Amazon and other outlets. For more details go to: https://alchemypress.wordpress.com

John Gilbert

LES VACANCES by Phil Sloman

At a time when families are in lockdown due to the threat of COVID-19 infection and are dreaming of the day in which they will be set free, it seems fitting that Phil Sloman should take as his protagonists Frank and Elizabeth, a couple desperate to escape their humdrum lives and lacklustre marriage. Escape in this instance is to a holiday home – a 'gite' – in an idyllic French hamlet.

All seems to be going well until they get lost on the road. Elizabeth is alarmed at the sight of a contorted crone on the road and Frank almost crashes the car. Not the most auspicious of starts to this once in a lifetime holiday, but things get worse when they discover that their rental property is situated on the site where a group of monks had been burned at the stake and buried.

Elizabeth begins to have nightmares about sinister torch-bearing brown-robed figures and begins to have suspicions about Frank when he takes more than a passing interest in Madeline, their attractive hostess. Her dreams become more intense and her fear increases as they appear to feature Madeline's mysterious mother. The holiday which was apparently sent from heaven quickly descends into hell as Frank and Elizabeth become embroiled in the local village's dark past which refuses to stay buried.

Les Vacances is a cleverly crafted tale in the currently trending folk horror genre, with well wrought characters, a slow, careful build and an denouement which, though not totally unexpected given the tragic trajectory of such tales, is nevertheless hugely satisfying. Phil Sloman, whose previous work includes the British Fantasy Award-nominated *Becoming David* and his short story collection *Broken on the Inside*, is certainly a talent to watch and, given his literary style, one who, I suspect, will quickly garner even greater audiences worldwide.

Les Vacances is published by The Alchemy Press and is available to purchase from their website, Amazon and other outlets. For more details go to: https://alchemypress.wordpress.com

John Gilbert

ROADSIDE PICNIC by Arkady & Boris Strugatsky

The Strange Potato Salad of the Cosmos

Allow me to take you on a journey. Since you're still reading I'm going to assume you agreed. Any problems you have with what's written after this are your own fault.

Imagine that you are a member of a sentient, dominant species of a planet. Perhaps you're bipedal, and the product of hundreds of thousands of years of evolution from some kind of hairy primate species. Or that a deity of some kind created you as you are for the ground up. Whichever scenario that offends you the least, really. It doesn't matter at this moment in the story and you can always change your mind later.

Now, you're this bipedal creature, and you think you're pretty on top of things. Maybe there's life outside your world, maybe there isn't. It doesn't much matter to you at the time because you have a job to go to, bills to pay, and media to consume. Mostly you're still worried about making it from one day to the next, in a not dissimilar way to your ancestors.

Then, all of a sudden, creatures from another planet or another dimension or from the sprinkles on your ice cream show up at several points across the planet. They don't stay long or seem all that inconvenienced by the military efforts set against them. Then, just as suddenly as they arrived, they leave. Up, zoom, gone.

Except, not everything about them is gone. There is much alien material left behind, almost all of it useful in some way, almost all of it dangerous. How do you think it would effect not only your life, but societies, civilizations, and the world as a whole?

That's the question in the world of *Roadside Picnic* by Arkaday and Boris Strugatsky.

The novel follows Redrick "Red" Schuhart, a stalker in North America (probably Canada.) A stalker is someone who goes into the zones – the locations of the alien visits – and recovers technology or material. It's a dangerous profession, and not least because many of these sojourns into the zones are illegal.

Much of what had been left behind by the visitors is dangerous in ways that no one on Earth has ever encountered before. There are places of intense gravity that can crush you to the thickness of a coin, there's slime that can decompose anything that touches it, and there are areas that can turn a person into a pile of dust and clothing. Something new, wondrous, and fatal is being discovered all the time, making the zones the most uncertain places to traverse.

Stalkers are romanticized, admired like astronauts or Western outlaws, or both. But the life of a stalker isn't easy, not only because arrest by governing authorities is a constant danger. This is an area that can re-animate the dead and cause the children of stalkers to be born mutated, and yet people still flock to the zones like people to the California gold rush, looking for their fame and fortune. Most of them die.

Roadside Picnic is an interesting book. The story premise is interesting, yes, but it's more about how the alien visitation affected the characters. The Strugatsky brothers have tackled sociological and philosophical implications of alien visitation and have done so in a way that's not academic or preachy. The characters deal with things that no human has ever had to even consider (mainly because so many things that show up in the zones are inconceivable) and still act in a believably human way.

The genre is usually identified as science fiction, but I'm not sure that's exactly right. I'd say it's cosmic horror pressed through a traditional science fiction filter. Science fiction tends to have a tone to it as something positive or negative – it passes a judgement on not only the events in the story, but also the society in which the story was written. *Roadside Picnic* doesn't, to me, seem to want to make a judgement call one way or another. It merely presents the way that the Strugatsky brothers believe humanity would react to all the complications (and there are many) that such an alien visitation would bring. Less teaching and more showing.

The story surrounding this book, much like the one it contains, is a strange one to those unfamiliar with the Soviet society it was published in. The edition that I have, the one available on Amazon at time of writing, contains a story at the back from Boris Strugatsky of its publication. Soviet literary censorship, like much of what the Soviets did, was a nonsensical, ideological maze that killed so many things. Indeed this novel almost didn't come about because of the difficulty created for the Strugatsky brothers for the most idiotic reasons.

It skates by pretty much free of "communism-good-capitalism-bad" (it's not even set in Russia) but it still can be a little off-putting for readers. That reason isn't ideologically or that it's from the late 1970s, but that it's a translation.

Prose within *Roadside Picnic* is much like what native English speakers are used to, but dialogue is structured oddly. It isn't a deal breaker by any means, but it's clear that it would flow differently in Russian than it does in English. If you aren't used to reading translated works, it's something you'll have to get used to.

Roadside Picnic should have its own Barnes and Noble classic edition. Not only is it up there with the greats in science fiction, like H. G. Wells or Ray Bradbury, but with the horror greats like H. P. Lovecraft and Robert W. Chambers. It's an eye opener to the casual, and probably the ravenous reader too. Like the stalkers in the book, traversing unusual and dangerous areas of literature can yield fortune. Or it can lead to disaster, but you have the advantage of being able to put the book down. Although, also like the stalkers in the book, it's unlikely that you'll be able to stop.

Roadside Picnic is published by Gollancz and is available to purchase from Amazon and other outlets.

Carl R. Jennings

PROJECT NOTEBOOK by Jason J. McCuiston

Here Come the Men in Black
(and the Commies and the Greys too!)...

Set mainly in Seattle and the state of Washington in 1947, *Project Notebook* follows the adventures of the clandestine government task force of the title, assigned, in part, to locate and solve the mystery of unidentified bright lights in the night skies that may be extraterrestrial in origin – little green men from outer space potentially!

The story is narrated by Project Notebook's wise-cracking, World War II veteran, pulp detective-style team leader, Elzabad "El" Summers, and begins with him, along with his colleagues – the attractive, though no-nonsense, Olivia Cornell, Lt. Thomas "Red" Edwards, a black man battling real world prejudices along with an otherworldly invasion of origin unknown, and the somewhat loose cannon "Wild" Bill Nowakowski – encountering the mysterious lights one night on a highway, which soon results in collective amnesia and them being temporarily split up.

When El, Olivia and Red soon regroup, it appears Bill has been arrested for attacking police officers, but there is something much more sinister going on, and as the trio investigate further they soon find themselves at the centre of a shady plot involving UFO witnesses, "Men in Black", Russian agents, and something not of this planet invading the skies of the Pacific Northwest…

As a self-confessed 1990s *X-Files* fanboy, this type of book is always going to appeal to my inner Mulder, however, from a more unbiased perspective, and while this type of conspiracy mystery has been done many times before, what really won me over was the characters and characterisation. The main trio are all fully-rounded, flawed (always the most interesting!) characters, with a compelling tension between them, and they leap off the page, especially the narrating lead of Elzabad. Another great strength is the pacing, combining the character moments and backstory/flashbacks excellently with the more action-driven sequences. There's an emotional core to proceedings – McCuiston knows his characters and cares about them. It also deals very well with the post-WW2 fallout of the era, race relations in America of the time and twentieth century history.

There is some greatly enjoyable stuff within *Project Notebook,* a supernatural conspiracy thriller based on real life events, including the modern day lore surrounding the meteorite incident in Tunguska, Russia in 1908, the Aurora, Texas UFO incident in 1897, and "Operation Paperclip" concerning Nazi scientists in the aftermath of the Second World War. The old pulp references add a lot of fun to the mix too.

Jason J. McCuiston is an author of exceptional talent, so I certainly recommend this offering by him, his first novel, especially if, like me, you have a particular fondness for this sub-genre of science fiction. Go check it out – the Truth really is in *Project Notebook* (sorry, I couldn't resist)!

Project Notebook is available to purchase from Amazon.

Trevor Kennedy

JAM by Yahtzee Croshaw (audiobook version)

Preserves Without the Preservation Part

Just in case you've been sequestered in the International Space Station or you're a member of a subspecies of humans that exclusively reside in basements, I should say that the world has been a little topsy recently. I'm sure turvy is on its way, but we're not quite there yet at time of writing. At the onset of what I'll call the International Anti-Social Funtime Hour, there were plenty who seriously considered what they would do in the event of an apocalypse. People did so before the International Anti-Social Funtime Hour, but this time it was less "idle interesting thought" and more "lets rush to the grocery store for toilet paper."

Since early 2020, people have been consuming more media related to the International Anti-Social Funtime Hour, which to me seems like having the urge to listen to *Disco Inferno* while you're on fire. I'm not judging you, you understand, I'm here to judge a book. Which is why I felt now it was time to revisit one of the most funny and absurd depictions of apocalypse on the market: *Jam* by "Yahtzee" Crowshaw.

The setting of *Jam* is Brisbane, Australia, that has been covered by carnivorous strawberry jam. No, you didn't just have a seizure: it is jammy substance that consumes organic matter. In this novel, that stuff that makes the J of PB&J wants to pack you for lunch too.

Our protagonist and narrator is Travis, whose life didn't amount to much before his city was submerged to the waist in lethal jam, and the event didn't do much to improve his prospects. Along his pinball journey across the city he is joined by his roommate Tim, a directionless man who saw his opportunity to shine in this misfortune; Angela, the barista with dreams of being a journalist; and Don, the game programer, and the only one of the group whose life was going pretty well before strawberry-scented death appeared.

Crashing into their dynamic is the mysterious X, the untrustworthy American woman who may have a connection to it all; and the muscular Y, the Grievous Bodily Harm charge that walks like a man, acting as X's guard and muscle. Together they traverse the city, encountering those who were also on the fringes of society and have coped in a far less healthy way.

What is easily the best thing about *Jam* is that it couldn't be more firmly set in British-style humor if it was written by a scone that had learned to read exclusively from Douglas Adams and G. K. Chesterton. This book is full of dry wit, hilarious word play, and the best thing about British humor: the routine clashing with the absurd. You would think that man-eating jam being spread over your city would radically change your life, but not with the residents of Brisbane. No, time and again these people try to force what they're familiar with to work in their new, ridiculous situation.

There's a downside to this kind of story structure, and it's that the characters can suffer. Not that they suffer throughout the story – that's typically a positive thing for the reader – but that they're more one-note. The main focus of *Jam* is spent going from event to event, while the main characterization of Tim, Angela, and Don is that they have a comic obsession. Not that they don't develop, but it's a minor thing and not the focus of the narrative.

The protagonist, Travis, is the most stark example of this. He is a very passive character, often times being literally pulled along the plot. It isn't that he has a flat arc, because the world doesn't change because of him, but things more happen around him. He shows some pep in his development with his desire to save Mary, the bird-eating spider that he and Tim find in a neighbor's apartment (comic obsession again), but even that is more to create tension in the plot later on.

This isn't to say that they're not interesting, because how they are quintessentially themselves in this disaster is pretty interesting and hilarious, it's just that their development isn't the focus, and they lose depth because of it.

The world isn't going to end because of the International Anti-Social Funtime Hour. I don't mind putting money down on that because I won't be out a dollar either way. So you might as well enrich your mind while you have the time.

Jam isn't exactly about an apocalypse, it's more about holding up a mirror to our notions of the end of the world and society as a whole. People cope in the worst way possible, and that is an unwillingness to adapt correctly. We all wonder about how we'd do, and *Jam* answers: not so well, and in the stupidest ways.

If you are a fan of Crowshaw's fast-talking game review YouTube show, *Zero Punctuation*, then you'll recognize the humor (and a few of the lines.) He narrates it as well for the audiobook and it is a joy to listen to. Even if you've never heard of him, *Jam* is a fantastic addition to the library of satirical humor. So grab your peanut butter sandwiches and dry pastries and dive waist-deep into it.

Jam is published by Dark Horse and is available in paperback, on Kindle and on audiobook from Amazon and other outlets.

Carl R. Jennings

STAR TREK: PICARD: THE LAST BEST HOPE by Una McCormack

Star Trek: Picard: The Last Best Hope acts as a preamble to the show *Star Trek: Picard* (2020) on CBS Access streaming service. This iteration follows the timeline of *Star Trek: The Next Generation* (1987-1994), specifically after the events of *Star Trek: Nemesis* (2002), the year 2379 in the Trekverse. The book fast forwards twenty years past that, placing the setting in the year 2399. By now Picard is an Admiral no longer assigned to his former ship, the Enterprise E. He is tasked with coordinating the relocation efforts of Romulan citizens to a new homeworld. Their sun is about to go supernova.

I thought this was a nice nod of correction to the *Star Trek* (2009) of the "Abrams-verse", aka the Kelvin timeline. There we were told that Romulus was threatened by a supernova. Ambassador Spock had an idea of how to prevent Romulus' destruction by the use of something referred to as "Red Matter" that would consume the explosion. Spock was not successful, the "Red Matter" created a black hole consuming the planet Romulus and its citizens. This gave rise to revenge by a Romulan Captain called Nero. He blamed the loss of his family and world on Spock. This main plot is introduced early to erase that convoluted version of *Trek* they tried to force down our throats with sleek lens flares.

So now it's left up to Picard to set the record straight. Makes sense to me. This time around he has a new First Officer in which to groom. Her name is Raffi Musiker and unlike Riker the two of them are on a first name basis. She often refers to him as "JL", short for Jean-Luc, of course. He in turn refers to her as "Raffi" and never by her rank. That's a vast difference from the Picard we've come to know on the bridge of the Enterprise E. I believe they call that character development. To assist Picard in the Romulan relocation, Starfleet commissions the help of a brilliant scientist by the name of Bruce Maddox. He is the Director of the Division of Advanced Synthetic Research of the Daystrom Institute, located in Okinawa, Japan. Against his best interest, Starfleet wants him to build a significant amount of synthetic lifeforms to speed up the relocation process of the Romulans.

This would seem simple enough, but in their haste to help the Romulans, Starfleet has totally ignored – and perhaps on purpose for a better good – Romulan folklore, looked upon as superstition. A significant faction of Romulan zealots are against synthetic life or what they refer to as "synths". Not to mention their top scientist Dr. Maddox doesn't have his heart in the project. He has other scientific ambitions that he wants to pursue. In his mind there can only be one Data and he is no Noonien Soong. This was the famous cyberneticist who created Data. Unsure if his personal goals will ever see the light of day, he begins to put them aside and follow orders. He meets a bright and beautiful student, Agnes Jurati, and they become lovers. She convinces him to pursue both projects.

Their relationship blossoms into a fine romance. So much so that conspirators sabotage his work on the synths causing Geordi La Forge to open up an investigation. Here Geordi acts as a Quality Assurance Officer for this project. He and Maddox appear to be acquaintances. This leads us up to the massacre and destruction of the shipyard facility on Mars. All of which brings Picard to give an ultimatum to the Federation, forcing him into an unwanted retirement.

Overall this is a good tie-in to the television series. Yet, I have one complaint and that's the amount of profanity used. It's even worse than what you hear on the show. This is *Star Trek* and this amount of curse words simply are out of place. What was the reason for adding this into the *Trek* lexicon? The phrase "Dammit, Jim!" is enough. Perhaps the producers were trying to attract a newer audience? If so, they have thrown manure towards a work of art. Part of Gene Roddenberry's premise was that bad social norms ceased to exist past first contact. It has no place here, or as Spock would say: it's "highly illogical."

Star Trek: Picard: The Last Best Hope is published by Pocket Books and is available to purchase from Amazon and other outlets in hardcover and paperback, and also on Kindle and Audiobook.

Abdul-Qaadir Taariq Bakari-Muhammad

THE ABOMINABLE by Dan Simmons

"We have absolutely no concept of what lies ahead for us."
– The Abominable

Dan Simmons returns to frozen climes again after his novel *The Terror*, but the difference this time around is that this book is one that is much less concerned with the supernatural and more in exploring themes of obsession, betrayal and the often appalling nature of self-discovery.

Simmons opens the novel with an introduction that is not extraneous to the pages that follow, as so often such prefaces can prove to be. Told from the writer's 'experience' meeting a dying old man in preparation for constructing an entirely different book, Simmons describes a set of circumstances that immediately begin blending the fictional with the factual. The author talks about his own initial doubts regarding the veracity of the retired climber's tale, but when he later receives a set of notebooks written by this Jacob Perry, long after his death, we are invited to take a literary 'leap of faith' and indulge in what is presented to the reader as the journals of a young American recounting his experience in the mid-1920s of a perilous expedition to summit Mount Everest.

Using this 'found journal' narrative device, Simmons is able to craft a tale that distils a terrifying journey that is itself awash with technical detail, religious history and, certainly towards the close of the novel, a good portion of sanguinary violence. Simmons/Perry posit a story that, much like Simmons' earlier work – specifically his novel *The Crook Factory* – takes a great many liberties with historical fact shot through with a suspense dynamic that is, as always with Simmons, confident and assured. Equipment preparation, the dangers of injury, whether it be from opthalmia, frostbite or altitude sickness ("mountain lassitude") are mixed in with the apparently meditative qualities of climbing, group paranoia and Tibetan-centric superstition.

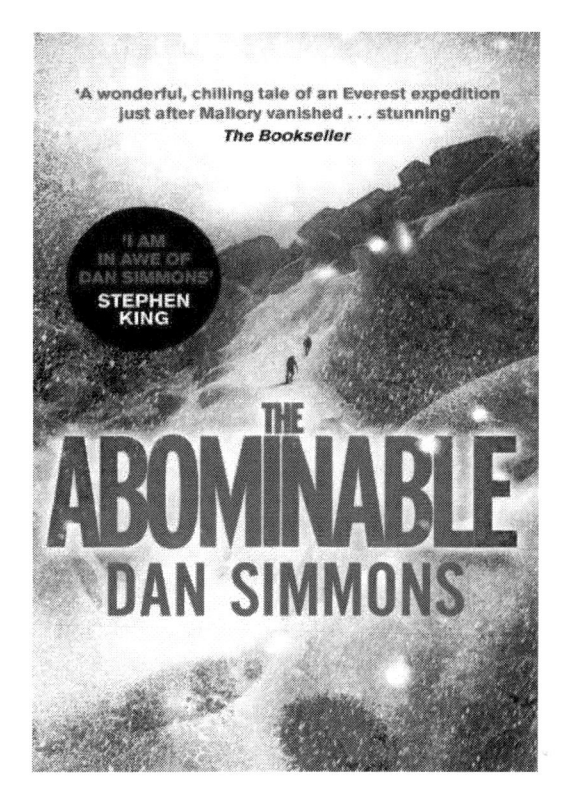

The problems with Simmons' narrative are that often the text is over-saturated with the technical side of climbing – there's a great deal of mechanical minutia here; everything from the improvement of crampon boots, the developments in ice-axe technology, pitons, ascending grapples, ropes, goggles, oxygen tanks, clothing, heating implements and so on. The reader may very well feel that after finishing this they'd be quite au fait with the early twentieth century history of mountain climbing, which is no bad thing in itself, but it does become mildly wearying in places. Also, there's the matter of exposition on the part of the author, which in places comes across as bizarrely clunky and artificial. There's an event quite early on in this lengthy tome where a climbing test of sorts is set for Perry and his young French comrade, Jean Claude, that is so obvious in its foreshadowing of what will occur later in the book that it appears calculated and predictably elliptical.

Very much like the central narrative theme of the novel, this is a reading experience that approximates the idea of a long mountain trek as it's really only in the last third of the book that Simmons' flair for suspense really kicks in. Subsequently the pages fly by as the author summits his own admirably literary endeavour and gives the reader a shocking coda to *The Abominable* that is perhaps not quite what the reader may be expecting.

This is a marvellous work of fiction from a writer who consistently delivers profound and intriguing works, but for those looking for a rather predictable scenario involving possibly supernatural elements they may feel somewhat short-changed here. The horrors here are far more insidious and thought-provoking than legendary mountain-dwelling creatures. A engagingly quixotic author whose work often incorporates disparate genres, he's fashioned a splendidly riveting tale here that's deeply affecting, beautifully written and diverting in the very best sense of the word.

4.5/5

The Abominable is published by Sphere and is available to purchase from Amazon and other outlets.

James Keen

CATS' PERIL and *THE ADVENTURE OF AN CUPLA* by Kevin L. O'Brien

Cats' Peril

Eile and Sunny are a couple who live and work together. One snowy night they find a cat on their doorstep, weak and near to death. They take it inside to nurse it. However, realising that it needs medical attention they take the cat to a local vet, Joyce Luasaigh. Once at the vet's, Eile and Sunny find out the cat's address from its microchip and decide to go and inform the owner. When they leave the vet's, the same taxi cab they took there is still waiting outside for them. The lady cabbie drives them to the address from the microchip and what they find is a neglected warehouse. They enter and find some sort of robot guards who escort them to the owner forcibly.

Meanwhile, Joyce starts to converse with the cat asking her what her name is. The cat tells the vet that her name is Snowrunner. This seems to mean something to Joyce as she tells Snowrunner she has heard of her and is honoured to meet her. Snowrunner tells Joyce that Mabuse caused her injuries. Joyce is angered by this as she knows who Mabuse is.

Back at the warehouse, Sunny and Eile are taken to Mabuse, who wants her cat back...

The Adventure of An Cupla

Snowrunner (the cat from *Cats' Peril*) has been adopted and renamed Snowshoe Kitty by Eile and Sunny. One night, whilst they are both sleeping, Snowshoe Kitty performs a ritual over them. Unbeknownst to Eile and Sunny, they have been sent into the Dreamlands at the request of Bast, Queen of Cats. They appear in the same dream and Sunny quickly figures out that it's not just a dream.

Descending down the Seven Hundred Steps of Deeper Slumber and finally emerging in the Dreamlands proper, they are taken by a cat named Shadow Stalker to meet the cat council in Ulthar. The Queen tells them that Mayv their friend is in danger and that they are 'The Twins' and the only ones who can save Mayv because they have special qualities. However, their bodies lie vulnerable in the waking world, and although time passes differently here – an hour in the waking world is the equivalent to a week in the Dreamlands – Eile and Sunny only have three days in the waking world before their physical bodies will start to die and they will be lost in Dreamlands forever. As their bodies lie defenceless in the waking world, Team Girl begins a journey across an unknown land to save Mayv and themselves.

They are assigned a guide in the form of a cat named Shadow-Stalker and a Zoog called Eolai. Following the river Skai, they head for Dylath-Leen to find Mayv. Eile is not happy about their predicament and voices her concerns to Sunny after they are attacked in the woods. Sunny is now scared because

Eile has always been the stronger, more stoic of the two girls. Despite their concerns, Team Girl continues on to the city of Dylath-Leen. Once outside the city, Shadow-Stalker tells them to lay low in the woods and they will go on ahead and ensure safe passage into the city. There will be eyes everywhere and they don't want a repeat of their encounter in the woods.

Agreeing to Shadow-Stalker's request, they are hiding in the woods when they hear the voices of men. When they listen closely, they overhear a conversation about themselves and Mayv being a sacrifice. Deciding they can't wait for Shadow-Stalker's return they follow the men into the city, oblivious to the danger they've put themselves in.

Following the men through the maze that is Dylath-Leen, they find themselves in a tavern and again overhear that Mayv is in the place with the broken spire. Believing that Mayv is being held captive, Team Girl searches the city skyline for the building with a broken spire. Once they find it, they sneak into the building and find Mayv, not being held against her will. Eile and Sunny have interrupted a very private moment which doesn't go down well with their friend Mayv, who doesn't need their help at all.

There are aspects of these books that I really liked. The LGBTQ+ representation in the form of Eile, Sunny and Mayv was refreshing to see as often these types of characters are antagonists not protagonists. However, I felt that the sex between Eile and Sunny was not always necessary and their love could have been portrayed through other physical contact. Another feature that I liked was the use of excerpts from *The Dreamlands for Dummies* at the start of each chapter. It was a nice way to feed into the world-building and correlate the experiences of Eile and Sunny with the lore of the universe.

The books rely heavily on the mythology of H. P. Lovecraft, which can be seen with the use of things like the Dreamlands and the river Skai. O'Brien has also dipped into a couple of other worlds too, most notably Tolkien – there's a mountain called Thorin. In O'Brien's favour he also uses a lot of Irish Gaelic words (he's obviously proud of his heritage) and there is a glossary at the end to help those of us who aren't fluent.

For me as a reader, what didn't work was the syntax of the characters. Sunny in particular says things like "Don'cha see?" and "Ya ditz". I felt that I wasn't quite sure what accent she was supposed to have, as it's not explained. Also, Mayv is spelt in two ways – Mayv and Medb – it's not until well into the story that there is an explanation as to why.

Finally, at the end of *Cats' Peril*, O'Brien has included a biography for each character. As an idea it's good, but in practice it has stereotypical features like Mabuse was "in at least one instance emotionally and physically abused and in another sexually abused". It just came off as a bit contrived.

On the whole, Kevin O'Brien has written two books that are like Marmite. He's used characters and settings from other people's work to help write his stories. I myself wasn't aware of this until I read it in the author's interview where he says, "I was a fan of a webcomic called *Girly*. I turned Otra and Winter into Eile and Sunny and Marshmallow Kitty into Snowshoe Kitty." The shame of it is that, like I have said, there are aspects of this that are promising.

Cats' Peril and *The Adventure of An Cupla* are published by Lindisfarne Press and are available to purchase from Amazon.

Helen Scott

ALMOST SURELY by Gavin Jefferson

You Were Fated to Read this Subtitle... Or Were You?

Do you ever think that your life is out of your control? That's probably a stupid question to ask anyone old enough to actually think about their life, but the answer isn't the point. It was a review technique to lead you to think about fate, so I'm going to give myself a pass on that one. Truthfully, I was going to give myself a pass anyway because I'm the one in front of the keyboard writing this, not you, so I get to make the rules.

By the last count, there's a fair number of people who believe in fate. It can be comforting to know that there is an order to things, even if that order isn't in your favor, or doesn't make sense to you, or is completely horrific. That there is *something* out there that has all its ducks in a row, and is making sure that what's supposed to be happening, happens, is a lot off a person's shoulders.

But have you ever considered *who* it is that actually makes sure what's supposed to be is what is?

By the way: buckle up because there are more sentences ahead that are corkscrews of tenses.

Almost Surely, by Gavin Jefferson, mainly follows Anthony Hopper, an Agent of Influence. What's an Agent of Influence, you ask? They are the *who* who are on the ground and making sure things go the way they're supposed to in the moment. What it is that's actually supposed to happen is decided/foreseen by four heralds: Armour, Collector, Gift, and Watcher, the embodiments of Love, Death, Opportunity, and Fate respectively.

Anthony, or Tony, or Tone, resides in 1956 Manhattan and is the agent of Fate for 2016 London. As difficult as it may be to believe, Tony is in a rut in his job. As fantastical as it is, jobs are still jobs at the end of the nine to five. Mainly it's because, as paradoxically as it seems, he's mostly in the dark about the direction of his life and his purpose. It isn't helped by the fact that he isn't challenged anymore by what he does – it's second nature to him to go through the motions.

Then one day two trainees are dropped on him out of the blue. They're the twins Henry and Jack, and their presence effects his rut of a life in ways he could never have predicted.

Right out of the gate what's impressive about *Almost Surely* is that Jefferson has an excellent balance of mystical and mundane. The prologue sets up the four heralds, showing the organization but leaving it clouded so it's still something mystical. The Agents of Influence have a co-worker-like comradery, and anyone who has ever worked in an office situation will easily relate to their interactions. He does something I love with books and movies with added bureaucracy to the preternatural. This requires a delicate balance: too much of the mundane and it's boring, too little and the bureaucratic elements just seem out of place and forced. Jefferson pulls this off well.

The story of *Almost Surely* is quite surely an intriguing one. It's not a mystery, per se. It's closer to a slice of life, that slice being from Anthony Hopper's life pie. At the start there isn't a plot in the traditional sense – that doesn't come in until after the appearance of the twins – but Tony has quite the interesting life. The twins start out as the reader's "in" to the story, and evolve into much more. Beyond several choice events, the story is rolling and the pages fly.

As an addendum to this point, Jefferson writes the characters much like it's from the perspective of someone from their specific time, or even outside time. It's a wonderful way to create authenticity and is especially noticeable when they're in 2016.

There really isn't much to complain about in the book. Probably the only thing is that sometimes, when they're all together in their co-worker environment, the voices of the different Agents of Influence can sound the same. They have a different way when talking to each other than when they're talking to anyone else (you know, as co-workers do), and it can muddle the speakers in conversation. This doesn't happen often at all, and is easily rectified by going back and looking at the conversation again, but it's something to look out for.

The concepts within *Almost Surely* are ones that are difficult for most people to get their head around when they're presented in an academic way. Things like fate are vague to most people, even if they believe in it. What Gavin Jefferson has done is to put structure to it, and show how fate works in a way that people can understand. Better than that, he does it in a way that's entertaining. These aren't easy feats and you owe it to yourself to bring that effort into your life. Just start by reading the back cover description and I know you'll be hooked. I don't know if you're fated to get the book or anything, but I would say it's a safe bet.

Almost Surely is available to purchase from Amazon.

Carl R. Jennings

CORPSE WHISPERER SWORN by H.R. Boldwood

Follow Allie Nighthawk to exciting New Orleans where she raises the dead, puts down rotters, and dabbles in the mystical world of hoodoo. She's on the trail of an evil necromancer who will stop at nothing to rule the world with his army of deadheads. Is her magick strong enough to save the day? Or will this necromancer from her past kill her before she gets the chance?

She figures she's got a fifty-fifty shot. Make that forty-sixty.

Praise for the *Corpse Whisperer* Series:

"One of my favorite paranormal writers, her books are insanely fun to read. Love that her female protagonist is an ass-kicking, funny-as-hell, take-no-prisoners, next-level zombie hunter. Allie Nighthawk. She can raise them when necessary and she can put them down."
(Christiana Miller, author of the *Toad Witch Mysteries*)

"If Anita Blake and Stephanie Plum had a lovechild, it would be Allie Nighthawk. One of the funniest and freshest takes on the zombie genre I've read, with genuine heart at the core of the humor and gore."
(Dana Fredsti, author of the *Ashley Parker* and *Spawn of Lilith* series)

Get Your Copy NOW!

Available from:

Apple: https://books.apple.com/us/book/id1511106255

Kobo: https://www.kobo.com/us/en/ebook/corpse-whisperer-sworn

Google Play:
https://play.google.com/store/books/details/H_R_Boldwood_Corpse_Whisperer_Sworn?id=pIngDwAAQBAJ

Nook:
https://www.barnesandnoble.com/w/corpse-whisperer-sworn-h-r-boldwood/1136955158?ean=2940163010356

Amazon:
https://www.amazon.com/Corpse-Whisperer-Sworn-Nighthawk-Mystery-ebook/dp/B088DCM3Q7/

Find other works by H.R. Boldwood at:
https://www.amazon.com/H.-R.-Boldwood/e/B01LWY22MD

Contact H.R. Boldwood at:
www.hrboldwood.com
hrboldwood@gmail.com

FILM

NOTE: Due to cinemas throughout the world being closed because of the ongoing coronavirus situation, for this issue we have decided to review films available on streaming services along with some older classics.

THE HUNT (2020)

<u>Directed by Craig Zobel.</u>
<u>Written by Nick Cuse and Damon Lindelof.</u>
<u>Starring Betty Gilpin, Hilary Swank, Ike Barinholtz and more.</u>

Rather like the *Purge* franchise, Blumhouse's *The Hunt* is little more than a single political-satire high concept extended to feature length. But it's done with such wit, panache and (mostly) efficiency that it's difficult not to love – unless, of course, you're of the opinion that serious matters can only be treated seriously.

Indeed, had it not rapidly disappeared from cinemas as a result of the pandemic, it's not difficult to imagine that it might have become a minor success.

The fun starts early, with a prologue onboard an airplane signalling how random, gory and slightly absurd the movie's violence will be, followed by an unashamed rip-off of *The Hunger Games*'s Cornucopia sequence. The single best cinematic joke of the movie follows, with a rapid-fire series of deaths that include all the obvious "leads", leaving the less charismatic standing.

One of them, Betty Gilpin, will be the star. And if her character's backstory seems slightly contrived, well, so is the whole thing. (It was written by *Lost*'s Damon Lindelof along with Nick Cuse.) But underneath it lie some serious and even sharp points, all the same.

The Hunt repeats the idea of the upper classes killing the low for sport, as seen for example in *The Purge: Anarchy*, and there are echoes of *Get Out*'s secretly murderous liberals as well.

But here there also seem to be meta-themes about conspiracy theories and fake news. We have arrogant (and hilariously mocked) liberals hunting rednecks and conservatives, a ridiculous notion that is not too different from (say) the anti-vaxxers' beliefs, but then we also find out that the entire project began when a joke about eliminating "deplorables" was taken seriously, as evidence of a conspiracy theory.

Maybe, then, Hilary Swank – as the mastermind of the hunt that now pursues Gilpin *et al* – is a kind of victim too, losing her job over the joke and only *then* deciding to execute the fiendish plan in reality. Prejudice and craziness are equal-opportunities wreckers of life on both sides of the political divide, it appears.

The fact that much of the movie seems to take place in Croatia, despite the participants being told they are still in America, might also nod to the indeterminate eastern European origins of much dubious online news.

These ideas never dominate individual moments of the film; *The Hunt* is led by action (a little too much of it in the climactic fight, which despite superb editing and a nod to *Clockwork Orange* in its Beethoven soundtrack is overlong).

And even the characters who aren't actually thrown away in the early scenes are mostly throwaway. For example, Amy Madigan and Reed Birney contribute the movie's best performances as a sweet old couple running a country store who aren't what they seem, but they too must be sacrificed to director Craig Zobel's relentless need to keep Gilpin and everything else moving forward.

The Hunt is very slight, then, more a progression of events unpeeling an idea than a tale of real human beings with real problems. But it is supremely watchable, often very funny, less than 90 minutes long, and smarter than it looks. What more can you ask for?

The Hunt is available on Amazon Prime Video in the UK; other countries may differ.

Barnaby Page

THE HOLE IN THE GROUND (2019)

Directed by Lee Cronin.
Written by Lee Cronin and Stephen Shields.
Starring Seána Kerslake, James Quinn Markey, Kati Outinen and more.

It droops briefly to dull silliness at the conclusion, but for much of its 90 minutes *The Hole in the Ground* exploits effectively the typical strengths of recent Irish cinema – great performances, imaginative use of kitchen-sink locations, and new perspectives on much-filmed issues.

This tale of a young woman and her child, moving away from trouble to a new home and discovering things that go bump in the woods behind their refuge, also makes nice use – in a relatively low-key way – of genre tropes (the dark house, the child's bedroom, the sinister forest).

Writer-director Lee Cronin's feature debut fits snugly into at least three horror traditions: the city folk in the wilderness (the song *Rattlin' Bog* conjures up *The Wicker Man*), the unsettling child (there are echoes of *The Babadook* and *Brightburn*, to name but two), and physical possession *(Invasion of the Body Snatchers)*.

Meanwhile, it doesn't pass up an opportunity to exploit the obviously rich symbolism of holes, finding them in wallpaper patterns and coffee cups as well as the ground. There's even a touch of found footage.

All this could suggest a frantic attempt to cram in as many horror concepts as possible, but even if the tantalising early hints that we might be watching a movie about mental illness rather than evil ultimately come to little, *The Hole in the Ground* brings together its disparate threads efficiently and entertainingly enough that there's no pause to worry about how derivative it is.

The big revelation is unsurprising, but it's followed by a more satisfying last-minute twist and a pleasing, if slight, ambiguity at the close. Earlier there is one highly successful jump-scare.

Stephen McKeon's score, similarly, won't win any prizes for originality but supports the narrative usefully.

The real strength, though, is in the acting: especially Seána Kerslake as the mother (running through a wide range of emotions and moods without letting any of them become extreme), James Quinn Markey as the boy (his expression when mum takes him to the doctor is wordlessly chilling), and old hand James Cosmo as the husband of a local woman who may or may not know more than he's letting on.

That's the same beguiling sense we get from the film, at least for most of its running time: it, and the eponymous pit in the woods, know more than they're telling us. And if the secret at the bottom of the hole turns out to be a familiar one, our descent to its discovery is entertaining and at moments genuinely disquieting.

The Hole in the Ground is available on Netflix in the UK; other countries may differ.

Barnaby Page

RATTLESNAKE (2019)

Directed by Zak Hilditch.
Written Zak Hilditch.
Starring Carmen Ejogo, Theo Rossi, Emma Greenwell and more.

There is little original about this tale of a woman who must kill someone –

anyone – before sunset to repay a supernatural debt. But writer-director Zak Hilditch (known for the Stephen King adaptation *1922*, also Netflix) invests it with genuine tension, and there are sterling contributions from director of photography Roberto Schaefer (*What They Had* recently) as well as many of the small cast.

Debrianna Mansini is suitably spectral as the mysterious old woman who saves Carmen Ejogo's daughter from a snakebite, plunging Ejogo into her rather Faustian unasked-for bargain: she now has to take a life to compensate for her daughter's being spared. David Yow is a frightening gun dealer (with, chillingly, what seems to be a painting of a hooded Abu Ghraib figure in his garage – inexplicable but spooky).

Joy Jacobson is outstanding as the daughter of a dying man Ejogo briefly considers euthanising; it's only a little part but she fills the character with believable humanity; we sense she has a full past. And Ejogo herself is full of emotional energy, while Emma Greenwell is touchingly drained of it as the abused girlfriend of another potential victim.

Schaefer, meanwhile, effectively exploits locations – a half-dead Texan town, elaborate desert rock formations.

Some of the scares are tired if not precisely *predictable*, as a sequence of apparitions warns and/or threatens Ejogo. But there are moments of real eeriness too, not least towards the close, alongside some well-observed touches (Jacobson's husband unconcernedly watching TV sports by his father-in-law's hospital bed).

Rattlesnake is pure B-movie, but at 85 minutes it never outstays its welcome, and if it is derivative and a tad shallow – well, those are not terminal faults.

Rattlesnake is available on Netflix in the UK; other countries may differ.

Barnaby Page

A FIELD IN ENGLAND (2013)

Directed by Ben Wheatley.
Written by Amy Jump.
Starring Reece Shearsmith, Michael Smiley, Julian Barratt, Peter Ferdinando, Richard Glover and more.

During the English Civil War, a group of deserters with opposing allegiances find themselves, whilst on the way to an apparent alehouse, in a remote field and under the control of an alchemist named O'Neil, who forces them to search for a hidden (and possibly non-existent) treasure in the surrounding area. An odd, inexplicable, hallucinatory journey into the unknown soon awaits the men… and the viewer.

Shot in black and white and released simultaneously in cinemas, DVD and television in 2013 (quite a big game-changer at the time), *A Field in England* is an unsettling, haunting, surreal folk horror classic.

The plot, on first viewing, is somewhat obscure, intentionally so, but this is definitely the sort of film that very much improves on repeat viewing, akin in a way to Robert Eggers' *The Lighthouse* from last year, which has a similar brooding atmosphere, surrealist elements and also shot in B&W. Or maybe even the work of David Lynch, but crossed with *Witchfinder General* and *The Wicker Man*. The viewer will certainly gather a better informed opinion after watching it more than once (is it O'Neil causing the strange events, or is the field itself – which may be alive in some unnatural way – behind it all? Are they in Hell or Purgatory? Is it connected to the "black planet" glimpsed at? Or are they all just spaced out on magic mushrooms? Perhaps it's a combination of all of these factors, or maybe something else altogether??).

The dark humour and witty dialogue serves to break up the intensity of proceedings when it makes a welcome appearance, giving the viewer a moment to catch their breath.

Ben Wheatley is masterful in his direction as he seamlessly moves in and out with the camera angles whilst giving nods to his cinematic influences; the blood dripping off the grass, for example, the camera in the pit. You can almost smell the pox off the characters and how gross they are, but they're still relatable at the same time. It's like going back in time for real, making things even more disorientating. The field in question is like a psychedelic sea as it rolls in the wind, coupled later with the sort of imagery that wouldn't look out of place in a 1990s rave era music video.

There is also the argument that the script is an allegory for the English Civil War itself, which is just as viable a take, in our opinion.

Additionally, the story, and character of O'Neil with his scrying mirror, is quite possibly an allusion to the Anglo-Welsh astrologer, occultist and advisor to Queen Elizabeth I, John Dee, along with the obvious conflict in there between Christianity and the black arts too.

The performances by the small cast are sublime, especially Belfast actor Michael Smiley as the threateningly sinister O'Neil and *The League of Gentlemen*'s Reece Shearsmith as the religiously repressed "coward" Whitehead, a character who goes on one of the greatest journey arcs witnessed on screen in many years, at least for ourselves anyway.

In a movie chock-full of disturbing imagery, one (now famous) scene in particular – featuring Shearsmith's Whitehead being driven insane after being exposed to something (is it some sort of dark, possessive magic or does O'Neil rape him??) in a tent – really does stand out as one of the most powerful in modern cinema.

Add to this the beautifully shot cinematography (those theatrical "posing"/Brechtian technique-style, fourth wall-breaking shots are extremely effective) and practically perfect score/soundtrack (which includes a dreamlike version of *Lady Anne Bothwell's Lament*), and you have one of the best – and trippiest – folk horror films in recent times, one that is arguably art house with shades of Shakespeare in its delivery and will remain with you for quite some time.

Watch this film, but after you have viewed it, watch it again. It is a character-driven visceral experience, a feeling. It matters little that the plot is rather absurd and it's quite refreshing to have some real intrigue within a modern horror film.

Trevor Kennedy and GCH Reilly

NEAR DARK (1987)

<u>Directed by Kathryn Bigelow.</u>
<u>Written by Kathryn Bigelow and Eric Red.</u>
<u>Starring Adrian Pasdar, Jenny Wright, Lance Henriksen, Bill Paxton and more.</u>

Near Dark is a cross-genre film if I ever saw one. Usually anything with the word 'Western' in its description is swiftly dismissed in my books.

The casting – perfection. The story line – unique. The hearsay is that a film of the past is one that you grew up with and unless you viewed this back in your youth, it tends not to resonate as well on a contemporary level or it lacks that childhood charm. I watched this gem back in 2017 for the first time during a Halloween movie saga (in what would have been its thirty-year anniversary) and I am disappointed not to have latched on to it sooner.

Being a fan of Lance Henriksen and Bill Paxton (who feature heavily in my sci-fi collection), I cannot for the life of me figure out HOW this one slipped through the net!

The DVD cover alone is powerfully dark – alongside the film's phrase 'Pray for Daylight', it projects Bill Paxton's Severen as the ultimate badass, as he and his vampire chums (led by Henriksen's Jesse Hooker) rove the blood-barren countryside for new recruits.

The frantic keyboard sounds set the scene as screenwriter/director Kathryn Bigelow casts aside anything that is the vampiric norm – throughout the film there is no mention of strings of garlic, over-exaggerated bats, nor wooden stakes. While the evil gang prey on their human counterparts, the main enemy is purely the Sun.

This neo-Western/horror all starts when our teenage boy Caleb (Adrian Pasdar) attempts to seduce vampire Mae (Jenny Wright) which, of course, completely backfires. He *actually* gets bitten. As he slowly turns, he finds it deeply difficult to succumb to the brutal ways of vampirehood (yes, this is my own invention – like brotherhood but with vampires...).

You can see where Tarantino secured his inspiration when making *From Dusk Till Dawn*, especially in Bigelow's bar scene where the gang of terrorising vampires make an infamous kill, coaxing Caleb to commit to his 'vampire trial' which, naturally, he rebels, allowing his kill to escape like a frightened rabbit into the night.

This sees Caleb torn between his 'turning' into a vampire to become one of Jesse's crew whilst striving to stay human amongst his blood relatives, one of whom is his little sister who is revengefully abducted by the gang. Caleb spurs a stand-off between himself and Severen – a Wild West-style showdown in a desolate night-time town setting which is absolutely stunning to watch, even for a Western-pooper like me.

One of the most exhilarating scenes follows – the adrenaline-pumping climax where we actually see vampires exposed to the Sun: they do not just smoulder, they perish.

I know the secret behind how they do it with the make-up and special effects, but it is literally magnificent. For a brief moment, when you see each of the vampires awaiting his or her death (bar Mae who has 'turned' for the better) as each one melts down to a cinder (akin to The Wicked Witch in *The Wizard of Oz* but a zillion times better), genuinely, you feel a sense of empathy for this species. They are only trying to survive, preserve their existence, keep the blood pumping...

While in lockdown, I re-watched this film and hand on heart, I can confess that this is one I will never tire of. *Near Dark* is a true '80s classic.

Allison Weir

ED WOOD (1994)

<u>Directed by Tim Burton.
Written by Rudolph Grey (book), Scott Alexander and Larry Karaszewski.
Starring Johnny Depp, Martin Landau, Sarah Jessica Parker, Patricia Arquette, Jeffrey Jones, Bill Murray, Lisa Marie and more.</u>

Set in Hollywood in the 1950s and based on the life of infamous B movie director Edward D. Wood Jr., an enthusiastic, though struggling, young wannabe auteur runs into many difficulties whilst trying to find funding for his ambitious film projects. He soon befriends ageing, troubled *Dracula* star Bela Lugosi, whose own personal demons are taking their toll on him. When

Lugosi agrees to appear in some of Wood's rather offbeat productions, the duo, along with a bunch of other misfits – including fake psychic Criswell, television star Vampira and Swedish wrestler Tor Johnson – embark on an emotional and oft comedic journey together, culminating in the premiere of the cult classic *Plan 9 from Outer Space*.

Film biopics can be somewhat tricky for me. They are almost always a blend of fact and fiction, dramatic licence often used quite liberally. A few issues have been raised concerning some of the real-life people and events portrayed in this one. For example, Wood's one-time girlfriend, Dolores Fuller (who incidentally went on to write songs for Elvis Presley), according to reports, had a problem with the lack of addressing of Wood's alcoholism (a deleted scene apparently *does* reference this side of the man), citing this as the real reason she left him, adding that she also had no issue with his transvestism either (she does in the film), and actually supported it. Bela Lugosi's son was allegedly unhappy with the swearing used at times by the screen version of his father, as he was more of a classy man who never used curse words. However, if you are prepared to cast all this aside and enjoy this comedy-drama on its own terms then there is a hell of a lot to relish in *Ed Wood*.

The true heart of the film is, of course, the strange friendship between Wood and Lugosi, both played sublimely in career-defining performances by Johnny Depp and Martin Landau respectively, Landau earning a well-deserved Best Supporting Actor Oscar for his work. It is a relationship wrapped in pathos, both men fated to be tragic, though fondly remembered, characters. The supporting cast also works very well, especially Patricia Arquette as Kathy O'Hara, Lisa Marie as Vampira and Bill Murray as Bunny Breckinridge. You just can't help but like these guys, even more so because of their eccentricities. You're rooting for them, you want them to succeed, despite their limitations. Edward D. Wood Jr. is portrayed as a loveable, resourceful guy, who always encouraged and supported his friends during their efforts to realise his visions, against great odds.

Many critics, usually rather smugly, mock and scorn the real Edward Wood, labelling him the worst director of all time. I strongly disagree with this. His films are far from perfect, of course, but they're a lot of fun and come from a place of passion and an almost childlike love for the telling of wacky, over-the-top stories. Some of them – *Glen or Glenda* especially – are quite personal, too. For me, there will always be a certain degree of great charm to these types of films and, by extension, also an affection for their directors, such as Wood and the more contemporary Tommy Wiseau.

Edward D. Wood Jr. was a complex man and although it may not be a one hundred per cent accurate depiction of his life, *Ed Wood* certainly feels like a warm and fitting tribute to him. It's a true underdog movie, very emotional at times, and one of the best films to come out of the 1990s.

Trevor Kennedy

THE HATEFUL EIGHT (2015)

Directed by Quentin Tarantino.
Written by Quentin Tarantino.
Starring Samuel L. Jackson, Kurt Russell, Jennifer Jason Leigh, Walton Goggins, Demián Bichir, Tim Roth, Michael Madsen, Bruce Dern and more.

Set in wintry Wyoming during the mid-to-late 1800s, a bounty hunter named John Ruth (Kurt Russell) is delivering the criminal Daisy Domergue (Jennifer Jason Leigh) to the town of Red Rock to be hanged. On the way, they encounter a former American Civil War officer, Major Marquiss Warren (Samuel L. Jackson), and the new sheriff of the town (Walton Goggins), and reluctantly agree to give them a lift in their carriage. The group soon takes shelter from the oncoming blizzard in a cabin peopled by a collection of strange and somewhat sinister characters. As the storm hits and the residents of "Minnie's Haberdashery" realise they are going to be trapped in the cabin together for a number of days, it appears that some of those present are not quite what they first seem and not everyone is guaranteed to get out alive…

You may be asking yourself why I am reviewing what is, from the outset, a western in what is supposed to be a magazine dedicated to horror, fantasy and science fiction, but for me this eighth film by Quentin Tarantino definitely verges on the horror, due to the explicit bloodshed and gore, and has quite a "locked in" paranoid thriller element to it as well. The director has openly admitted that it was inspired by John Carpenter's *The Thing* (released in 1982 and also starring Kurt Russell) and his own *Reservoir Dogs* from 1992, of which there are many plot similarities to. However, it is much more than that and the other westerns it pays homage to. It is also a "whodunnit" mystery brimming with atmosphere that Agatha Christie would be proud of (brutal violence aside, perhaps) and an uncompromising commentary on racism, the West and the nature of war and man's inhumanity to man. The ultra-violence is indeed extreme, but done in Tarantino's trademark comic book style. Certain other scenes pertaining to male rape, violence against women, and the (arguably) gratuitous use of the "N" word are bound to upset many viewers (and have), but it could also be debated that QT is one of the very few filmmakers around today with the backbone to address uncomfortable, but important, real-life issues. The West was indeed wild. History is complex and bloody. Racism exists in the real world (just like it did in the past), as does violence. Tarantino's films simply reflect these realities through his very unique and stylistic brand of storytelling, that many others have tried to imitate, but failed. He certainly doesn't bend to the likes of studio demands and interference in his realisation of his visions, and that to me is a breath of fresh air in itself.

There's plenty of the usual quick-witted dark humour in there that you would also expect from Tarantino and the characterisation is sublimely written, something I feel QT excels at, with his more character-based films such as *Jackie Brown*, *Inglourious Basterds* and the recent *Once Upon a Time... in Hollywood* being his best.

The cast is superb, especially Samuel L. Jackson, Kurt Russell (doing a John Wayne impression), Jennifer Jason Leigh and Walton Goggins, alongside the absolutely stunning exterior cinematography and score from a diverse group of contributors including Ennio Morricone (look out for the genius use of his "Regan's Theme" from *Exorcist II: The Heretic* near the beginning), Roy Orbison and The White Stripes.

The Hateful Eight is a greatly entertaining pulp western/horror that doesn't hold back and which works on multiple levels. It won't appeal to everyone, that's for sure, and it has had a lot of critics since its release in 2015, but to be honest I don't think Quentin Tarantino makes films for anyone but himself anyway, and for that he certainly has my full respect.

Trevor Kennedy

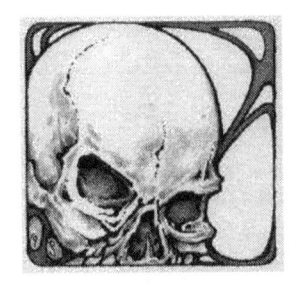

TELEVISION

STAR WARS: THE CLONE WARS (season 7)

<u>Created by George Lucas.</u>
<u>Showrunner: Dave Filoni.</u>
<u>Starring Ashley Eckstein, Dave Filoni, Dee Bradley Baker and more.</u>

A long time ago, a galaxy far, far away was sold to Emperor Mickey in control of the Disney Empire. He bought it for a cheap price and eventually more than tripled his investment. Since this acquisition a slew of *Star Wars* media has graced itself across many platforms. I think the midichlorians would be proud. Yet, all was not perfect. A successful animated television show known as *The Clone Wars* was cut short. The new parent company insisted that it planned to go in a different direction. This was almost a fatal mistake. Rule number one: if it ain't broke, then don't try to fix it. Many other licensed properties were told to stop production and await further orders. If it wasn't for the public outcry to bring the show back on television, season 7 (available on Disney+) would not exist.

A cool dude named Dave Filoni was given the green light to produce one more season. These episodes were long overdue. There are only twelve eps, but that has proved to be more than enough.

The first four episodes deal with a group of clones known as "The Bad Batch." They are autonomous from their clone brethren in terms of programming. It is a misnomer that they have this notion of being misfits. They each have unique combat abilities as well as character that give them strength and the Republic an edge. I like to look at them as the *Star Wars* version of *The A-Team* (1983) that gave rise to the likes of Mr. T. I hope to see them again in perhaps another animated series. I'm curious to know what happened to them during and after Order 66.

The next four episodes, despite some people's criticism, were a present gift wrapped and hand delivered. If you are a gamer such as myself you have probably played at least one *Star Wars* game. Part of the deal Disney made with George Lucas back in 2012 included ownership over several of his intellectual properties such as Lucas Arts. This is the gaming section that was working on a title called *Star Wars 1313*. The premise of this was that a player would assume the role of bounty hunter Boba Fett. This would take him down to Level 1313 of Coruscant's underworld. There he would traverse the level until he uncovered a criminal conspiracy. I was really looking forward to getting a better view of ordinary life on Coruscant. No Jedi, Sith, clone/stormtroopers, or twisted politicians that the films portray. Just ordinary people living their lives one day at a time.

Again, thanks to Dave Filoni, with the new season of *The Clone Wars*, he gave us a glimpse of what could have been through the lives of the Martez sisters, who just happen to live on Level 1313. Ahsoka shows up eventually, befriending them both, despite their dabbling into questionable criminal activities just to get by. She swallows her Jedi morality to keep her true identity hidden, but more importantly sees things that aren't necessarily black and white. As this arc comes to a close, Bo-Katan, a Mandalorian warrior, shows up to ask for help in removing Darth Maul from Mandalore. Maul has managed to align himself with a splinter group from Manadalore calling themselves the Death Watch. Now what Filoni manages to do next is, you've guessed it, not only another story arc but something similar to a *Rogue One*'s (2016) ending. Against Bo-Katan's advice, Ahsoka seeks out help from the two Jedi she trusts the most – her former Master Anakin Skywalker and Obi-Wan Kenobi. Kenobi basically tells her no and for good reason. They receive notice that General Grievous, second only to Count Dooku, has attacked Coruscant and even worse, captured Chancellor Palpatine. Anakin promotes Rex to Commander and sends him and a small battalion of clones to help Ahsoka. Soon we see two significant things grace our televisions. One, the infamous siege of Mandalore, and also a visit to the front door of *Revenge of the Sith* (2005). In a very emotional scene we see the last time Ahsoka will see her former Master. At least from a certain point of view.

As the very last two episodes play out, they run concurrently to a portion of *Revenge of the Sith*. Although Ahsoka, Bo-Katan and the clones are successful, it appears that the siege of Mandalore is not over. That was just the first of perhaps several more battles. Ahsoka defeats Maul in an incredible lightsaber battle that shows her maturity as a Jedi. Clearly she has become a fully-fledged Jedi Knight, even if it is unofficial. With Maul captured, she and the clones head back to Coruscant to turn Maul in, totally unaware that their lives will be upended in a matter of minutes. The musical score playing at this moment reminded me of the track "Lament", also played in *Revenge of the Sith*. A beautiful score all around. This one is even more poignant because she disobeys Master Windu's orders, which was to remain in the temple, while he and other Jedi Masters confronted Chancellor Palpatine. In his decision making we see him make a historic mistake. And as he does so the music just carries us to destiny's end. So, much like the instance with Ahsoka as she contemplates her life as a Jedi to Rex. To bring some clarity of substance they both agree that had things turned out differently they never would have met. Keep in mind that during this scene on the bridge it had me full of anticipation. I could feel that something was about to happen. I knew something had to happen but I didn't know exactly how or what.

Then Rex is told that he has a message from Coruscant. He leaves Ahsoka to receive that message. Darth Sidious appears on a holo-screen informing him that "the time has come to execute Order 66." The camera shifts back to Ahsoka in the other room. Immediately she feels a disturbance in the Force as countless numbers of Jedi are systematically killed by their clone comrades. Rex is probably one of the few clones to at least try and reject his programming. We all know he will because he and Ahsoka show up in *Star Wars: Rebels* (2014), set fourteen years later. Needless to say, she removes his inhibitor chip and frees Maul so they can all escape death. They do so after a fierce battle, but not before Maul manages to escape, as he always does, destroying the cruiser's engines and plummeting it towards an icy world. The ship crashes leaving only Ahsoka, Rex, and some familiar looking droids as the only survivors. Out of respect, they give posthumous burials to the clones that were once their friends. Saddened and speechless, Ahsoka drops her lightsaber, leaving the audience to guess what's next for her and Rex.

Filoni loves and listens to the fans. In the finale scene we are treated to one last gift and that's a time jump. It's unclear of the date but if the presence of stormtroopers guarding an Imperial shuttle didn't give viewers an idea, then perhaps the guy dressed in all black and breathing heavily did. Yes, Darth Vader in all his evil glory shows up. Yet, why is he there? Did the Emperor instruct him to do so? Or did he go there to see if his former Padawan survived Order 66? Is this an early sign that deep down there is some good in him, as Padme said on her deathbed. Only time will tell. I don't think we have seen the last of pre-*Rebels* Vader. He collects her lightsaber that he once made for her. Then, in a moment of ambiguity, he walks back towards his shuttle.

Abdul-Qaadir Taariq Bakari-Muhammad

A DISCOVERY OF WITCHES

<u>Showrunner/head writer: Kate Brooke.</u>
<u>Starring Teresa Palmer, Matthew Goode, Edward Bluemet, Louise Brealey, Malin Buska, Owen Teale, Alex Kingston and more.</u>

Here is a TV series that you can sink your teeth into during these hard times – the fantasy drama *A Discovery of Witches*, based on the book series by Deborah Harkness.

If you loved the teen book series *The Twilight Saga*, then you will love this TV show. A Romeo and Juliet story, dealing with supernatural forces and a forbidden union between a vampire named Matthew Clairmont (Matthew Goode) and a witch named Diana Bishop (Teresa Palmer).

In a world where witches, vampires and daemons live discreetly among humans, Diana Bishop is the last in a long line of distinguished witches. Unwilling to embrace her heritage she has immersed herself in a career as a historian.

Her particular interest is alchemy and she visits Oxford to research some of Elias Ashmole's papers. She requests "Ashmole 782" and as soon as she receives it she knows there is something uncanny about it. When she opens it she is shocked and learns that "782" had been presumed lost for a very long time and that each species of creature desires it. She is besieged and threatened by Peter Knox (Owen Teale), a high-ranking witch, Diana's ex-friend and a fellow witch Gillian Chamberlain (Louise Brealey), and Satu Jarvinen (Malin Buska), a Finnish witch.

She encounters the enigmatic vampire Matthew Clairmont, who offers to help her. Their mutual attraction is immediate, undeniable and inexplicable because they both know that witches and vampires are not supposed to trust each other. Diana makes her choice, however, and accepts Matthew's help.

Throughout the series, Diana's powers start emerging at a fast pace but she discovers that she is "spellbound", which means she can't use magic. She discovers that her parents spellbound her to protect her from drawing the attention of other witches. She also discovers that her father Stephen could magically travel in time. This results in us seeing Diana and Matthew travel back to the Tudor era.

Season 2 is currently in post-production. It is based on the second book, *Shadow of Night*. We are really keen to find out how Diana handles living in the Tudor era. We picture Diana sticking out like a sore thumb and fitting in will prove to be quite difficult.

We rate this TV series 9 out of 10. It would have been rated higher but there were small oversights with the post-editing of episode 4.

If you wish to hear more about *A Discovery of Witches*, check out our film review podcast *Boys 'n' Ghouls*:

https://boysnghoulsfilmreviewpodcast.podbean.com/
https://anchor.fm/boysnghoulsfilmreview

Sarah Stephenson and Michael Stephenson

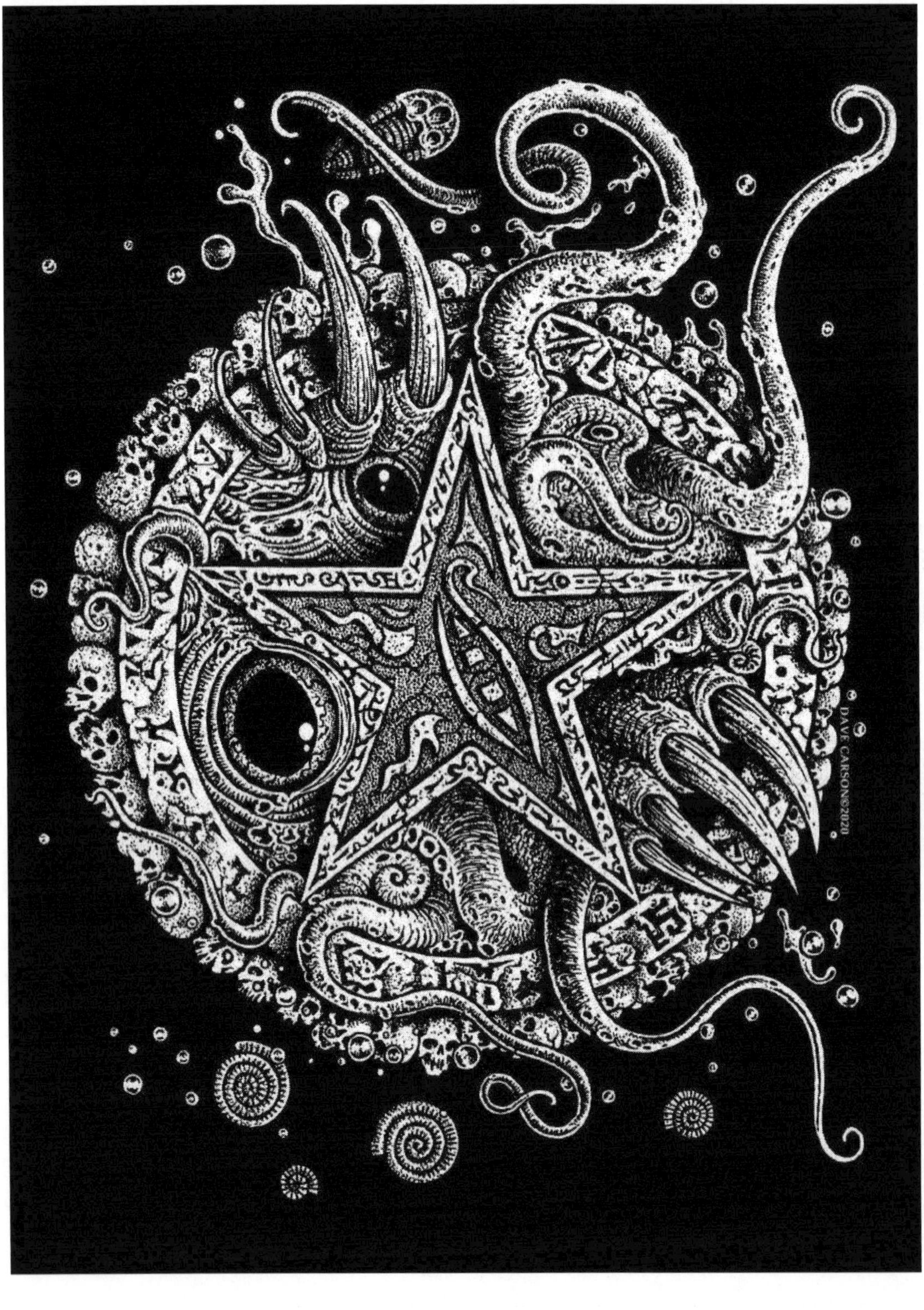
DAVE CARSON©2020

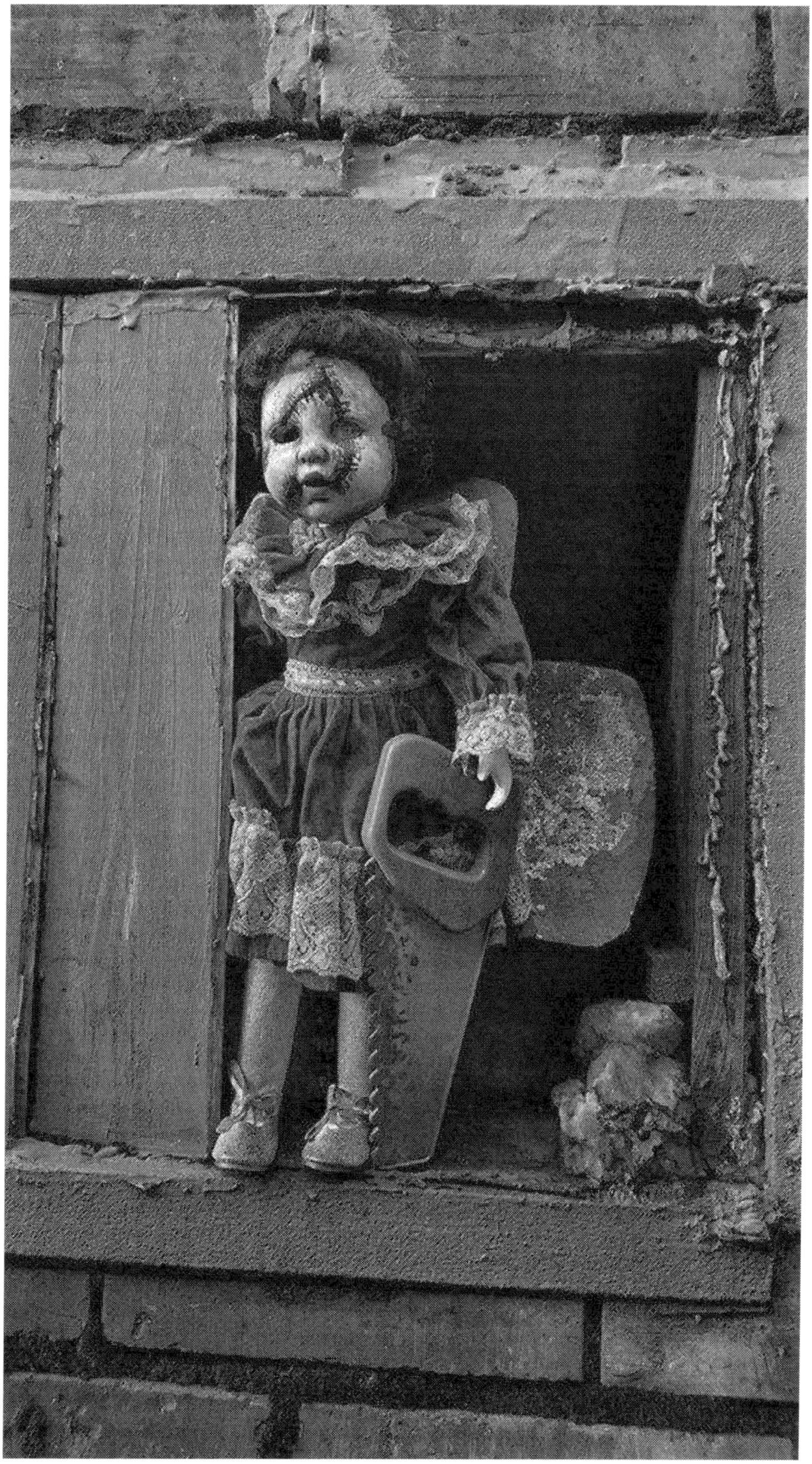

ACKNOWLEDGEMENTS

Page 1: Artwork copyright © Allen Koszowski.
Page 6: "Editorial: The Case For Catharsis" copyright © Trevor Kennedy.
Page 10: Graham Masterton interview copyright © Marc Damian Lawler, Graham Masterton and *Phantasmagoria Magazine*.
Page 10: Picture copyright © Graham Masterton.
Page 11: Image copyright © Sphere.
Page 12: Image source: Google Images.
Page 15: Image copyright © of the relevant publisher.
Page 22: Image copyright © of the relevant publisher.
Page 30: Picture copyright © Graham Masterton.
Page 31: Extract from *The House of a Hundred Whispers* copyright © Graham Masterton and Head of Zeus.
Page 33: Artwork copyright © Jim Pitts.
Page 35: "Eye Creature" artwork copyright © Dave Carson.
Page 36: Aidan Chambers interview copyright © *Phantasmagoria Magazine* and Aidan Chambers.
Pages 36-43: Images copyright © Aidan Chambers and the relevant publishers and artists etc.
Page 44: *Dead Trouble & Other Ghost Stories* review copyright © Trevor Kennedy.
Page 44: "Head Spot" copyright © Randy Broecker.
Page 45: "Two Skulls" from "The Ghostly Skulls of Calgarth Hall" copyright © Randy Broecker.
Page 47: "Seeing is Believing" copyright © Randy Broecker.
Page 48: Image copyright © PS Publishing.
Page 49: Lynn Lowry interview copyright © David L. Tamarin, Lynn Lowry and *Phantasmagoria Magazine*.
Page 49: Picture copyright © Lynn Lowry.
Page 51: Picture copyright © Pittsburgh Films.
Page 53: Picture copyright © Cinepix Film Properties/DAL Productions.
Page 54: Picture copyright © Cinepix Film Properties/DAL Productions.
Page 55: Picture copyright © 15th Street Films/Armor Films Inc.
Page 57: Picture copyright © Penny Spent Films/Rebel Idol Films/Morgue Art Films.
Page 58: Picture copyright © Cat Scare Films.
Page 59: Picture copyright © Audubon Films.
Page 60: Image copyright © The Alchemy Press.
Page 61: "The Many Faces of Frankenstein... and His Creations" feature copyright © John Gilbert.

Page 61: Picture copyright © Universal Pictures.
Page 64: Picture copyright © Universal Pictures.
Page 66: Picture copyright © Hammer Films.
Page 68: Picture copyright © Venture Films/Crossbow Productions/Jouer Limited.
Page 69: Picture copyright © Davis Entertainment/Twentieth Century Fox/MPC.
Page 70: "Stephen Jones' *The Best of Best New Horror*" feature/review copyright © Trevor Kennedy.
Page 70: Image copyright © PS Publishing.
Page 73: Image copyright © PS Publishing.
Page 74: "John Stewart: A Forgotten Artist of Fantasy and Supernatural Horror" feature copyright © James Doig. All feature artworks reprinted by kind permission of the Estate of John Stewart. They are also subject to the copyright © of the various publications they originally appeared in.
Page 74: Photograph of John Stewart from the back flap of Centipede Press's *John Stewart: A Portfolio*. Copyright © Centipede Press.
Page 88: Lynda E. Rucker interview copyright © Allison Weir, Lynda E. Rucker and *Phantasmagoria Magazine*. Interview pictures and images copyright © Lynda E. Rucker and her relevant publishers and artists etc.
Page 97: Simon Fisher-Becker interview copyright © *Phantasmagoria Magazine* and Simon Fisher-Becker.
Page 97: Picture copyright © Simon Fisher-Becker.
Page 99: Image copyright © Fantastic Books Publishing.
Page 100: Picture copyright © BBC.
Page 101: Picture copyright © BBC.
Page 104: Picture copyright © Simon Fisher-Becker.
Page 105: Artwork copyright © Allen Koszowski.
Page 106: "The Many Wars of the Worlds" feature copyright © Raven Dane.
Page 106: Picture copyright © Paramount Pictures.
Page 108: Picture copyright © Paramount Pictures.
Page 109: Picture copyright © Mammoth Screen/BBC/Creasun Media American.
Page 110: Picture copyright © AGC Television/Canal+ /De Wereldvrede
Page 111: Artwork and picture copyright © Stephen Clarke.
Page 112: "Evolution of a Classic: The Story of the *Planet of the Apes* Franchise. Part One: *Planet of the Apes* (1968)" feature copyright © Dave Jeffery.
Page 112: Picture copyright © APJAC Productions/Twentieth Century Fox.
Page 114: Image copyright © of the relevant publisher and artist etc.
Page 117: Picture copyright © APJAC Productions/Twentieth Century Fox.
Page 119: Picture copyright © APJAC Productions/Twentieth Century Fox.
Page 120: "Old Ones" artwork copyright © Dave Carson.

Page 121: Artwork copyright © Allen Koszowski.
Page 122: "*Phantasmagoria* Fans' Euphoria" copyright © *Phantasmagoria Magazine* and the authors of the individual comments and material. All section artworks copyright © Jim Pitts.
Page 125: Artwork and picture copyright © Stephen Clarke.
Page 126: "Behind the Masks" artwork copyright © Jim Pitts.
Page 127: "The Fragile Mask on His Face" copyright © David A. Riley.
Page 127: "The Fragile Mask on His Face" artwork copyright © Jim Pitts.
Page 144: Artwork copyright © David A. Riley.
Page 145: "Fair Dues" copyright © Mike Chinn.
Page 149: "Salin Thur" artwork copyright © Mike Chinn.
Page 150: Artwork copyright © Mike Chinn.
Page 151: "The Amazing Xandra Lee vs Ned Swann" copyright © Adrian Baldwin.
Page 160: "Prey" copyright © Joe X. Young.
Page 162: Artwork copyright © Allen Koszowski.
Page 163: "A Place For Junkmen" copyright © Connor Leggat.
Page 179: "Saturn" artwork copyright © Peter Coleborn.
Page 180: "Greasehead" copyright © Conor Reid.
Page 183: "My Pillow is a Ship" copyright © Marc Damian Lawler.
Page 184: "Ghost" artwork copyright © Peter Coleborn.
Page 185: "I Should Not Be" copyright © Richard Bell.
Page 186: "Skelly B" artwork copyright © Peter Coleborn.
Page 187: "As Silver Dusk Suffuses Red" copyright © David A. Riley.
Page 187: Artwork copyright © Jim Pitts.
Page 188: "Byron's Burning Bones" copyright © Emerson Firebird.
Page 188: "Skull" artwork copyright © Peter Coleborn.
Page 189: Artwork and picture copyright © Stephen Clarke.
Page 190: "Batman Triumphant: How the Dark Knight Rose From the Ashes to Begin Again" feature copyright © Nathan Waring.
Page 190: Picture copyright © Warner Bros./Syncopy/DC Comics/Legendary Entertainment/Patalex III Productions Limited.
Page 192: Picture copyright © Warner Bros./PolyGram Filmed Entertainment.
Page 195: Warner Bros. Animation/Warner Bros. Television.
Page 198: Picture copyright © Warner Bros./Syncopy/DC Comics/Legendary Entertainment/Patalex III Productions Limited.
Page 199: Picture copyright © Warner Bros./Syncopy/DC Comics/Legendary Entertainment/Patalex III Productions Limited.
Page 200: "Demon" copyright © Peter Coleborn.
Page 201: "*AVPR: Aliens vs Predator – Requiem*: The Most Underrated Movie of Them All" feature copyright © Owen Quinn.

Page 201: Picture copyright © Twentieth Century Fox/David Entertainment/Brandywine Productions/Dune Entertainment.
Page 203: Picture copyright © Twentieth Century Fox/David Entertainment/Brandywine Productions/Dune Entertainment.
Page 205: Picture copyright © Twentieth Century Fox/David Entertainment/Brandywine Productions/Dune Entertainment.
Page 206: Artwork copyright © Allen Koszowski.
Page 207: "Dracula" artwork copyright © Peter Coleborn.
Page 208: "The Family Are Not What They Seem: A Look At the Domestic Horror of *Twin Peaks: Fire Walk With Me* (1992)" feature copyright © Michael Campbell.
Page 208: Picture copyright © New Line Cinema/CiBy 2000/Twin Peaks Productions.
Page 210: Picture copyright © New Line Cinema/CiBy 2000/Twin Peaks Productions.
Page 212: Picture copyright © New Line Cinema/CiBy 2000/Twin Peaks Productions.
Page 214: Picture copyright © New Line Cinema/CiBy 2000/Twin Peaks Productions.
Page 215: "*Twin Peaks: Fire Walk With Me*-Inspired Artwork" artworks copyright © Franki Beddows.
Page 217: Byddi Lee interview copyright © *Phantasmagoria Magazine* and Byddi Lee. Interview pictures and images copyright © Byddi Lee and her relevant publishers and artists etc.
Page 223: Artwork copyright © Allen Koszowski.
Page 224: Casey Biggs interview copyright © Owen Quinn and Casey Biggs.
Page 224: Picture copyright © Casey Biggs.
Page 226: Picture copyright © Paramount Television.
Page 228: Picture copyright © Paramount Television.
Page 230: "Retrospective: The Horror Film Years: 1960s" feature copyright © David Brilliance.
Page 230: Picture copyright © Alfred J. Hitchcock Productions.
Page 231: Picture copyright © Metro-Goldwyn-Mayer British Studios.
Page 233: Picture copyright © Hammer Films/Seven Arts Productions.
Page 234: Picture copyright © Tigon British Film Productions/AIP.
Page 234: Artwork copyright © Jim Pitts.
Page 236: "Reading R. Chetwynd-Hayes: 'The Underground'" feature copyright © Marc Damian Lawler.
Page 236: Image copyright © William Kimber & Co and the relevant artist.
Page 243: Artwork and picture copyright © Stephen Clarke.
Page 247: Artwork copyright © Jim Pitts.
Pages 247 to 275: All book cover images copyright © of the relevant publishers, authors and artists etc.

Page 247: *The Wise Friend* review copyright © Trevor Kennedy.
Page 249: *Warts and All* review copyright © John Gilbert.
Page 251: *A Small Thing For Yolanda* review copyright © Con Connolly.
Page 253: *The Curse of the Fleers* review copyright © Trevor Kennedy.
Page 255: *Talking to Strangers and Other Warnings* review copyright © John Gilbert.
Page 257: *Les Vacances* review copyright © John Gilbert.
Page 259: *Roadside Picnic* review copyright © Carl R. Jennings.
Page 262: *Project Notebook* review copyright © Trevor Kennedy.
Page 263: *Jam* review copyright © Carl R. Jennings.
Page 266: *Star Trek: Picard: The Last Best Hope* review copyright © Abdul-Qaadir Taariq Bakari-Muhammad.
Page 268: *The Abominable* review copyright © James Keen.
Page 270: *Cats' Peril* and *The Adventure of An Cupla* review copyright © Helen Scott.
Page 273: *Almost Surely* review copyright © Carl R. Jennings.
Page 275: Artwork copyright © Jim Pitts.
Page 278: *The Hunt* review copyright © Barnaby Page.
Page 278: Picture copyright © Blumhouse Productions.
Page 280: *The Hole in the Ground* review copyright © Barnaby Page.
Page 280: Picture copyright © Savage Productions/Backside Films/Wrong Men North/Hand Gear Films/Metrol Technology.
Page 281: *Rattlesnake* review copyright © Barnaby Page.
Page 281: Picture copyright © Campfire/Netflix.
Page 282: *A Field in England* review copyright © Trevor Kennedy and GCH Reilly.
Page 283: Picture copyright © Film4/Rook Films.
Page 284: *Near Dark* review copyright © Allison Weir.
Page 285: Picture copyright © F/M/Near Dark Joint Venture.
Page 286: *Ed Wood* review copyright © Trevor Kennedy.
Page 287: Picture copyright © Touchstone Pictures.
Page 288: *The Hateful Eight* review copyright © Trevor Kennedy.
Page 289: Picture copyright © Visiona Romantica/Double Feature Films/FilmColony.
Page 290: Picture copyright © Visiona Romantica/Double Feature Films/FilmColony.
Page 290: Artwork copyright © Jim Pitts.
Page 291: *Star Wars: The Clone Wars* (season 7) review copyright © Abdul-Qaadir Taariq Bakari-Muhammad.
Page 291: Picture copyright © CGCG/Cartoon Network/Lucasfilm Animation Singapore/Lucasfilm Animation/Lucasfilm.
Page 293: Picture copyright © CGCG/Cartoon Network/Lucasfilm Animation Singapore/Lucasfilm Animation/Lucasfilm.

Page 294: *A Discovery of Witches* review copyright © Sarah Stephenson and Michael Stephenson.
Page 294: Picture copyright © Bad Wolf.
Page 295: Artwork copyright © Allen Koszowski.
Page 296: "Cthulhu Cult" artwork copyright © Dave Carson.
Page 297: Artwork and picture copyright © Stephen Clarke.
Page 315: Artwork copyright © David A. Riley.
Page 316: "Bookplate" artwork copyright © Dave Carson.

PARALLEL UNIVERSE PUBLICATIONS

A LITTLE LIGHT SCREAMING — Johnny Mains

KATE FARRELL — AND NOBODY LIVED HAPPILY EVER AFTER — Introduction by Reggie Oliver

FISHHEAD — The Darker Tales of IRVIN S. COBB

ANDREW DARLINGTON — A SAUCERFUL OF SECRETS

INTO THE DARK — a novel by ANDREW JENNINGS

MOLOCH'S CHILDREN — DAVID A. RILEY

PARLOUR TRICKS — CARL BARKER

THE CRABIAN HEART — Erik Hofstatter

KITCHEN SINK GOTHIC — Selected by David & Linden Riley

THE CHAMELEON MAN & Other Terrors — DAVID WILLIAMSON — Veteran author from The Pan Books of Horror and The Black Books of Horror

BLACK CEREMONIES — Charles Black

THE FANTASTICAL ART OF JIM PITTS — ROLLING BACK THE YEARS...

For full details of all our books please check our website:

http://paralleluniversepublications.blogspot.co.uk/

Creeping horror... twisted tales...

Creeping Crawlers

A bumper anthology of creeping, crawling, slithering horror, Science Fiction and Fantasy by 19 of today's top authors. Edited by award winner, Allen Ashley.

Including stories by Adrian Cole, Storm Constantine, Andrew Darlington, John Grant, Andrew Hook, Mark Howard Jones and others. (£11.99)

Worse Things Than Spiders

Samantha Lee can tell a great story... These are dark stories indeed, told with just the right dollop of horror to thoroughly unnerve the reader.

Samantha Lee is the author of several SF, fantasy and horror novels, including Demon, Demon II, Amy, The Belltower and The Bogle. (£8.99)

Get them at Amazon.co.uk / Amazon.com
From the publisher at: https://www.shadowpublishing.net/shop
Text 07484 607539

Shadow Publishing

Jim Pitts Prints

Each print is on high quality A4 paper, approved and signed by the artist before being sealed for protection inside a plastic envelope.

Colour prints are £7.00 each incl p&p

Black & white prints £5.00 each incl p&p

Any orders for 5 or more prints qualify for a 20% discount.

To order please email paralleluniversepublications@gmx.co.uk, listing which prints you would like. You will then be emailed a Paypal invoice.

Jim Pitts is an award-winning artist (two-times winner of the prestigious British Fantasy Award, plus Science Fiction's Ken McIntyre Award), whose work has appeared in numerous magazines and books, both professional and small press.

Check our website: paralleluniversepublications.blogspot.com/

The new book from Alli Weir…

Oveds of Ohncara tells the story of a young arachnid called Tarah-Entula who is trying her best to fit into a lost community and loving family.

She must quickly learn the ropes of survival in human territory and across the districts of Ohncara whilst also being there for others when the chips are down.

Just when the tiny creature thinks she is winning with regained trust and blossoming friendships, the weird Wallingtons decide to move into the area…

A fantasy-must for the curiously imaginative – those who relish obscure adventure, drama and multiple twists!

Available from Amazon and Coffee & Heroes (Belfast)

(Cover design by Adrian Baldwin, www.adrianbaldwin.info)

Short Sharp Shocks! available from Demain Publishing on Amazon priced at just 99p each (eBook)!

(Cover design by Adrian Baldwin, www.adrianbaldwin.info)

Currently on sale from Amazon...

Mister Posted and the Brain Freeze Goddess

Carl R. Jennings

On sale from Amazon in paperback (£8.99)
and e-Book (£6.99)...

BEFORE YOU BLOW OUT THE CANDLE...

EDITED BY MARC DAMIAN LAWLER

Currently available from Amazon in paperback and on Kindle...

Heroin Is The Answer

A Memoir of What I Can Remember

Russell Holbrook

Available from Amazon and Forbidden Planet Belfast, Trevor Kennedy's first two solo books…

(Cover designs by Adrian Baldwin, www.adrianbaldwin.info)

Some titles currently available from Amazon...

(Cover design by Adrian Baldwin, www.adrianbaldwin.info)

~~~~~

If you would like to contact us at *Phantasmagoria Magazine* with feedback or submissions we are available through the following:

Email: tkboss@hotmail.com

Facebook: https://www.facebook.com/PhantasmagoriaMagazine/

Twitter: https://twitter.com/TKBossPhantasm

Instagram: https://www.instagram.com/tk_pulp_phantasmagoria/

Back issues are also available to purchase from **Amazon** in print and on Kindle; and also in print form from **Forbidden Planet Belfast**.

Phantasmagoria Magazine will return at the beginning of August 2020

Phantasmagoria
Horror, Fantasy & Sci-Fi

Printed in Great Britain
by Amazon